Claimed by a

Mi

Woman

Three intense, luxurious romances from three
beloved Mills & Boon authors!

In January 2010 Mills & Boon bring you two classic collections, each featuring three favourite romances by our bestselling authors

CONVENIENT BRIDES

The Italian's Convenient Wife
by Catherine Spencer
His Inconvenient Wife
by Melanie Milburne
His Convenient Proposal
by Lindsay Armstrong

MILLIONAIRE'S WOMAN

The Millionaire's Prospective Wife
by Helen Brooks
The Millionaire's Runaway Bride
by Catherine George
The Millionaire's Reward
by Angie Ray

Millionaire's Woman

HELEN BROOKS

CATHERINE GEORGE

ANGIE RAY

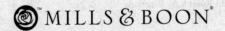

MILLS & BOON®

First published in Great Britain 2010
Harlequin Mills & Boon Limited,
Eton House, 18-24 Paradise Road, Richmond, Surrey TW9 1SR

MILLIONAIRE'S WOMAN © by Harlequin Enterprises II B.V./S.à.r.l 2010

The Millionaire's Prospective Wife, The Millionaire's Runaway Bride and *The Millionaire's Reward* were first published in Great Britain by Harlequin Mills & Boon Limited in separate, single volumes.

The Millionaire's Prospective Wife © Helen Brooks 2005
The Millionaire's Runaway Bride © Catherine George 2006
The Millionaire's Reward © Angela Ray 2005

ISBN: 978 0 263 88095 3

05-0110

Printed and bound in Spain
by Litografia Rosés S.A., Barcelona

THE MILLIONAIRE'S PROSPECTIVE WIFE

BY
HELEN BROOKS

Helen Brooks was born and educated in Northampton. She met her husband at the age of sixteen and thirty-five years later the magic is still there. They have three lovely children and three beautiful grandchildren.

Helen began writing in 1990 as she approached that milestone of a birthday – forty! She realised her two teenage ambitions (writing a novel and learning to drive) had been lost amid babies and family life, so set about resurrecting them. Her first novel was accepted after one rewrite, and she passed her driving test (the former was a joy and the latter an unmitigated nightmare).

Being a committed Christian and fervent animal lover Helen finds time is always at a premium, but walks in the countryside with her husband and their Irish terrier, meals out followed by the cinema or theatre, reading, swimming, and visiting with friends are all fitted in somehow. She also enjoys sitting in her wonderfully therapeutic, rambling old garden in the sun with a glass of red wine, (under the guise of resting while thinking, of course!).

Since becoming a full-time writer Helen has found her occupation one of pure joy. She loves exploring what makes people tick and finds the old adage "truth is stranger than fiction" to be absolutely true.

CHAPTER ONE

THE moment Cory let Rufus off the lead she knew it was a big mistake. The powerful Labrador cross golden retriever shot across Hyde Park like a bat out of hell, mothers whisking toddlers up into their arms at his approach and elderly couples leaping out of his way with a nimbleness they probably thought had been lost to them years before. Even the group of young people who had been ambling towards them clad in strategically slashed jeans and with piercings in seemingly every nook and cranny lost their cool aplomb, scattering with shrieks and cries which—on the whole, Cory was thankful to note—were good-humoured.

For the first minute or so of following in the dog's wake Cory shouted apologies to all and sundry, then, when Rufus showed no signs of slowing down, she kept her breath for running.

Why hadn't she listened to her aunt? Cory silently berated herself as she panted after the dog, wasting valuable breath every twenty yards or so by screeching his name. But Rufus had been so docile and obliging on the walk down Bayswater Road from her aunt's house, sitting at all the right times without being told and keeping to heel like an old pro. And the deep brown eyes had been so imploring once they'd entered the park, the doggy expression of longing as he'd watched other canines chasing balls and playing making her feel like the wicked witch of the west.

'Keep him on the lead, Cory,' Aunt Joan had warned as she'd seen them off at the door, her left leg encased in plaster due to a nasty fall a couple of weeks before. 'I can

5

just about trust him to come back now but I don't know how he would react with someone else. He's perfectly friendly, of course, and just adores children and other dogs, but the original owners kept him confined all the time as well as neglecting him in other ways, as you know. The poor darling.'

'The poor darling' was not the phrase she'd choose to describe the dog right at this moment, Cory thought grimly. Her lungs felt as though they were going to burst and her throat and chest were on fire. There were various choice names which sprang to mind but poor and darling didn't feature in any of them.

Rufus having made a couple of lightning stops to sniff the certain part of other canines' anatomies which dogs found so interesting, Cory now found herself closer to him than at any time since the undignified chase had begun. Summoning all her strength, she bellowed, *'Rufus! Stay!'* just as the animal prepared to take off from socialising with a French poodle. The golden head turned, brown eyes considering her with a faintly amazed expression as though he couldn't understand why she wasn't entering wholeheartedly into this wonderful game he'd organised. Seizing the opportunity, Cory growled, *'Come here. Heel, Rufus.'*

There was still a good fifty yards between them but she couldn't run any more, the stitch in her side excruciating. Whether it was her ferocious voice or the fact that she had slowed down to a walk, Cory didn't know, but the big dog suddenly seemed to realise all was not well. After one more moment of hesitation he took off again, but this time headed straight for her, determined to impress her by the speed with which he obeyed. It was doubtful he even noticed the tall, well-dressed figure about to cross his path. There was one endless moment when man and dog met and then five or six stone of sheer canine muscle sent the unfortunate figure hurtling into the air.

A very nice leather briefcase went one way, the suit jacket which had been slung over one shirt-clad arm another, and all Cory could do was to look in unmitigated horror. The man landed on his back with earth-shaking force and even Rufus realised he'd committed a *faux pas*. He was slinking obsequiously around the prostrate figure on the grass when Cory reached them, his ears flat to his face and his floppy jowls shaking as though he was about to burst into tears.

'Oh, I'm sorry, I'm so, so sorry.' Cory went down on to her knees in a flurry of blue denim jeans, pink shirt and tumbled hair the colour of rich dark chocolate. 'Are you all right?'

The man remained perfectly still for another moment and then drew air into his body with something of a tortured groan. It probably wasn't the moment to notice it was an exceptionally fit body—tall, lean and muscled with an aggressive masculinity that was rawly sexy—or that the jet-black hair topped a face that was out-and-out dynamite.

Cory swallowed. Pierce Brosnan, Orlando Bloom, Brad Pitt—eat your hearts out. She had to swallow again before she could say, 'Have you broken anything?'

A pair of very blue eyes met hers. In spite of his prone position and the fact he'd had all the air knocked out of him—or maybe because of it—they were lethal, the one rapier sharp glance saying more than mere words could ever have done. When Cory went to help him as he sat up he motioned her hands away with a cutting action that was savage. It was unfortunate Rufus chose that moment to make his apology by means of a long slobbery lick across one chiselled cheekbone. The man froze for a second but still didn't say a word before he rose to his feet.

He was tall. Cory found herself looking up some distance as she too stood up. Very tall. And angry. Very, very angry. 'Is it yours?'

'I'm sorry.' She was still frozen by the icy eyes and the way the set of his hard mouth gave the handsome face a harsh cast, and her brain wasn't working properly.

'That.' He gestured furiously in Rufus's direction. 'Is it—? Hell!' The original sentence was cut off. 'What's he eating?'

Oh, no. Please, no. This couldn't be happening. She took the mobile phone out of Rufus's wet jaws but the damage was already done. Neither of them had noticed the dog snuffling in the discarded jacket. 'Was...was it expensive?' she asked in a small voice whilst already knowing the answer. It was a state of the art, super dooper technological miracle of a phone. What else? But it hadn't been designed to withstand the power of those big jaws.

He ignored the outstretched hand with the chewed phone and took a deep breath, retrieving his briefcase and jacket and wincing slightly as he did so.

He *was* hurt. But then of course he would be. Meeting an express train in the middle of Hyde Park on a Saturday morning was something even Superman would have found a little hard to take. 'I'm sorry,' she said again. 'I shouldn't have taken him off the lead.'

Dark eyebrows climbed sardonically. 'Really?'

He wasn't being very gracious but she supposed she couldn't blame him. Cory took a deep breath. 'I'll pay for any damage, of course,' she said with a little upward jerk of her chin which wasn't lost on the man in front of her. 'To the phone, your suit...anything,' she finished lamely.

The eyebrows went a touch higher. 'Am I supposed to say thank you here?' he drawled silkily.

What a thoroughly unpleasant individual. Cory found she

could ignore the beauty of the sky-blue eyes quite well now. It wasn't so much what he said but the way that he said it which was so nasty. 'Not at all,' she said curtly, her whole body stiffening. 'I'm merely making the point, that's all.'

Rufus had seated himself at the man's side as though he had disowned her and was now looking the very picture of docility, his big head moving interestedly from one to the other as they had spoken. Cory found she could have throttled him. Preparing to clip the lead back on his collar, she said, 'Rufus, come here,' just as the flirtatious French poodle the dog had been eyeing up earlier sauntered past.

Her despairing, 'Rufus, *no!*' was lost as he sprang up, blind and deaf to anything but his hormones.

He had only gone a few feet when one bitingly sharp, deep 'Sit!' brought him skidding into the required position seemingly in mid-air. *'Heel,'* followed with equal success, the dog performing a perfect Crufts manoeuvre to arrive in ingratiatingly quick time pressed close against the man's legs. As an authoritative male hand stretched out for the lead Cory handed it over. The next moment both lead and dog were returned to her.

'Thank you.' It was said with extreme reluctance.

'You can't suggest he does what he's told,' the man said with irritating coolness. 'It's all in the tone.'

'You're an expert on dogs?' Cory responded before she could stop herself.

'No.' In a leisurely exercise which stopped just short of being insulting, heavily lashed blue eyes wandered over her hot face. 'I'm an expert on being obeyed.'

Somehow she didn't doubt that.

'Obedience classes would be good for you,' he continued with insufferable condescension.

It didn't escape her notice that he had said good for her

rather than the dog. The fact that he had several bits of grass in his perfectly groomed hair gave her savage satisfaction. 'He's not mine,' she said shortly. 'My aunt recently acquired him from a dog sanctuary. They thought he'd been locked away in a shed from when he was a puppy and just thrown scraps now and again. She *has* been taking him to classes—' it was wonderful to be able to say it in all truth '—but she's broken her leg and so I offered to give him a walk this morning.'

The sapphire gaze left her face and turned downwards to the golden dog. 'Poor old boy,' he said directly to Rufus who wagged his tail furiously.

And then his voice lost the brief softness and returned to its former coldness when he looked at her again and said, 'For the sake of the dog and not least anyone in his path, keep him on the lead while your aunt is indisposed, would you?'

She bit her lip hard to prevent the spate of words which sprang to mind and counted to ten. 'I'd worked that one out for myself.'

'Good.'

It looked as though he was going to walk away and now Cory said quickly, 'Your phone; I meant what I said about paying for a new one. Do you want my telephone number and address?'

He raised his brow. 'Are you always so exceedingly generous in giving complete strangers your private details?'

He was deliberately needling her and she recognised it but still couldn't help being caught on the raw. 'I'm not in charge of a dog which knocks people down every day,' she returned smartly.

He muttered something she thought might be, 'Thank heaven for small mercies,' before saying, 'Don't worry about the phone, Ms...?'

'James. Cory James.' She looked at him steadily through velvet-brown eyes just a shade or two lighter than her hair. 'And I insist on paying for a new one, Mr...?'

'My name is Nick Morgan and, I repeat, forget about the phone.' He now took it from her, pocketing it nonchalantly.

'I can't do that.' The obstinate streak which ran through her slender frame like a rod of steel came into play. 'Rufus has ruined it and I wouldn't feel happy unless I make amends.'

The square male jaw tightened. 'It's not necessary.'

'*I* feel it is.'

'Are you always this—' he hesitated for the merest fraction of a second, and when he finished '—determined?' she felt sure that was not what he'd been about to say.

'Always.' She didn't smile and neither did he.

He folded his arms, surveying her for some moments without speaking. He was standing a couple of feet from her and in spite of herself her pulse was racing. It was his overwhelming masculinity that was sending the blood coursing, she told herself irritably, and she hated that he could affect her so. It wasn't attraction—it definitely, *definitely* wasn't attraction, she reiterated as though someone had challenged her on it—but more an awareness of the you Tarzan, me Jane type of definition of the sexes. What with his height, which must be at least six-three or four, and the hard look to his body, he was...well...

She couldn't find a word to describe what Nick Morgan was and so she gave up the struggle as he spoke again.

'A new phone will be provided the moment I walk into my offices,' he said evenly, 'but if you really feel the need for atonement?'

'I do.'

A thin smile curved across his mouth as though he found something amusing. The next moment Cory realised it was her reaction to his next words he had been anticipating with relish. 'Then I need a partner for a social occasion tonight and my proposed date has had to fly out to New York at short notice.' His eyes pierced her with laser brightness. 'Care to oblige?'

Cory took a moment to compose herself. She had never been so taken aback in her life. Was he joking?

Her face must have reflected her thoughts because the smile widened. 'I'm quite serious. Of course, if you have a previous engagement or a husband or boyfriend who might object…' He let his voice trail away but his gaze never left her.

She could lie. No, no she couldn't, she corrected herself in the next instant, because he'd know. Somehow she knew without question that he would be able to discern any fabrication a mile off. She looked at him squarely. 'I'm not in a relationship,' she said shortly. 'What exactly is involved tonight?'

'Cocktails, dinner, dancing.'

It wasn't a proper explanation and they both knew it. Cory waited for more.

After a few seconds had stretched themselves into what was to Cory unbearable tension, he said, 'I've recently taken over a particular company and this is a goodwill gesture by me for the senior management and their partners. Nothing heavy, you know? Merely a table at Templegate and us all getting to know each other on a social level.'

Cory stared at him, her mind buzzing behind the steady brown of her eyes. A table at Templegate for the evening? That was going to cost him an arm and a leg. She had never had the opportunity to see inside the most famous nightclub in London herself, but it was where the young, rich and beautiful went to see and be seen. Trendy magazines were always brimming with pictures of this or that celebrity dancing the night away there and it was common knowledge that dinner equated to a second mortgage. She swallowed hard. 'A party of how many?' she asked with what she considered commendable matter-of-factness.

'Just sixteen, or fifteen as of eight o'clock this morning,' he added wryly. 'My date was offered a modelling assignment she apparently couldn't refuse.'

His girlfriend was a model? But of course she was— what else? Cory asked herself waspishly. He was obviously filthy rich and enormously successful—if the takeover remark was anything to go by. That, added to his good looks, would make him the catch of the year and ensure women were lining up in their droves. This last thought caused her to say, 'But you must have someone else you can ask to stand in?'

'Must I?' he countered with lazy amusement.

'Well, haven't you?'

He didn't answer this directly. What he did say was, 'You wanted to make reparation for the dog and I suggested a way you could do so. If it's not to your liking, that's fine.'

It wasn't to her liking! Of *course* it wasn't to her liking. The kind of women who put in an appearance at Templegate wouldn't be seen dead in anything other than Versace or Gabbana or Armani; the shoes that clad their tiny feet would take a couple of months of her wages alone. And to spend the evening in the company of this complete stranger who was entertaining other complete strangers would be torture. She'd be terrified of saying or doing something wrong for a start, and what if they were all snooty and standoffish or just plain uncommunicative?

She took one swift glance around the park, which was bathed in warm June sunlight, as though it was going to help her before bringing her eyes back to the keen blue gaze. 'All right,' she heard herself saying with faint disbelief. 'If that's what you want, fine, although I'd rather just pay for the phone and be done with it.'

'Not the most gracious acceptance to dinner I've ever received.' The amusement was still very much in evidence as he reached into his briefcase and extracted a small gold-embossed card which he handed to her.

Cory glanced down expecting a formal business card, but it merely stated his name followed by four telephone numbers.

'Forget the first number, that's my home in Barnstaple,' he said a touch impatiently. 'The second is my London flat and the third my private line at the office. Obviously the mobile number is a little irrelevant now.' Piercing blue eyes fastened on Rufus for a moment and the big dog shifted guiltily at her feet. Nick's mouth twitched and then he glanced at the gold wrist-watch on one tanned wrist, his brow furrowing and the impatience more pronounced as he said, 'I'm late for an important meeting, Miss James. Ring the flat after six tonight to give me your address, or the office number if you need me before that. The table's booked for eight-thirty, incidentally, but we're meeting in the cocktail bar at eight. I would like to be at the club no later than seven-thirty. Is that acceptable to you?'

The vivid blue eyes raked her face again and her pulse gave an unexplained jump. She managed a nod while she took a deep breath. 'Look, I'm just an ordinary working girl,' she said a little breathlessly. 'I'm not used to places like Templegate, to be frank. If you find someone more suitable today who can help you then feel free to tell me tonight when I phone. I'll quite understand.'

He had been about to walk away but now he turned and looked at her. There was a swift assessment when his gaze moved over her from the top of her head to the soles of her trainers. His expression didn't alter and neither did the tone of his voice change when he said, 'I shan't change my mind, Miss James. Goodbye.'

Well! Cory's face was burning as she watched him walk away with long strides which soon put him far into the distance. He'd looked at her as if she was a horse he was considering buying!

She stood for a few moments more until a whine at her feet brought her out of the maelstrom of her thoughts. Glancing down at Rufus she saw he had the nerve to be looking hard done by at the inactivity. 'Don't even go there,' she warned him fiercely. 'This is all your fault.'

The dog grinned back at her before leaping to his feet and straining at the leash, his nose twitching as a cute Bearded Collie with a topknot tied with a big pink bow to keep the hair out of her eyes swayed past, a definite come-hither wiggle to her silky rear end.

'You definitely need a certain little operation, if you ask me,' Cory grumbled, before raising her eyes to gaze into the distance again. Blow, he'd gone. She shaded her eyes against the glare of the sun but after a moment or two was forced to accept he had disappeared from view.

All around the normal Saturday scenario was taking place—kids skateboarding, families strolling, couples stretched out on the grass sunbathing or reading, folk walking their dogs, groups of teenagers playing football or cricket or throwing Frisbees to each other—but she felt suddenly separate from it all. A run-of-the-mill walk in the park had suddenly turned into something extraordinary and, now he had gone, she had time to actually consider what had happened and she felt panic rise hot and strong.

She must be mad—stark staring mad—to agree to ac-company him to Templegate tonight! Not just accompany him but virtually act as hostess to a group of people she'd never seen before in her life. Why hadn't she said no? Why hadn't she taken the get-out clause he'd offered? What on earth had prompted her to acquiesce to such a ridiculous proposition?

She brushed the memory of a striking, evenly planed face and steel-hard body out of her mind determinedly. It wasn't *him* as a person, she told herself firmly as she began to continue the walk round the park. She wasn't interested in Nick Morgan, not in the least. That would be sheer madness. Anyway, he already had a girlfriend and the last thing she was looking for was a relationship of any kind. No, she'd felt obliged to make amends, that was all.

She glanced down at Rufus trotting happily at her side and groaned inwardly. Why had she let him off the lead? Aunt Joan had been specific and she'd ignored her advice—and not for the first time in her life, she added miserably. But she wasn't going to think of William Patterson now. She had enough problems right at this moment as it was, the most immediate being—what was she going to wear tonight? She would have to do some emergency shopping because she hadn't got a thing that would pass in Templegate's fabled surroundings.

As her feet quickened in time with the swirly butterflies in her stomach, Rufus had the most energetic walk he'd had for some time, and by the time the pair of them reached Cory's aunt's house they were both panting.

'Are you all right, dear?' her aunt asked mildly as she opened the door. 'You look a little warm.'

Warm would be great. Just being over-warm would be heaven right now. 'I did a silly thing,' Cory said miserably as she stepped into the cool hall. 'A very silly thing as it's turned out.'

'Really?'

She nodded.

'Ooh, lovely,' her aunt said happily. 'I'm always doing silly things and it's so reassuring when someone as together as you does too. The coffee pot's on, come and tell me all about it.'

Rufus settled in his basket, gnawing frenziedly at an enormous hide bone, and with a mug of fragrant coffee and a plate of chocolate digestives in front of her Cory felt a little better as she related the events of the morning. There was something terribly homely and nice in sitting in her aunt's farmhouse-type kitchen with a dog at their feet and bright sunlight picking the colour out of a bunch of marigolds in a vase on the windowsill.

When she'd finished explaining, her aunt was beaming. 'But that's wonderful,' she said enthusiastically. 'You'll have a wonderful meal in the most wonderful place and this man sounds—'

'Wonderful?' Cory interrupted wryly. There had been a sight too many wonderfuls as far as she was concerned. She was terrified, and here was her aunt acting as though she had just won the lottery or something.

'I was going to say very reasonable,' her aunt said reproachfully. 'He could have shouted or caused a fuss after all. Lots of people *would* have, and in this day and age of everyone suing everyone else at the drop of a hat…' She sighed, wagging her head in despair at the current trend. 'And all this Mr Morgan did was to ask you out to dinner at the most fabulous place. I mean, what's the problem?'

Put like that there wasn't one, but then her aunt hadn't seen Nick Morgan. Cory swallowed hard. 'I don't have a thing to wear,' she prevaricated, but even to her own ears it sounded weak. 'Not something that carries a million dollar label anyway.'

'Is that all?' The complacency was now most certainly of the Cheshire cat variety as Joan's smile widened. 'Darling go and see a friend of mine, Chantal Lemoine of Mayfair. She'll fix you up.'

This wasn't comforting. Cory loved her aunt—since her parents had died within a year of each other when she had been at university, her aunt was the only close relative she had—but Joan had never married and had made her career her life before she'd retired early at the age of fifty after a heart attack scare. She'd had a high-powered position in the world of fashion and hadn't thought anything of spending an exorbitant amount on a simple skirt or top. Since leaving university four years ago Cory, on the other hand, had felt drawn to work in the sector of social care, something which involved long hours, stress and a merely adequate salary. A salary which didn't lend itself to designer establishments.

Whether her aunt sensed what she was thinking Cory wasn't sure, but the next moment the older woman had picked up the telephone saying, 'I'm ringing Chantal, all right? It's your birthday in a few weeks' time and I didn't have a clue what to get you. This is the perfect answer. You go and choose something absolutely outrageously expensive. You've been an angel to me since my fall and I want to thank you.'

'I couldn't, Aunty.' Cory's cheeks were pink.

'You could and will.' And then Joan's expression and voice changed as she said softly, putting her hand on Cory's arm, 'Please, darling. For me. You're the daughter I never had and you never let me spoil you. Just this once indulge me, eh?'

Cory wriggled uncomfortably. It was true she looked on her aunt more as a mother than anything else. In spite of being an only child she hadn't been close to either of her parents, who had been so wrapped up in each other they hadn't needed anyone else, not even their daughter. It had been a lonely and not particularly happy childhood in many respects, and her Aunt Joan had often been an oasis in the desert. Whether because of her childhood or perhaps just the way she was made, she'd always been reserved and independent, preferring to help rather than be helped and to give rather than receive.

'Hello, could I speak to Miss Lemoine, please?' Her aunt had taken her hesitation as a yes. When Cory went to speak Joan waved her to silence with a raised hand. 'Chantal? Darling, how are you? It's Joan.' A few seconds and then, 'Yes, we must as soon as this wretched leg of mine is better. Perhaps lunch at Roberto's? Look, the reason I'm calling is to ask a favour. I'm sending Cory to you—you remember she's my niece? She has a very special occasion tonight—at Templegate. Yes, I know, it's very exciting. The thing is, she needs something really gorgeous and I thought you might be able to help. Could you see to her personally? Advise her on what suits her best? I'd come myself but with this leg... Oh, you're a sweetheart. Two o'clock will be fine. Thanks so much, darling. And put it on my account, would you, this is a little birthday treat. Bye-bye, Chantal.'

The receiver replaced, her aunt beamed at her. 'That's settled then. Sweetheart, you're going to have a perfectly lovely time and you'll look beautiful. Chantal will guarantee it.'

Cory smiled but said nothing. The day wasn't going at all as she had planned.

CHAPTER TWO

IT WAS five to seven and Cory was panicking big time, not least because she barely recognized the girl staring back at her out of the mirror. When she'd left Chantal earlier that afternoon, the little Frenchwoman's parting encouragement had been, '*Chérie*, make up your mind to enjoy a night on the tiles in haute couture style! Yes? You will look enchanting. As the late Gianni Versace once said: "If you make an entrance and nobody turns to look at you, my dear, find a back door and leave. And then find a new dress." I promise you, *chérie*, you will not have to find the door,' Chantal had said with great satisfaction. 'Not in that dress.'

It *was* beautiful. Cory's gaze left the frightened eyes in the mirror and travelled downwards. And in this case the clothes did definitely maketh the woman. The midnight-blue silk just missed being black, the cap-sleeved bodice with flattering collar-bone-skimming neckline topping a skirt with the same leaf transparencies and beading, and, as if all that wasn't enough to catch the eye, the skirt had vertiginous side slits. These had caused Cory to protest that she couldn't possibly wear the dress out before she had tried it on, but once Chantal had zipped her up she'd had to admit that it did something to her figure and skin that was riveting.

'This is the one,' the little Frenchwoman had cried. 'This is the dress that makes you a goddess.'

Goddess was going a bit far, Cory thought, her gaze returning to check her make-up for the umpteenth time. But the dress did do something for her that was amazing. She dreaded to think how much it had cost her aunt. None of the clothes in the exclusive shop had had anything so vulgar as a price label. Presumably if one couldn't take the heat one stayed out of the kitchen!

When she'd made noises about the cost, Chantal had merely tapped the side of her small nose and shook her beautifully coiffured head in disapproval. 'This is the gift, yes?' she had scolded, making Cory feel terribly unsophisticated. 'Your aunt will know and this is enough. Now…' She had gone on to recommend another couple of establishments where Cory could purchase suitable accessories but, although she'd thanked the older woman, Cory had known she wouldn't be stepping through their doors. Shoes and bags at several hundred pounds a go just wasn't an option on her salary.

Instead she had looked round various high street shops and market stalls, eventually finding delicate strappy sandals in just the right shade with a little purse to match in Covent Garden. Racing home to her flat in Notting Hill— the purchase of which had taken every last penny of her inheritance, but which had been supremely worth it—she had showered, washed her hair and set about moisturising and perfuming for the night ahead.

Should she have left her hair down? She glanced again at the silky smooth chignon she'd persuaded her shoulder-length waves into. It had seemed too fussy somehow, the dress being so stunning, but her hair had been up and down three times before she had made up her mind.

'Stop it.' She breathed the words out loud into the quiet, pastel-coloured bedroom. 'It's just a nightclub, they're just people like everyone else, *he's* just a man.' And he'd reduced her to talking to herself already after one brief meeting!

An authoritative buzz from the lobby entry intercom

brought her hand to her throat before she breathed deeply, willing the panic to subside. Walking through into the small square hall she steeled herself to press the button situated to the side of her front door. 'Yes, who is it?' she asked with a breathlessness she could have kicked herself for.

'Nick Morgan.' Succinct and to the point.

'I'll be right down, Mr Morgan. If you'd care to wait in the lobby…' She pressed the building's door release before flying back into the bedroom in a tottering scramble which warned her that the sandals didn't lend themselves to anything other than dignified sedateness, not unless she wanted to end up on her rear end, that was. And that was unthinkable in front of Nick Morgan.

Snatching up her purse, which was just large enough to hold her keys, lipstick, two twenty pound notes for emergencies—in case he didn't intend to see her home for example—and a few tissues, she walked carefully back to the hall, opening her front door and then making her way down the wide staircase which led to the lobby.

The old Victorian house had been converted to three fairly large flats, one on each floor. The ground floor flat was owned by a retired couple with a massive German Shepherd called Arnie who had a howl like a wolf's. This was the biggest apartment, having three bedrooms and its own tiny garden. Cory's flat and the one above each had two bedrooms and a large balcony off the sitting room French windows. The young married couple above her had made their balcony into a miniature garden, but Cory's contained a small table and two chairs and a large lacy palm in a big pot and that was all. Her work sometimes involved excruciatingly long hours for a couple of weeks or so and if a problem occurred in one of the families she was assigned to the last thing she wanted to worry about was watering plants.

She was concentrating so hard on descending gracefully, balanced as she was on her giddily high, needle-thin heels, that she didn't lift her head until she'd reached the safety of the tiled floor of the small entrance lobby.

'Wow.'

The deep male voice brought her head turning. Nick Morgan was leaning against the far wall, hands thrust in his pockets and black hair slicked back from his brow. He looked like something every red-blooded woman from the age of sixteen to sixty would love to find in their Christmas stocking. An exquisitely cut dinner jacket sat on shoulders broad enough to satisfy even the most demanding female, and the smile lighting up his blue eyes was electric.

Cory forgot to breathe as he walked towards her, only managing to mumble, 'Hello,' at the last moment.

'You look sensational.'

'Do I?' Oh, come on, you can do better than that. She wasn't totally without the ability of social repartee. She took hold of herself, adding, 'Thank you, you look pretty good yourself,' with a coolness she hoped he didn't know was completely feigned.

His gaze moved over her hair, eyes made up to look huge, and carefully painted lips, and there was a faint note of surprise in his voice when he said, 'You'll set tongues wagging tonight. They'll all want to know where I found you.'

He made it sound as though she was a stranded puppy he'd brought in from the cold. She forced a smile, saying lightly, 'I think it was the other way round, don't you? Or rather, it was Rufus who did the finding.' And then, because his comment really had caught her on the raw for some reason, she added sweetly, 'Perhaps it would be better if we didn't explain I had to pick you up from the floor.' She hadn't, not exactly, but if ever there was justification in stretching a point, Cory felt this was it.

He blinked, just once, but she knew she'd taken him aback. The smile dimmed a little for one thing. 'Quite.' He took her elbow. 'Shall we go?'

That had set the boundaries quite nicely; at least she hoped so. There was no way she was going to let this man patronise her, even if he did have the clout to take half of London to Templegate as his guests. Wealth did not equate to lordship, not in her book.

Once outside, even the heavily laden city fumes couldn't obliterate the beauty of a perfect June evening. The air was soft and warm, the buzz of the city lazy and evocative. Cory felt a little thrill of anticipation she wouldn't have thought herself capable of just minutes before.

Instead of the taxi she'd been expecting, she found herself led to a chauffeur-driven Mercedes. After seating her inside the vehicle, Nick Morgan joined her. 'Templegate, please, George,' he said easily, before settling himself more comfortably beside her. She could feel the imprint of a hard male thigh against her hip but didn't dare move. She wouldn't give him the satisfaction of thinking he bothered her in any way—if he was thinking along those lines, which he probably wasn't, of course.

Burningly aware of the way the slits in the dress revealed a tantalising amount of leg, Cory tried to think of something else. Nothing came to mind.

Too late she realised he'd said something and she'd missed it. 'I beg your pardon?' she said politely.

'I asked you if you'd been to Templegate before.'

It was slightly stiff as though he was offended about something. Cory suddenly wondered if he usually had to repeat himself when he was taking a woman out for the evening. She rather doubted it.

The surge of adrenalin this caused enabled her to say quite airily, 'No, I haven't as it happens although I've heard about the place, of course. One goes to see and be seen, I understand?'

'I wouldn't know about that.'

Oh, no. Right.

'The chef there is second to none, however.' He looked her full in the face as he spoke, forcing her to meet his gaze. The blue of his eyes was like the deepest ocean, something to drown in. 'And the guy in the cocktail bar, Luigi, is a master of his art. His drinks carry a sting in the tail that have made many a grown man wake up with the mother and father of a hangover the next morning.'

'Thanks for the warning,' she said tightly. He was too close. The confines of the luxurious car were too intimate. Her dress was too revealing. She turned her head to look out of the window.

There was a long pause when the air between them hinted at the delicious sensuality of his aftershave.

'Relax, Cory.'

It was the first time he had called her by her Christian name and it acted on her overwrought nerves like a cattle prod. 'Relax?' Her gaze shot to meet his again. 'I don't know what you mean. I'm perfectly relaxed.'

'Yeah?' He glanced meaningfully at her lap and for the first time she realised her hands were tight fists.

'Look, you won't be expected to do anything tonight,' he said quietly. 'Just enjoy yourself, okay? There are no hostess duties, if that's what's worrying you.'

She wasn't sure exactly what was worrying her but playing hostess was only part of it. She managed a little bounce of her head which could have passed for a nod. 'Your girlfriend,' she said awkwardly. 'She's not going to get the wrong idea about this?'

'Girlfriend?' Dark brows furrowed and then cleared. 'Oh, you mean Miranda? The model? No, she'll be fine. And, incidentally, she's a friend without the girl in front of it, if you get my meaning.'

She did. And she wasn't sure if that made her feel better or worse. Probably a bit of both. Which went with the general craziness of this whole evening.

'If we're supposed to be a couple—' again her eyes shot to his and he smiled innocently '—at least as far as my guests are concerned, I should know a bit about you, shouldn't I? Your work, hobbies, things like that.'

It sounded reasonable. It would have *been* reasonable if it was anyone but Nick Morgan. Which wasn't fair, Cory acknowledged silently. She didn't know him, not in the least, and he might be a very nice person under the arrogance and good looks and blatant wealth. William had been all those things too and she'd given him the benefit of the doubt, more fool her.

She smiled a brittle smile. 'I'm a social worker, working with disfunctional families on the whole. The hours are long, but when I'm not working I'm either eating, sleeping or preparing to do one or the other. Okay?'

He didn't say a word, merely continuing to observe her as the Mercedes purred through the evening traffic. Much to her annoyance, Cory found she was the one who looked away first.

She didn't know why she was loath to reveal anything about herself and her private life to this man, but the check was there, in her spirit. In truth she had lots of friends with whom she socialised and, although she had to do the odd intense stretch at work where she had no time to see anyone, these didn't occur all the time.

It was a good minute or two before he spoke again, and then his voice was bland. 'No time for fun then?'

'Not much, no.'

'Pity.'

'I don't think so.' He was really annoying her now, not by what he said but the tone in which he said it. But then it was her fault if he was pitying her. 'I love my work.'

'I enjoy mine but I still have a life outside it.'

'Like tonight?' she asked with a touch of sarcasm.

'Tonight, I admit, I'm combining work and pleasure.'

He didn't rise to her bait and Cory found herself feeling somewhat ashamed. She was being awful and she didn't understand why.

And then he slid shut the glass partition which gave them privacy from the driver, leaning towards her as he said softly, 'Are you always this prickly or is it me? Have I done something to offend you, Cory?'

She wished he wouldn't say her name like that, in that deep smoky way. Say something, she told herself. Anything to pass this off. She found she couldn't, her thought processes seemed to have faltered and died.

She cleared her throat, moistening her lips and then wishing she hadn't as the piercing gaze followed her tongue. 'I guess I'm just a little nervous,' she managed at last. 'Meeting your guests and so on.' She waved a vague hand. It wasn't the people though, just one person and he was sitting right beside her.

'You are more than a match for them.'

It was dry and she wasn't quite sure if he was complimenting her or not.

Her face must have revealed her thoughts because his searching gaze was replaced by a smile. 'You have a very open face,' he said, the smile lingering at the corners of his mouth. 'I would have thought that would've been a handicap in your line of work.'

She arched an eyebrow. 'I can be deadpan when I want

to be,' she assured him evenly. It was just that this capability didn't seem to work around Nick Morgan, although she wouldn't give him the satisfaction of admitting to it.

He settled back in the seat again and Cory breathed an inward sigh of relief as the space between them expanded.

'So the reason for your single status is down to work obsession?' he asked smoothly after a small pause.

She didn't answer this directly. 'I do not have a work obsession.'

Her voice had been clipped and again the corners of his mouth twitched. 'What else would you call it when a beautiful woman eats, sleeps and drinks her job?' he asked mildly.

'A career?' She couldn't remember when she'd last felt so mad with someone.

'A career doesn't exclude having friends—'

'I do have friends.'

'Or going on dates,' he continued as though unaware of her interruption.

'*Look, Mr Morgan*—'

'Nick.' The tone was amiable. 'Call me Nick or else my guests will think I've hired you for the evening.'

He had in a way. She put that fact to one side and concentrated on her main line of attack. 'I'm sorry but I really don't see that my lifestyle is any of your business,' she said hotly. 'You asked me to stand in for your girlfriend—'

'She's not my girlfriend. I thought we'd already ascertained that.'

'Whatever.' She put a wealth of disinterest into the word. 'Anyway, you asked me to stand in for her and I have. I don't think that that merits the third degree.'

'You think a little polite social intercourse qualifies as the third degree?' he asked with reproachful innocence.

Cory swallowed the words she wanted to say. They still

had the rest of the evening in front of them and some pretence at togetherness would be required, besides which she was blowed if she was going to rise to his bait. She breathed deeply, counted up to ten and smiled sweetly. 'One's definition of politeness can vary so much from person to person, don't you think, depending on background, upbringing, just how nice someone is?' she said with saccharine civility.

He knew exactly what she was really saying. Vivid blue eyes held defiant velvet-brown for a few moments and then, to her surprise, he threw back his head and laughed. 'You're a formidable lady, Miss Cory James. I have to admit I wondered how a slender young thing like you would be able to take on some big butch parent or other shouting about their rights. Now I know.'

Cory frowned. 'Do you usually stereotype people so harshly?' she said sharply. 'Most of my families are great people who are struggling to keep it together after a rotten start in life. They deserve every little bit of help and support they can get. It's people like you—' She stopped abruptly. The evening would certainly be over if she told him what she thought of people like him, and with her aunt paying a fortune for this dress and it having taken her hours to get ready she might just as well see the inside of Templegate!

It was very quiet in the car now. Then Nick said, 'You don't like me, do you.' It was a statement, not a question.

Cory chose not to say anything. The truth was apparent in her silence anyway.

'Why is that, I wonder?' he mused thoughtfully.

How long had he got? She nerved herself to glance at him. Bearing in mind he had been pretty reasonable about Rufus, as her aunt had pointed out, she prevaricated, 'I don't know you so how could I not like you?'

'If you'd put just the tiniest amount of warmth into that

I might have attempted to persuade myself you meant it,' he said drily. 'Is this state of hostilities going to continue all night because I think my guests might have severe indigestion at the end of it if so.'

She glared at him. 'I promised I'd accompany you and I wouldn't dream of being other than courteous to your guests.'

'I'm aware of that. I just thought they might find the evening something of a strain with you savaging their host at every opportunity.'

The underlying amusement in the deep voice made her want to hit him. Instead she called on all her self-control and said calmly, 'There's no question of that. I wouldn't do or say anything to embarrass them.'

'So I can count on you to give the impression we're the perfect couple?'

'Utterly,' she said with biting sarcasm.

'Love's young dream even?' he drawled lazily.

The quirk to his eyebrows and complete refusal to be affronted by her bad humour brought a reluctant smile to Cory's face. Impossible man!

'That's better.' He grinned at her and it did something powerful to the ruthlessly handsome face that made her heart race. 'Now, let me give you a quick who's who of who'll be there tonight, OK? They're a nice bunch on the whole but one or two are still a bit tender after the takeover. Understandable, but not conducive to good working relations. Hence this evening.'

Cory nodded. His tone had suddenly become very businesslike and that suited her down to the ground.

By the time the Mercedes drew up outside the chrome and glass building that was Templegate she'd absorbed most of the background information Nick had given her. She knew that five of the couples were married, including the big chief, Martin Breedon, and that Martin and his wife had recently been presented with their first grandchild. 'Good talking point,' Nick said cold-bloodedly. 'Folk are always gaga over their grandchildren.' The remaining four consisted of a couple who both worked at the company and who were seeing each other, and a David Blackwell who was bringing a date.

The chauffeur opened the car door but it was Nick who assisted her out of the vehicle before saying, 'Bring the car at three, OK, unless I ring before that,' whereupon he took her arm and led her into the building.

Three o'clock? This was going to be one long night. And then Cory's mind was washed clear of everything but her immediate surroundings. The place was as expensively luxurious as she had expected and huge, but as Nick ushered her into the cocktail bar, which was fairly buzzing, she spotted at least three celebrities without even trying.

Closing her mouth, which she knew had fallen open, and trying to appear as if she was completely au fait with the milieu, Cory took the seat Nick had pulled out for her at a table which overlooked the vast nightclub below. After glancing at the cocktail menu, she tried to look for the least alcoholic drink. She needed to keep all her wits about her tonight and doubtless it would be one where the drinks were flowing.

'If you're not sure, how about a champagne cocktail?' Nick suggested quietly. 'I've ordered champagne for the table.'

'Lovely.' She smiled brightly. Once he had walked across to the massive circular bar which ran round three-quarters of the room and behind which a number of waiters were busy shaking mixers and juggling bottles with amazing dexterity, Cory studied the ingredients. Brandy, a couple of dashes of angostura bitters, dry champagne and a white sugar cube. That didn't sound too lethal, certainly not compared to the Negroni, which was comprised of Campari, sweet vermouth and gin, or a Margarita, which looked pure dynamite. And she'd make the one last.

When Nick returned she took the champagne flute with a smile of thanks, lifting it in a salutation as she said, 'To a successful evening.'

'To a successful evening *and* my beautiful companion.'

She smiled again before taking a sip of the sparkling drink. It was delicious. She could well understand why the cocktail had been a favourite of stars of the silver screen in the forties; it epitomised the elegance and sophistication of that wonderful era beautifully.

'Well, this is very civilised.'

It could have been a pleasant social comment but she'd seen the wicked glitter in his eyes and knew he was making a point after her antagonism in the car. She decided to ignore it and take the words at face value. 'Isn't it,' she agreed lightly. 'And what a place this is. Like a film set.'

'The owner's always been a sucker for the sort of lavish decadence of the Fred Astaire, Ginger Rogers age. He set out to appeal only to the rich and famous, and he succeeded. There are more film stars, models and footballers here per square yard than anywhere else in the world.'

There was something, just the merest inflexion in the deep voice, which suggested he didn't altogether approve. Cory stared at him curiously. 'You're here,' she pointed out quietly, 'so you must enjoy all that too.'

'Must I?' It was laconic. And then as she continued to keep her eyes on him, he said, 'It's amusing to drop in now and again and undeniably useful for tonight's sort of occasion.'

'But you don't like it?' she persisted.

'I didn't say that.' The blue eyes surveyed her under

brows which suddenly had a moody tilt. 'It's just that I've found that wealth and fame don't always equate to good manners and acceptable behaviour. The desire to be a sensation and fêted and adored can be ugly when it becomes an obsession. Alex has made a fortune with Templegate and knows just how to keep the latest celebrity purring, whilst being able to take any tantrums and smooth ruffled plumage. I couldn't do that.'

She didn't doubt that for a minute. 'Alex?' she asked interestedly. 'Do you know the owner then?'

'We were at university together.' He paused, finishing his cocktail in one swallow before he said lazily, 'Care for another?'

'I'm fine.' She'd barely touched her own drink.

This time he raised a hand and immediately a waiter was at his side. After he'd given his order, Nick pointed out a well-known politician who had just entered the bar with a glamorous female on his arm who was easily young enough to be his daughter, if not his granddaughter, and then went on to mention other well-known faces he'd seen at Templegate. It wasn't until much later that Cory realised he'd turned the conversation away from himself most adeptly.

When the others arrived the atmosphere was a little tense at first, but Cory's misgivings about Nick's guests being standoffish were soon put to rest. With the exception of perhaps David Blackwell, the man who had brought along a date in the form of a tall willowy blonde who smiled a lot but who said little, she immediately felt at ease with them.

After cocktails, they were led to their table in the main section of the nightclub and Cory wasn't surprised it was in a prime position at the edge of the dance floor. The food was excellent, the floor show which entertained them while they ate equally so, and with the armour of the extravagant dress in place Cory felt as good as any of the other women in their designer evening wear.

The circular shape of the table prompted dialogue in which everyone could share, and she soon realised Nick had set himself out to be both charming and amusing. He was winning them all over, she mused, finishing the last of her pudding—a creamy orange charlotte—which had tasted heavenly, with real regret. Not that she would have eaten another morsel, she admitted to herself reluctantly, but each spoonful of the light, tangy dessert had been the stuff dreams were made of.

It was as the floor show ended and coffee arrived at the table that Cory noticed the look on David Blackwell's face. Everyone was laughing at something Nick had said, their amusement ably enhanced by the amount of very fine champagne which had been consumed, and David, who had just been to the men's cloakroom, was within a few feet of the table when she happened to glance his way. His bitter expression shocked her before he became aware of her gaze and immediately stitched a smile in place.

What was all that about? Cory asked herself, returning David's smile briefly before she turned back to Martin on her right as the older man spoke to her. What axe was David Blackwell grinding that made him so full of resentment towards Nick? And then she shrugged the thought away, telling herself it was none of her business and that it didn't matter anyway. After tonight she wouldn't see any of them again, including Nick, so any problem or disputes between Nick and David were unimportant to her. She was here to fulfil an obligation, that was all.

As though Nick had been aware of her thoughts, he now reached out a hand and covered one of hers where it was resting on her wineglass. 'Enjoying yourself?' he asked softly as her startled gaze met his. 'In spite of the reason you agreed to come?'

His flesh was warm and firm and a thousand little pin-pricks shot out through her nerves at his touch. Ridiculous, she told herself. Ridiculous to react like this to a man you don't know and have no particular wish to know either. 'Yes, thank you,' she returned politely, slipping her hand away from under his on the pretext of reaching for her napkin to dab at the corners of her mouth.

'Good.' If he had noticed her withdrawal he didn't comment on it. 'Let's dance.'

'What?'

Before she'd had a chance to protest he had drawn her to her feet, his cool smile washing over the others as he said, 'The night's young, folks. Enjoy it.'

Before she knew where she was Cory found herself in his arms on the dance floor. There were only a few couples taking advantage of the slow, easy number the jazz combo were playing, but it wasn't that which had caused the sudden tension radiating through every nerve and sinew. His body was hard and strong, and held close to him like this his height was emphasised, making her feel fragile and feminine. It was a nice feeling. And she didn't want to have nice feelings around Nick Morgan. Neither did she want to acknowledge what the sensual scent of his aftershave was doing to her equilibrium.

She lifted her head, determined to say something to break the curiously intimate spell which seemed to have woven itself around them. His eyes were waiting for her, their blueness riveting, and causing the words to die in her throat as his body betrayed what her closeness was doing to him. 'You're one beautiful, sexy woman, Cory James,' he murmured huskily.

A tingle of excitement fluttered over her skin. It was a

warning and she knew it. William had said all the right things and before she'd known it she'd been in way over her head. She was never going to let that happen again. 'It's the dress,' she said, carefully and deliberately, forcing a flatness into her tone. 'Not me.'

He continued to look down at her and she prayed the trembling which had begun in her stomach wouldn't transfer itself to the rest of her body. The incredible width of his shoulders, the male squareness of his chin enhanced by the merest cleft and the ruggedness of the handsome face all proclaimed a virile masculinity which was overwhelming.

'No, it's not the dress,' he said softly, his eyes dark and intense. 'Although it's stunning.'

Stunning it might be but she regretted wearing it right now. No, no she didn't, she qualified in the next moment. She wanted to look sexy and beautiful to him. But then again it was the last thing she wanted. Which didn't make sense... Their gazes were still locked and she forced herself to break it, pulling back a little and glancing round the room as she said, 'It's a present, the dress. I didn't have anything remotely good enough for this place.' Suddenly the need to make him see they were poles apart was paramount.

'Who from?'

'What?' She glanced at him again.

'A present from whom?' he asked quietly, a look on his face now that Cory couldn't quite pin down.

'Oh, my Aunt Joan.' The music had changed and now a livelier number had drawn more people on to the dance floor. Cory noticed they were the only couple still entwined but when she tried to disentangle herself from his arms they merely tightened.

'Your Aunt Joan.' His face had cleared. 'Not an admirer then?'

'An admirer?' She stared at him, mingled surprise and outrage vying for first place. 'Of course not. As if I'd accept a present like this from a man.'

'It happens.' His voice was dry.

'Not with me it doesn't.' She glared at him.

'I'm very pleased to hear it.'

He was laughing at her! Oh, not openly, but she knew amusement was there in the tone of his voice and the way the firm, hard mouth was trying not to smile. 'You can let go of me for this dance,' she said frostily.

'Perhaps I don't want to let you go.'

'People are looking.'

'Let them look.' He bent his head and skimmed her mouth with his lips. 'There, that'll give them something to talk about,' he said evenly.

For one giddy instant the room swam. The caress had been too fleeting to be called a kiss but she'd felt the contact right down to her Covent Garden shod toes. She blinked. 'Don't do that, please,' she said as firmly as her breathing would allow. 'It's not in the agreement.'

'We didn't discuss the finer points, if I remember correctly.'

Cory ignored the little flame that had been ignited deep inside and frowned at him. 'Perhaps because I thought it wasn't necessary and that you were a gentleman.'

He grinned, completely unabashed. 'Big mistake,' he said cheerfully.

She ought to be furious at the arrogance but instead she found herself trying not to smile. But she couldn't let him suspect that. 'Shall I spell it out for you then?'

'Please do,' he said politely, laughter glinting in his eyes.

'I agreed to come here tonight because I'm in your debt about Rufus, but acting as your—'

'Girlfriend?' he put in helpfully.

'*Companion*,' she corrected firmly, 'only necessitates the most elementary bodily contact.'

He looked as though he was enjoying himself. 'Define elementary,' he said interestedly, his hand at her waist finding bare skin through one of the carefully positioned leaf transparencies and stroking it almost absent-mindedly.

Cory took a steadying breath. 'In this context elementary means straightforward, simple.' Her skin was melting. '*Rudimentary*,' she added desperately.

His head tilted as though he was considering what she'd just said. 'Sorry, can't agree to that.' His eyes danced over her hot face. 'Call it the interest on the debt if you like, but for this evening you're my consort and I'm not the kind of guy who is happy with…elementary bodily contact.'

In the same moment that the music finished Cory noticed David and the blonde at their elbow, the other man's close set eyes fastened avidly on their faces. It was enough to break the spell of Nick's closeness, and it enabled her to jerk away out of his arms. 'I'd like to sit down now, please.'

'Sure.' He took her hand, weaving his way through the couples on the dance floor and pulling out her chair for her when they reached their table.

Had David Blackwell been listening to their exchange? Cory tried to think exactly what had been said and what impression an eavesdropper might have formed as she sipped at her champagne, but it was difficult with the music and conversation all around. Making the excuse that she needed to visit the Ladies' cloakroom, she rose from the table, vitally aware of Nick's eyes on her as she left the room although she didn't glance his way.

Once in the relative quiet of the reception area she found the cloakroom—an elaborate affair of marble and mirrors— and sat down on one of the cream cushioned seats in the outer area to repair her lipstick. As her mind continued to dissect all that had been said on the dance floor she had to stop herself from groaning out loud. It might have sounded almost as if she was a hired escort of the most basic kind to anyone who didn't know the true facts.

She put the lipstick back in her purse, fiddling with her hair as her mind sped on. But then what she'd thought earlier still applied—she'd never see any of these people again so it didn't matter how they viewed her. She just didn't like someone like the Blackwell man getting the wrong idea, that was all. Admittedly she didn't know him but the guy gave her the creeps.

She straightened her back, her eyes narrowing as she stared at the reflection in the mirror. She wasn't going to worry about David Blackwell or anyone else for that matter. She'd fulfil her obligations tonight and make sure she went home alone in a taxi in view of Nick's earlier comments. She wasn't sure if he would be crass enough to try anything on when she'd made it clear how she felt, but she wouldn't give him the chance. The man was dangerous— she refused to qualify to herself that it was her response to him that was dangerous—and she didn't need any complications in her life at the moment.

When she stepped out of the cloakroom Cory had only taken a couple of steps when David caught hold of her wrist. He made her jump, having come up behind her, and her voice was sharp as she shook her hand free and said, 'Don't do that, please.'

'Sorry, sorry.' He was smiling but she'd noticed before that his smiles didn't reach his eyes. 'I just wanted a word with you, that's all.'

'Couldn't it have waited until we're at the table?'

'In private.' His voice was low. 'I wanted to speak to you in private, Cory.'

She didn't like the way he spoke her name in that slightly conspiratorial tone and her voice reflected this when she said, 'I don't know you. How could we have anything to discuss privately?'

'Look, I'll come clean.'

He was too close and the amount of aftershave he was wearing was making her feel nauseous. It had a sickly sweet scent with a tang of something else beneath it, much like the man himself, she suspected.

'I couldn't help overhearing what you and Nick were saying on the dance floor and I take it you aren't his actual girlfriend?'

Cory stared into the weasely face. Was this a come-on, because if it was he'd get more than he'd bargained for.

When she neither confirmed nor denied this, he went on, 'The thing is, I suppose you know he's just taken over the firm, lock, stock and barrel? A lot of people were upset at first but they've all gone quiet, pay-offs I suppose,' he added bitterly.

Where was this going? 'That's nothing to do with me.'

'I know that but—' He paused. 'Look, it was clear from what he said that he fancies you and that you aren't inter-ested. Most women fall in adoration at his feet.' Again hot resentment came through loud and strong. 'That being the case, I'd make it worth your while if you could find out a couple of things for me.'

'What?' She stared at him in absolute amazement.

'If you just jollied him along I'm sure he'd talk to you. You know, pillow talk. You could ask him about the take-over and how people were, whether he paid on the quiet to

get Martin's co-operation, things like that. I reckon I'm the
only one who hasn't had a backhander and it's not fair.'

He wanted a backhander? She'd give him one right
round his nasty little face if he said another word. And
pillow talk? How dared he? 'If you want to know anything
about Mr Morgan's dealings with the rest of your associates
I suggest you ask him yourself,' Cory said icily. 'OK?'

His eyes narrowed at her tone but then a wheedling note
came into his voice. 'That'd be no good, facing him head
on like that. It's the ladies who are his weakness. You could
get more out of him with just being friendly than I could
in a month of Sundays. He wouldn't suspect anything if
that's what's worrying you. He's used to women throwing
themselves at him all the time.'

'Really?' If she'd been anywhere else but her present
surroundings, Cory would have socked him on the jaw.
'And I wonder why that is? Could it be that he is a real
man rather than a snivelling little excuse for one? You
picked the wrong woman to ask to do your dirty work, Mr
Blackwell, and the minute I go back into that room Mr
Morgan will be told of your proposition, all right?'

'That won't be necessary.'

The deep, cold voice behind them made them both jump
a mile, and Cory found herself tottering on the exorbitantly
high heels for a breathtaking moment. Like David, she'd
spun round with more haste than care. Righting herself, she
saw a different Nick from the one she'd known all evening.
This one was frightening.

'Nick.' David's voice was sickeningly obsequious. 'This
isn't what you think.'

'Save it.' The blue eyes could have been cut from granite. 'This isn't the time or the place. My office on Monday
morning. Eight o'clock sharp.'

'But let me explain—'

'There's no time, you're leaving.' Nick raised his hand and as though by magic one of the staff was at his elbow. 'Would you be so good as to tell Miss Miller on table twelve that Mr Blackwell is waiting out here for her, please?'

As the man hurried away David tried again, and Cory felt like telling him it was no use.

Nick cut into David's servile excuses after the first sentence. 'We might just keep this civilised if you disappear right now,' he said grimly, 'but don't push your luck, David. Not tonight. Ah, Fiona…' As the blonde appeared with a puzzled expression on her pretty face, Nick waved his hand at David, saying, 'I'm afraid David is indisposed but I'm sure he'll see you safely home. Goodnight.'

As Nick took Cory's arm and walked her away, he murmured, 'Do you want a few minutes to compose yourself before we join the others?'

Did birds fly? Her head was spinning and she didn't know if she was on foot or horseback. She nodded, and the next minute she found herself ensconced in the cocktail bar, which was now almost completely deserted. Sinking down on to a seat, she said faintly, 'What will you do to him?'

'Don't worry about David Blackwell; his type always come up smelling of roses.' As the waiter came over, Nick said to her, 'Another cocktail?'

'Is it possible to have a coffee instead?' She felt a little tipsy as it was.

'Make that two, please.'

The waiter looked as though he was going to protest for a moment, but after a glance at Nick's face he said quickly, 'Two coffees it is, sir,' and disappeared.

'For the record, there have been no hand-outs.' Nick looked her straight in the eye. 'It's true Martin didn't want to relinquish the reins but we reached a compromise where we're both happy. Unfortunately the guy's too soft for his own good and has carried a lot of dead wood for years—like David Blackwell—so there will be changes to be made. I'm sure David's got wind of that and is feeling threatened.'

'I think he feels a lot more threatened now.'

'With good cause.' And then so suddenly that it made Cory catch her breath, his face changed, his voice warm and throaty as he said, 'Thanks for being on my side out there.'

She didn't know what to say. She shrugged uncomfortably. If he'd heard the bit about the hand-outs he'd been there longer than she would have liked.

Like before, he seemed to know what she was thinking, his voice now holding a thread of amusement when he murmured, 'I especially liked the bit about me being a real man.'

'A gentleman wouldn't mention he'd heard that,' she said, knowing she'd gone a bright crimson.

'I thought we'd already ascertained that I'm not a gentleman.' His smile lit the flame inside again and this time it burnt stronger.

Cory was very glad when the coffee arrived a moment later.

were both happy. They threaten the equies, so I'll tell his
own good and be carried ever as clear wood the ret???
like David Blackwell, so, they will be chances to d?? made.
'I'm sure David is a very careful, responsible man,' she said.
'I think he works a lot more than you'd now.'

CHAPTER THREE

CONTRARY to what she had expected after the unpleasant
incident with David Blackwell, Cory found she thoroughly
enjoyed the rest of the evening.

When they returned to the table Nick said briefly that
David was feeling unwell and had had to leave early.
Which was true in a way. The other man had certainly
looked green about the gills when they'd left him.

No one seemed particularly concerned or interested that
David and Fiona were no longer with them; in fact with
the young man's departure the whole group seemed more
relaxed and natural, in Cory's opinion. She wondered just
how much David had been whispering in people's ears
about Nick. A little yeast could very quickly work through
a batch of dough, and David had seemed resentful of Nick
as a person as well as an employer, as the remarks about
Nick being popular with the ladies had shown.

Everyone stayed right to the end of the evening at three
o'clock, whereupon they all declared they'd had a night to
remember. Cory could agree with this as a good part of it
had been spent in Nick's arms on the dance floor.

She'd put the idea of going home in a taxi to one side.
Somehow the episode with David had taken her and Nick
beyond such a thing. Now, as everyone said goodnight
amid hugs and handshakes, the possibility that Nick might
expect more than a goodnight peck was at the forefront of
her mind. It excited her as much as it scared her. She
couldn't get involved with Nick—every nerve and bone in

her body was telling her so. He was way, way out of her league in every respect.

He'd probably not want to see her again anyway. Men the whole world over seemed capable of nipping in and out of bed with this woman or that without it really meaning a thing to them and, from what David had said, Nick was never short of female company.

But she was jumping the gun here. He hadn't suggested bed. He hadn't suggested anything.

Slow down, she warned herself silently. Stop panicking. You are a grown woman of twenty-five who is more than capable of taking care of herself in every way, not a fifteen-year-old schoolgirl.

They waited until all of Nick's guests were safely on their way home in the fleet of taxis he'd ordered, and then he led her over to the Mercedes, which was parked across the road. 'Care to come back to my place for a nightcap?' he asked softly as he opened the car door for her.

'No.' It was too quick and now she moderated her refusal with a smile as she said, 'I'm exhausted; it's been a long day.'

He nodded, joining her in the car and sliding the glass panel which separated them from the driver to one side. 'Back to Miss James's place please, George,' he said quietly before closing it shut again and then pulling a blind down so they were now quite private.

Cory went into overdrive. More flustered than she'd ever been in her life, she searched for something, anything, to distract him. Then she found herself saying, 'I wondered if we'd see your friend, Alex, tonight but he didn't appear.'

'He's in the States.'

'Really?' She was burningly aware of a hard male thigh against hers. 'On holiday or business?'

'Holiday.'

'In what state?' she gabbled. 'America's such a huge country, isn't it, and so fascinating. I think—'

She never did tell him what she thought because he kissed her. Really kissed her. And it was everything she'd imagined it might be. Hot, stunningly sweet and altogether mind-blowing.

She could tell he was devastatingly experienced, a man who would know a woman's weakness and just how to use it for his own advantage in the seduction stakes. The warning in her mind was there but it didn't mean a thing while his mouth was working its magic and his arms were pressing her close to his hardness.

Almost leisurely, he explored her mouth until her heart thudded wildly against the steady beat of his and she was kissing him back in total surrender.

This was crazy, insane. She knew that, knew she had to call a halt before things got out of hand, but it was impossible with her blood singing through her veins and molten lava in the pit of her stomach. His hands were clever, stroking her arms and the smooth roundness of her shoulders until her skin was on fire with his caresses.

She gave herself over totally to the kiss, knowing the danger of letting herself become vulnerable to this man but unable to help herself. He kissed so well; she had never been kissed like this in all her life. She'd found most men used a kiss as a preliminary to other things but Nick seemed in no hurry to progress, seemingly enjoying her mouth as much as she was relishing his.

His hands moved up to her hair and within a moment it was falling down about her shoulders, silky soft and smelling of apple blossom shampoo. His fingers tangled themselves in the rich strands, using them to draw her head backwards to allow him greater access to the sensitive skin of her throat.

Cory moaned softly, her hands sliding over the powerful male chest muscles flexing beneath his shirt. The faint scent of aftershave she'd noticed earlier was teasing her nostrils again, its essence wild and dangerous, feeding her desire with its elusive aroma.

She heard him whisper her name as his mouth came back to hers, his voice husky. She knew what he wanted because she wanted it too, and it didn't seem to matter where they were or what the rest of the world was doing.

The thought was enough to bring her abruptly to her senses. This was a William Patterson situation all over again. *He'd* had charisma and that extra something which was undefinable but which made a woman go weak at the knees. *He* had pursued her, using his wealth and magnetism to dazzling effect until she hadn't known if black was white. She'd been wary at first. Why would a man like William, fifteen years older than her, rich, successful, be bothering with a little nobody fresh out of university? She'd been right to be wary. She should have gone on being wary...

She had stopped kissing Nick back and unconsciously stiffened as the memories had flooded in, and now she became aware that he had picked up on her withdrawal as he drew away. 'What's wrong?' he asked very quietly, but without the annoyance or irritation she'd half-expected.

'I...I don't do this, not on the first date.' Although it wasn't a date, as she'd reminded him this evening. Which made everything a hundred times worse.

'You don't kiss?'

His voice was still without expression and, because she could only catch glimpses of his face now and again by the light of passing streetlamps, she had no idea if he was angry or not. She didn't know how to answer him. How could she say that what they'd just shared had been more than a kiss, at least to her? That would give all the wrong signals. And to admit she had presumed it was the prelude to something more would be even worse.

Cory swallowed. 'Not like this, no.'

'Like this?'

'In...in the back of a car.' She swallowed again. 'A goodnight kiss on the doorstep is one thing, but this is more...'

'Intimate?' he finished for her.

'Yes.'

'Nice, though.' There was warmth in his voice now and she was glad of the darkness to hide her burning cheeks. There was a pause and then he said, 'OK, no more kissing until I deposit you on your doorstep.' Before she could resist, his arm had gone round her and he drew her into his side, holding her against him, pushing her head down on to his shoulder. 'Relax,' he said softly. 'Shut your eyes and think of that doorstep.'

'Nick—'

'No more talking, not unless you want me to remember I'm not a gentleman.'

Relax he'd said, with every nerve she possessed twanging and her heart thumping fit to burst at his closeness.

It seemed a long, long time until the Mercedes purred to a halt outside the flat. Cory knew exactly how a jelly must feel.

'Your doorstep awaits, Ma'am.' The deep voice was smoky with amusement.

From some unexpected reserve of self-preservation, Cory managed to feign sleepiness as she raised her head from the pillow of his shoulder. 'Are we here?' she mumbled, pretending to yawn. 'I must have been dozing.'

He didn't challenge her on the lie, but there was a distinctly quizzical slant to his mouth as he exited the car and then helped her out.

The night air wasn't cold—in fact there was a humid balminess to the shadowed street which suggested another hot June day in store—but Cory shivered as his big hand closed over her fingers. When she was standing on the pavement she tried to gently disentangle herself from his hold, but Nick was having none of it.

Instead he pulled her to the front door of the house. 'Come on,' he said coolly. 'In we go.'

'There's no need for you to come up,' she protested quickly. 'Thank you for a lovely evening and—'

'I'm seeing you to your front door.' It was spoken in a tone which brooked no argument. 'I'd never forgive myself if a mad axeman was lying in wait,' he added with every appearance of seriousness.

She didn't trust the solemnity any more than she trusted him. 'I hardly think that's likely.'

'No? You want to look at the news and read the papers more often. Rape, pillage, mayhem and destruction are all part of the world we live in,' he said cheerfully. 'Do you want me to open the door?'

'I'm quite capable, thank you.' Having said that the keys had got themselves jammed in the lining of the purse some-how, and it took a few moments to yank them free under his amused gaze.

Once inside the hall, Cory whispered, 'You'll have to be very quiet. The people on this floor have a dog that hears the slightest thing and then barks enough to wake the dead.'

'Wonderful,' Nick murmured sarcastically.

'It is, actually. It makes everyone feel very safe.'

'Haven't they heard of burglar alarms?'

A low growl from across the hall persuaded Cory to give up the argument. She slipped off her sandals preparatory to climbing the stairs and, as she straightened, he whispered, 'You've just lost about five inches. What have you been walking on all night, stilts?'

She couldn't help giggling. 'You wait till you see my glass eye and wooden leg.'

'I can't wait.'

As they reached the first landing where her flat was all amusement left Cory however. Was he expecting to be asked in for a nightcap? Was he expecting to be asked in for something else? Or both? But she'd made it plain how she felt in the car—she hoped. But if he kissed her again…

'Thank you for a lovely evening,' she began.

'You've already done that bit.' He had to bend further to kiss her this time now she was minus the sandals, and it was still more satisfying than the most expensive chocolate. All the feelings he'd aroused in the car were there, and her arms were just beginning to snake up to his shoulders when she was free. 'Goodnight, Cory,' he said blandly.

Goodnight? She stared at him, totally taken aback, before she pulled herself together. 'Goodnight,' she said quickly. 'And I meant what I said, by the way. It was a lovely evening.'

He smiled, his eyes glittering in the dim light on the landing. 'I thought so.' His hand reached out and stroked the silky skin at the side of her face below her ear.

Cory had never realised there were so many nerve-endings in one place. Should she ask him in and blow the consequences? The force of the temptation was so strong it was enough to kill it. Besides, he had already turned and walked to the head of the stairs.

'Sleep well,' he said lazily.

He wasn't going to ask to see her again. Well, she'd expected pretty much that, hadn't she? And if he had, she'd determined she'd say no anyway.

'Fancy lunch tomorrow?'

Her heart did an Olympic leap and then raced for gold. The moment of truth. *Remember William.* She didn't want to remember William, she wanted to say yes. Which was why it had to be no. 'Lunch?' she repeated weakly.

'You know, that meal in between breakfast and dinner?'

It was easier when he was being sarcastic. 'I don't think so, thank you.'

'Why not?' He rested his arms on the banister, his face full of sharply defined planes and angles in the shadows.

'Because—' She hesitated. Should she lie and say she had a prior engagement? But he'd only suggest another time. 'Because I'm not dating at the moment.'

'The work thing.' He shook his head. 'Not a good enough reason when your dog damn near broke my back.'

'I've made recompense for that,' she said indignantly. 'And Rufus isn't my dog anyway.'

'You were in charge of him.' He grinned. 'Do you want to see my bruises?'

'Not particularly.' He was doing the charm bit again and it was lethal. Good job William had made her immune to such ploys.

'There are women who'd die for the privilege.'

'I don't doubt it.' She was determined not to smile.

'I'll be back at midday. There's a great little pub I know where the roast beef melts in the mouth and the Yorkshire puddings are more than puffs of air.'

'I've told you, I'm not dating,' she said severely.

'And I've told you, this isn't a date but more paying off your debt. I don't like to eat Sunday lunch alone.' He straightened. 'OK?' he threw over his shoulder as he began to walk down the stairs.

Not OK. Definitely not OK, but it was like saying no to a brick wall. She followed him to the top of the stairs, looking down at his back as she hissed, 'Nick, I'm not having Sunday lunch with you.'

'Twelve sharp.' He turned just long enough for her to see the flash of his white teeth in the darkness. 'And I'm not backing off, Cory, so accept with good grace.'

'Nick!'

He was in the hall now and his voice was low and reproachful when he murmured, 'Quiet, remember the dog.'

She muttered something very rude about the dog just as the front door closed behind him.

In spite of the late hour, after Cory had showered and removed her make-up she found she was wide awake. The events of the evening were spinning through her head like a fast moving film and sleep was a million miles away. She tossed and turned for an hour or more before getting out of bed and padding through to the kitchen.

A mug of hot milk and half a packet of chocolate digestive biscuits later, she tried to get a handle on the way her life had been turned upside down in less than twenty-four hours.

The man was a human bulldozer, she told herself irritably. It would serve him right if she was out tomorrow when he called.

But she wouldn't be.

She sighed. This was madness. Getting involved with a man like Nick Morgan, even briefly, was asking for trouble. Unbidden, thoughts of William intruded and for once she was too muddled and over-tired to stop them.

When she had met him she had left university six months earlier and had been training for her present job. She and her colleagues had treated themselves to a Christmas meal at an expensive restaurant and it had been there she'd bumped into him—quite literally. The heel of one of her shoes had suddenly snapped and she'd fallen against him.

She reached for another biscuit, needing the sweetness to combat the acidity of the memories.

She had known from the beginning that William was wrong for her, that he was the type of man who would never be happy settling down with just one woman. But he had pursued her, probably because she was a challenge. Normally women fell into his lap like ripe plums and it had been something of a novelty for him to be the hunter for once. She had known that, in her head, but in spite of that she had found herself falling for him. Some little grain of sense, of sanity—call it what you would—had prevailed, however, and in spite of all his efforts he hadn't got her into his bed.

Then he had asked her to marry him.

The packet of biscuits had almost gone now. Feeling mad at herself for the self-indulgence, Cory stuffed the remainder back in the biscuit barrel and turned off the kitchen light, padding back to her bedroom and climbing into bed.

She had been over the moon at William's proposal. It had meant he wanted her, *really* wanted her and not just as a sexual conquest. For the first time in her life she had felt loved, the hang-ups from her lonely childhood and teens fading into the distance.

He'd suggested a weekend in Paris to celebrate the engagement, declaring he knew the most perfect little jeweller's shop there where she could choose her ring. She'd said yes—who wouldn't? Of course she'd known that 'celebrating' would probably mean more than the limited lovemaking she'd allowed so far, but they were going to be married…

Why she had called unannounced at the advertising agency William owned the night before they were due to leave for Paris, she didn't really know. She had been visiting a problem family in Soho, and rather than go straight home she'd decided to stroll the mile or so to the agency in Mayfair. With hindsight it had been the worst—and the best—thing she could have done.

Nearly everyone had left by the time she got there, but after assuring William's secretary—whom she'd met at the door—that she'd surprise him, she had made her way to his office on the top floor of the building. And she'd surprised him all right, as well as the partially clothed blonde he had been writhing with on the couch.

The scene which had followed had been ugly. He'd accused her of being frigid, an emotional cripple and plenty more besides in an effort to justify himself. She had walked out and had never seen him again from that day to this. A very messy end to an affair which never should have started in the first place.

Cory sighed, turning over in bed and hammering at her pillow, which felt as if it was packed with rocks. She had to get some sleep; she'd look like a wet rag in the morning. She began the technique she'd perfected in the months after William's betrayal, relaxing all her muscles, one by one, from the bottom of her feet to the top of her head.

Half an hour later she was as wide awake as ever, but this time it was Nick Morgan who was featuring on the screen in her mind.

She must have drifted off at some point after it became light, because when the alarm woke her at nine o'clock she was in the middle of a particularly erotic dream which made her blush to think about it.

How could she imagine such antics with a man she'd only met the day before? she asked herself in the shower. She could still feel the electricity racing through her veins which she'd experienced in the dream when Nick had touched and tasted her, and the heat in her body was nothing to do with the warm water cascading down on her. Crazy. She turned the dial to cold. It didn't help much.

He was early—fifteen minutes early—but as Cory had spent the last two hours agonising over what to wear, she was ready. Her bedroom looked like a bomb had hit it and almost every single item of clothing she possessed was on the bed or floor, but Nick wasn't going to go in that particular room so it didn't matter. She closed the door firmly. In fact she'd made up her mind he wasn't going to set foot in the flat let alone her bedroom. This lunch was going to be the end of the road. Just the state she'd got in over what to wear had convinced her of that.

After William she hadn't had a date for some time, but when she'd felt ready to go into the arena again she had made sure any hopeful suitors understood pretty quickly that what she had to offer was limited. Fun, friendship, the odd kiss and cuddle but nothing heavy. She had no intention of letting a man into her life, her mind or her body. She needed to be in control of any relationship from the beginning, and she ended things immediately if any man couldn't keep to the rules of engagement.

She didn't want to suffer pain again. As she pressed the intercom and told him she would be straight down, Cory's mouth was tight. Her parents had been unable to love her as parents normally did and William had just reaffirmed that there must be something lacking in her. Something which caused people not to want her like she wanted them. So she'd concentrate on her work, on making a difference in an area where she *was* needed. And that would suffice. It would, because it had to.

She hadn't opened the front door of the building for him this time, so when she stepped out into the hot June day

Nick was leaning against a snazzy little black sports car parked across the road. He looked…disturbing. His pale blue shirt was tucked into the flat waistband of his trousers and was unbuttoned just enough at the neck to show the beginning of the soft black hair on his chest.

Narrow-waisted and lean-hipped, he had a flagrant masculinity that was impossible to ignore. It was intimidating, and that made her annoyed because she didn't want to feel intimidated. It put her at a disadvantage even though he couldn't know how she felt.

'Hi.' He walked towards her, his thickly lashed blue eyes appreciative as they took in the pale rose jeans and bubble gum pink flounced strapless top she was wearing. She had left her hair loose today, wearing only a touch of mascara and lip gloss, the wide silver hoops in her ears completing the picture of casual elegance for a hot summer's day. She had been determined not to dress up too much and by the same token wore the minimum of make-up; she hadn't wanted him to think she was making an effort—even if it had taken over two hours to decide on her look.

'Hello.' She knew her cheeks matched her top but she couldn't do a thing about it.

'I'm glad you decided to come,' he said softly.

Decided to come? She'd been railroaded by an expert and he knew it. She sucked in a shaky breath but her voice was surprisingly firm when she said, 'The way I remember it, I had little choice?'

'Ouch.' He pretended to wince. 'You were supposed to say, preferably with a sweet smile, that you were glad I'd asked you, that you've been looking forward to it, something like that.'

'Really?' She provided the sweet smile. 'But I don't lie very well.'

He grinned at her, apparently totally unabashed. 'Then

I'll just have to work hard today to make sure you're looking forward to our next date, won't I?'

No way, no how. If ever she'd needed proof she'd inadvertently caught a tiger by the tail, it was in that grin.
The word charm had obviously been invented with Nick
Morgan in mind. She tried very hard to ignore her racing
heart. 'Surely your model—Miranda, isn't it?—is back
from the States soon?'

They had just reached the car and he brought her round
to face him with both hands on her shoulders. He gave her
a hard look. 'One, Miranda isn't *my* anything. Two, I've
no idea when she returns because she's not obliged to report her whereabouts to me. Three...' His frown changed
to a quizzical ruffle. 'Three, have you any idea what the
feel of your bare shoulders is doing to me?'

Possibly. His shirt was thin and the dark shadow beneath
it suggested his powerful chest was thickly covered with
hair.

Cory took the coward's way out. 'No Mercedes today?'
she said brightly, hoping he wouldn't notice the slight
croakiness to her voice as she turned and pretended an interest in the car. 'Is this yours too?'

'Weekend runabout.' He opened the passenger door.
'Purely to impress my legion of women, of course.'

She decided to ignore the sarcasm. After sliding into the
car, which gave the sensation that one was sitting at a level
with the road, she straightened her back and folded her
hands in her lap so she wouldn't make the mistake of
bunching them again and betraying her tenseness as she'd
done the night before.

When Nick joined her, it took all of Cory's control to
maintain the pose. The close confines within the car was
the ultimate in travelling intimacy and wildly seductive.

As he started the engine she glanced at him. 'Where are we going?' she asked with careful steadiness.

'Surprise.'

'I don't like surprises.'

'Tough.' The blue eyes did a laser sweep of her face. 'But don't worry, I'm not into spiriting women away and forcing my wicked will on them. Not on a Sunday lunchtime anyway,' he added lazily.

'I never thought you were.' She hoped the haughty note had come through in her voice.

'No?' He swung the streamlined panther of a car smoothly into the Sunday traffic, his gaze on the road. 'You could have fooled me. I'm getting the distinct impression you view me as the original Don Juan.'

'Not at all,' she said stiffly, refusing to dwell on how large and capable his hands looked on the leather-clad steering wheel, or how those same hands had caressed her last night in the back of the Mercedes.

'Good.' It was casual, as though he didn't care much one way or the other, and as she glanced at him again she saw a small smile was playing about the firm mouth. 'So, tell me a bit about yourself,' he went on. 'I gather you have an aunt living around here with a broken leg. Any more family? And what about siblings to take turns with Rufus the terrible?'

Cory's heart plummeted. She didn't want to talk about herself, not to him. She had the feeling that the less Nick knew about her, the better. Still, she could hardly refuse to tell him the basics. 'My parents died some years ago,' she said flatly, 'and I don't have any brothers or sisters. My Aunt Joan is my closest relative.'

'And you get on well with her?'

'Oh, yes.' She was unaware of the sudden warmth in her voice but the big man at the side of her noted it. 'She's always been more than an aunt to me. My parents…well, they were busy people. They didn't have a lot of time…' Her voice trailed away as she became aware she was in danger of revealing too much.

'A peaceful childhood then? With lots of friends to make up for the lack of brothers and sisters?' he asked casually.

Lots of friends? She had never been allowed to bring friends home or invite anyone round for tea, neither had she been permitted to go to other children's houses when they had invited her. It had been too much trouble for her parents, interfering with their plans. The string of au pairs her parents had had all through her childhood had been instructed to make sure that, once she had been given her tea, she was despatched up to her room to do her homework. After that she had been allowed to read or watch TV, but never encouraged downstairs except to say goodnight. Her room had been spacious with its own *en suite* bathroom, and the TV and all her things had been of the best, but it had still felt like a prison.

Cory's stomach clenched. She looked away through the side window so he had no chance of seeing her face if he glanced at her, the silky curtain of her hair swinging forward. 'It was quite peaceful at home,' she agreed evenly.

If he noticed that she had only answered half his question he didn't comment on it. 'Any pets?'

In her mother's immaculate surroundings? 'No, no pets,' she said quietly. 'What about you? Do you have family living near?'

'Depends whether you think Barnstaple is near. I was brought up there and my mother still lives there although my father died five years ago.'

There was a note in his voice which prompted her to say, 'I'm sorry. Were you close?'

'Very. He was a great guy. But my mother has my two

sisters and their families to keep her busy; they both live within walking distance from the old house. I have a property in the area too, but due to the business I'm away more than I'm at home. Hence the flat in London.'

'So you had a happy childhood?' she asked curiously, drawn by the affection in his deep voice as he'd spoken about his family.

'The best.' They had just drawn up at some traffic lights and again the blue gaze raked her face. 'Hence the nicely rounded, well-adjusted individual you see in front of you,' he said quietly.

The lights changed in the next instant but, as the car purred on, the content of his last words stayed with Cory. Had he been hinting that she wasn't those things or was she being over-sensitive here? she asked herself silently, her mouth unconsciously tightening. If it was the former then he'd got a right cheek because she was fine, just fine. But it could be the latter...

She risked another sideways glance through her eyelashes. It probably wasn't the moment to notice the way his dark hair curled ever so slightly into the base of his neck. It wasn't short and it wasn't long but it suited him perfectly. She wondered how it would feel if she sifted her fingers through the soft strands. And then she caught the errant thought quickly and looked straight ahead before he caught her observing him.

She was going loopy here. What on earth was she doing fantasising about this man? In fact, how come she was with him in the first place? She wanted her head examined!

By the time they reached the pub, which was close to Hampstead Heath, Cory just wanted out of the car. She couldn't ever remember being so aware of every little movement or action by another human being. Nick, on the other hand, appeared perfectly relaxed and at ease, chatting about this and that and keeping the conversation strictly impersonal now.

Once inside the pub, which was all brass and copper and leaded windows, he led her straight through and out into the small, flower-bedecked garden at the rear. 'This is our table.' He pointed to a table for two set next to a lattice of climbing roses which were scenting the air with their rich sweetness.

'How do you know?' The pub had been packed inside and out here the few tables there were were full.

Nick reached out and removed a reserved sign from the table. 'Trust me,' he said, smiling. 'I know the owner.'

'Not another university friend?'

'Boyhood friend this time. John and I grew up together.'

'And he always keeps this table for you?'

'If I ring up and request it, yes. Which I did first thing this morning.' He pulled out a sun-warmed seat and she sank down, the perfume of the flowers and the caress of the sun on her skin blissful.

'They do a great Brunello here,' Nick said, still standing. 'Do you like red wine?'

'Love it.'

'I'll get a bottle. I shall limit myself to one glass as I'm driving but I guarantee once you taste it, you'll be unable to resist another. Shall I order two roast dinners while I'm at it?'

Cory nodded. This was nice, too nice.

So was the wine when it came. The intense chocolate and nutty aroma was a ripe explosion of taste in the mouth, and she closed her eyes and just breathed in the aroma made all the more potent by the hot air. 'This is gorgeous,' she murmured, taking another long sip.

'Don't tell me I've found the way to your heart?' Nick

had sat down opposite her, his eyes slightly closed against the sun and his long legs stretched out in front of him.

Forget about the roast dinner, Cory thought wryly. He looked good enough to eat. She raised an eyebrow. 'With one glass of wine?' she said severely. 'I think not.'

'The bottle's there, feel free.'

She smiled. 'I've always believed in moderation in all things.'

'All things?' The blue eyes were wicked.

'*All* things,' she insisted firmly, refusing to acknowledge the innuendo.

'Then it's as I thought,' Nick said with obvious complacency. 'Your education in certain areas has been sadly neglected and I look upon it as my duty to set things right. What you need to do from this point, Cory, is to look upon me as your teacher and guide into the ways of the flesh. OK?' And he took a long, satisfying drink of wine.

She laughed. Well, there was nothing else she could do really, because she couldn't take him seriously. In spite of the bolt of lightning that had shot through her.

'I'm more than up to the task,' he assured her softly, putting down the glass and taking one of her hands in his. He turned her fingers over so that the soft, vulnerable underside of her wrist was exposed, stroking it with first one finger and then—shockingly—as he raised her hand to his mouth, his warm lips.

'Don't!' She snatched her hand away, almost knocking the wine over. 'Don't do that.'

'Why not?' He sat back in his chair, his eyes on hers. 'It's nothing.' His smile was lazy.

It *was* nothing and yet it suggested everything—all the forbidden delights of her dream were in those warm, knowing lips. She knew exactly what he was trying to do and she was determined not to acknowledge her own desire and need. She shrugged. 'I don't play those sort of games,' she said shortly.

There wasn't even a hint of a smile on his lips when he said, 'Who's playing games?'

CHAPTER FOUR

CORY could have kissed the little barmaid who arrived at the table with their food just after Nick had spoken. In the ensuing activity the moment for her to respond to him came and went, and she made sure she tucked into her meal without further ado. The Sunday roast with all the trimmings was delicious, as was the hazelnut and cherry pie which followed, all washed down with another large glass of wine by Cory and sparkling mineral water for Nick.

Nick's friend brought their coffee, pulling up a chair from a table which had been vacated when Nick invited him to join them for a glass of wine. 'Here.' Nick poured the last of the wine into his empty glass and passed it to John. 'Cory insists she's had enough.'

'Potent stuff, isn't it?' John was a slight blond man and he grinned at Cory as he spoke. 'My favourite ever since Nick introduced me to it years ago. Bit expensive for the pub trade but I always make sure a bottle's in for when this guy turns up.' He punched Nick lightly on the shoulder. 'I can only stay a minute or two, though. Lucinda—the wife,' he added in an aside to Cory, 'will be on the warpath if she catches me slacking.'

'Are you man or mouse?' Nick put in.

'Where Lucinda's concerned? Definitely rodent.'

He was only halfway through the glass and in the middle of relating an incident from their childhood—about the time when he and Nick had been caught scrumping from a farmer's orchard—when the said Lucinda appeared. Big, buxom and definitely Italian, she bustled over to their table, throwing her arms round Nick and then scolding him for staying away for too long, before she clipped her husband round the ear. 'You creep out here without telling me and then you drink the last of Nick's wine,' she remonstrated in a heavy accent. 'You are the impossible man. You see what I have to put up with?' she appealed to Nick. 'And who is your beautiful lady?' she added, turning a beaming smile on a bemused Cory.

'Cory James meet Lucinda Robinson,' Nick said, laughter in his voice. 'And her bark's worse than her bite.'

'Says who?' said John, rubbing his ear. 'She used to do that when she was a little thing the size of Cory but I could keep her in her place then. She packs a fair wallop now.'

'Oh, you.' Lucinda planted a smacking kiss on John's lips, pinching his bottom as she added, 'I keep you warm at night though, yes?'

'That you do, wench.' John smiled at his wife and for a moment the look the two exchanged brought a lump to Cory's throat. This was love, true love. It was shining out of their faces. For a second she envied the other woman from the bottom of her heart.

After a few more minutes, during which time Lucinda had extracted a promise from Nick that he would attend her thirty-fifth birthday party in the middle of July—Cory having ducked her invitation by saying she would have to check her diary—the two disappeared back into the pub, leaving them alone. They were the last ones in the garden now, apart from a cheeky robin who was busy pecking a morsel of gateau under a nearby table and chasing off a horde of hopeful sparrows when they got too near his plunder.

'How long have they been married?' she asked Nick as they finished the last of their now cool coffee.

'Ten years.'

'Have they any children?'

He shifted in his seat. 'Lucinda can't have any. They tried everything but...' He shrugged. His eyes lifted to hers as he continued, 'It was a bad time. She comes from one of those huge Italian families where every daughter pops one out a year. They were living in Italy then but when she had a nervous breakdown John brought her over here for a change of scene for a while. That was five years ago and they haven't looked back since.'

'And John doesn't mind? About not having children?'

Nick looked at her levelly. 'He minds like hell, but the way he sees it he didn't fall in love with Lucinda because she was some sort of baby-making machine. He loves *her*, he always has from the day he first set eyes on her.'

Cory stared at him. She wanted to cry but he would think she was mad. Nevertheless her voice was thick when she said, 'They're lucky, the way they feel about each other, I mean.'

'Yes, they are, but they're not unique.' His eyes were holding hers now and although she wanted to break the contact she found she couldn't. 'That's what you were thinking, wasn't it,' he said softly, and it was a statement not a question. 'That they're unique. I could read it in your face.'

She wanted to deny it but he would know she was lying. 'Not unique,' she prevaricated. 'More...unusual.'

'Why do you think that way?'

It was straight for the jugular but she was recognising he was that sort of man. She couldn't answer him. She let her hair fall to cover her face. 'I don't want to continue this conversation.'

'OK.'

It was immediate and almost nonchalant and the tone shocked her. Which was ridiculous, she told herself angrily.

She hadn't wanted him to pursue the matter so why should she feel so let down that he didn't seem to care?

'Let's go for a stroll on the Heath to walk the lunch off and get ready for dinner,' Nick said easily as she raised her head again.

Dinner? Who had said anything about dinner? 'I don't think—'

'Good. Don't think. I like you better that way.'

'Now look—' And then she noticed his smile. Weakly, she said, 'You're trying to wind me up.'

'Me?' He leant forward as he stood to his feet and kissed her on the top of her nose. 'As if. Finish your wine while I go and settle with John. We'll leave the car in the pub car park for now.'

He was gone before she could object.

Cory had wanted to stay remote and detached on the Heath but she found she couldn't. The beautiful day had brought many Londoners out into the fresh air, the fathomless blue sky above too perfect to waste time indoors.

They walked hand in hand, talking now and again, and unlike in the pub garden she found herself relaxing, waves of contentment flowing over her like a balmy breeze.

'You're beginning to burn.' Nick pulled her into the shade of an old tree, the bottom of its trunk splotched with lichens and velvety moss. The grass was thick and warm as they sat down, and in the distance two young boys were throwing a Frisbee for a shaggy mutt of a dog who was barking enthusiastically as he ran.

Cory turned her head. Nick was stretched out beside her, hands clasped under his head and his eyes shut. He opened one eye. 'We've had the walk, now it's time for a nap.'

This was far too beguiling. 'You make us sound like a

couple of old-age pensioners,' she said flatly, aiming to break the mood. 'And I don't nap during the day.'

'Try.' He reached out one arm and pulled her down beside him, settling her head on his chest. 'Even a pillow provided,' he drawled lazily, idly stroking her hair. 'Now shut your eyes like a good girl.'

She was as tense as piano wire for a few minutes but then, as he made no move to kiss her or do anything except slowly stroke her hair, she found herself relaxing. The heat of the day, the dappled shade through the leaves of the tree, the muted sounds in the background all combined to unknot her nerves and make her drowsy. At the most she had only managed two or three hours' sleep the night before and the Sunday lunch had left her comfortably full, not to mention the soporific effect of the wine. She slept.

When she next opened her eyes, Nick was looking down at her. He was propped on one elbow and her head was now resting on his middle. 'Hello,' he said, very softly.

Still dazed with sleep, she murmured, 'Hallo yourself.'

When he bent and kissed her it seemed the most natural thing in the world to lift her arms about his neck. She still wasn't awake enough to fight the realisation that she had been waiting for this moment all day, the moment when he would really kiss her again.

He made no attempt to touch any other part of her body yet every nerve came alive, twanging with sensation as the kiss deepened.

When he drew away he was breathing hard, his voice gruff as he said, 'Any more and I shall forget where I am, and we don't want to frighten any little children, do we.'

She smiled as she was meant to, but she couldn't help wondering if she had imagined the note of what had sounded like surprise in his voice.

He seemed to confirm, it, however, when he said, 'I'm

not sure what you do to me, Cory James, but it could get to be like a drug.'

'Is that good or bad?' She heard herself flirt with a little stab of amazement, but it all seemed to be part of the lazy afternoon.

'Depends.' One finger traced the outline of her lips.

'On what?'

'How often I can get a fix.'

Enough. She sat up, brushing her hair out of her eyes as she said, 'I told you, I don't—'

'Date. Yes, I remember. So when do you see that changing?'

'What?'

'You'll want to settle down one day, surely, so how do you intend to find Mr Right if the opposite sex is out of bounds?' he asked smoothly.

She found his presumption galling to say the least. 'Why should I want to settle down? Because I'm a woman?'

He stared at her, the riveting blue of his eyes betraying nothing of what he was thinking. 'I've found most of your sex are inclined towards ultimate monogamy, babies, that kind of thing.'

'Well, I'm not,' she said firmly.

'You don't want babies one day?'

'No. Yes. I mean—' What did she mean? 'Babies are not part of my plans for the future.'

'That's a little harsh, isn't it?' he asked mildly.

'Not if it prevents them just being mere incidentals in someone else's life.' She'd spoken too quickly and from the heart without considering her words, and now she could have kicked herself as she watched the piercing gaze narrow.

'Incidental? Is that how you saw yourself in your parents' lives?'

Cory made a conscious effort at self-control. She couldn't believe how they had arrived at talking like this. She had known some of her friends for years and years and they had never remotely touched on such intimate subjects. She had known Nick for a couple of days and here he was giving her the third degree. 'Let's change the subject,' she said stiffly.

'Let's not.' He rose to his feet, pulling her up with him and then keeping her within the circle of his arms when she made to pull free. 'Cory, most kids grow up knowing they are the most precious things under the sun to their parents,' he said softly. 'I'm sorry, heart sorry, if it wasn't that way for you, but don't let anyone else's mistakes push you down a path where you don't really want to go.'

'How do you know where I want to go?' His words had bit into the secret recesses of her heart like acid. 'You don't know me. You didn't know my parents either so don't make any snap judgements on them or me.'

He was quite still for a moment, then he said, 'It'd be a crying shame if someone as beautiful and sensitive as you shut herself away from life. Don't you see that?'

'Life meaning sex?' she asked with a baldness that shocked her. 'And sex meaning your bed, I suppose?'

'My bed is certainly big enough to accommodate the two of us,' he said mildly, 'but I wasn't necessarily referring to it. I can actually think about something other than sex occasionally.'

'Then you're one of the few men who can.' Again she could have kicked herself, What was she *doing*? She had to calm down. He was far too perceptive for his own good—or maybe that should be *her* good. She tried to prise his arms away but they merely tightened.

'What was his name?'

'Whose name?' she hedged, swallowing hard.

'The guy who let you down. Because you have been let down by someone, haven't you, Cory? Was it recently?'

Her frozen state resembled a rabbit caught in the headlights of an oncoming car.

'You can tell me to go to hell,' he said grimly, 'but I'd rather hear if it's really over, at least from your side.'

'It's over,' she said dully.

'In your heart or in your head?'

He really didn't seem to know when to stop. The thought brought enough adrenalin for her to break free and take a step backwards, her voice a snap when she said, 'Both, OK? Both. Is that what you wanted to hear?'

'Yes, it is.' And he didn't sound in the least apologetic about his temerity.

'His name was William Patterson and he was rich, good-looking and very sure of himself. He asked me to marry him and then I found him making love to someone else. Is that enough information? Oh, and it was over three years ago now.' She had put as much sarcasm into her voice as she could to stop it trembling.

He didn't say anything for what seemed like a very long time to Cory's overwrought nerves. Then he stuffed his hands into his pockets, his eyes still on her. 'Her name was Joanna and we *were* married,' he said quietly. 'She was killed instantly when a drunk driver on the wrong side of the road knocked her car straight in front of a lorry on Christmas Eve. She'd popped out to get some bulbs for the lights on the tree so it would be ready when I walked in from work. The drunk driver had bruises, nothing else.'

'Oh, Nick.' She was scarcely breathing.

'It was a long time ago, Cory, thirteen years to be exact. We had only been left university for six months. We were still two kids, playing at being married but enjoying every moment. I was twenty-two but I grew up very quickly that night. After that…' He shrugged. 'I threw myself into work and the next year started my own business. It was good to have something to drive at.'

'And you've never… I mean, there hasn't been anyone else you've wanted to—' She stopped abruptly, aware she was putting it badly.

'I've had relationships since Joanna,' he said, 'one or two of them long-term. If you're asking me if I was ever tempted to get married again, then the answer's no.'

Cory nodded. She didn't know what to say. She'd had him down as a love 'em and leave 'em type—which he might be now—but she had to admit she hadn't thought about what might have made him that way. 'It must have been very hard for you,' she said at last.

'For a while.' He shrugged. 'But it seems like another lifetime now. The boy Joanna knew was very different to the man I've become, I guess. Who knows whether we would still even be together if she had lived? We were very young, that's for sure. And typical students. We married in a registry office one wet Saturday afternoon; she wore a long skirt and a jumper with bells round the bottom and I wore jeans and a scruffy T-shirt.'

'Bohemians.'

'Something like that.' He smiled at her, reaching out and taking her hand, and she let him pull her into his side as they began walking again.

Even as she was making all the right noises, Cory found her mind was working on a different plane altogether as they strolled back to the pub. Nick Morgan was inveigling himself into her life somehow, and it frightened her. She was sure he hadn't made up the story about his young wife, but had he told her about Joanna hoping it would soften her attitude to him? William had been full of little tricks like that. In fact, once their relationship was over she'd realised William had played her like a master virtuoso. She frowned to herself.

'You're thinking again.' The deep voice was amused.

'What?' She wiped her face clear of expression as she glanced up at him.

'I'd bet a pound to a penny I was featuring in your thoughts and not favourably,' he drawled. 'Right?'

'Don't be ridiculous.' She could feel her cheeks burning.

'Something along the lines of wondering if I'd spun you a yarn, yes?'

'No.' Her voice carried a note of indignation that couldn't be misconstrued. 'Of course I believe what you told me. I know you wouldn't make something like that up.' Even as she spoke Cory wondered how she knew. But know she did. She decided to look at that one later.

'Then you're wondering *why* I told you,' he persisted doggedly.

Wretched man. She turned her head, pretending an interest in two screaming toddlers whose harassed mother was trying to persuade them back into a double buggy. 'I don't know what you're talking about.'

'Little liar.' It was soft, indulgent, and took the sting out of the words.

Cory decided she could do some plain speaking herself. She stopped, looking up into the clear blue eyes as she said, 'OK then, why *did* you tell me?'

'I don't know.' He didn't blink, his face oddly vulnerable. Cory didn't like what it did to her treacherous heart. Then, with a wry smile, he said, 'It's not something I usually drop into the conversation on the second date. In fact it's not something I usually talk about at all.'

How could someone who was so big and male and dangerous look so boyish for a moment? She told herself she'd had enough of aching heartstrings for one afternoon and

answered his smile with one of her own, saying lightly,
'Looks like we're both in the dark then. And we're not
dating, remember? This is my penance.'

He chuckled and her heart thudded with pleasure that
she could make him laugh, even as a hundred alarm bells
went off in her head. He was the most exciting man she
had ever met, she'd known that yesterday, but today she'd
realised there was much more to Nick than met the eye.
He probably had a lighthearted little romance in mind, a
few romps in bed until the next woman came along, a
woman more suited to his complex and captivating personality. But she wasn't *like* that.

They walked on, the warm evening air redolent of
woodsmoke from a distant bonfire somewhere, but Cory's
mind was racing.

How did you tell an experienced man of the world like
Nick Morgan, a man who by his own admission had had
more than one woman in his bed in his time—lots more—
that you had never actually…

She groaned inwardly. He would laugh at her and somehow—somehow she couldn't bear the thought of that.

Of course she had had her moments in the days before
she had tangled with William. Her friends at university had
been popping in and out of bed with the current boyfriend
as though it was as simple and easy as having a cup of tea.
They had said she was too intense, that she was making
too big a deal out of what was the most natural thing in
the world, but something had always stopped her from
making total bodily commitment with the lads she had gone
out with.

She supposed she'd been waiting for the Mr Right Nick
had spoken of earlier. Her lip curled at her naïvety. Even
though she'd always doubted anyone would feel that way
about her in her heart.

They reached the pub within a few minutes and after saying their goodbyes to Lucinda and John walked to the car. As they drove back along the route they had travelled earlier, Cory said tentatively, 'I brought some work home I really ought to look at before tomorrow. If you wouldn't mind dropping me back at the flat now, please.'

'I do mind.' He spared her one piercing glance before going on, 'We're doing dinner, Cory. Relax and you might even enjoy it.'

She wriggled in her seat. 'Where are we going?'

'A nice little place I know.'

'You know so many nice little places,' she said with a touch of acidity.

He chose to ignore it. 'That's true, but this one is special. Trust me.'

That would be a grave mistake.

Her face must have spoken for itself because she became aware of him laughing softly, and when she looked at him his eyes were brilliant with sparks of humour. 'You're priceless,' he murmured. 'Do you know that? And so good for keeping my ego on the ground.'

'I don't think I'll feel sorry for your ego,' she said, thinking of all the other women he had said he'd known and feeling ridiculously jealous. Which just showed how crazy she was and how this had to be the end of things.

The light banter continued as they drove on, but when they drew up in one of the streets close to Richmond Park Cory stared about her. 'This isn't a restaurant,' she said accusingly.

'Who said anything about a restaurant?' Twilight was beginning to fall as he slid out of the car, walking round the sleek low bonnet and opening her door for her.

Cory remained sitting. She raised her eyebrows at him

and he stared innocently back. 'So?' she said meaningfully. 'Where are we?'

'Outside my London flat.'

She'd already arrived at that conclusion herself but had been determined to make him spell it out. She opened her mouth to tell him to take her home but he forestalled her.

'Before you say anything, it's only dinner that's on the cards, by the way. I know you'd like to get your hands on my body but you'll just have to restrain yourself.'

Cory glared at him. 'This isn't funny, Nick.'

He crouched down so that his head was on a level with hers. She tried hard to ignore the way his trousers strained over muscled thighs but it was difficult. 'Only dinner, Cory,' he repeated softly. 'I thought it would be nice to eat in, that's all. That way I can enjoy a bottle of wine with you and call a taxi to take you home.'

'You can cook?' she asked doubtfully.

'My dumplings have been known to make women swoon.'

She giggled, she couldn't help it. 'Really, *can* you cook?' she persisted.

He smiled. 'Tonight we're starting with spiced chicken salad with papaya and avocado. I cheated and got that ready before I left this morning. The main course for madam is pork and ginger stir-fry with noodles and prawn crackers. And for dessert…'

'What's for dessert?' Her mouth was watering.

'That'll be a surprise.' He stood up again, holding out his hand which she took a little reluctantly, still unsure of what she was doing.

Once she was standing on the pavement she eyed him warily. He was certainly full of surprises, and she didn't mean the dessert! Who on earth would have guessed he could cook? He was too…male. And then she couldn't believe she'd been so sexist.

'Come on.' He led her over to the large terraced house in front of them. As soon as he opened the front door Cory knew his flat was going to be sumptuous by the splendour of the marbled lobby complete with lift.

Nick's flat was at the top of the house and, when he stood aside for her to enter after opening the front door, Cory looked about her interestedly. She saw immediately that she had been right. It *was* sumptuous, but not overpoweringly so. It was also severely male, no frills or fancies littering the contemporary feel of the flat.

The lounge area which opened from the front door had pale cream walls and an oatmeal carpet, the huge sensation of space enhanced by the absence of doors between it and the dining room. The designer had left the chimney breast only as a natural division, and Cory could see by the charred logs in the grate that this was a real fire.

Three black leather two-seater sofas and several black lacquer oval occasional tables dotted the lounge, and in the dining room the monochrome effect continued with a black dining table and chairs.

Several striking pieces of sculpture and bark wall hangings and a row of steel-framed mirrors added to the air of uncompromising stark beauty. There were no plants, no ornaments, no vases of flowers or photographs on view, nothing to give any idea of the personality of the man who owned the place.

Cory turned to look at Nick, who was watching her intently. 'Is your house in Barnstaple like this?'

The hard face relaxed into a smile. 'No,' he admitted softly, 'but that's home. This is part of my work. It's where I bring colleagues, clients, people I want to impress.'

Cory nodded. She knew his international electronics firm

was huge and still growing. He was a very successful and intelligent man and she supposed this flat reflected this. She wouldn't want to live in it though.

'Come through to the kitchen,' Nick said, the twist to his lips suggesting he had read her mind again. 'It's where I spend most of my time when I'm here, that and the bedroom. I tend to get in late and leave early unless I'm entertaining.'

The kitchen was a smart combination of brushed stainless steel and solid wedge wood, and the impression of space and light was continued here by the ceiling having been removed, revealing the timbers of the original structure which were painted white. A large corner breakfast bar which was really a small table had two high stainless steel chairs with coffee-coloured upholstered seats tucked beneath it and, after pulling one out, Nick said, 'Sit down while I see about dinner. I'll open a bottle of wine. A nice Chardonnay, I think, to go with the salad and then the stir-fry.'

She had half been expecting that he would give her a tour of all of the flat, including his bedroom, and now as she sat on the chair she had to confess to a slight feeling of disappointment. She would have liked to see where he slept, to be able to picture him there at night. *Dangerous.* The word reverberated in her head as loudly as if someone had screamed it in her ear. She didn't need to picture him anywhere; he had no part in her life. This was one weekend out of the norm and it would remain like that. A pleasant but acutely disturbing episode that would soon fade from her memory if she put her mind to it.

Oh, yeah? challenged a little voice in her head. And pigs might fly.

The Chardonnay was as delicious in its own way as the Brunello at lunch. Cory didn't know much about different wines but it was obvious Nick did. All part of the image, she told herself, before feeling a little ashamed of the cattiness which had prompted the thought.

'Can I help?' she asked as she sat watching him deftly cut the pork loin into thin strips before covering it and putting it with the other ingredients he'd pulled out of the fridge, already prepared for cooking—a man who thought of everything.

He took a swallow of his wine before saying, 'You could set two places in the dining room if you like.'

'We're not eating in here?' The dining room table was enormous for two, besides which the informality of the kitchen was less conducive to a romantic tête-à-tête, surrounded as they were by gleaming pans and kitchen utensils.

'Is that what you'd prefer?' And, as she nodded, he said, 'So be it. Cutlery and everything else you'll need is in the cupboard to your left.'

They ate the first course almost immediately and it was truly delicious. Nick seemed determined to be the perfect host, making her laugh with one amusing story after another and displaying none of the intuitive and disconcerting probing which had so bothered her during the afternoon.

He wouldn't let her help with the main course, so Cory sat sipping her wine as she watched him cook the pork strips until they were brown all over, at which point he added the garlic, ginger, spring onions, pineapple chunks and other ingredients.

He was perfectly relaxed and at ease in the kitchen, adding the oyster sauce to the stir-fry with one hand and dealing with the noodles and prawn crackers with the other, whilst talking of inconsequential things. Cory could only marvel at him. She wasn't too bad a cook when she put her mind to it, but she didn't particularly like an audience and certainly couldn't have coped with Nick watching *her*.

Cory ate the ginger and pork stir-fry in a delicious haze of well-being, only protesting very slightly when Nick re-filled her empty glass. 'This food is so *good*,' she said, wrapping a noodle round her fork and transferring it to her mouth. 'I can't make my meals taste like this.'

He smiled lazily. 'The secret is in using fresh ingredients, like the root ginger and garlic. I never buy my herbs and spices in packets.'

Cory gave a hiccup of a laugh and then put down her glass of wine which she had just picked up. She suddenly realised she'd had quite enough. It was deceptively potent stuff.

'What's funny?' he asked softly.

She tried very hard to pull herself together. 'Just that I never imagined we'd be discussing the pros and cons of herbs and spices,' she said in a voice which was shaky with the amusement she was trying to quell. 'You didn't strike me as that sort of man when I met you, that's all.'

'What sort of man did you think I was then?' he asked lightly.

Cory considered her answer, forgetting she wasn't going to drink any more wine and taking several sips as she sur-veyed him through dreamy eyes. 'A he-man type,' she stated.

'And they don't cook?'

'I don't know.' Wrapped in contentment and lulled into a false sense of security she forgot to be careful. 'They might do. You do, so other men might, I suppose.'

'What about William?' Nick asked softly. 'Didn't he spoil you by at least cooking breakfast now and again?'

'I never had breakfast with William. I've never had breakfast with anyone.' She finished the last of the wine, holding out her glass for a refill as she spoke out the thought in her head without thinking about what she was revealing. 'I suppose you have to sleep with someone to wake up to breakfast with them.'

There was the merest of pauses before Nick said, 'It helps.'

There was a quality to his voice which brought Cory back to earth more effectively than a bucketful of cold water.

Much later she realised that at that point she could still have saved the situation if she hadn't lost her head. She could have made some light innuendo which suggested that bed wasn't the only place people made love or deflected the assumption she had heard in his voice in some other way. Then maybe—*maybe*—she might have fooled him.

As it was, she stared at him with wide horrified eyes, the effects of the wine completely burnt up in the mortification she was feeling. She set the wineglass down on the table. 'Not that I haven't had lots of offers though,' she blurted out before realising that made everything ten times worse.

Jumping to her feet she took the coward's way out. 'Can I use the bathroom?'

'Sure.' Nick was magnificently unconcerned but it didn't help. 'First door on your right outside the kitchen.'

Cory fled.

She stood in the bathroom for a good few seconds feeling utterly wretched before her surroundings registered through the maelstrom. Then she glanced about her in awe. The white tiled walls and floor were offset with midnight-blue granite surfaces and illuminated recesses which stored white bath-linen and toiletries, and the massive raised bath, shower cubicle, pedestal basin, toilet and bidet were white with elegant silver fittings. Two exquisitely worked granite sculptures of storks stood either side of the shower cubicle, a mosaic of white and blue taking up almost one wall over the bath.

The stark use of white and blue, the voyeuristic ceiling which consisted totally of glass and the carefully positioned lighting made this a bathroom where modesty would go out of the window. Cory walked gingerly across to the basin, fiddling about for a few moments before she realised it had a thermostat mixer and sensor which was activated when the occupant held their hands beneath it.

But of course it would, she told herself cantankerously. What else? She wouldn't be surprised if you only had to wish for the bath to fill up and it happened.

She glanced up at the ceiling again when she had dried her hands on the big fluffy towel and then her eyes moved to the huge bath which would easily take two people, if not a whole rugby team. This room had been designed for other activities than merely getting clean. She put her hands to her hot cheeks. Which made what she'd revealed to Nick doubly humiliating. He wouldn't have any concept of how she felt.

She stayed in the bathroom for as long as she dared but eventually she squared her shoulders and lifted her head. She would have to go and face him and get it over with. She breathed very deeply. But definitely no more wine. No more wine, no more leading conversations, no more of anything!

He was sitting where she'd left him, but now their plates had been cleared away and dessert dishes and spoons were on the table. 'Hi.' His smile was easy and unhurried as she joined him. 'Vanilla parfait with chocolate rum truffle or apricot whisky mousse?'

Cory forgot to be embarrassed as she stared at the two rich concoctions in front of her. 'You made these?' she asked in amazement.

'Almost.' His eyes drifted over her face. 'But my local gourmet store helped a little.'

Her smiled was strained. She didn't want to eat dessert with him in this gleaming super-technological kitchen. She wanted to go home and lick her wounds.

As soon as she had finished her portion of vanilla parfait with chocolate rum truffle, Cory slipped off her seat. 'I must go home and do that work,' she said quietly. 'Thanks for a lovely day. I'll hail a cab from the end of the street.'

'Don't be silly, I'm coming with you.'

'There's no need.'

He inhaled deeply and audibly, and let his breath out. 'I'm coming with you,' he repeated steadily, rising to his feet.

His tone was exactly what one would use with a difficult and annoying child, and it caught her on the raw. She stared at him and piercingly intent blue eyes stared back. He seemed very big and very dark and Cory couldn't help looking at his mouth as he stopped speaking. It was a sexy, cynical and purposeful mouth. She swallowed. 'As you like,' she said casually, shrugging as she turned away.

The next moment she was turned around again by a firm hand on her shoulder. 'I do like,' he said with silky control. He put his mouth to hers, stroking her sealed lips as one hand held her in the small of her back and the other brushed her hair away from her face.

When her lips opened slightly beneath his he plunged immediately into the undefended territory, his hand leaving her face to thread deftly into her hair, supporting her head. The kiss deepened with a sensuality that started her senses reeling.

'You're delicious, you know that, don't you,' he murmured, a sound—almost like a groan—coming from deep in his throat. 'Specially tasting of rum truffle.'

The hand that had been tangled in her hair had shifted to fit her face into the curve of his neck and now he stood cradling her close, so close she could feel every inch of his arousal. Cory stood absolutely still. She was having trouble with her breathing and her heart was pounding. The overpowering passion which ignited every time this man touched her had taken her unawares again, and now all her doubts and fears came back in a rush to reproach her.

Act nonchalant, she told herself silently. Finish this with a modicum of self-respect. If nothing else, let him remember you as the one who got away.

She straightened, pulling away and smoothing her hair with a light laugh before she said, 'Red wine, white wine and now rum truffle. You're a bad influence.'

'I hope so.' The unreserved warmth in his eyes brought colour into her cheeks, especially as the feel of his body was still imprinted against her. 'But we've a long way to go yet.'

Cory looked at him guardedly but made no reply. The only place she was going was home, and then from this night on she'd make sure she refused any invitations from Nick Morgan. If he asked her to see him again, that was. She ignored the chasm that her stomach had fallen into at the thought of never seeing him again, and said brightly, 'Shall we find a taxi now?'

'Let's.' It was dry.

They didn't say much on the way to Cory's flat, but the air in the back of the taxi was electric with tension. At least, Cory felt so. Nick, on the other hand, sat with his arm round her, the hand resting on her shoulder playing idly with a lock of her hair and his legs stretched out lazily in front of him.

His kisses didn't mean anything. The refrain went over

and over in her head as she tried to convince herself. Not a thing. To a man like Nick, kissing a woman was little more than a social habit.

Why had he stopped kissing her? The thought which had assailed her as they had left his flat kept jabbing at her. Because it hadn't been her who had stopped initially. It *should* have been, she acknowledged miserably, but it hadn't. Was it because of what she'd unwittingly revealed? Had it put him off? Did he feel he couldn't be bothered with someone as inexperienced as her? Or perhaps, like her friends at university, he thought she was too intense, too emotional—slightly...odd?

She continued to go round and round in circles until the car drew up outside the house and then, to her surprise, she had a feeling of very real panic at the thought of not seeing him again. Which was ridiculous, utterly and absolutely. Nevertheless it was there.

'I'll see you to your door,' Nick said, and this time she didn't object. He told the taxi driver to wait and then escorted her across the pavement, following her inside the house after she had opened the front door.

When they were finally standing outside her own door, she looked up at him. How had he managed to become such a part of her life in two days? It was scary. So, so scary.

'Don't look at me like that,' he said roughly.

'Like what?' she asked, genuinely hurt by the thread of anger.

'Like you expect me to treat you badly, manhandle you, hurt you.'

She supposed she did expect him to hurt her if she got involved with him, but not in the physical sense he was talking about.

'*Hell*, Cory.' He was suddenly furious and it showed.

'Give me a break, won't you. I don't know how this William guy behaved but I'm not him. OK? It might be stating the obvious but I need to say it.'

'I know you're not him,' she said shakily.

'Do you? I don't think you do, not yet.' And then he echoed her earlier thought when he said, 'It's been two days and yet it feels like much, much longer. Do you feel that?'

She wanted to make some clever, witty comment and then send him on his way, or even just shake her head. She nodded instead.

'Do you see the age gap as a problem?'

'What?' It had been the last thing she'd expected him to say.

'I'm ten years older than you. Does that bother you?' he asked softly.

She didn't know what to say. Something was happening here and she seemed to have no control over it. She shook her head because she couldn't have spoken to save her life.

'You're going to tell me we inhabit different worlds, aren't you?' he went on.

She hadn't been but now he'd mentioned it it was absolutely true.

'And you're right,' he said quietly. 'For the last thirteen years I've worked like a dog and loved every minute, and any woman I've got involved with has known the score. At first I was so cut up about Joanna it was easier to keep relationships from developing into anything but physical ones. There are plenty of career women out there who aren't looking to settle down until way on in their timescale of things, and they suited me as I did them. Fun, friendship, someone warm in bed but no emotional commitment. Then, as time went on, I found I was becoming autonomous because I *liked* it that way, not because of any lingering loyalty to Joanna. The freedom of being self-determining and independent was heady.'

She stared at him, her eyes wide. Was he being brutally honest at last? Was he going to say that any relationship with him would be purely physical and only last as long as he wanted it to? His other women had obviously been happy with that.

And then he disabused her of that idea. 'You might be a career woman but you aren't like them, are you.' It was a statement, not a question. 'You think differently.'

This was all because of what she had inadvertently told him before dessert. That she was a virgin. A twenty-five-year-old virgin. Was this his way of telling her he wasn't going to see her again because she wasn't like the other women, wasn't what he wanted?

Her chin rose a notch. 'Nick,' she began, but he put a finger to her lips.

'We come from different ends of the pole, Cory, but you know as well as I do that there's a spark there. It's there when I touch you and it's there when I don't. And I like that. It makes me feel alive,' he added wryly. 'I didn't realise till I met you that I was growing stale. So, how about we see each other once in a while, take it nice and easy and see how things go? Sure there'll be hurdles, but we'll take them one at a time and see what happens. What do you say?'

Every single brain cell was telling her to say no. It was the sensible, the *safe* thing to do. She had been this way once before with William and it had ended in disaster. This would too. She knew it at heart. Nick would grow bored with her; it was inevitable with a man like him. No was the only answer to give.

But she couldn't do it. She couldn't tell him to walk away from her. Not yet.

Cory was unaware of the play of emotions across her face, but when he pulled her to him she realised he'd guessed something of what she was feeling. 'So, do we start doing the dreaded "d" word?' he asked drily.

She looked into the blue eyes. From somewhere she found the strength to be as cool and laid-back as him. 'I guess we'd better give it a shot for a while,' she said airily. 'If only to stop you growing stale.'

CHAPTER FIVE

'OH, DARLING, that's absolutely wonderful. I'm so pleased. Haven't I said you need another boyfriend, if only to spite William?'

Cory smiled at her aunt. For someone who had lived most of her adult life in the crazy and often promiscuous world of fashion, Joan could be terribly ingenuous. 'For one thing, Nick's not my boyfriend,' she said gently, not wanting to disappoint the older woman. 'We're just going to date sometimes, that's all. And, considering I haven't seen William for three years, I doubt very much if anything I do would affect him in the slightest. He didn't care when we were together as he proved only too well. He'd hardly take any interest now.'

'What do you mean, he's not your boyfriend?' said Joan, ignoring the rest. 'You said Nick wants to see you. It's not one of these modern open sort of things, is it? Where he can do what he likes and so can you?'

'Not exactly.' To be truthful, she wasn't sure what it was, but she couldn't very well say that.

'I'd like to meet him,' stated Joan definitely.

Cory's nerves jangled. Joan had only met William once and it had been such an unmitigated disaster that they hadn't repeated it. 'I've only seen him twice myself,' she objected. 'I can hardly ask him round for an inspection by you.'

'Not an inspection.' Joan fixed her with a look that said she wasn't about to be deflected. 'Just to dinner.'

'Not yet,' Cory said firmly. Maybe not at all. She was

due to go out to the theatre with him in the middle of the week and she was preparing herself already for the possibility that things might have changed between them. The weekend they had just shared had been...good—she wouldn't allow herself a more enthusiastic summing up—but they might meet again and there would be nothing there. For him at least. And that would be fine, it *would*. She was expecting nothing from this relationship that wasn't really a relationship at all. She was *ordinary*, for crying out loud.

She had spent most of the day in the house of a family who hadn't a clue about personal hygiene or the most elementary social graces, trying to ascertain if the children were neglected out of intent or simply because their young parents didn't have a clue.

She had returned home exhausted and stinking of the smell peculiar to the Massey family—a mixture of cat's urine, dirt, cooking smells and body odour—which permeated every nook and cranny and ingrained itself into clothes, hair and nails. After washing her hair and having a long, hot bath she had gone round to her aunt's house for dinner as she did every Monday, only to find that the odour seemed to have lodged itself somewhere between the end of her nose and her brain.

She could just imagine Nick's reaction if he had seen her earlier. She almost laughed to herself. Nick, with his incredible flat, cars, designer clothes and immaculate appearance. No, they were miles, tens of thousands of miles apart. It was never going to come to anything. He was like a bright shooting star and she was like a damp squib.

'Not yet?' Joan was the original British bulldog when she wanted to be. 'When then? Now your parents are gone I feel responsible for you.'

Now Cory did laugh out loud. 'You know as well as I

do that Mum and Dad barely knew I was alive,' she said, just the merest trace of bitterness showing through. 'And they would never have claimed to be responsible for me.'

'Their loss.' Joan sighed, looking into the lovely young face opposite her and wondering how two intelligent people like Cory's parents could have been so criminally blind to their own daughter's needs. 'But I do worry about you. I can't help it. And I know you are a perfectly modern woman who is in control of her life and her destiny, but still...'

Cory wasn't at all sure about the control bit. 'Maybe in a couple of months,' she said placatingly. If they were still seeing each other then. Which she doubted. The tug at her heartstrings which followed was worrying.

'I shall keep you to that,' Joan said with great satisfaction. 'Now, have a piece of the shortbread I made this afternoon with your coffee. I'm really getting the hang of this cooking lark, aren't I, Rufus,' she added to the dog sitting drooling at her feet. 'After all those years at work when I ate out or had a ready meal in front of the TV, I've found it's very satisfying to start a meal from scratch with fresh ingredients.'

'You and Nick are going to have a lot to talk about,' said Cory wryly.

They did. Two months later—months in which she and Nick had seen each other almost every night—Cory found herself watching him charm his way into her aunt's affections. He had arrived at the house with a vast collection of herbs, all in little plant pots—'thought it'd go down better than a bunch of flowers', he'd murmured to Cory, who'd arrived early to help her aunt with the dinner—and an enormous hide bone for Rufus. The dog had promptly claimed Nick as his own personal companion, sitting on his foot all through dinner and then plonking himself down at the side of Nick's armchair when they'd retired to Joan's conservatory overlooking her pretty little garden.

The doors had been open to the warm August evening and in the distance somebody had been cutting their lawn, the drone of the lawnmower soothing. When Nick and her aunt had begun an in-depth conversation concerning the merits of certain herbs in certain dishes and other gastronomic delights, Cory had found herself beginning to doze. She'd had a hard week with a particularly harrowing case, and now the big meal, comfortable chair, mellow evening sunshine and general sense of well-being was seductive.

She was woken by a lingering kiss on her lips. She opened her eyes to find her aunt was nowhere to be seen. 'Where's she gone?' she asked Nick drowsily.

'Your aunt? Taken Rufus for a quick walk in the park. Apparently they have a little routine at nights now her leg's better. Rufus has a chance to meet Oscar—an Old English Sheepdog,' Nick explained knowledgeably, 'and Periwinkle—a German Shepherd. According to your aunt, they are the canine version of the Three Musketeers and Rufus is bereft if they don't meet up.' His expression changed. 'Were you bored earlier?' he asked softly.

'Bored?' She gazed into the hard handsome face and wondered if he was aware of how devastatingly gorgeous he was. 'How could anyone be bored listening to the merits of basil and thyme, or curd cheese over butter icing?'

He was used to her chaffing him. She had decided in the very early days that the only way she was going to hold her own in this relationship was not to fall foul of his charm.

He grinned at her now and she caught her breath as the blue eyes crinkled sexily at the corners. 'Worked though, didn't it,' he said with a great deal of satisfaction. 'Your aunt is putty in my hands.'

So was she but she wasn't about to let him know that. 'I'll set her straight another time,' she promised drily.

'Come here.' His voice had changed and as she stood up he pulled her into his arms, his tone husky as he said, 'I've been wanting to do this all evening.' His kiss was fierce, hungry, and she matched him in fierceness and hunger. It was always like that. And she knew the day was fast approaching when he would want it all, want her in his bed. She wanted it too. It had never been that way with William. Nothing was as it had been with William. That ought to be comforting but it wasn't because she just couldn't bring herself to believe that the bubble wouldn't burst.

They stood moulded together and swaying slightly as their hands explored each other while their mouths fused. Nick nipped and sipped and savoured the sweet taste of her, pressing the tip of his tongue against her throat where her pulse pounded in reaction. He knew just what buttons to press, exactly how to please her. She knew going to bed with this man would be an experience she'd never get over. She would be his slave for ever.

'Pity your aunt's going to be back any minute.' Reluctantly he raised his head, his voice husky as he adjusted her clothing.

His eyes had turned a deeper blue than usual and she smiled at him, the thrill she always felt at knowing how much he wanted her sending little ripples down her spine.

'I want you, Cory.' He ran one fingertip down her throat and into the dip between her breasts and she shivered. 'And you want me. Not in little snatched moments or an evening here and there.'

Wanting was dangerous. Needing even more so. She

stared at him, her eyes enormous in the shadows which were encroaching as night fell.

'I love you,' he said very softly. 'Do you love me?'

She had known it would come to this one day. The summer had been so wonderful, so magical, but underlying every day had been a complicated web which had got stickier the more they had been together. The gap between them was as immense as it had ever been. He spoke of love but what he really meant was that he wanted her. Not just physically, she knew he wasn't as crass as William and that he enjoyed being with her, but as for it lasting…

She drew back a little in his arms as she looked up at him. She had to be honest here. It was the only way but she was frightened this would be the moment he would get tired of her. 'I'm not sure I know what love is,' she said carefully. 'My parents had this feeling between them they said was love but to me, on the outside, it was more of an obsession. It made them cruel to…to other people without them even knowing it.'

'To you?' he murmured, retaining her in his hold, his eyes narrowed on her face which was pale with emotion.

She nodded. 'One of my flatmates at university said I'd been programmed from birth to accept the fact I was unloveable and unworthy. I hated her for it at the time—she wasn't a particularly good friend and was always analysing everyone because she was doing psychology—but she might have been right. She said because I'd never experienced love when I was young—the old thing of give me a child until he's seven and I will give you the man—I'd never know it in my adult life.'

Nick swore, just once but so explicitly Cory was shocked. 'Get that out of your head,' he said roughly. 'That's rubbish and the woman wants locking away.'

'She got a First.'

'She'd get a darn sight more if I got my hands on her.'
He shook her gently. 'Listen to me, Cory. Life is what you
make of it, OK? You don't play with the cards you would
have liked, you play with the ones you've been dealt and
some of them can be lousy. Look at Lucinda. The woman
was built to have babies—big, fat, Italian babies—but can
you honestly say she is grieving her life away? Look at her
at her birthday party; she was happy and making the most
of what she *did* have.'

They had had a whale of a time at the party, which had
gone on all night until everyone had been served breakfast,
but now Cory said, 'She knows John loves her, really loves
her, and she loves him. She's not confused or inhibited.
She trusts him.'

'Dead right. But if they could have had children their
love would have flowed over and encompassed each one.
You see that, don't you? Because it's real, it's not selfish
or restricting. You said yourself what your parents had was
more obsession than love, so how the hell can you weigh
anything they said or did to you in the balance and find
yourself wanting? Of course you're loveable. Damn it, I
could eat you alive.'

She didn't return his smile. How could she explain to
him that she knew deep inside the day would come when
he didn't want her any more? She didn't have the power
to inspire real love. If she didn't have it for her parents then
why would anyone else love her? 'William said he loved
me,' she said flatly.

'William was a piece of dirt.'

She raised tortured eyes to his. 'You can't say that. You
have never even met him.'

'Let's hope I don't, for his sake,' Nick said grimly.
'Cory, the guy was on the make and he strung you along.

There are men like that out there but we're not all the same. I have never lied to you and I never will.'

No, but that wouldn't make it any the easier when he got tired of her. He could have any woman he liked. Why on earth would he stay with her?

'You think if you let yourself love me I'll treat you like William, right?'

She could tell he was struggling to remain calm and she couldn't blame him. She wished he would let go of her. She couldn't think clearly when he was holding her. She shook her head. 'I've told you, I don't think you're like him. Maybe at first, but not when I got to know you.'

'So where is the problem, for crying out loud?'

Me. I'm the problem.

The sudden arrival of Rufus shooting through to the conservatory followed by Joan calling out she was back brought the very unsatisfactory conversation to a close. Cory got her wish because Nick let go of her, bending down to stroke the dog as Joan came bustling through.

'Sorry we've been a while but Rufus is so popular it's always difficult to get away,' she said, for all the world as though she'd been accompanying a sought after celebrity to some event or other. 'Now, coffee, yes? And you must try one of my demerara meringues, Nick. They don't have the cloying sweetness of meringues made with white sugar. Have you ever tried your hand at meringues?'

Cory made an excuse and left them to it. When she reached her aunt's neat pink and cream bathroom she locked the door behind her and sank down on the edge of the bath. She was trembling and she didn't seem able to stop. He had said he loved her but he'd probably said the same thing to the women he'd had long-term relationships with in the past. Love didn't necessarily equate to staying together or fidelity or dependability or any of those sorts of things.

She ran her hand through her hair before groaning softly. Was she being too possessive and clingy here? Thousands of women the whole world over were quite happy to give themselves body and soul to a man without the promise that it was going to work out, or even that they would stay together for more than a short while. If things went wrong they picked themselves up, brushed themselves down and got on with their lives. She worked with women like that and there had been plenty among her friends at university. Strong, determined, independent women.

She got up and walked over to her aunt's basin, washing her hands with a rather strong-smelling lavender soap before drying them on a rose-embroidered towel, her head buzzing.

When William left her life so unpleasantly she hadn't crumbled. She might have been crying inside but she'd gritted her teeth and presented the normal capable Cory to the rest of the world. Only her aunt had understood what his betrayal had meant to her. Of course she hadn't given herself wholeheartedly to William, not in mind or body. But if she stayed with Nick she would do that.

She raised her head and stared at the wide-eyed girl in the mirror. *Because she loved him*, she thought sickly, facing it for the first time. She had been lying to him downstairs. She knew what love was since Nick had come into her life, and the affection she had felt for William before he had hurt her was a pale reflection in comparison. Her pride and fragile self-esteem had been hurt when William had treated her so badly but her heart hadn't been broken.

She sank down on the edge of the bath again, staring at the rose tiles without really seeing them. Right, she thought grimly. Where did she go from here? If she went into this for real it would involve staying at his place and him at hers, that much had been clear from what he'd said downstairs about not wanting her in little snatched moments or the odd evening. It might even involve them living together. How would she survive if—when—it finished?

A coldness invaded her limbs in spite of the warm August night and she shivered. What sort of heartache would she be letting herself in for? How would she pick up the pieces and carry on? True, she'd have her work. Somehow that was supremely unimportant. And her friends and Aunt Joan. Not even in the equation.

She squeezed her lids tightly shut and tried to *think*. She was afraid to care and afraid to be cared for. That was what it boiled down to. Nick would expect that she would trust him and she would, in so far as other women were concerned. He wouldn't play the field when he was with her; he wasn't like that. But if he fell out of love with her and in love with one of the glamorous, exciting businesswomen he met every day…

She took a long shaky breath. And she couldn't expect anything else to happen long-term, not realistically. He had made it clear when they first met that his work was his life and women fitted into the niche he'd allowed for them. He needed his independence, he'd said, had found he liked autonomy, no complications in his love life.

An increase of pressure from somewhere inside her chest made it difficult for her to breathe. She had known from the beginning that she should have sent him packing after that first weekend. But she had miscalculated. She had thought it was Nick who was dangerous but in fact it had been her own feelings that were the real hazard. From the first time she'd met him she had known she could love him. But she had been too cowardly to face that then and do something about it. And now everything was a million times worse.

She couldn't be what he wanted. She rose and began pacing back and forth. And that was it in a nutshell really. She wouldn't be able to let him go gracefully when the time came; in fact, she wouldn't be able to let him go at all. And then it would all turn horribly messy and nasty. It happened, all the time.

But not to her. She stopped the pacing and became very still. Because she wouldn't let it. This was the point where she had to take control. OK, it was hellishly late in the day but better late than never. She smiled bleakly.

Nick and her aunt were sitting eating demerara meringues and drinking coffee when she joined them.

'Excuse us starting, darling, but you were such a long time.' Joan gazed up at her, her smile changing to a frown of concern. 'Are you all right, Cory? You look terribly pale all of a sudden.'

'I have a headache.' It was true, she did. Her head was pounding fit to burst.

'Oh, I'm sorry, sweetie.' Her aunt jumped up. 'I'll get some aspirin.'

When Joan had disappeared into the house, Nick leant across and took one of her hands. 'You're cold,' he said quietly. 'You must be sickening for something. Do you want me to take you home?'

What she wanted was to turn the clock back to the time before she had met him. A time in which there had been no crazy highs and lows, just a steady calm stroll through life. She nodded, wincing as the movement sent pain shooting through her eyeballs. A migraine. She hadn't had one of these in years.

By the time she had swallowed the aspirin and they had

made their goodbyes, bright lights were flashing at the back of her eyeballs. Cory knew the signs. She had had a series of migraines at university which the doctor there had put down to excess stress. She would be nauseous soon; she could feel her stomach beginning to churn already.

She stumbled as Nick helped her into the car and didn't protest when he fastened her seat belt for her. He could have stripped her stark naked and she wouldn't have cared.

'You need a doctor.' His voice sounded so loud he could have been shouting, her hearing sensitised a hundredfold.

'It's just a migraine,' she whispered through numb lips, praying she wouldn't vomit all over his beautiful car.

'Do you have them often?'

The engine was such that it fairly purred but tonight it resembled a jet preparing for take-off. 'No, not often.' Please don't make me talk.

He must have heard the silent plea because he said no more, pulling out of her aunt's drive and into the road beyond slowly and smoothly.

Even in the midst of the pain Cory appreciated his thoughtfulness. Slow was not normally a word which featured in Nick's driving vocabulary.

When they reached her flat Cory just had time to dive into the bathroom where she lost Joan's delicious plaice florentine down the toilet. She was vaguely aware of Nick helping her to her feet and then using a wet flannel to mop her face. 'I'll be fine, now, thanks,' she whispered painfully. 'I'm only ever sick once. I shall just go to bed and stay there for twenty-four hours.'

He made no reply to this, taking her arm and leading her through to her bedroom as though she was a frail old lady. Mind you, that was exactly what she felt like right at this moment, Cory thought painfully.

Once she was sitting on her bed, she said again, 'I'll be fine now. You go.'

'You're far from fine and I'm not convinced this is a migraine. What if you've got food poisoning or something?'

'Aunt Joan would love to hear you say that.'

'Not through her cooking; your aunt and I aren't affected. What did you eat for lunch?'

She really didn't want to do this right now. Forcing herself to reply, Cory murmured, 'Tagliatelle and it was perfectly all right. I've told you, this is a migraine. Now, if you don't mind, I want to go to bed.'

'Fine. I'll help you. Where's your nightie or whatever you wear?'

Cory opened one eye and then wished she hadn't as the equivalent of a laser blast hit her brain. 'I'm quite capable of undressing myself,' she said irritably, wincing as her voice added to the drums beating in her head. 'Now, if you'll just go and leave me alone so I can sleep.'

'I'll wait outside until you're in bed.'

For heaven's sake! After the door had closed, Cory slipped out of her clothes without opening her eyes and moving the least she could. She didn't bother trying to find her nightie, which was folded up in the bedside cabinet, sliding under the thin summer duvet with a sigh of relief.

A few minutes later she heard the door open and then a deep voice at the side of her said, 'There's a drink of water beside you if you need it.'

'Thank you.' Go, just go.

'Are you warm enough? You were cold earlier.'

In actual fact she was still cold; migraines always seemed to make her feel that way. There was a quick debate in her aching mind as to whether she should admit to it or just send him home. 'There's a hot-water bottle in the bottom of the chest of drawers,' she said, her eyes closed. 'It's got a Winnie-the-Pooh cover on it.'

A moment's pause, and then he said, 'I've got it.'

In no time at all he was back. When she heard the door open Cory slid an arm from under the covers. 'Thanks.' She was feeling worse if anything. She'd had special medication prescribed for her at university, but since the migraines had waned and then disappeared altogether once she was working she hadn't renewed the prescription. She wished now that she had. Her aunt's aspirin wasn't even touching the pain.

'Anything else I can do?'

'No. No, thanks,' she added, knowing she'd been too abrupt.

'I'll leave you to get some sleep then.'

She was aware of his lips brushing her brow and then the door closed again.

She lay completely still because the slightest movement jarred her head unbearably, and after a few moments she heard the front door close. He had gone. Tense muscles relaxed. If she was sick again at least she could do it without an audience!

Then she berated herself for being so nasty when Nick had tried to be so nice. But she'd lied to him when she'd said the nausea only happened once; often it was two or three times, and throwing her heart up in front of him wasn't exactly the picture she wanted him to carry home in his mind.

The aspirin must have worked to a small degree because she dozed for a while. She had no idea of how long she'd been in bed when she suddenly knew she had to get to the bathroom again.

Throwing back the duvet, she struggled to her feet but after making the mistake of opening her eyes once she didn't try it again, feeling her way out of the room. She reached the bathroom without mishap, only to find the waves of nausea receding. She felt behind her gingerly for the bath and sat on the edge of it as she tried to decide if she dared go back to bed.

'What are you doing?'

The shock of Nick's voice brought her eyes open and a thousand daggers pierced her brain. She was as naked as the day she was born and here he was spying on her! 'What am *I* doing?' she croaked furiously, grabbing a bath towel and pulling it round her. 'What are you doing? I heard you go ages ago.' She glared at him, colour flooding her face.

'I went to a local pharmacy for something a bit better than aspirin,' he said with magnificent aplomb. But then he wasn't the one with no clothes on. 'I was going to give you a couple of pills when you woke up.'

'You've been here all the time?' She shut her eyes again, partly because the pain was too intense to keep them open, but mainly because she didn't dare look at him a moment longer. He had seen her stark naked and not in a nice romantic way either. No—his first sight of her totally in the buff had had to be when she was feeling like death and no doubt looking it too. And he had added insult to injury by switching on the light as he'd walked in the bathroom. Her cellulite would have been positively screaming at him.

'I've been kipping in the chair in the sitting room.'

That would have been fine if he had stayed there.

'Come on, get back to bed and I'll fix you a hot drink so you can have a couple of these pills,' Nick said comfortably, as though he hadn't just put her through her worst moment ever. It didn't help that in the brief glare she'd indulged in she'd noticed a dark stubble on his chin which made him look ten times more sexy than usual, if that were possible. That and the open-necked shirt and rumpled hair.

'It's three in the morning, so if you have a couple now you might start feeling better towards lunchtime when you wake up. I'm assured these knock you out like a light.'

She wished he'd woken her up when he'd fetched them then. Before she'd decided to lumber blindly about the flat in her birthday suit.

Cory pulled the towel tighter round her and stood shakily to her feet, allowing him to lead her back to the bedroom because it was easier than arguing. Once she was in bed she lay listening to the sounds from the kitchen, but the pain was so bad again her embarrassment had vanished. Nevertheless, she made sure the duvet was wrapped round her like a second skin when she sat up to take the warm milk and pills Nick brought.

'Thank you.' It was reluctant, which wasn't very nice, she admitted to herself.

'My pleasure. Drink it all up.'

He didn't actually add, like a good girl, but he might as well have, Cory thought bitterly, swallowing the pills and finishing the milk before she snuggled under the covers again. Obviously the sight of her in the altogether hadn't stirred him in the least.

'You really can go now,' she said as she heard him walk towards the door. 'You said yourself I'll sleep till lunch-time.'

He didn't answer, merely closing the door gently behind him, which was somehow more aggravating than any argument.

The next time Cory opened her eyes there was a chink of bright sunlight stealing through where the curtains had parted a little, but she found it didn't cause her to wince any more. She felt incredibly tired and somewhat fragile, but the piercing pain was a thing of the past, just a normal sort of headache remaining.

She moved her eyes carefully to the little alarm clock on her bedside cabinet, experience warning her that any sudden movements could remind the pain to return. One o'clock. *One o'clock?* She really had slept till lunchtime, she thought in amazement. But there was no doubt she felt better, much better.

Was Nick still here? Now she could open her eyes without fear of the laser, she slowly sat up and reached into the cabinet for her nightie. Once it was on she felt better, even though she was dying for a bath.

He wouldn't still be here, surely? But then she would never have dreamt he would remain last night. Her cheeks flamed as she remembered the incident in the bathroom. But it *had* been nice for him to be so concerned. She hadn't expected that somehow.

She swung her legs out of bed and rose to her feet. Her head thudded a little, otherwise she didn't feel too bad. She found her bathrobe and fluffy mules, brushing her hair through at her dressing table and groaning at the sight of her white face. She looked awful, just awful. Still, she'd probably looked even worse last night. It wasn't particularly cheering.

She visited the bathroom, cleaning her face with the lotion she used and then brushing her teeth vigorously. She compromised on the bath by having a quick sluice down, promising herself a long hot soak later. Five minutes later and she was in the kitchen, looking at Nick who was busy cooking bacon. He had looked round and smiled at her entrance before saying, 'I was going to bring you a tray but now you're here we'll eat at the breakfast bar.'

Her tiny kitchen was nothing like his and the breakfast bar was barely big enough for two but Cory didn't point this out, merely sitting with a little plop on one of the stools. She was still more shaky than she'd thought.

'How are you feeling?'

The blue eyes briefly met hers again and Cory found she had to lick dry lips before she could reply. His five o'clock shadow was definitely designer stubble now. If she'd thought he looked sexy before it was nothing to now. 'Lots better,' she managed huskily. 'And thanks for staying and the pills and everything.'

'All part of Nick Morgan's bedside manner service.' He cracked eggs expertly into a bowl and began to whisk them. 'Help yourself to orange juice and pour me one, would you,' he said over his shoulder.

She stared at his back. Considering what she had decided the night before in her Aunt Joan's bathroom, Nick making himself so at home here was not a good idea. It was too cosy, too…poignant. It spoke of things which could never be and she was going to find it hard enough as it was once he had gone from her life. But she couldn't very well tell him to leave, not when he'd spent the night on her sofa because he'd been concerned about her. It wouldn't have been so bad if she'd had a guest room for him to sleep in, but her second bedroom was her study and clutter room.

He turned round, putting a rack of toast on the breakfast bar before skimming her mouth with his lips. He had returned to the bacon before she could react. 'Peppermint,' he said thoughtfully.

'What?'

'Your taste this morning. Peppermint.'

'I brushed my teeth,' she said unnecessarily. 'Nick, we have to talk. What we were discussing last night at my aunt's, I don't know…' She faltered, not knowing how to go on.

The muscles across his back had tensed but his voice

sounded perfectly normal when he said, 'Not before breakfast. I'm starving and I can't talk on an empty stomach.
Besides which, you need something inside you so you can
have another of those pills. Just one this time, though.'

'I'm not hungry.'

He turned with two plates, putting one in front of her
and sitting beside her as he began to eat. 'Eat, Cory,' he
said softly. 'We can talk another time. Don't worry.'

She risked a glance at him and then wished she hadn't.
She wanted him. She wanted him so much. She reached
for a slice of toast and put a little of the scrambled egg
from her plate on it. Mechanically she began to eat.
Another time he had said. So she didn't have to say goodbye today. It was worth the migraine.

CHAPTER SIX

CORY sat staring at the case file spread out on the desk in front of her but her mind was miles away. Should she have taken the bull by the horns and said something before Nick had left yesterday? She'd had plenty of opportunities because he had stayed most of the afternoon.

She wriggled in her seat. But it had been so *nice*, she wailed silently. Special. She had lain with her head in his lap on the sofa and he had stroked her hair as they had talked a little and dozed quite a lot. He had been tender and gentle and relaxed; it had been one of the few times when she'd been with him and had not been assailed by a hundred and one different emotions, all of them disturbing.

He had looked after her, she thought with a feeling which was half pain and half pleasure. He hadn't thought of his own needs at all; he'd just been wrapped up in caring about her.

The phone on her desk rang and she picked it up automatically, still thinking of Nick. 'Miss James. How can I help you?'

'I can think of a good few ways and all of them X-rated.'

'Nick?' She could hear the warmth in her voice herself and tried to moderate her tone as she continued, 'What are you doing ringing at ten in the morning?'

'Enquiring how my favourite girl is,' he said smokily.

Cory shut her eyes. She could just picture him sitting at his desk, black hair slicked back and face freshly shaven. He would probably have discarded his suit jacket as soon as he'd got to the office and for certain his tie would be hanging loose. He hated the constriction of a tie. She took a deep breath. 'More or less back to normal, except for feeling ridiculously tired, but a few early nights will fix that.'

She wondered if he'd picked up on the subtle hint that she wouldn't be seeing him that night. She had known as she'd waved him goodbye the evening before—after a kiss which had set her toes tingling, never mind the rest of her—that she had to cool things down rapidly. It was time to take a big step backwards and maybe if she did that he would do the same. If this relationship could just wane naturally it would all be for the best. Wouldn't it?

'Sure,' he agreed lazily. 'Best thing.'

She frowned at the phone. He wasn't supposed to say that. And then she caught the pique, angry with herself for her inconsistency. She wanted him to bow out of her life gracefully on the one hand but on the other she wanted him to fight tooth and nail to see her every moment. She was a bundle of contradictions and she was driving herself mad, never mind Nick. Nevertheless her voice was cool when she said, 'That's what I thought.'

'The other reason I'm ringing is to say I'm out of town for a few days from this afternoon. I've been putting off a trip to Germany for some time but certain reasons make it imperative I go this week.'

'Oh, right.' Suddenly the sunshine streaming through her office window was less bright, the sky less blue. 'I...I hope it goes well,' she said in a small voice.

'It will.' He sounded positive and forceful and clearly couldn't care less that for the first time since they'd been seeing each other they would be spending some time apart.

Cory was suddenly furiously angry with him. She knew it was unreasonable but she couldn't help herself. She also knew she had to wait a moment before she spoke because the last thing she wanted was for him to pick up on how she was feeling.

'Cory? Are you still there?'

'Yes, sorry. Someone was handing me something,' she lied quickly.

'I'd better not keep you any longer. Look after yourself and don't work too hard. I'll ring you.'

'Yes, all right. Bye.'

'Bye, sweetheart.'

The receiver went click at the other end but Cory stared at the phone in her hand for some seconds before slowly returning it to its stand. Sweetheart. She couldn't remember him calling her that before and his voice had been different when he'd said it—warm, soft, as though he'd really meant it.

Stop it. She was thinking again and she thought too much. She had decided action was the only answer to this incredible tangle she'd got herself in, and action spelt distance in this case. She just hadn't expected it would be Nick who would do this distancing. But that was fine, just fine. It *was*. It had to be.

Nick rang just as she was getting into bed that night. 'Cory? It's Nick. I haven't got long but I wondered how you're feeling. Headache still under control?'

She sat on the edge of the bed stupidly, her mouth opening and shutting, her heart pounding at the sound of his voice. She hadn't expected him to call. 'I feel fine,' she said at last, her voice thankfully steadier than she felt. And then, as a burst of laughter came down the line, she added, 'Where are you?'

'Out to dinner with some people. Sorry, it's a bit noisy but it's the first chance I've had to call.'

'You shouldn't have bothered.' That sounded awful.

'You've plenty to think about without worrying about me,' she qualified quickly.

'Perhaps I want to worry about you,' he said softly, or as softly as the background din would allow. 'Anyway, it's unlikely I'll be able to call the next day or so and I wanted to tell you to keep the weekend free. I'm taking you somewhere.'

'Taking me somewhere?' She was so surprised she forgot to tell him she couldn't possibly go. New regime and all that.

'Somewhere nice.'

'Somewhere nice?'

'Cory, you're repeating everything I say,' he said patiently. 'Look, I've got to go.' The noise swelled even more. 'I'll see you Friday evening. Pack a bag.'

'Nick—'

'Dream of me.' It was husky and deep and she felt the impact trickle over her nerves like warm honey. 'Only of me.'

'Nick—'

'Because I'll be dreaming of you, especially now I've seen exactly what I'm missing.'

Cory blinked. She had been quite impressed that he hadn't mentioned her *faux pas* yesterday; she might have known he couldn't keep it up. 'That was below the belt,' she said with what she hoped was haughty displeasure.

'Below the belt, above the belt, I saw it all.'

She knew he was grinning. She could hear it in his voice.

'And very nice it was too. More than nice...'

She heard someone call his name. A female voice.

'Look, I have to go,' he said quickly. 'They've brought us out for dinner after a meeting that went on for hours; they're so hospitable.'

Yes, well, they would be, wouldn't they? Cory thought

waspishly. She bet 'they', whoever they were—and there was certainly one woman among them, at least—didn't get many British visitors who looked like Nick Morgan. 'Nick, about this weekend—'

'Bye, sweetheart.' The line went dead.

Two sweethearts. Cory stared at the carpet. Two sweet-hearts *and* a weekend away somewhere. This was definitely the lead up to the big seduction scene. Maybe he had even planned the trip to Germany to make her miss him and be more receptive when he got back?

And then she immediately dismissed the thought, telling herself not to be so cynical. Nick wasn't into mind games the way William had been. If she didn't believe that she wouldn't still be with him.

But she couldn't go away somewhere, to a lush hotel or whatever, and then tell him that far from sleeping with him she actually was going to end their affair. She would have to talk to him as soon as he got back to England; failing that, when he arrived to pick her up on Friday evening. That was if he didn't call her again in the meantime.

She rubbed her hand across her face to wipe away the tears seeping down her cheeks. How would she bear not seeing him again? How was she actually going to say good-bye? But far better to do it now than in a few months, a year, even a couple of years, by which time she would be unable to exist without him. This was self-preservation at its rawest.

By Friday evening Cory was a nervous wreck. In spite of knowing she was determined to go nowhere with Nick Morgan, she found herself packing an overnight case—just…in case. Which really made her a candidate for the funny farm, she told herself wearily, glancing at her watch. Six o'clock. Nick knew she usually arrived home from work about five-thirty. He could be here any minute. Her stomach turned over and she had to sit down suddenly. Of course he might be much later.

She had missed him more than she would ever have believed possible this last week. She had dreamt about him when she was asleep and when she was awake and had made some elementary mistakes at work which had caused her to start checking her paperwork over and over again. She hadn't felt the slightest bit hungry all week—that was the only bonus in days and nights of misery because she had lost three pounds.

She had phoned his office at lunchtime but his secretary had told her he was arriving back in England some time in the afternoon, and no, she didn't have any idea if Mr Morgan was coming into the office or going straight home. Cory didn't know if she altogether believed this, but the secretary would say exactly what Nick had told her to say, that was for sure. He must have known she was less than enthusiastic about going away for the weekend by the tone of her voice when he'd called her from Germany. That being the case, his astute and intelligent mind would know he had far more chance of persuading her if he stood before her in the flesh than by speaking to her on the telephone.

And he was absolutely right. Cory groaned out loud. In all her dreams she'd woken filled with a raging hunger for his embrace, an intense longing to feel his arms round her and his mouth on hers. He was just too good at everything he did, that was the trouble, and his lovemaking was top of the list.

When the door buzzer went a moment later Cory jumped so much she nearly fell off her chair. Telling herself she had to be the most feeble woman in the world, she walked over to the intercom in the hall. 'Hallo?' she said flatly as the butterflies in her stomach did the tango.

'It's me.' Just two words but they had the ability to make her start trembling.

'Hi.' She breathed deeply, willing herself to calm down. 'Come on up,' she said, leaning with one hand against the front door as her legs threatened to give out.

She was still standing in exactly the same position when he knocked on the front door moments later.

You can do this, she told herself firmly, ignoring the racing of her heart. Just be cool and calm. No tears, no hysterics, no big scene. The 'we can still be friends' scenario, even though you know you can't.

She opened the door. Nick was leaning against the stanchion, an enormous bunch of flowers in his hand. He wasn't smiling; in fact, his expression was one she hadn't seen before, almost brooding. The next moment she was in his arms, the flowers tossed carelessly on to the carpet.

He covered her lips with his in a kiss of such explosive desire that the world stopped, or Cory's world at least. He'd kissed her hungrily before, passionately, until her legs had become weak and her mind befuddled, but nothing—nothing like this.

Her arms had wrapped round his waist and she pressed against him, wanting to absorb his heat and his strength, needing to fuse their bodies together. Curves melted against hard angular planes, rock-hard thighs against soft feminine places until neither of them could have said where one body began and the other finished.

Nick pulled his mouth away for a millisecond to fill his lungs, but then his mouth returned to hers as though he couldn't bear even a moment of separation. His tongue touched hers, probing, urging her to respond, and she gave herself up to the wonder of pure sensation.

He had moved one hand to her head to hold her in place, one leg slid between hers to bring his lower body in alignment with her hips as he moved her against the hall wall, pinning her against him. The action both eased and increased the rocketing sensations shooting to every part of her body and she caught her breath at the sharp pleasure.

'Hell, I've missed you.' He lifted his head slightly so he could look into her face. 'You've no idea...'

She had. Oh, she had.

'I've dreamed of doing this every hour of every damn night.' He bent his head again to tease one corner of her mouth with his tongue, before kissing her cheek, her jawline, then forging a burning trail to her ear.

'Say you've missed me,' he murmured, his breath in her ear making her shiver with delicious anticipation. 'Say it.'

'I've missed you.' She arched against him, her body saying it too. 'So much.'

He shifted her in his arms, his hands running over her soft curves and cupping the fullness of her breasts through the soft fabric of her top. She gasped against him and he smiled, a slow, masculine smile that made her toes curl. 'You feel great,' he said very softly. 'You taste great. You are great.'

'So are you.'

He chuckled into her mouth. 'Not good enough. You've got to give your own accolades, not steal mine.'

Her eyes were heavy, her mouth swollen with his kisses. 'You're amazing,' she murmured dazedly. 'Will that do?'

'For starters.' He shifted her in his arms but then, instead of continuing to make love to her, he reached down and picked up the discarded flowers. 'Put them in water before we go,' he said quietly.

If she hadn't noticed his hand shaking slightly she would have thought he was totally in control, despite the hard ridge of his arousal which had been forged against her only seconds before. The sight was comforting; she was trembling so much she knew he must see it. She took the flowers without saying anything, walking with them into the kitchen where she buried her hot face in the fragrant freesias and soft white roses. She drank in their perfume, not thinking, not allowing any thought to come into her mind. Then she filled a vase with cool water and put the bouquet in it just as it was. She would arrange them properly when she came back.

Because she was going. She was going to have this one weekend if nothing else, she told herself, still a little dazed and numbed by the powerful emotions which had been released between them. It was probably the most stupid thing she would ever do in her life, a guarantee of emotional suicide at some point in the future, but suddenly she didn't care. He was here, here with her, and for the moment that was enough.

'Where are we going?'

They had been travelling for some miles before Cory asked the question, her voice low and husky. She was still registering the sensations which had taken her over at the flat—the way their bodies had fitted together, the pleasure given and received, the wonder of the world of passion and need and hot desire he'd taken her into.

'Guess.' He gave her a quick smile. 'You know about this place but you've never been there.'

'That applies to more parts of Britain than it should.' She wrinkled her nose. 'I'm not exactly a seasoned traveller.' She kept her eyes on him as she spoke although his gaze had returned to the road through the windscreen. He looked hard and dangerous and too sexy by far. He was dressed more casually than usual and she knew he must have gone to the flat before coming to see her. His formal suits or tailored trousers had been replaced by well-washed black jeans, tight across the hips, and his open-necked black denim shirt emphasised his flagrant masculinity more than any silk shirt could have done.

Suddenly it dawned on her. 'We're going to your home,' she said. 'The house in Barnstaple.'

'Quite right.' He reached for her hand and brought it up to his mouth, kissing her knuckles. 'I thought it was about time you saw where I live.'

'You live in your flat.'

'No.' The blue eyes flashed her way for a moment. 'I only occupy that. There's a difference.'

She stared at the dark profile. He'd shaved recently; there was a tiny nick on his chin where he'd cut himself. The rush of feeling this produced was scary.

'Besides which I thought you might like to meet a few of the family,' he continued casually.

'Your family?'

'I was thinking of the one next door,' he said with gentle sarcasm. 'Of course my family. Why? Does that bother you? They're really quite normal.'

Cory didn't know what to say. She wanted to ask if he usually took his girlfriends home to meet his family but she didn't dare. Of course it was highly likely that he did, she warned herself quickly when her treacherous heart did a few cartwheels.

'It seemed a good time with my mother's birthday being on Sunday,' he added.

'Your mother's *birthday*?' She sat bolt upright in her seat, all the nice floaty sensations that had stayed with her from the episode at the flat gone in a moment. 'It's your mother's birthday and you didn't tell me? I haven't got a card or a gift for her.'

'She won't be expecting one,' he said with typical male denseness regarding the niceties of such occasions.

'Of course she will.' Cory was horrified. 'Have you bought her anything?'

'I'll get something tomorrow,' he said calmly, his voice stating there was no need to get in a panic. 'When I've asked her what she wants. Something for the house, maybe.'

Men! Cory shut her eyes for a moment. 'A nice new vacuum cleaner, perhaps?'

He seemed quite oblivious to the sarcasm.

'Nick, your mother is a woman, in case you haven't noticed,' Cory said evenly. 'Do you ever get her something for herself? Chocolates? Flowers? A book? Clothes?'

'Clothes?' She could have suggested something obscene, such was his scandalised expression. 'Of course not. I have bought her chocolates and flowers before, though.'

There was some hope for him then. 'And I bet she loved them, didn't she?'

'My mother always loves anything I buy her.' There was a definite note of hurt in his voice now. 'It's the thought that counts, isn't it?'

So they said. And it must have been a man who coined the phrase. 'We'll shop tomorrow,' she said, 'for something for you to give her and something for me. What's she like? Describe her to me.'

'My mother?' His mouth twisted in a wry smile. 'She's quite a woman.'

She would have to be to have a son like you.

'She and Dad had the sort of relationship where they'd be hammer and tongs one minute and then falling into each other's arms the next—two strong minds, you know?'

She nodded.

'But us kids never doubted how much they loved each other or us. Dad was the more staid, upright one, very conventional—typical lawyer, I guess.'

'Your father was a lawyer?' Somehow she'd assumed he would have been a businessman like Nick.

'A damn good one.' There was a wealth of affection and pride in his voice and it touched her deeply. 'Mum...' He smiled again. 'Mum is one on her own. A true original. Nonconformist, feisty, stout-hearted. Dad used to say she was sent to keep him humble.'

Cory smiled but she thought Nick's mother sounded a bit scary. 'Does she work?'

'She was involved in animal welfare when Dad first met her but while we were young she did the housewife bit and thoroughly enjoyed it. Once my youngest sister was at school she started doing one of her great loves—painting—and also went back to the animal welfare thing, but in a smaller way. She does voluntary work at a local sanctuary. On the painting side—' he paused briefly while he executed a driving manoeuvre Cory was sure was illegal and which caused several other motorists to make use of their horns '—she's done very well. She sells all over the country now.'

Cory was feeling more nervous by the minute at meeting this Superwoman. 'What about your sisters?' she asked a little weakly, feeling she didn't really want to hear the answer.

'Rosie's thirty years old, married her childhood sweetheart at eighteen and has two kids, Robert who's ten and Caroline who's eight. She's utterly content being a wife and mother and is in nature a carbon copy of our father. Jenny's twenty-eight, travelled the world with a backpack from eighteen to twenty-three, married an artist who has his own pottery business and had twin girls four months after the wedding.' He raised a laconic eyebrow. 'That was a couple of years after Dad died, which is just as well as he'd have blown a gasket.'

Cory giggled. 'The twins are about three, then?'

'A few weeks before Christmas.'

'You sound like quite a family.'

His mouth curved upwards in a crooked smile. 'When Jenny and Rod called the girls Peach and Pears, Mum thought the names were terrific and Rosie and her husband were horrified. There isn't a more devoted aunt and uncle than Rosie and Geoff though. Sums us up, really.'

'What about you?' she asked interestedly. 'What did you think about the names?'

'Jenny had survived what proved to be a traumatic birth when she haemorrhaged and we nearly lost her and the twins were well and healthy. They could have called them Noddy and Big Ears as far as I was concerned.'

Male logic. Cory smiled. 'I like Peach and Pears,' she said very definitely. 'I don't see why people are locked into tradition about names. Flower names are considered perfectly proper so why not fruit or anything else for that matter?'

'Do I detect a smidgen of bohemian coming through? Is it possible that in the future you might be considering artichoke or cabbage, or even New York if the unfortunate infant was conceived away from home?'

Her smile faded. She didn't reply for a moment and then she said flatly, 'I don't intend to have children.'

'Perhaps all for the best if cabbage is a possibility.'

His voice was light and easy and he was smiling, but the warm intimacy in the car was gone and they both knew it. Cory felt a moment of deep regret that she had broken the mood.

The nifty little sports car fairly ate up the hundred and seventy miles or so to Barnstaple once they were out of London, but it was still almost dark when they neared the coast.

For some reason Cory was feeling an illogical sense of panic at the thought of seeing Nick's house. She couldn't actually have said why. It wasn't so much that this was the weekend she would finally take the plunge and go to bed with him, more that this house—his *home*—would reveal more about him than the flat ever could. And what if she didn't like what it revealed? Certainly the flat, beautiful as it undoubtedly was, didn't do a thing for her. But then he had said he didn't *live* in the flat, merely occupied it.

The morning star was high in a sky which was turning from mauve washed with midnight-blue to deep velvet-black when the car finally turned off the wide, pleasant avenue they'd been travelling along for a minute or so. A smaller road, almost a lane, took them past several houses set in beautifully manicured grounds. After several hundred metres there were no buildings at all, just the high stone wall one side and to their left rolling fields in which the round white bodies of sheep stood out in the evening shadows. Then the stone wall curved round in front of them, forming the end of the lane, and after drawing to a halt Nick opened the wrought iron gates set in the wall by remote control.

This was going to be some property! Even before they drove on to the long gravelled drive winding between established flower beds and mature trees, Cory was preparing herself for her first sight of Nick's home. And then there it was in front of her. A large mellow-stoned thatched building flanked either side by magnificent horse chestnut trees, its leaded windows on the ground floor lit by lights within the house.

'Good,' Nick murmured at the side of her. 'Rosie's remembered to leave the lights on. She always comes in and stocks up the fridge when she knows I'm coming home,' he added as they drew up in front of the huge stone steps leading to the front door.

'Nick…' For a moment Cory was devoid of speech. 'This is beautiful, just beautiful.'

He smiled at her in the shadows, his blue eyes glittering. 'I fell in love with the place the first time I ever saw it,' he admitted softly. 'It dates from 1703, although bits have been added here and there. Come in and have a look.'

The minute Cory stepped into the wide gracious hall she knew the inside of the house was going to match the outside. Warm-toned oak floorboards stretched into every room on the ground floor, their richness interspersed with big rugs. The huge sitting room, which overlooked the grounds at the back of the house, had big squashy sofas, one wall lined with books, low coffee tables and an enormous fireplace with a pile of logs in one corner ready for burning. The dining room, big breakfast room, Nick's study and the farmhouse-style kitchen complete with Aga were all beautifully decorated but with a cosy feel to them which ran throughout the house.

By the downstairs cloakroom off the hall an open tread wooden staircase led to four generous-sized double bedrooms, all with *en suite* bathrooms, and a gigantic master bedroom. This room caused Cory to take a sharp breath when she first entered it. It wasn't the walk-in dressing room, which would have swallowed her sitting room at home, or even the *en suite* bathroom, which was more luxurious than the one in Nick's flat that was the trouble. It was the bed. It was unlike any bed Cory had ever seen. In fact, it was more of an ocean of billowy space than anything else.

That he had been expecting her discomfiture was obvious in the amused tilt to his mouth when he said, 'You might have guessed I had the bed made specially. I'm a big boy; I like a lot of room.'

'You've certainly got that,' she squeaked weakly, wondering how many of his women he had shared it with.

It was set in front of huge windows, which had the same outlook as the sitting room below, the three carpeted steps which led to it the same length as the bed. The duvet and numerous pillows and cushions were various shades of coffee and taupe and this colour scheme was reflected through the whole suite. The bed was sensual and outrageous and sinful; it dominated the whole room and declared without any apology that pleasure was its chief aim.

Cory had to clear her dry throat before she could say, 'The...grounds look very nice from what I can see in the dark.' Nick had switched some outside lights on before he had begun to show her round the house, and now an area stretching some distance from the building was revealed.

'Oh, it is nice, Cory,' he said seriously.

Too seriously. She glanced at him sharply. He was laughing at her. She knew it, but she also knew she needed at least two glasses of a good wine before she could relax enough to contemplate that bed with any confidence or, more to the point, the man who slept in it.

She could just imagine the model type beauties who normally graced its languorous folds, she thought miserably. Suddenly all her imperfections had ballooned to giant size—particularly the vastness of her bottom and the dimples she could see at the tops of her legs when she looked hard enough. And Nick would be looking.

'What's outside, exactly?' she asked with what she hoped was cool dignity.

'Exactly?'

He grinned that fascinatingly sexy grin and Cory upped the wine to three glasses.

'Let's see. Covered swimming pool and sauna which can be reached via a door off the kitchen as well as from outside. I'll show you when we go downstairs. Plus a tennis court and croquet lawn, an orchard and a walled garden, which is very old-fashioned but quite cute. And lawns and trees and bushes, of course.'

'Wow.' Her eyes had widened. 'Quite a bit of land then.'

'A bit, but manageable. I have a gardener come in once a week for a few hours.'

She nodded. Another world really. Her parents hadn't been badly off and she had certainly never wanted for anything materially, but this sort of wealth was a thing apart. Of course she'd known his little empire was successful— he'd told her early on in their relationship that he'd been in the right place doing the right thing at the right time— but confronted with this beautiful house the reality of how rich he must be hit her for the first time.

She became aware that he was studying her face, the amusement gone from his eyes. 'Relax, Cory,' he said softly. 'This is Nick, not William, remember? You're allowed to leave this room without being ravished if that's what you want. I wanted you to see my home, that's all.'

That was only half true and she knew it. He wouldn't be human if he wasn't hoping for more from this weekend and he had been patient, allowing her time. They couldn't go on as they had been doing; their relationship either had to end or go on to the next stage.

And then suddenly he took her hand, his voice quite normal when he said, 'Come and look at the pool and then we'll see about some supper and a glass of wine. It's a gorgeous night, how about we take it outside?'

'That'd be nice.' Her relief was overwhelming. No doubt girlfriends in the past had just gaily stripped off and jumped into bed without a thought in their pretty heads except how

to please him and how he could please them—young, carefree, eager beauties who were self-assured and modern
without any hang-ups. She envied them. How she envied
them.

The pool complex was gorgeous but they didn't tarry
there. The very capable Rosie had packed Nick's fridge
with everything needed for a romantic supper for two, and
within a short while they were sitting outside at the patio
table, which was spread with all sorts of delicious delica-
cies. Nick had apparently asked his sister to put a bottle of
champagne on ice, and after pouring two glasses he handed
her one, saying, 'To us.'

It was a perfect summer's night. Stars overhead, the
stone beneath their feet still retaining the day's heat and
the garden bathed in a moonlit silence which was magical.
The air was rich with the perfume of scented stock and
fragrant night lilies which were in pots all around the patio,
a faint breeze carrying the delicious scents on its meander-
ings.

Cory breathed very deeply and took a sip of the ice-cold
champagne that tasted faintly of strawberries. 'I wonder
that you can bear to leave here for the city.'

'So do I tonight.' His voice was husky and his blue eyes
held hers in the glow from the candles he had lit before
switching off the outside lights. The house behind them and
the grounds stretching in front had all been relegated to the
shadows of the night; it was as if they were the only two
people in the world in their flickering circle of light.

Cory shivered suddenly but the chill was from within,
not without. She wished he had been an ordinary sort of
man—one who did a nine to five job, who was perhaps a
little overweight, who maybe had smelly feet. There might
have been a chance he wouldn't grow tired of her then. But
that was silly—he wouldn't be Nick and she wouldn't love

him if he was any different. She'd ignored the caution light even when it had turned from amber to red, flashing its danger sign in great big letters. *Don't let him into your heart and your life.* Yes, she'd ignored it. She only had herself to blame.

But she wasn't going to think of all that now. She gave a mental shrug. There was tonight, this entrancing garden and Nick. Her blood heated, singing along her veins. If this one weekend was all she had, then it would be enough.

CHAPTER SEVEN

WHEN they had finished the dessert Rosie had brought—a wickedly frothy concoction of raspberries, dark chocolate and meringue topped with lashings of thick cream—Nick disappeared into the house with the dishes and empty champagne bottle to make the coffee. He refused to let Cory help, kissing her very thoroughly before he left until she felt she was drowning in the taste and feel of him.

She sat in the balmy quiet of the scented garden, wrapped in a sensual glow that didn't fade before he returned. As he placed the coffee tray on the table she wrapped her arms round his neck, pulling his mouth to hers. 'I've missed you,' she said throatily, half smiling.

'I'll have to leave you more often.' He kissed her again before he straightened, adding, 'Drink your coffee. It's one of my specials.'

'Specials?' She picked up her cup, running her tongue dreamily over the creamy foam. It tasted wonderful. 'I didn't know coffee could taste like this. What's in it?'

'I told you, it's one of my specials. I've quite a range,' he said lazily. 'This one's got spices and whipped cream and a coffee liqueur a friend of mine from Brazil brings me when he's in this neck of the woods.' He sat down in his seat again, stretching out his long legs, his body relaxed and at ease.

Cory glanced at him from under her eyelashes as she sipped at the fragrant drink. The black denim added to the aura of masculinity and he made her legs weak. Tonight he would take her into that enormous bed. The morning could take care of itself.

They talked of inconsequentials as they sat there, the flickering candles slowly burning down and the star-studded sky above. When Nick at last rose to his feet, pulling her up with him, Cory felt a brief moment of panic.

She wasn't experienced like his other women. She didn't know any little tricks or moves to keep a man interested in bed. She just had herself to offer and suddenly that didn't seem nearly good enough.

As he put his arm round her she shivered. 'Cold?' He pulled her tighter into the warm protection of his body. His hands began caressing her, their touch as light as down and unthreatening. Slowly she relaxed, her head falling back against his shoulder, her eyes drowsy with desire as they met his. He lowered his head, nipping and teasing at her lips between planting little kisses on her chin, her nose, her closed eyelids. When his mouth finally took hers, his tongue thrusting deep into the warm moisture within, it was a kind of consummation, a woman accepting the powerful thrust of a man inside her body and Cory moaned softly.

He led her into the house still wrapped in his arms and they walked slowly up the stairs, each step punctuated with more caresses and soft murmurings. When they reached the landing Cory didn't realise for a moment where he was leading her. Then, as he opened the bedroom door and she stared into the pretty room beyond, her eyes opened wide. 'But I thought…'

'What did you think, sweetheart?' he asked softly.

She stared at him, so taken aback she didn't know what to say.

'That coming away with me for the weekend was some sort of sexual blackmail?' he continued silkily. 'I told you before, I'm not William.'

'I know.' Her voice was barely a whisper and his face gentled.

'No, you don't, not yet. Make no mistake, Cory, I want you. I want you so much I walk the floor some nights when cold showers don't do the trick. But you're not ready yet. Did you think the reason I told you I loved you before I went to Germany was to set you up for this weekend?'

Now he had voiced it she realised it had been at the back of her mind all the time. But she shook her head. 'No, of course not.'

'I've told you before, you don't lie too well,' he said with a faint little smile. His eyes searched her face. 'I want your trust as much as your body, Cory. Can you believe that? And this minefield of your past has to be cleared before that can come about. The only way I know to make it happen is to show you who I am. If you don't trust me then anything we have will be built on shifting sand; the first strong wind that comes against it will send the whole pack of cards tumbling.'

Cory's throat was locked and she couldn't utter a sound. She had never felt more confused in her life.

'You're bound up by fear; you know that, don't you?'

'Fear?' It unlocked her voice. 'I'm not afraid.'

'Yes, you are. I thought it was of me to begin with but the more I've got to know you, I see it's not that. It's Cory James who frightens Cory James.'

She took a little step away from him. 'I don't know what you're talking about,' she said, backing into the bedroom.

'You're frightened that the person you are isn't good enough or worthy enough or whatever it is.' A note of anger was in his voice for the first time. 'It's a legacy from your parents and it's rubbish, Cory. You know there's a part of me that could almost feel sorry for William if the guy hadn't been such an out-and-out jerk.'

'*What?*' Now she was angry. It put adrenalin where it was needed and burnt up the feeling of a few moments before which had had her wanting to cry. 'Why?' she snapped.

'Because you were waiting for him to let you down, weren't you? All along. And when it finally happened it confirmed you had been right. He had followed the pattern. You damn near led him into it.'

'I did not!' Her face was flushed; she glared at him, her hands clenched at her sides. 'How dare you say that?'

'Think about it,' he ground out. 'You picked a low-life who was programmed to treat you badly because that's the way he treats any woman in his life. It's a kind of victim mentality.'

'*Victim?*' It was fortunate that Nick had brought her to his home rather than a hotel because Cory's shout of sheer outrage would have woken every guest in the place.

She didn't have to think about what to do next. Her hand shot out with such speed it surprised them both, but Nick more so. Her last sight of him he was nimbly springing backwards as she slammed the door shut with enough force to have broken his nose but for his quick reflexes.

How dared he? How *dared* he say those things to her? She called him every name under the sun under her breath. And to think she had been going to sleep with him tonight; she must have been stark staring mad. She would never forgive him for this, never. If it wasn't the middle of the night she'd be straight out of here to find the nearest railway station.

She stood, breathing hard, glaring at the door, half-expecting he might knock or at least try to speak to her but there was no sound at all. He wasn't going to apologise. As the realisation swept in she became even madder.

She swung round to survey the bedroom. Her overnight

case was on a chair by the bed so he had obviously intended that she would sleep alone even when they had arrived at the house. Her cheeks began to burn but the anger was mixed with humiliation now. He must be having a good laugh at her expense.

She marched across to the *en suite* bathroom, opening the door and surveying the expanse of cream and gold which echoed the colour scheme in the bedroom. She was glad to see there was a nice big bath because if ever she needed a long soak rather than a shower it was now.

Thirty minutes and a refill of hot water later, Cory's rage was beginning to be replaced by self-pity. Half an hour after that she began to ask herself if there was a grain— just a grain—of truth in Nick's accusations. At three o'clock in the morning, after two hours in the bath and with her skin resembling the texture of a shrivelled pinky-white peach, she finally admitted to herself that he did have a point.

But she hated him. She rubbed herself vigorously with a towel before wrapping herself in an enormous bath sheet and padding through to the bedroom, her hair dripping wet. He needn't have been so offensive, and as for saying he felt sorry for William!

He hadn't actually said he felt sorry for William, a little voice in her head reminded her fairly.

As good as, she answered it militantly. Oh, yes, as good as. Well, that was fine, just fine. At least she knew where she stood now. He obviously thought she was off the wall and as weird as a cuckoo; if only he'd made that clear before he invited her down here it would have saved them both a lot of trouble. And she didn't give a damn what he thought anyway.

The tears came about four o'clock, but after a good howl she fell fast asleep and slept through until a knock on the bedroom door woke her. She opened her eyes to a room filled with sunlight and lay for a second of absolute confusion as to where she was. Then she remembered. As another knock sounded she scrambled up in bed, glancing around frantically as though a hole would open up in front of her.

Calm, girl, calm. As her thudding heart threatened to jump into her throat, she forced herself to take a deep breath. He was a rat and she loathed him. That being the case, she would treat him with utter contempt this morning and be on her way out of his life as soon as she was up and dressed. She refused to reflect on what she must look like with no make-up, eyes swollen from the tears of the night before and her hair—which had dried itself—one giant tangle.

'Come in,' she called tightly, adjusting the duvet under her armpits with her arms lying across her lap and her hands clasped.

'Good morning.'

He had the nerve to smile at her, she noticed, as he came into the room carrying a tray holding a cup of tea and a small plate of biscuits. She also noticed that he was wearing a black cotton robe and matching pyjama bottoms, and his hair was damp from the shower. He hadn't shaved either. He was devastating. 'Good morning,' she answered grimly.

'Sleep well?'

Swine. 'Perfectly well, thank you.'

'Breakfast will be another half an hour or so, but I thought you might like a cup of tea. I assume it is tea you drink in the mornings rather than coffee?'

She stared at him. She always had at least two cups of tea before she could begin to function in the mornings but she was blowed if she was going to admit that he was right about anything today. She shrugged, taking the tray as he came to stand close to the bed before nodding her thanks. 'Not really,' she lied coolly. 'Either are fine.'

'Funny, I'd got you down as a tea girl.'

He'd got her down as a lot of things as he'd made only too plain the night before. After taking the tray she refused to look at him, keeping her eyes on the teacup. 'Really?' she said, putting a wealth of disinterest into the one word.

'You're mad at me.'

Dignified contempt, remember, she warned herself silently. She raised flinty brown eyes. 'Why would I be mad at you?' she asked coldly.

'I don't know, unless it's because I've made you face up to a few things.'

The sheer arrogance took her breath away, that and the way the tight black curls on his broad chest—visible through the loosely tied robe—gleamed like oiled silk in the sunshine spilling into the room. 'Hardly,' she said stiffly.

'You sulk beautifully.'

The thread of amusement in his voice was reflected in the quirk to his mouth and Cory was sorely tempted to throw the tea over him. She just couldn't bear to spoil the exquisite broderie anglaise cover on the quilt, though—that and the inch-thick cream carpet. Besides, she told herself, she'd decided on cool disdain and that was what she was sticking to. 'Where is the nearest railway station?'

'Why?' he asked calmly.

'Isn't it obvious?'

'Not to me.'

'Well, I wouldn't dream of bothering you to run me back to London when you've only just got here,' she said with heavy sarcasm.

'Good.' He had been standing looking down at her but now he sat on the bed. Cory's senses went into hyperdrive.

'But you aren't going anywhere other than to do some shopping with me today, so cut out the childish tantrums and finish your tea.' He leant forward as he spoke, depositing a firm but swift kiss on her lips before standing again and walking to the door. 'I mean it, Cory,' he said evenly, all amusement gone from his face and voice. 'You're spending the weekend here. You're meeting my family. End of discussion.'

She glared at him, hot colour burning her cheeks. How could he make her feel like a recalcitrant child when he had been the one who was way out of line? 'You can't keep me here by force,' she said tightly.

'No, I can't, nor would I want to.' He stood with his hand on the door handle, eyeing her with the piercing blue gaze which seemed to look right into her soul. 'I was being cruel to be kind last night, can't you see that?'

'I thought that was the excuse people normally trot out when they are caught mistreating someone or something.'

'Then you thought wrong, in this case at least. I spoke as I did because I care, Cory. Think about it.' He opened the door and exited the room before she could answer.

She sat, trying to ignore the dull ache in the region of her heart that his last words had produced. She wanted to stay mad at him. She *needed* to stay mad at him. By his own admission he had been cruel last night. How could he say he had been like that because he cared about her?

Her parents had never had sufficient interest in her to tell her any home truths, either as a child or a young woman.

The thought hit her with the force of a ten ton truck. She couldn't remember a time when they had actually focused on her or got angry with her like Nick had done last night, she thought sickly. They had spoken sharply many times, usually to send her back to her room if she had left it for too long or if she was asking for their attention over something or other. But to take time to think about her or worry about her or even wonder why she behaved the way she did just hadn't been in their scheme of things. They hadn't cared enough.

She sat quite still, the tea cooling in her hand. Nick had said he cared. He'd also said he loved her before he had gone to Germany. But what exactly did he mean by that? How much? How much did he care?

With the tea now quite cold she got out of bed and carried the cup into the bathroom, tipping the contents down the basin. When she raised her head she caught sight of herself in the mirror and immediately any other thought was swept away by the sight of the scarecrow looking back at her. Her face was pale except for her eyes, which were faintly puffy and red-rimmed. Her hair gave the impression she had been pulled through a hedge backwards.

Whatever had he thought? She groaned. Even in her worst days at home she looked better than this.

Once she had showered and put a little light moisturising cream on her face she applied some careful make-up, which improved things no end. She brushed the tangles out of her hair with the help of a leave-in conditioner, looping it into a high ponytail once it was smooth and wavy.

Better. She inspected the result as she sprayed a dab of perfume on each wrist and the back of her neck. Much better.

Once in the bedroom she dressed swiftly in a sleeveless linen shift, sliding her feet into a pair of flip-flops and fixing small silver studs in her ears. She glanced into the full-length mirror by the bed. Casual, cool, without appearing to have taken too much effort. As a damage control exercise it would have to do. She took a deep breath. Now to face Nick downstairs.

He was sitting in the breakfast room, its French doors open to the fresh scents from the garden and a row of covered dishes at one end of the big pine table. He looked up as she entered, throwing the newspaper he had been reading to one side as he rose to his feet.

He had waited to eat with her. She felt a glow of pleasure out of proportion to the act of courtesy.

'Hi,' he said, very quietly. 'How about we start over again?'

She stared at him. 'Yes, please.'

'Does that mean shopping and lunch later?'

She nodded.

'Good.' He grinned at her. 'I thought I was going to have a fight on my hands. I wouldn't have let you go, you know.'

She wanted to ask him why but she dared not. 'I still don't think you put it very well,' she said, determined to have her say before they put it behind them. 'And that remark about William was uncalled for. But overall...' She hesitated.

'Overall?'

'There was some truth in what you said.'

'Thank you.' The grin widened. 'That was hellishly hard to say, wasn't it?' he added sympathetically.

She didn't trust the sympathy any more than she trusted her weakness where his charm was concerned. 'Hellishly,' she agreed crisply, determined not to smile. 'Could I have some juice, please?'

'Help yourself.' He waved a hand at the table. Besides the covered dishes there was a mountain of toast, preserves, a jug of freshly squeezed orange juice and a pot of coffee.

Cory suddenly found she was ravenously hungry and more happy than she would have dreamt herself being an hour ago. She filled her plate with scrambled egg, bacon, mushrooms and crisp hash browns, sitting down and beginning to eat with gusto.

Nick had done the same although his plate was filled with twice as much. She had just put a particularly succulent mushroom in her mouth when she sensed his gaze on her. She looked up. 'What?'

'I'm so glad you're not one of those women who push the food round on their plate for half an hour, or sit with a nice juicy something on their fork while they talk on and on,' he said appreciatively. 'The times I've wanted to lean across and tell a woman to get on with her food.'

She frowned at him. 'How rude.'

He chuckled softly. 'I've never claimed that patience is one of my virtues.'

And yet he had been terribly patient with her in the last couple of months since they'd met.

Her face must have betrayed something because now it was Nick who said interestedly, 'What?'

'Nothing.' She wasn't about to give him any accolades after last night. He might be right in essence about William but she hadn't quite forgiven him for pointing it out so brutally. And she definitely didn't agree with the victim bit.

It was a new experience for Cory to go shopping with a man and she found she loved it, probably because the man in question was Nick, she admitted to herself ruefully. It was nice shopping too—not trundling around a busy supermarket or anything like that.

She purchased a fairly generic card for Nick's mother, and then watched with concealed amazement as he scanned all the different verses in the 'son to mother' cards on display. The one he eventually chose was surprisingly sentimental.

'She places a lot of importance on the words,' he said

somewhat defensively as they walked out of the shop. 'She always maintains the best ones were the cards we made ourselves when we were children. She's kept them all.'

Cory smiled and said something appropriate but his words had hurt her. She would have given anything for a mother like that.

She hadn't let Nick call his mother and ask her what she wanted that morning before they had left the house. 'She would love a surprise,' she'd told him firmly. 'All women do. And not anything practical. OK?'

And so here they were after just an hour, with Nick having bought an elegant Louis XVI-style chair and matching footstool made from kiln-cured beech, the fabric being cream linen with velvet leaf appliqué. Nick had assured her his mother would go ape for the chair and had paid a hefty charge for it to be immediately delivered. 'She's been looking for something like this for her bedroom for years,' he said with a great deal of satisfaction. 'She'll love it. Trust me.'

Cory's comfort was rooted in the fact that the chair and footstool would at least be a surprise.

She had opted for a pair of exquisitely fashioned silver earrings from a small jeweller's in the heart of Barnstaple. The tear-shaped drops were inset with onyx, the semi-precious agate used to dramatic effect against the precious metal.

Nick had approved of her choice with reservations, as she had with his.

Later that afternoon he dropped the bombshell that they were in fact expected to attend a family party in honour of his mother's sixtieth birthday. They were sitting enjoying a relaxing cup of coffee in an enchanting little patisserie at the time. 'Nothing formal,' he assured her when her countenance changed dramatically. 'Just a casual get-together this evening.'

'How casual?' she demanded, her brain immediately doing an inventory of the clothes she had brought with her.

'Nibbles, drinks, dancing.'

'Where?'

'At a local hotel.'

She wondered if the owners of the little patisserie had ever had a man strangled in their establishment.

The next hour was spent in a frantic search which yielded a black and silver asymmetric dress in silk linen, which went perfectly with the black ankle-strap sandals she had thrown into her case at the last moment.

They arrived back at the house at six-thirty and were due at the hotel for drinks with the immediate family before the other guests started arriving at seven-forty-five.

Cory tore up to her room like a mad thing, clutching the bag with the dress in it. She had less than an hour to transform herself into an elegant creature of the kind usually seen on Nick's arm.

She was back downstairs at seven-fifteen; made-up, coiffured and feeling a lot more confident in the black and silver silk linen than she would have done in the smart-casual dress she had brought with her for evenings.

She found she had to take a deep breath at the sight of Nick. He had dressed up in black dinner jacket and tie. He had been sitting waiting for her in the hall, one leg crossed over the other knee, and now he stood up at her approach. The blue eyes stroked over her in a way that made her hot.

'You look good enough to eat,' he said softly. 'But the taxi's arrived so I'll have to restrain myself.'

'Pity.' She smiled brightly. 'But we don't want to keep your family waiting, do we?'

She'd decided she would emulate his other women tonight. She was going to be sophisticated and vivacious, carefree. The dress had cost more than she would have ideally liked, but when she'd slipped it on earlier a certain devil-may-care attitude had come with it. She was tired of being herself; she wanted to be someone else for a change. Nick had accused her of being childish and it had rankled. Tonight she'd show him she was very much a woman.

'Remembered the present?' he asked her as he opened the front door.

'It's in my handbag.' The jeweller's had wrapped the earrings beautifully.

'Then we're set.' He smiled at her, taking her arm as they walked to the waiting taxi. Just for a moment she saw them as an outsider would see them. A wealthy and handsome man with a well-dressed woman on his arm. Elegant, glittering, the sort of couple who had everything. Funny how different things could be from what they appeared on the surface.

Once in the taxi Nick pulled her close, his arm round her shoulders. It was a nice way to travel, more than nice. She could detect the hint of primitive musky male beneath the clean, sharp aftershave he was wearing. It was a heady combination.

He must have appreciated her perfume because after a few minutes he said huskily, 'What's that scent you've got on tonight?'

It had been an expensive Christmas present from Aunt Joan and she didn't wear it often. 'Why?' She turned her head to look up at him. 'Don't you like it?'

He took her hand and placed it on the hard ridge in his trousers. 'Need I say more?'

'Nick.' He had shocked her and it showed. So much for the cool sophistication.

He chuckled and she knew he'd got the result he wanted.

'You're beautiful, Cory, inside and out,' he said softly. 'And the wonder of it is you really don't think so.'

'I'm not beautiful.'

'You are.' He kissed her. 'Like a rare orchid or a precious stone.' Another kiss. 'Or a shooting star that leaves a trail of silver.' His lips were warm and erotic. 'Or a cactus flower that only blooms every few years.'

She wrinkled her nose. 'Cactus are spiky.'

'I know.' His smile was gentle. 'But the flower is worth waiting for.' This time he took her lips in a soul-stealing kiss that made her weak at the knees.

When she had regained her breath, she said, 'Do you think your mother will like me, Nick?'

She hadn't meant to ask but it had bothered her all day. She had been wondering how many women had been introduced to his mother and whether any of them had been particular favourites with Mrs Morgan.

'No, she won't like you,' he said softly. 'She'll love you, like I do. They all will.'

She stared at him, her eyes wide.

He held her gaze. 'Do you believe that?' he said quietly as the taxi sped on through the late August evening. 'That I love you?'

She hadn't expected this now, not here. But Nick was the sort of guy who was full of surprises. Unable to speak for the violent pounding of her heart, she settled for a slight nod of the head.

'That's an improvement on the last time I said it.' He ducked his head to nibble at her earlobe. 'It's still not the response I'm looking for,' he said after a moment or two when she had to bite her tongue to stop herself moaning out loud, 'but it's an improvement.'

Just then the taxi bumped over a hole in the road and they were thrown even closer together, his arms tightening as her rounded curves pressed against his hardness. 'Do you think we'd be missed if I told him just to keep driving all night?' Nick murmured in her ear.

'Possibly.' But she was game if he was.

When the taxi drew up outside the sort of hotel that featured in glossy magazines, Cory's nerves jangled. Meeting his family *en masse* suddenly seemed like torture. She found herself clutching Nick's arm so hard he actually winced, at which point she let go. 'Sorry.'

'The others'll be in the lounge bar,' Nick said quietly once he'd paid the driver and they were standing outside. He tucked her hand through his arm. 'Now relax, OK?'

'I don't think I can,' she said shortly.

'It's no big deal.' He turned her round to face him with his hands on her shoulders. 'They'll love you, Cory. I know they will. But even if they didn't it wouldn't make any difference to us. I'm a big boy now, in case you haven't noticed. I don't have to ask for my family's approval on my girlfriends.'

She knew that but it didn't help because she so wanted them to like her. She lifted her chin and now it was she who slipped her arm through his. 'Come on,' she said evenly. 'We don't want to be late.'

When they walked into the lounge bar it was immediately obvious where the Morgan contingent was by the calls and waves that met them. 'This is Cory,' Nick said as they approached the corner where three tables had been drawn together.

She smiled at the blur of faces and everyone smiled back, then Nick was kissing his mother and sisters and after a moment or two there were introductions all round. Nick's mother wasn't at all as Cory had expected from his description. Instead of a somewhat fierce Amazon, a small, dainty and very beautiful woman smiled at her, kissing her on both cheeks before she said, 'Cory, how lovely to meet you. I'm so glad you could come.'

His sisters were equally warm in their welcome, Jenny proving to be a carbon copy of her mother whereas Rosie was big, stolid and hearty. So was her husband, a tall blond man with red cheeks, whereas Jenny's husband was slim to the point of boyishness with floppy shoulder-length hair and an easy grin.

The only person who didn't seem pleased to see Cory was a voluptuous redhead whom Nick's mother introduced as, 'Margaret, my god-daughter. Margaret's a lecturer at Leeds University and doing awfully well.'

Margaret's handshake was cool, her smile more so, but Cory noticed it hotted up a good few degrees when the redhead turned her lovely green eyes on Nick. 'Nick, darling.' The voice was upper-class and well modulated. And warm, very warm. 'Why haven't you called me lately, you naughty boy?'

Cory kept her smile in place with some effort. So that was how things were? This woman liked Nick. In fact, from the way she was devouring him with her eyes, Margaret liked Nick very much. She watched as Nick gave the other woman a perfunctory kiss on the cheek, much as he had done with his sisters, before moving on to shake the hands of his brothers-in-law.

'Darling, my beautiful chair and stool. I love them, they're perfect. And what a surprise. I couldn't believe it when Hannigan's van drew up and the man said it was a special delivery for me.' Nick's mother reached up and kissed him, her eyes glowing. It was clear she was thrilled.

Nick's face was full of love as he looked down at the diminutive woman in front of him. 'I'm glad you like them,' he said softly. 'But the surprise part was Cory's idea. I was going to ring up and ask what you wanted.'

'Happy birthday, Mrs Morgan.' Cory handed Nick's mother the small package from her handbag along with her card.

'Oh, call me Catherine,' Nick's mother said, touching Cory's arm in a quick, friendly gesture before taking the gift. 'May I open it now?'

'Please do.' Cory would rather she'd waited until there wasn't quite such an audience, but as the tiny box revealed its contents Nick's mother was delighted. 'They are exactly what I would have chosen,' she said warmly. 'How did you know? I've always been a bit of a gypsy,' she added in an undertone to Cory, 'and I just love dangly earrings. These go perfectly with what I'm wearing tonight.' So saying, she whipped out her present earrings and substituted the ones Cory had bought, moving her head slightly so that the tear-drops swayed against the line of her jaw.

'Looks like we both chose well,' Nick whispered in Cory's ear a moment or two later. He had just ordered champagne cocktails all round.

She nodded. 'Your mother's lovely,' she said quietly. 'You're very lucky, Nick.'

'I know it.' He was looking into her eyes as he spoke and his voice was deep and soft.

The next moment Cory became aware of Margaret at their side. All the others had sat down again and now, as Rosie reached out and touched Cory's arm, asking her if she had been to Barnstaple before in an obvious effort to be friendly, Cory had no choice but to smile at Nick's sister and take the seat Rosie patted beside her.

All the time she was talking to Nick's sister she was vitally aware of the two people at the perimeter of her vision, however. Nick appeared to be his usual relaxed self from the odd glance she managed to throw his way, but Margaret seemed to be talking very intensely, her voice low but her body language suggesting it wasn't a normal conversation.

After a few minutes Nick took the seat on Cory's other side, putting his arm round her shoulders as he leant across to join in the discussion she and Rosie were having about the advantages and disadvantages of being near the coast. Cory welcomed his nearness; she had felt a bit odd talking to Rosie with Nick and Margaret so intent on each other.

By the time they had transferred to the big function room where the party was being held and the other guests had started arriving, Cory knew she liked Nick's family very much. His two sisters were as different as Nick had indicated, as were their husbands, but underlying their dissimilarity Cory sensed a bond that was unbreakable.

Catherine Morgan was very much the matriarch of the family but in the nicest possible way, and her respect for her children and their individuality was obvious. That each child adored their mother was also obvious, and as Cory noticed the easy relationship Catherine had with both her sons-in-law she reflected that Nick's mother was a wise as well as loving mother.

The nibbles Nick had spoken of turned out to be a full-scale buffet at ten o'clock, and as Nick had paid for an open bar all night everyone was enjoying themselves to the full—some a little too much. But everyone was pleasant and happy and the band was excellent, and as far as Cory was concerned it was wonderful to be in Nick's arms again on the dance floor.

She had danced with Nick's brothers-in-law and he had danced with his sisters a couple of times, as well as his mother, but Cory noticed he hadn't asked Margaret to dance. Margaret had stuck to their table like glue, slipping into a seat on the other side of Nick when folk had first begun to occupy the tables scattered around the dance floor.

It was around one o'clock in the morning, when Nick was having a last dance with his mother—Catherine having stated a minute or so before that she had called a taxi to take her home but that the rest of them must continue enjoying themselves—that Cory found herself in a conversation about Margaret with Jenny. Nick's sister was standing at the buffet table idly chewing on a stick of celery when Cory joined her, with her eyes fixed on her husband and Margaret, together on the dance floor.

'Look at her,' Jenny said in an undertone, with the candidness that was typical of her. 'She can't resist trying to bewitch every man who crosses her path. Poor Rod looks scared to death. He's not used to dancing with a praying mantis. And it was me who told him to ask her to dance, with her not having a partner. He'll never forgive me.'

Cory couldn't help laughing. Jenny's husband did have a hunted expression on his face. 'Why didn't she bring someone? I can't imagine she'd have any problem in finding a date.'

'Because of Nick, of course.' And then Jenny clapped her hand over her mouth. 'Sorry, that was incredibly tactless.'

Cory's stomach had done a flip but she managed to keep her voice casual. 'No, it's all right. I'd gathered she likes him.'

'Likes him?' Jenny eyed her grimly. 'She's like a leech at any family do but with her parents being great friends of ours Margaret's always been around. Funnily enough, her mum and dad are really nice. You'd like them. They're away in the Caribbean at the moment, though.'

Cory nodded. She wasn't interested in Margaret's parents.

'Look, let me explain something.' Jenny took her arm, leading her to a quiet corner. 'Nick would kill me if he knew I was talking like this so don't let on, but I think it's better you should know. So you don't get the wrong idea.'

Cory kept her face bland even as her heart sank like a stone. She wasn't going to like this, whatever it was.

'Margaret's always had a thing for Nick, right from when we were all kids together. She's Rosie's age and with our parents all being friends she was always at our house, supposedly to play with Rosie and me but in reality to traipse after Nick and his pals. When Nick married Joanna, well…' Jenny paused as if not knowing how to go on.

'Margaret didn't like it?' Cory put in.

'That's putting it mildly. She was nearly eighteen when we heard Nick and Joanna had done one of these sudden registry office things but even at that age she thought she was the cat's whiskers. I honestly don't think it had occurred to her that Nick might not want her. Then Joanna was killed.' Jenny shook her head. 'It was a bad time.'

'I can imagine.' His shock and grief must have been terrible.

'Nick came home for a while, more to decide where his life went from that point than anything else, but Margaret was never off the doorstep. It must have driven him mad. It certainly drove him away,' she added bitterly.

'That's a shame.' He would have needed his family desperately.

'Then, all of a sudden, she was off to university and seeing this boy and that. I mean she *really* put it around,' Jenny said darkly. 'She got a First, went on to greater and greater things, got married, then divorced, and we all thought she was over Nick. Then a couple of years ago she and Nick had a bit of a fling over the summer. Just a no strings attached type of affair. She actually told me herself that's what they had decided. She'd got this terrific job at the university—I mean she's brilliant, quite brilliant—and

Nick's always made it plain where he stands on commitment.'

Jenny stopped abruptly, looking at her anxiously.

'It's all right.' Cory forced a smile. 'He's made it plain to me too.'

'But since then she's been...odd. She's trying to get him back, I'd swear it.' Jenny sighed deeply. 'So just watch out for her, that's all I'd say. I wouldn't trust her an inch.'

'You don't like her.' Cory stated the obvious.

'Loathe her.' Jenny shrugged. 'But she's Mum's god-daughter and Mum likes her. Feels sorry for her a bit, I think. The thing is, if someone thinks your child is the bee's knees you can't help liking them, I suppose.'

Great. Had Nick's mother always hoped he'd marry Margaret so everything in the garden would be hunky-dory? If so, she'd view all his girlfriends as obstacles.

As Jenny bounced away to rescue Rod as the dance ended, Cory's mouth drooped. She watched Jenny join Margaret and Rod, who were walking off the dance floor with Nick and his mother, and Catherine had one arm through Margaret's and the other through Nick's. It looked cosy. Natural. Happy families.

Nick's eyes were searching the room and then as he saw her he lifted his hand and waved, leaving the others. She couldn't see the expression on Catherine's face as she was obscured by a young couple walking by, but Margaret looked straight at her, her eyes deadly.

Then Nick reached her, taking her in his arms as he murmured, 'I've missed you. We've been apart for five whole minutes. Mum's going now; come and say goodbye till tomorrow.' All the family were going to Catherine's for Sunday lunch.

For the next hour or so until the party finally broke up Cory said and did all the right things. She laughed and joked with the others, danced with Nick and avoided Margaret's lethal green gaze.

On the way home she pleaded exhaustion when Nick asked her why she was so quiet, and, refusing a nightcap—which would be much more than a mere liqueur coffee if Nick's smouldering gaze was anything to go by—went straight up to her room. And then regretted bitterly that she hadn't stayed with him.

She sat down on the bed with a little sigh, feeling as flat as a pancake. Which was crazy when she thought about it because nothing had changed. Nick had said he loved her. Fine. He had probably loved all his women, or the long-term ones at least. She *knew* that, so what difference did it make if he and Margaret had slept together a couple of summers ago and Catherine Morgan would like her god-daughter as a daughter-in-law too? He wasn't going to marry Margaret any more than he was going to marry her, so feeling upset and jealous and put-out was plain stupid.

It didn't matter if she was here on sufferance as far as Nick's mother was concerned. It didn't matter that Margaret was far more a part of Nick's life long-term than she was. It didn't even matter that Margaret was going to be at Nick's mother's tomorrow where she'd no doubt be a limpet attached to his side.

None of it mattered. She burst into tears.

One good cry, a scrub of her face and a brush of her teeth later, Cory climbed into bed, the exhaustion she'd spoken of real. It had been a long day after just a couple of hours' sleep the night before. She was asleep as soon as her head touched the pillow.

CHAPTER EIGHT

A GOOD night's sleep worked wonders. Cory awoke wide awake and alert—not a normal occurrence for her—at nine the next morning, and she was in a different frame of mind entirely. Climbing out of bed, she walked across and drew the curtains and immediately bright sunlight flooded the room. It was another gorgeous day. Flinging the windows wide, she leaned on the sill and breathed in the scent of the climbing roses beneath her, their heady, rich scent a wonderful start to the day.

She wasn't going to let all this about Margaret get her down. She turned from the window, staring across the room. She *wished* she'd stayed downstairs with Nick last night but there you were, she hadn't. She groaned softly. No use crying over spilt milk. But today was another day. And she was here in his home and Margaret wasn't.

That was when the idea came to her. Nick had brought her tea in bed yesterday morning. OK, why didn't she return the compliment? And once she was in his bedroom...

She hurried into the bathroom, had a quick shower and then brushed her hair until it shone with health. After putting a coat of mascara on her eyelashes and a dab of perfume behind each ear, she cleaned her teeth. She hoped he wasn't up yet but they had been terribly late last night and it *was* a Sunday. He was probably still dead to the world.

Her nightie was a floaty negligée type which consisted of very little, another gift from her aunt a couple of Christmases ago. She knew it was one of those horribly expensive designer things but she had never worn it until this weekend. She considered herself critically in the mirror. What the transparent film did to her body would have been enough to make her love her aunt for life if she didn't already.

Cory sped down to the kitchen with wings on her heels, hoping Nick wasn't already there. He wasn't. She made a pot of tea in record time, setting a tray with two cups and saucers, sugar bowl and milk jug, and adding a little plate of biscuits for good luck.

She had actually got to the door of the master suite when she stopped abruptly. What was she doing? Was this a good idea? She was going against all reason here. Hadn't she told herself that if she once got totally involved with Nick it would be emotional suicide? What would she do when he left her? And one day he *would* leave her.

It was too late anyway. She answered herself with total honesty. She loved him. Utterly and absolutely. She wanted to be with him for as long as he would stay with her. It was as simple as that. It probably was the biggest mistake she would ever make in the overall scheme of things because she didn't know how she'd survive when she had to do without him, but that was the future. This was the present. And the present was all that mattered.

She opened the door to the bedroom very quietly, tiptoeing into the room and over to the enormous bed. It was empty. She stared at it, utterly taken aback. And then she heard whistling in the bathroom.

Putting the tray on a small table which was half covered with Formula One magazines, she walked over to the bathroom door, which was open a chink. She didn't think about what she was doing, she was just drawn there by an invisible cord.

Nick had obviously just stepped out of the shower and was drying himself down. He was nude. Cory's heart did the sort of giant leap for mankind the astronauts had spoken of.

Six foot plus of lithe, tanned muscle and he was breathtaking, that was the only word for it. The wide shoulders and broad chest were strong and sinewy, his lean hips and hard buttocks unashamedly male. The hair on his chest narrowed to a thin line bisecting his flat stomach before forming a thick black mass wherein his masculinity stood out in startling white. He was a perfect specimen of manhood. A male in his prime.

Cory had stopped breathing. She was just looking. And looking. And then it dawned on her just what she was doing. Invading his privacy, spying on him, behaving like the worst sort of peeping Tom. What would she say if the tables were turned and she had caught him sneaking up on her?

She swallowed, panic rising up hot and strong as shame overwhelmed her. Stepping backwards, she stood trembling and weak, her cheeks flaming but her senses still stirred by the magnificence of him. She had to get out of here. She would die, die on the spot if he found her ogling him like a lovesick adolescent.

As the whistling stopped it prompted her to the door like a silent rocket and she shot along to her room with her feet hardly touching the ground. Once inside, she flung off the nightie, pulling on the first clothes which came to hand, which happened to be jeans and a T-shirt. Stopping just long enough to pull her hair back into a ponytail, she hightailed it back down to the kitchen.

She had to be cooking breakfast when he came down. He had to think she had just put the tray in his room and come down here. And then she groaned. Two cups. Two cups of tea on the tray. Well, she'd just say she thought he was probably thirsty in the mornings. She shut her eyes tightly. He would think she was mad but that was better than thinking she was some sort of sex-starved nymphomaniac!

She got busy cracking eggs into a bowl and putting bacon and tomatoes under the grill with a couple of minute steaks she found in the fridge. The toaster doing its job, the coffee pot bubbling and fresh juice on the table, she relaxed for a second. Her hands were shaking.

What had she been doing creeping about up there? That wasn't her; she wasn't like that. But that was the trouble, she didn't know what she was like any more. Since she had met Nick her whole world had been turned upside down and she didn't know if she was coming or going most of the time. And thinking she could seduce him with a flimsy nightie and a tray of tea! She groaned softly.

'What's the matter; are you feeling ill?'

She swung round, knocking a pile of toast on the floor in the process. 'You made me jump,' she said breathlessly, trying to see him as he was—clothed in jeans and a shirt—rather than stark naked.

'Sorry, but you made a sound as though—'

'I was thinking about a case I'm working on.' She was lying more and more since she had met him too. She wasn't even getting any better at it if the look on his face and his raised eyebrows were anything to go by.

'Right.' Thankfully he didn't pursue the matter. 'Do you want me to do the scrambled eggs because the bacon's burning,' he said helpfully.

'Damn!' She couldn't even cook a simple breakfast now.

Between them they salvaged the bacon and cooked the eggs, and once they were sitting down Nick reached across and took her hand. 'The tea in bed was nice of you,' he said softly, 'but I was hoping the other cup had been intended for you.'

Cory forced a brittle smile. 'Of course it wasn't.' She knew her cheeks were fiery and hoped he'd put it down to the mad scramble with the food. 'I wanted to cook breakfast for you. You did it yesterday, remember.'

'So I did.'

'And I thought we wouldn't want to eat too late if we're going to your mother's for half-twelve.'

'Quite right.'

'So that's why I got going on it.'

'Yes, you don't have to spell it out. I've got the idea.'

She was gabbling. She crammed a piece of bacon into her mouth to stop herself saying anything more. It was hot, burning hot. She spat it out as her tongue caught fire and then said, 'I'm sorry, that's awful, but it was hot and—'

'Cory, have I missed something this morning?'

'What?' She stared at him, horrified. 'What do you mean?'

'You're like a cat on a hot tin roof.'

She relaxed slightly. 'It's sleeping in a strange bed,' she improvised hurriedly. 'I never sleep well in a strange bed and then when I wake up I tend to be a bit…jumpy.'

'Oh, I see.' He took a bite of steak and chewed it slowly, swallowing before he said lazily, 'I thought it was because you saw me in the shower.'

She stared at him, utterly bereft of words.

'I didn't mind,' he added calmly, reaching for a slice of toast and spooning some scrambled egg on it. 'In fact, I think I rather enjoyed it. Of course I'd have preferred you to stay, but by the time I came into the bedroom, you'd vanished.'

He knew. She prayed for the ground to open up and swallow her, or at least for her to be able to think of something to say rather than sitting staring at him with her mouth open like a stranded fish.

Eventually she managed to croak, 'It's not what you think.'

'I don't think anything.' The blue eyes held hers and they were glittering with suppressed laughter. 'This is an excellent steak, by the way. You've cooked it just how I like it.'

Blow the steak. Cory swallowed. 'I thought I'd give you a cup of tea in bed as you'd brought me one yesterday,' she said stiffly. 'As I was leaving, the door was ajar and I just happened...'

'Ah, I thought that might be the case.'

She stared at him. 'You didn't actually see me then?'

'Of course not.' He smiled serenely. 'Do you think I wouldn't have pulled you in there with me if I'd seen you?'

'Then how...?'

'The two cups of tea were something of a give-away.' He was positively smug. 'I just put two and two together.'

Cory called him a name which nice, well brought up ladies didn't say—not often, anyway.

'What's the matter?' He looked at her with an injured expression. 'It was me in the nude, not you.'

'I know that,' she said through gritted teeth.

'So why are you the one complaining?'

'I'm not complaining,' she said icily, her voice in stark contrast to her cheeks, which felt as though they were melting. 'I just don't like being tricked, that's all.'

'But if I hadn't got it out of you you'd have been suffering a guilty conscience all day,' he said with insufferable complacency. 'This way we've cleared the air and everything is back to normal.' He took another bite of toast as he added, 'Did you like what you saw, by the way?'

She glared at him.

'OK, end of discussion.' He smiled, reaching out and stroking one hot cheek as he said, 'I love it that you can blush. It's a lost art, you know. Most women are so hard-boiled these days nothing bothers them.'

Most women wouldn't run like startled rabbits if they saw a man in the nude. She took a swallow of juice because it was easier than having to think of something to say.

'You were a great hit last night, by the way.' He smiled over the top of his coffee cup. 'My sisters are crazy about you.'

'What about your mother?' It was out before she could stop it, and something in the tone of her voice must have alerted him that all was not well.

'Mum, too.' The piercing blue gaze homed in on her.

'Good.' It was flat.

'Really.' He reached out and took her hand, lifting it to his lips in one of the little endearing gestures she found so special. 'My mother likes you; you must have sensed that?'

She nodded. 'I like her too.'

'What is it?' His voice was quiet, all amusement gone. 'Was something said I don't know about?'

She couldn't let Jenny down. She forced a smile to her face. 'Don't mind me,' she said quickly. 'Just feeling insecure being the new kid on the block, I guess.'

'You did great,' he said, but it was automatic. 'Cory, you'd tell me if something was wrong? If someone's upset you?'

How could she say that she knew she wasn't really wanted, by his mother at least? That Margaret was destined for him? It would look as though she was criticising Catherine for a start and she wouldn't want to do that. She didn't blame Nick's mother for wanting the best for her son, and Margaret, with her stunning looks and super-intelligent brain, had more to offer him than she did. 'Nothing's wrong.' She had to defuse the tension. She reached out and touched his hand. 'I had a lovely time last night and it was great to meet everyone.'

I love you so much. I don't want to be a ship that passed in the night in a few years.

She couldn't bear to look at him a moment more without saying something they would both regret. She took her hand away and reached for her coffee cup instead, beginning to make light conversation about his sisters and their children. Nick fell in with her mood, making her laugh about some of the antics of the twins in particular.

After breakfast Nick loaded the dishwasher while she wiped the table in the breakfast room, and then they went for a stroll in the grounds to work off the breakfast.

The tennis court and croquet lawn were immaculate, and the trees in the small orchard were gently basking in the summer sunshine, but it was when Nick led her to the walled garden that Cory became absolutely enchanted. It was set behind the orchard and clearly very old, as the ancient walls, mellow and sun-soaked, proclaimed. Nick opened the gate which creaked as they stepped inside, and Cory just stood and stared for a moment.

The stone walls were brilliant in places with trailing bougainvillea—purple, red and white flowers all jostling for space beside the green and red of ivy. There were a host of scents in the air, a winding path meandering past squares and circles of raised flower beds, old trees, borders of hollyhocks and marigolds and secluded bowers with seats surrounded by climbing roses.

'Nick.' She clutched his arm as she spoke but continued to feast on the scene in front of her. 'This is just the most perfect place in the world.'

He smiled, his voice soft as he said, 'It was neglected and overgrown when I bought the house but still beautiful. My gardener is an old guy with a great deal of soul. He gentled it all back to perfect health by letting the garden tell him what it wanted.'

She looked at him, surprised. He'd sounded almost poetic.

He caught the look and his smile widened, crinkling the corners of his eyes. 'That's what he says, anyway. Come in and have a wander.'

The path led them past sweet-smelling shrubs and bushes specially chosen for their individual fragrances, an old statue of a little girl with a puppy at her heels cast in bronze and weathered by time, the odd fountain or two tinkling their music into ancient stone troughs and crumbling stone bird tables all bearing traces of seeds. 'Albert loves the birds,' Nick said as he caught her glancing at the seed.

'I like Albert.'

The garden was an oasis of peace and tranquillity, the only sound the gentle hum of bees going about their business and the twittering of birds in the branches of some of the old trees above their heads. There were butterflies galore, bright and colourful as they fluttered from one sweet-smelling bush to another. It was a magical place. A place she'd remember all of her life.

'I would spend hours just sitting if I owned anything like this,' Cory said dreamily. 'Sitting and watching and letting the garden talk to me.'

'You'd get on like a house on fire with Albert,' Nick said wryly. 'He takes it as a personal insult that I don't inhabit the place twenty-four hours a day.'

'How often *do* you come in here when you're home?'

He shrugged. 'Not often.' And as she continued to look at him. 'Rarely.'

'What a waste.'

'Albert enjoys it.' They had reached the gate again, having done a full circle, and now they stood together looking at the colour in front of them. 'And I've been tied up with the business the last umpteen years. There hasn't been any time for sitting and watching and listening to gardens talk.'

'That's a shame,' she said quietly. 'To work as hard as you do just for other people to enjoy what you have.'

He stared at her, clearly taken aback. 'It won't always be that way.'

'When won't it be?' she asked directly. 'When is enough, enough?' And then she turned away. 'But it's nothing to do with me, of course.'

For a moment he didn't speak. Then he said, 'You of all people should understand how it's been for me. You said yourself your career is your life and that you don't want anything else to come before it.'

Had she said that? She supposed she had. But since she had got to know this complex individual at the side of her it had gone out of the window. There were other things which could work alongside her career, things which ultimately could come before it. In a strange sort of way she felt she had been sleeping the last twenty-five years and had only just woken up.

She kept her eyes on an exquisite red admiral butterfly sipping nectar from a profusion of scarlet and white lily-type flowers. 'Perhaps I was wrong,' she said softly. Perhaps she had been wrong about a lot of things. She might appear to be sure about where she was going and what she wanted from life, but the self-analysing she'd done since getting involved with Nick had shown her she was still the shy, nervous little girl who had been pro-grammed never to reach out to anyone. And she didn't want to live the rest of her life like that. Whatever happened between her and Nick, she didn't want to carry on the way she had been. It was a startling bolt of self-discovery.

'Perhaps you were.' He touched her mouth tenderly with

his finger, his voice deep and holding a note she couldn't quite discern.

She glanced at him, her eyes narrowed against the brilliant sunlight dappling the garden as she searched his face. But before she could say anything, he turned, pulling her out of the garden and shutting the gate behind them. 'It's twelve o'clock,' he said practically. 'We've half an hour to get changed and make it to my mother's.'

'Oh, my goodness.' She hadn't realised how late it was; the time had flown. It always flew when she was with Nick.

But instead of rushing her off, he took her into his arms, kissing her hard until she relaxed against him. 'I want us to talk when we get back tonight,' he said, raising his head and stroking her mouth with his lips as he spoke. 'We can't go on like this. You realise that, don't you?'

She looked back at him and her eyes were dark with the desire he had aroused, that and the slight chill she'd felt at his words. Had he finally got tired of her? Had seeing Margaret made him realise he couldn't be bothered to deal with someone who had so many hang-ups, someone who was such an emotional mess? And then she caught the thoughts. She was doing it again, she thought wretchedly, letting the anxious, uncertain little girl out of the closet. She nodded, trying to remove any trace of her fear from her voice when she said, 'Yes, I know.'

'Good. No argument, then?'

He hadn't actually added—for a change—but the words hung in the air between them along with his smile. She tried to smile back but it was hard. 'No argument,' she said weakly.

'You're in danger of being reasonable. I shall have to bring you to the walled garden again if it has this effect on you.'

The mocking quality to his words was enough to clear

the weepy feeling and enable her to say, half joking and half meaning it, 'Don't push your luck, Nick Morgan.'

'As if. I seem to remember the last time I did that with you I nearly lost part of my face.'

She smiled sweetly. 'Don't exaggerate. I had great faith in your agility.'

'Agile I might be, but the long jump done backwards isn't exactly my forte.'

'Are you saying there's something you're *not* good at?'

They continued to spar on the walk back to the house, Nick's arm round her shoulders and his hard thigh brushing hers. She wondered what he would say if she suddenly stopped and told him that she loved him, that she knew there would never be anyone else in the world for her and that he had become the centre of her universe.

Probably nothing, she answered herself wryly as they entered the house. He'd be too busy running in the opposite direction. Like Jenny had said last night, commitment wasn't an option as far as Nick was concerned, not the for ever type anyway. Love was one thing, devotion quite another.

Once in her room, Cory changed into a sleeveless cream crêpe dress which was hand-painted with squiggles in a rich chocolate shade that matched her hair. It was the dress she'd brought with her for evenings and it was eminently suitable for a Sunday lunch at which Margaret would be present, she thought, turning this way and that in front of the mirror. Classy, understated elegance. Exactly the look she needed for today.

After making up her face very carefully to emphasise her eyes, she put her hair up in a casual knot at the back of her head, leaving a few loose tendrils about her face. Standing back, she surveyed the overall result. Cool and tasteful. She frowned. Should she had gone for warm and sexy instead? But she couldn't compete with Margaret's flamboyant colouring and lovely figure, which was on the voluptuous side in all the right places. This was her, Cory James. She would never be a Page Three girl.

She squared her shoulders, picking up her handbag. She glanced in the mirror one last time with the sort of look that said, once more into the breach, dear friends. Margaret—beloved god-daughter, brilliant lecturer and old flame—I'm forewarned this time. And forewarned meant forearmed.

Nick's mother's house turned out to be a rambling old place, beautifully furnished with some lovely antiques but the carpets were worn in places and the sofas were the type where you didn't have to worry about dropping cake crumbs. Vibrant colours, lots of big throws, magnificent paintings on the walls—some of them Catherine's own— and a general air of the house being a home rather than a showpiece. Nick had told her that his mother's success with her paintings and his father's shrewd handle on investment and financial matters meant Catherine was a very wealthy woman, but material things meant very little to her. Her dogs—seven at the last count—and cats—five—were her priority.

'Every time there's a dog or cat that stays at the sanctuary for a while because no one wants it, home it goes to join the crazy gang,' Nick said, once they had patted and fussed the sea of animals about their feet on entering the house, and had managed to go through to the garden where Catherine had decided to hold a barbecue.

'The crazy gang?' Cory was sitting with a drink in one hand and her other in Nick's as they swayed in a big swing seat under a shady parasol, Catherine opposite them in a garden chair. None of the others had arrived yet.

'That's what the children call my babies,' Catherine said with a severe look at her son. 'They're not at all crazy. One or two were a little…disturbed when they came, but plenty of love and discipline in that order soon put things right.'

'Bertie—that's the big hearthrug,' said Nick, pointing to a Bearded Collie lying by Catherine's chair, 'used to eat paper. Right, Mum? Newspapers, magazines, books, they'd all get swallowed and digested. He'd actually take a book out of the bookcase when he fancied a snack.'

'That was because he'd been left alone from when he was a puppy and he'd developed bad habits because he was bored,' Catherine said protectively. 'He soon stopped that with me.'

'That cat, there, the black one with the white paws, only walks sideways. Like a crab,' Nick continued.

'She was hit by a car and has got brain damage but apart from the walking she's fine,' Catherine said, her tone sharper.

'And the mutt with the big grin—' Nick pointed to a little shaggy dog that did look like it was grinning from ear to ear '—starts howling if it hears music. Any kind.'

'Yes, well, I don't know why he does that, I must admit,' Catherine said reluctantly. 'But I've got used to it now.'

'Mother, they're all crackers in some way or other, that's why you've got them,' Nick said with a touch of exasperation in his voice. 'Crazy gang is kind; I can think of more appropriate names to call them. Especially him.' He eyed a little Jack Russell with only three legs who nevertheless was as nimble as the others and who'd nearly had Nick over as they'd walked into the house, by scooting under his feet. 'That wasn't an accident when we first walked in, you know,' he added to Cory. 'That's his party trick. He thinks it's great fun if he can actually land you on your back.'

'He never does it to women, though, only men,' Catherine said defensively.

'Great. You're telling me he's a gentleman now?'

'I think they're all lovely,' said Cory, smiling at Nick's mother, who smiled back. 'And taking the ones who really need you is brilliant. It's exactly what I'd do if I was in a position to work at home.'

'Don't encourage her.' Nick frowned darkly and then, as a big fat tabby cat with one eye missing jumped on his lap and settled itself down, purring gently, he began absently to stroke the thick fur.

Cory caught Catherine's eye and the two women exchanged a smile.

Rosie and Geoff joined them within a few minutes, their children, Robert and Caroline, politely introducing themselves to Cory before they disappeared to the end of the garden for a game of football with their father. All the dogs joined in, one or two barking frenziedly, while most of the cats retired to the fence where they sat looking down on the antics below with consummate disinterest. It was suddenly a lot noisier.

Jenny and Rod arrived next with Pears and Peach. The two small girls were identical twins and looked angelic, great big blue eyes looking out from under shiny blonde fringes and tiny rosebud mouths widening into smiles as Cory said hallo.

'Angelic?' Jenny snorted when Cory said what she'd thought. 'Don't you believe it. They're monkeys, the pair of them. I can't let them out of my sight for a minute.'

Within seconds the din in the garden had increased tenfold and Jenny smiled at Cory over the top of her wineglass. 'See what I mean?' she said resignedly. 'They have this effect wherever they go.'

It was another half an hour before Margaret appeared,

and Cory knew instantly that the other woman had timed her entrance for maximum effect, knowing everyone would be here. She looked stunning, her hour-glass figure filling out a low-cut black linen catsuit and her red hair styled in flirty fullness about her face. Red lips and talons completed the picture of a lady who meant business.

The men were all occupied with the barbecue and the women, having brought out the salads, french bread and all the extras, were sitting having another glass of wine when Margaret walked into the garden by way of a side gate at the end of the house.

'Wow.' Jenny was sitting by the side of Cory now in the swing seat, and her eyes widened. 'Impressive. Tarty and over-the-top and totally without taste, but impressive.'

Catherine had jumped up at her god-daughter's entrance, hurrying to meet her and then escorting her to a chair and fetching her a glass of wine. Cory schooled her face into a smile as Margaret glanced her way but then, to her shock, the other woman looked straight through her.

Whether Jenny had noticed the little exchange, Cory wasn't sure, but Nick's sister's voice had a definite edge to it when she drawled, 'Won't you be a little warm in that today, Margaret? Black's not ideal when it's so hot.'

Margaret's lovely green eyes were cold as she looked at Jenny. 'I don't feel the heat.'

'Lucky old you.' Jenny grimaced. 'Still, I dare say Mum can find you an old cardigan or something if you start to burn.'

Margaret raised perfectly shaped eyebrows before turning and engaging Catherine in conversation, although Cory noticed the redhead's gaze was fixed on the men at the barbecue. Or one man in particular.

The afternoon passed pleasantly enough. They all ate too much; the children wound the dogs up more and more until

Catherine banished them into the house—the children that was, not the dogs—until they calmed down. They drank wine, glasses of homemade lemonade, which were absolutely delicious, talked, even dozed a little. It was relaxed and comfortable, or it would have been if Cory hadn't been aware of every single glance Margaret sent Nick's way. And there were plenty.

To be fair, Nick seemed quite oblivious to the other woman's concentrated attempts to get his attention. Even when the redhead managed to brush up against him several times, ostensibly while fetching more food from the barbecue, which Nick was in charge of, he barely spoke to her. He was courteous but cool, Cory noticed. And she didn't know if that was a good or bad thing. Did it speak of unfinished business? Of something bubbling away under the surface? A lover's tiff maybe?

Jenny and Rod left just after tea time to take the twins home, declaring the two little girls would need at least an hour to settle down before they could put them to bed. 'They adore being with Robert and Caroline,' Jenny said, as she hugged Cory goodbye, 'but they do get overexcited.' Then, her voice soft, she added, 'It's been lovely meeting you, Cory. You're so good for Nick. I've never seen him so happy.'

Cory stared at her, taken aback. 'Thank you.' She didn't know what else to say.

They had all wandered out to Jenny and Rod's car to wave the little family off, and once indoors Cory let the others walk through to the garden and disappeared to the downstairs cloakroom. It was as she was leaving it that she stopped dead as she heard Margaret's voice somewhere near.

'Please, Nick, you have to listen to me. I can't bear it

when we're apart. I'll come down to London, I'll do anything but I want to be with you.'

'Don't start this again, Margaret.'

'I know you don't want marriage or anything like that and I accept it. I do. We don't even have to live together if you don't want that.'

'Margaret, move on. I have.' Nick's voice was cold, flinty.

'You're not talking about that little nincompoop you've brought with you? Darling, you'll be bored with her in a month or two. I guarantee it.'

'Leave Cory out of this. I'm talking about us having nothing left, Margaret, not Cory or anyone else. Whatever you're searching for, it's not me. It never was. You've always wanted me only because I didn't fall at your feet like most men you meet. Even as a child you always had to be the centre of attention and it wears thin.'

'You wanted me once.' It sounded sulky.

'We had a few dinners, a few laughs and that was all it was,' Nick ground out stonily. 'Face it. You were between partners and so was I.'

'This is because I said I loved you, isn't it?' Margaret's voice was quivering. 'Because I wanted us to be together always. It scared you off.'

She heard Nick sigh impatiently. 'Margaret, once you went to university you found the big world of men and you never looked back. I've lost count of the number you had before, during and after your marriage. You have no idea what love is unless it's love for the reflection in the mirror. You know damn well that's true; you've as good as admitted it in your better moments. I'm a challenge, the one who won't play ball. That's all. Now, cut the heartbroken act because it doesn't wash.'

There was a screaming silence for a few seconds and

Cory found she was holding her breath. Then Margaret said, a different note to her voice now, 'We're two of a kind, Nick, you and I. You'll never settle down with one woman, just like I'll never settle down with one man. But we could at least have some fun for a while.'

'Thanks, but no thanks.'

'Because of her?' Margaret said petulantly.

'Because I don't want you. End of story. Now go and say your goodbyes to my mother like a dutiful god-daughter. I've told Rosie and Geoff to take their leave too. You may not have noticed, but mother is getting older and a weekend like this shows it up, not that she'd ever admit it.'

'I'm always around when you grow tired of little Miss Perfect. You only have to pick up the phone and call and I'll drop everything.'

'Margaret, you always drop everything when a man calls.' It was said drily, the double meaning clear, and Cory waited to see how the redhead would respond.

Surprisingly there was a reluctant giggle before Margaret murmured, 'You're a wicked man, Nick Morgan, but irresistible. I shall live in hope.'

She couldn't hear Nick's reply to this because they were moving away, presumably going into the garden. Cory stood quite still. He didn't want Margaret, at least she knew that now, but from all that had been said the redhead was his type of woman. Two of a kind, Margaret had said. The kind who didn't want emotional commitment or monogamy.

Her heart was thumping madly and she put her hand to her breast. But she had known Nick was like that all along, so why did she feel so devastated now? Just because he had let her into his life to some extent, had been tender, understanding, it didn't mean he had changed his views about anything. He wasn't a cruel or manipulative man like William had been; of course he would be gentle and sympathetic to the woman he was seeing.

She stood for a few minutes more, knowing she had to get a handle on how she was feeling before she joined the others. Then, when she really couldn't delay any longer, she lifted her head and marched out into the garden.

'Hi.' Nick rose immediately as she walked through the French doors on to the patio. He sent the Jack Russell a warning glance which made the little dog slink away under Catherine's chair. 'I was beginning to wonder if you were all right,' he said, reaching her in three long strides.

She smiled up at him, into the blue, blue eyes that had the power to make her dream impossible dreams and long for what she could never have and hadn't even known she wanted before she met him. Because with Nick she wanted it all. Commitment, marriage, babies, for ever. But it wasn't going to be. 'As you can see, I'm fine,' she said softly, loving him and knowing she had to leave him.

When she had heard Margaret confirming all her worst fears she knew she had been fooling herself. She wouldn't be able to continue seeing Nick, sleep with him, stay at his house and he at hers, and then be able to get on with her life when it finished. It would break her. This way it would be crucifying, she knew that, but at least it would end cleanly and without dragging on and turning into something which ultimately would be distasteful to him and shameful for her. She didn't want him to remember her begging him not to leave her and falling to pieces, and she would if she let this continue.

Rosie and her family took their leave shortly afterwards along with Margaret, the latter kissing Catherine's cheek, giving Nick a swift but full kiss on the lips before he could object, and smiling a tight, hard little smile at Cory.

Cory didn't smile back. 'Goodbye, Margaret,' she said politely, keeping her gaze steady and cool. After a moment or two Margaret tossed her head, muttering something about it having been nice to have met her, and without further ado left.

Cory glanced around at the remains of the barbecue and the general mess. Then she looked at Nick's mother. Catherine *did* look tired. 'Why don't I make you a nice cup of tea and then Nick and I will clean up a bit while you put your feet up?' she suggested quietly.

Catherine protested a little but not too much, which spoke volumes. Once she had fed all the dogs and cats—a major feat in itself as several were on special diets and two of the cats were diabetic—she went into the sitting room with her tea and Cory and Nick got to work.

Once they had loaded the dishwasher with the first lot of dirty dishes and utensils they set about restoring order in the garden. By the time they had cleaned the gas barbecue, sluiced down the tables and one or two of the chairs which were sticky with lemonade spilt by the children and put all the toys in the small outhouse Catherine used for that purpose, the second dishwasher load was purring away.

While Nick washed all the animals' bowls in the deep stone sink in the utility room and put them away, Cory whipped over the surfaces in the kitchen and tidied up.

'We make a good team.' Everything finished, Nick came through to the kitchen and put his arms round her, nuzzling his face into her neck as she stood looking out of the kitchen window into the gathering twilight. A blackbird was singing at the bottom of the garden, and where the barbecue had stood before they'd wheeled it into the outhouse a flock of starlings were squabbling over tasty morsels. Nick was used to Sundays like this, times when all the family joined together and just enjoyed being with each other. Cory felt unbearably sad.

She turned into him, laying her head against his throat for a moment but not saying anything, and his arms tightened around her. They stood together in the quiet of the old house for some time before Cory stirred, her voice husky as she said, 'We ought to go and leave your mother in peace.' It was strange, but in all their passionate times she had never felt so close to him as she had for the last few minutes.

Catherine was dozing as they entered the sitting room, an array of dogs at her feet and a cat snoozing in her lap. 'Don't get up,' Cory said, smiling. 'We'll see ourselves out.' She bent over the back of the sofa and kissed the older woman's cheek.

'You'll come again soon?' Catherine asked. 'Just the two of you for dinner so we can get to talk a little. The family *en masse* always turns into something like a chimpanzees' tea party.'

Cory kept the smile in place with some effort as the sadness increased. She would have liked to come again and get to know this woman whom she felt instinctively she could have loved. 'Thank you,' she said. 'I've so enjoyed today.' And she had, in a way.

Once they were in the car and on their way to Nick's house to pick up their things, Nick said warmly, 'That was nice of you, to suggest we stay and clear up. I appreciate it.'

'It's all right.' A terrible consuming emptiness was filling her. He had said he wanted to talk and she knew what he would say. He wanted to know how she felt about them as a couple, where she saw them going, what she envisaged happening between them in the next weeks and months.

And that was fair enough. He had a right to expect some answers from her after all these weeks.

'Is anything wrong, Cory?' He flashed her a concerned glance but she didn't respond for a moment. 'Cory?'

'You…you said you wanted to talk about things earlier,' she said flatly.

'What? Oh, yes.' His brow furrowed slightly. 'But it doesn't have to be today. We're later leaving Mum's than I expected and we've got the drive back to London. We can talk tomorrow.'

'I'd rather it be tonight.'

'You would?' They were just approaching the lane leading to his house. 'OK. Once we get in, why don't you pull your things together and put them in the car while I make some coffee. We can talk then.'

She didn't wait for him to open her door when the car pulled up in front of the house, jumping out with more speed than grace and nearly going flat on her back in the process. She saw the quizzical glance he shot her but pretended that she hadn't, rushing straight up to her room once he had opened the front door. Bundling her things into her case and clearing the bathroom of her bits and pieces, she was downstairs again in a minute or two, stowing her case into the back of the sports car as Nick had suggested.

Then she stood for a moment on the drive, staring up into one of the huge trees bordering the house. You've been here for over a century, she said silently. You've seen so much. People come and go, heartache, trials, loss. And you're still here, weathering the storms and feeling the sun on your leaves and branches in the good times. Life will go on after Nick, I know that, but nothing will be the same. And I just don't know how I'm going to bear it.

'All packed?'

He called her from the doorway and she lowered her eyes

to his. He looked very big and dark standing in the shadows dappling the house, and in the strange half-light she couldn't see the expression on his face. 'All packed,' she said, walking to join him and taking the hand he held out to her.

'Cory, what's wrong?' As they walked through to the sitting room he spoke softly. 'You were fine earlier but something has changed.'

'You were right this morning.'

'Right?' he said, puzzled.

'About us having to talk. We do.' She sank down on to one of the sofas and watched him as he poured coffee from a tall white jug into slender china mugs. He added cream and sugar to hers and passed it to her before he sat down with his own beside her. She wished he had sat opposite her. She didn't want to say what had to be said with the feel of his thigh against hers.

'So you agree we have to talk,' he said, and his voice had changed. The softness had gone and it was cool, wary. 'Why do I feel I'm not going to like this?'

'I don't think we should carry on seeing each other.' She hadn't meant to put it so baldly but really there was only one way to say it. 'I don't think it's working.'

There was absolute ringing silence for a moment. 'May I enquire why?'

'I told you at the beginning that I don't date.' She had decided in the car coming home that she wasn't going to tell him what she had overheard. He might get the idea that she was trying to blackmail him into saying something he didn't want to say, that she was hinting he let her know that he wanted her in a different way to Margaret, that he was prepared to offer more. But she would never hold him to ransom like that. She went on with the lines she'd prepared. 'The last few weeks have been good but I'm getting behind with my work and things are slipping. I… I can't have that.'

'And so I'm to be sacrificed on the altar of your career?' he said silkily.

The tone didn't fool her. The powerful body at the side of her had stiffened and tensed as she had talked on. She cleared her throat. 'I wouldn't put it quite like that.' Her voice had croaked on the last word and she took a sip of coffee to moisten her dry mouth.

'How would you put it?'

'We're different sorts of people, we want different things from life.' For the first time she could speak the truth and, unbeknown to her, her voice carried weight because of it. 'We have had something great, I admit that, but if we go on we'd lose it.'

He swore, just once, but explicitly. 'Rubbish. I don't accept that. Is all this because I told you a few home truths the other night, because I got near? Is that it? I got under your skin and it rankles.'

She put the coffee mug down on the occasional table in front of them and stood to her feet. She had to put space between them. Then she turned to face him. 'I'm sorry you think that but it's not true.'

'Neither is the garbage you're telling me.' He rose slowly without taking his eyes off her white face. 'I've held you, damn it. Felt you quivering in my arms, moaning, begging me to take you all the way. Oh, not in so many words,' he said, as she went to interrupt him, 'but your body was saying what your mouth wouldn't admit. We're not so different, Cory.'

'You're talking about sex.'

'Yes, I am,' he said with no apology in his tone, 'and it's a damn good place to start. But there's more than that between us and you know it.'

'Whatever is between us I don't want it to continue.' She stared at him, desperate, her heart breaking. She had to go through with this now; it was the only way, so why did it feel so wrong, so cruel? She hadn't expected him to look at her the way he was looking now. It made her feel so horribly guilty.

'What was all that about earlier in the walled garden then?' he said furiously, anger coming to the fore for the first time. 'When you said you were wrong about your career being your life?'

'I didn't say that exactly.'

'The hell you didn't.'

'I said *perhaps* I'd been wrong about it, but on reflection I don't think so. I've been thinking about everything this afternoon and now I know what I want.' And it's you. For ever and ever. Impossible.

'Well, bully for you.' There was a look on his face which made her want to cringe. He despised her. Hated her even.

'I… I thought you'd at least try and see it my way.'

'Sorry to disappoint you,' he said bitterly.

'Nick, I didn't want it to end like this.'

Her lip trembled but then he almost made her jump out of her skin when he barked. '*Enough.* No tears. Damn it, it'd be the last straw. Drink your coffee.'

He walked out of the room without looking at her again and she heard him go up the stairs, presumably to his room. A minute later he came back with a jacket slung over his arm and, his face set, he said, 'Are you ready to leave?'

She nodded, walking past him and then out of the house to the car. He opened the door for her and shut it once she was in her seat, striding round the bonnet with a face like thunder.

She felt herself shrinking when he joined her, the only thought in her head being, how was she going to get through the next three hours until she was home?

CHAPTER NINE

THE journey back to London was the sort of unmitigated nightmare Cory wouldn't have wished on her worst enemy—not even Margaret. At least the mood Nick was in meant that it didn't take as long as on the way down. In fact he cut a good half an hour off the time, and he hadn't driven slowly before. Cory was sure she saw at least two or three cameras flash, but she didn't mention it.

When they reached her flat he got out of the car and fetched her case from the boot, walking with her to the front door. 'I'll stand in the hall until you've gone upstairs and opened your door.'

'You don't have to.' She had been fighting the tears all the way home and her voice was a husky whisper.

'Just open the damn door.'

Cory was all fingers and thumbs with the key hindered as she was by the mist in her eyes, but eventually the door was open and she walked into the hall, Nick behind her.

'Here.' He handed her the case, his face cold.

She walked over to the stairs and then turned on the bottom step to face him. She couldn't let him go like this, she just couldn't. Her face tragic, she said, 'I'm sorry. I mean it, I'm sorry.'

'Go on up, Cory,' he said flatly.

'Nick, please—'

'What the hell do you want from me, woman?' he growled before an answering growl came from the direction of the downstairs flat.

Oh, no, please, not now. Cory cast agonised eyes towards

the Wards' flat just as Arnie went into full action, the sound
of the big dog's savage barking horribly loud in the dead
of the night. She could hear Nick swearing even above the
din the German Shepherd was making, but before she could
say anything the door to the flat opened and there stood Mr
Ward holding on to Arnie's collar, Mrs Ward standing behind him clutching what looked like a rolling pin.

Cory saw Nick shut his eyes briefly.

'Cory, is that you?' Mr Ward peered into the hall, his
eyes enormous behind the strong glasses he wore. 'Is everything all right?' he shouted.

'Everything's fine, Mr Ward.' She found she was yelling
at the top of her voice to make herself heard.

'Are you sure, dear?' Mrs Ward screeched back.

'Quite sure.'

Mr Ward was now in the process of trying to drag the
dog back into the flat but Arnie was having none of it. He
hadn't had excitement like this for a long time.

It took both of the Wards to manouevre the dog in
enough to shut their door, Mr Ward pulling with all his
might and his wife getting in front of Arnie and using her
ample body as a sort of battering ram. Nick stood watching
them as though he couldn't believe his eyes, his arms
crossed over his chest and his face dark.

They had no sooner shut their door when, above the
sounds of, 'No more, Arnie!' and 'Quiet, boy, quiet! Lie
down!', a timid voice above Cory said, 'Is everything all
right down there?'

Cory turned round and stared into the faces of the young
couple from the top flat who were hovering on her landing.
'Everything's fine,' she said again, wishing the inoffensive
pair to the ends of the earth. 'Go back to bed.'

Something in her voice must have convinced them not

to prolong the discussion because they vanished immediately.

She turned back to Nick, who hadn't moved a muscle. 'I didn't want us to part like this.' She stared at him but the hard, handsome face didn't change. 'I thought we could be—'

Don't say friends.'

'Civilised. I was going to say civilised.'

'I'm not civilised where you are concerned, Cory. I thought you knew that.'

For a moment she couldn't speak.

'Go to bed.' It was toneless, final.

She opened her mouth to argue but suddenly there was so much anger in his face that she shut it again. And then she saw him visibly get his temper under control again. 'I mean it, Cory. Before I do or say something I'll regret.'

When she reached the landing and opened her door, switching on the light, Cory paused for a moment. Then she heard the front door to the building open and close. He had gone.

How long she sat on the sofa in the sitting room with her bag at her feet Cory didn't know. Eventually she rose, walking into the kitchen on legs that were shaky. She made herself a mug of milky coffee, carrying it back into the sitting room.

Her hands cupped round the warmth of the mug, her brain seemed to kick in and come to life again. They were finished. She was never going to see him again. It was over. Why had she done it, why? She had made the biggest mistake of her life.

She swayed back and forth a few times, her eyes dry now she could cry at last. Suddenly the emptiness of what she saw before her was too consuming for the relief of tears.

If she had stayed with him who knew what the future might have held? He might have grown to love her like she loved him; he *might*. Anything was possible. People could change, mellow. He could have decided at some point down the line that he wanted more than a semi-bachelor existence. Marriage, even children might have presented themselves as attractive.

She finished the coffee before standing up and beginning to pace the room, twisting her hands in front of her like a demented woman. She had burnt all her bridges tonight because Nick was a proud man and he would never forgive her for this. Even if she begged him, he wouldn't take her back now.

How could she have done it? Why had she been so stupid? It had seemed so right earlier after she had listened to him talking to Margaret, but now it seemed just as wrong. She didn't understand herself. She didn't understand herself at all. He had said he loved her. OK, it might not be the roses round the door and ring on the finger kind of emotion when he spoke about the word, but at least it had been a start. Now...

After a while she forced herself to go into the bedroom and get undressed. She had a shower, standing under the warm flow of water for some time, but nothing helped the terrible grinding pain in her heart. After brushing her teeth, she pulled on an old pair of pyjamas that had seen better days but which were fleecy and warm and climbed into bed. Half an hour later she was back in the sitting room again, not knowing what to do with herself.

She would go and see him in the morning. Eat humble pie. Crawl if necessary. She glanced at the clock. It was only three o'clock in the morning. How was she going to endure the next few hours without going mad?

The buzzer on the intercom in the hall brought her eyes widening and her heart thudding. She suddenly had a mental picture of a policeman standing at the front door with the news that Nick's car had crashed and he was dead. He had driven like one of the Formula One drivers he admired so much on the way back from Barnstaple.

She rushed to the hall, flicking the switch on the intercom with trembling hands. 'Yes, who is it?' she croaked.

'Cory?'

The relief she felt in hearing Nick's voice almost made her faint. Somehow she managed to say, 'Nick? What are you doing back here?'

'I've asked myself the same question.' It was dry and sardonic, but there was none of the furious rage of earlier. 'Can I come up?'

'What? Oh, yes, yes.' She pressed the switch to open the front door almost numbly, unable to believe he was here. That he was back. And then it suddenly swept over her. She had to tell him. This was her moment. She didn't know what had brought him back but she couldn't miss it again.

She opened the flat door, stepping out on to the landing just as he reached the top of the stairs. 'Nick!' She flung herself at him with enough force to have taken them both down the stairs if he hadn't braced himself at the last moment. 'Oh, Nick, Nick. I didn't mean it. I was stupid, crazy. I don't want us to finish, I don't.' The tears which had been on hold all night had burst forth in a torrent, her voice a wail.

She was aware of him picking her up when she continued to cling on to him like grim death, also that Arnie was barking again downstairs and the flat door above had just opened. Nick carried her into the flat, kicking the door shut behind him and walking over to the sofa, where he sat down with her on his lap. She still had her arms round his neck in a stranglehold, terrified he was going to leave before she could say what she had to say. The only trouble was, she couldn't get anything out with the tears blocking her voice and her nose streaming.

He let her sob for a minute or two against his chest before prising her arms away and reaching into his pocket for a handkerchief. After wiping her eyes, he held it to her nose. 'Blow.'

She blew, gulping and then saying, 'Nick, oh, Nick.'

'Whatever I expected, it wasn't this.' There was a thread of amusement in his voice but she didn't care. *He was here.*

'I was so stupid.' She tried desperately to stop crying but now she had started she didn't seem able to control the tears. 'And I didn't mean it. It's just that with you not wanting commitment and all that, I thought it was for the best. But it's not.'

'Slow down, love, slow down.'

Love. He had called her love. Suddenly she could see a light at the end of the tunnel again.

'What's all this about me not wanting commitment?' he asked softly, getting her to blow her nose again.

She must look a fright. Cory became aware of her tear-ravaged face and runny nose at the same time that it registered that she was wearing the most un-sexy pair of pyjamas in the world. It helped stem the tears. Shakily she said, 'I look awful; these are my oldest pyjamas. I bet none of your other girlfriends ever wore anything like this, did they?'

'Cory, none of my other girlfriends have been remotely like you,' he said very drily. 'None of them refused to have anything to do with me until I had to resort to blackmail to get a date; none of them viewed me with suspicion and downright dislike; none of them had me walking the floor at night and having cold showers like they were going out of fashion, and none of them nearly took my nose off with one of my own doors. Having said that—' he adjusted her more comfortably on his lap, stroking her hair back from her damp, blotchy face '—none of them were as sweet as honey without a trace of malice in the whole of their bodies; none of them cared about struggling families and folk who couldn't do a thing in return for them, and certainly none of them would have thought about clearing up for a tired old woman who needed to put her feet up.'

'Your mother isn't old and she would kill you for saying so,' Cory said shakily.

'A tired woman then.' He smiled at her. A heavenly smile. 'And none of them have given me the run-around like you, sending me away and then welcoming me back in a manner that took my breath away.'

She looked at him, unsure if he meant it or not.

'Now, I repeat, what's this about my not wanting commitment?' he asked softly.

'You don't. You never have.' She stared at him earnestly. 'You told me so, and when you were talking to Margaret today—' She stopped. This was what being truthful led to.

'You heard us?' He pulled her to him, kissing her hard before he said, 'There is absolutely nothing between Margaret and I; there never has been, not really. A couple of summers ago I took her for dinner a few times, to the theatre and things like that, but that was all. It didn't go any further.'

'You didn't go to bed with her?'

'I'd as soon bed the wicked witch of the west.' He kissed her again. 'That was never on the cards, not with Margaret. She knew that from the start. But she was a bit low—her own fault, there had been a divorce case in which she was named as the scarlet woman—and I provided a shoulder to cry on.'

She smiled. 'I'm glad you didn't.'

'I'm glad you're glad.' He brushed her mouth with his lips. 'And, as for me not wanting commitment, that was the bilge I talked before I met you. Don't you know that?'

She shook her head, not daring to hope he was saying what it sounded like he was saying.

He groaned. 'Look at me, woman. I'm a nervous wreck. Do you think I'd put up with what I've put up with if I wasn't head over heels in love with you? I've never waited for any woman like I have you; I've never had to,' he added wryly.

Now that she could believe. They queued up for Nick Morgan.

His mouth sought hers and he kissed her with increasing ardour, his hands moving over her body, caressing and fondling. He raised his head. 'What are these things made of?' he asked, glancing at the pyjamas with definite dislike.

'I don't know. Something woolly.'

'You won't be wearing anything like that on our honeymoon.'

'What?' Her eyes stretched wide. She couldn't have heard right.

'I'm asking you to marry me, darling Cory.' Suddenly he was deadly serious. 'I love you. I want to spend the rest of my life with you. I want to fill our house in Barnstaple with lots of little Corys and one or two Nicks. I want to make up to you for what your parents did and convince you you're loved more than you'd have dreamt possible. Every morning or our lives I want to tell you that Iadore and worship you. I want to take all the bad memories out of here—' he touched her forehead with a gentle finger '—and fill it with joy. Will you let me? Will you let me do that?'

She nodded wordlessly, incapable of uttering a sound.

'I wanted to tell you all this after we'd talked in the walled garden,' he said, 'but I was going to lead in to it slowly. The damage your parents did—' he shook his head '—I knew it would take time to diminish and I'd rushed in like a bull in a china shop. It had all happened too fast for you, hadn't it?'

His insight amazed her, especially as she hadn't looked at it that way herself. But it was true. Again she nodded. And finally she told him the words he'd been waiting to hear. 'I love you,' she said. 'With all my heart.'

'And I you, my darling. Never doubt it. You're my sun, moon and stars. Flesh of my flesh and bone of my bone. My special, funny, beautiful, incomparable Cory.'

'And you're my Nick.'

She put her arms around him and the blue eyes smiled.

THE MILLIONAIRE'S
RUNAWAY BRIDE

BY
CATHERINE GEORGE

Catherine George was born on the border between Wales and England, in a village blessed with both a public and a lending library, and fervently encouraged by a like-minded mother she early developed an addiction to reading.

At eighteen Catherine met the husband who eventually took her off to Brazil, where he worked as Chief Engineer of a large gold-mining operation in Minas Gerais, which provided a popular background for several of Catherine's early novels.

After nine happy years the education of their small son took them back to Britain, and soon afterwards a daughter was born. But Catherine always found time to read, if only in the bath! When her husband's job took him abroad again she enrolled on a creative writing course, then read countless novels by Mills & Boon® authors before trying a hand at one herself. Her first effort was not only accepted, but voted best of its genre for that year.

Catherine has written well over sixty novels since and won another award along the way. But now she has come full circle. After Brazil, and in England the Wirral, Warwick and the Forest of Dean, the family home is now in the beautiful Welsh Marches – with access to a county library, several bookshops and a busy market hall with a treasure trove of second-hand paperbacks!

CHAPTER ONE

SHE locked the car, and set off at a run past such a long line of parked cars she felt horribly guilty. The party was obviously in full swing and the guest of honour was late. As she raced up the drive towards the house the door flew open, but before Anna Maitland could start scolding Kate gave her a hug and a penitent kiss.

'Sorry, folks,' she panted.

'The late Miss Durant!' Ben Maitland grinned and gave her a bear hug.

Anna elbowed her husband aside. 'You said you were about to leave when I rang, Kate. Where have you *been*?'

'I went on painting too long. And at the last minute I remembered that my party gear was still packed, so I had to wear something that didn't need ironing.' Kate pointed an accusing finger at her friend's clinging beaded dress. 'Hey— just look at that cleavage! You said dress code was casual.'

'*Smart* casual,' scolded Anna, frowning at Kate's jeans.

'Are we going to stand out here all night?' inquired Ben.

'No, indeed—get a move on, Kate,' ordered Anna. 'Take your things up to the spare room.'

Kate saluted smartly, and ran upstairs to dump her bag and toss her coat on the bed. She replaced suede boots with black silk slippers with high silver heels, tugged her silver satin camisole into place and teased a loose strand from her upswept knot of hair. She renewed her lipstick, hung silver and crystal icicles from her ears and ran downstairs to join her friends.

'Smart casual after all, Cinderella,' said Anna, relieved.

'Ready for the fray?' asked Ben.

Kate grinned. 'You bet. Lead me to the champagne.'

Anna seized Kate by the hand to tow her through the crowd of people in party mood, taking her on a round of greetings to old acquaintances and introductions to new ones before she left her with a fair, attractive man ordered to take good care of her. Richard Forster was obviously only too happy to do so, and Kate was quickly absorbed into a convivial group, blissfully unaware that she was under surveillance.

In the adjoining conservatory, half concealed by greenery, a man stood answering questions about his company's latest regeneration project. His answers were courteous and informative but his covert attention was on the new arrival. Unlike the other women she wore jeans with some shiny thing that looked like underwear. Her lean, boyish figure had fuller curves above the waist now, but her hair still shone like the conkers they'd once collected under his father's chestnut tree. And, instead of looking the odd one out, she made the other women seem overdressed.

'That's Anna Maitland's friend, Kate Durant,' said the man next to him, following his look. 'Want an introduction?'

Still unaware that she was under scrutiny, Kate sipped champagne and contributed her fair share to the conversation in the group. But when she turned her head slightly her fingers clenched, white-knuckled on her glass, as she recognised the tall man wending his way towards her. The mane of black waving hair was shorter, the build more formidable and the angular planes of the face harder, but one look at him was like a blow to the heart.

'Hello, Katherine,' he said casually, as though it had been days instead of years since their last encounter.

'You've met Jack Logan?' asked Richard Forster, and Kate pulled herself together, smiling with hard-won composure as she held out her hand.

'Why, yes, many moons ago. Hello, Jack. Fancy meeting you here.'

'Kate and I are old friends from way back.' He included the group in his smile as he put a hand under her elbow. 'Forgive me if I steal her away for a minute.'

'Sorry I couldn't introduce you.' She took her arm back once they were out of earshot. 'I didn't get all the names.'

'I know most of them.'

'And they all know you, of course.'

'Big fish, small pool.' His eyes held hers. 'You look good, Kate. A touch rounder these days, but it suits you.'

'Thank you.' Kate peered past him round the room. 'Where's your wife?' she asked pointedly.

His eyes narrowed in surprise. 'She's in Australia.'

'On holiday?'

'Dawn went to live with her sister in Sydney straight after the divorce. She married an Aussie years ago.'

Divorce? Kate covered her stupefaction with a smile. 'I hadn't heard.'

He smiled coldly. 'Can't be easy, keeping track of all your ex-fiancés.'

Her answering smile was colder. 'I can't boast *that* many.'

'And none at the moment, I hear.' His eyes moved over her bare shoulders with a look Kate felt like a brand on her skin.

'Who's your informant?' she asked.

'The Maitlands' next door neighbour, Lucy Beresford. Her husband's company does a lot of electrical work for me. They moved here after you left for the big city.' Jack smiled blandly. 'I didn't tell her I'm on the list of ex-lovers.'

'Why would you?' She gave him a bright, social smile. 'Will you excuse me? Good to talk to you again, Jack, but I must see if Anna needs help.'

Kate stalked into the kitchen, her eyes stormy as she beckoned Anna away from the caterers. 'A word in private, please.'

Anna took one look and chivvied Kate into the pantry and closed the door. 'What's up?'

Kate glared at her friend. 'What on earth possessed you to invite Jack Logan here?'

Anna looked taken aback. 'Why ever shouldn't I? Not that I did invite him,' she added, pulling a face. 'Apparently he gave George Beresford a lift home tonight and Lucy convinced our local celeb I'd be delighted if they brought him along to meet you. My jaw dropped when I found Jack Logan on my doorstep, believe me. He never goes to parties.'

'He only came to this one out of curiosity.' Kate took in a deep breath. 'He's the man I was engaged to before I met you.'

'*What?* You're kidding!' Anna goggled in amazement.

'I haven't seen him since we broke up.' Kate's mouth twisted. 'It was rather a shock to find him here tonight.'

'I bet it was!' Anna shook her head in wonder. 'I was in shock myself. And, gush as I might, my faultless hostess act didn't deceive the man for a second. He knew I felt awful for not inviting him. Anyway, he apologised very charmingly for gatecrashing, and Ben gave him a drink and took him on a round of introductions. But he wouldn't have needed many. Logan Development's a household name round here.' Anna gave her a wicked look. 'You should have stuck with him. He's loaded.'

Kate's eyes flashed ominously. 'We didn't break up over money!'

'I'm sure you didn't.' Anna patted her hand. 'But whatever the reason, don't let it spoil the party for you. This whole shebang is in your honour, remember.'

'I know, and I appreciate it.' Kate gave her an apologetic hug. 'Let me give you a hand with your guests.'

Kate helped her friend supervise while the catering staff served the buffet supper, exchanged banter with those who knew her and pleasantries with others—and without making it obvious managed to avoid Jack Logan entirely. By the time the last guest was served she was beginning to regret her killer heels and agreed with gratitude when Anna filled a plate for her and insisted she take a break.

'Sneak off to the study with this—if those jeans let you eat!'

Kate made her escape along the hall to the study, but almost turned tail again when Jack Logan rose from the sofa, plate in hand.

'Looking for sanctuary?' he asked. 'Maitland rescued me from people determined to talk shop. But I can find somewhere else.'

She shrugged indifferently, and settled behind the desk with her supper. 'Stay if you want.'

He looked amused as she attacked her meal. 'You're obviously hungry.'

'I was too busy to eat lunch today.'

There was a pause while they ate in fraught silence, Kate determined to get the food down, even if it choked her.

'Are you up for the weekend?' Jack asked at last, as though he were a polite stranger instead of the man who'd once broken her heart.

'Longer than that.' Kate munched on a mouthful of cheese torte for a moment. 'Actually,' she said, looking him in the eye, 'I've left London for good. I live here now.'

He stared at her incredulously. 'Alone?'

'No.' She held the hard gaze steadily. 'I live with my niece.'

'Ah, I see.' His eyes softened. 'I was very sorry about your sister. Tragic accident.' He raised a quizzical eyebrow. 'But I'm curious, Kate. What brought you back to this neck of the woods? At one time you couldn't get away fast enough.'

'My aunt left me a house here in Park Crescent. When Elizabeth and Robert were killed—'

'I was at the funeral.'

She stared at him, startled. 'Were you? I didn't see you.'

He shrugged. 'It seemed like a bad time to intrude. But I was there.'

'Why, thank you, Jack, that was very kind,' she said quietly. 'After it was over I brought my niece to stay here with Anna and Ben. Joanna was desperate to leave London after her parents died, and she liked it here so much I resigned my job, sold my flat and moved to Park Crescent to make a home for her.'

'Amazing.' Jack's eyes were cold. 'Not,' he added, 'the admirable aim to make a home for your niece, but to provide it here instead of London. At one time a career there was all you wanted in life. You thought I was mad to stay here and work with my father.'

Kate shrugged. 'It was your choice to make. Mine was different.'

'Obviously the right one. I heard you climbed pretty far up the tree in your job. Was your niece your only reason for leaving it?'

'It was the deciding factor, yes, but I'd had a move in mind for a while. The chain of department stores I worked for merged with a bigger outfit a while back. I stayed on for a year or so after the takeover, but it wasn't the same with the new regime. So when Liz and Robert died I decided to accept the company's very generous pay-off and make a life for Jo back here.'

'So what will you do now? Look for a job here in town?'

'I've already sorted one,' she said, and got up with her empty plate. 'Can I get you some pudding?'

He stood up. 'Let me bring some for you.'

She shook her head. 'No, thanks, Jack, I must get back to the fray. In case you didn't know, Anna gave the party just for me—a sort of welcome home for the prodigal.'

'I did know. Lucy Beresford told me.'

She gave him a mocking smile. 'Yet you still came?'

'It was the sole reason *why* I came. I rarely go to parties, let alone turn up at one uninvited. Tonight curiosity won over manners.' His eyes locked with hers. 'I'm glad it did. It's good to see you again, Kate.'

'You too, Jack.' Kate gave him a cool little smile, and hurried back to the sanctuary of the dining room.

'There you are, Kate.' Anna trickled damson sauce over two plates of hazelnut meringues and handed them over. 'I promised Richard you'd join him to eat these.'

'Richard,' repeated Kate blankly.

'Richard Forster, the man I invited for you!'

'Are you matchmaking again?' said Kate, exasperated. 'Give it up, Anna. It's no sin to be single and thirty-something.'

'Thirty-four, if we're counting,' Anna reminded her. 'And I'm not asking you to marry the man, just talk to him for a bit. You've hardly spoken two words to him yet.'

'Sorry, sorry, situation remedied right now.' Kate went off to hunt down her quarry and found him in the conservatory, looking out at the moonlit garden. 'Hi,' she said, handing him a plate. 'I hope you like this kind of thing.'

In actual fact Richard Forster actively disliked sweet things, but wasn't fool enough to refuse food, or anything else, offered by a woman like Kate Durant.

'Thank you.' He began on his meringues with apparent relish while he asked her how she was settling back into small town life after her years in the capital.

'It's quite an adjustment,' she admitted. 'But I grew up here, so I don't feel totally alien. And I've been so busy with my new job and setting my house to rights I haven't had time to miss my old life. Friends and colleagues, yes, but not the hours I put in, or the endless meetings.'

'I'm with you there,' he said with feeling. 'Until recently I worked in a City law practice.'

'What brought you back here?'

His face shadowed. 'My father's health began to deteriorate. I left London to lighten his load in the family firm.'

'Of course.' Kate clicked her fingers. 'That's why the name rang a bell—your father was my aunt's solicitor. He's been very helpful to me.'

'Great man, my dad.' He smiled at her. 'So, Miss Durant, you and I have something in common; we're both newly returned to the fold.'

'Has settling back here been hard for you?'

He sobered abruptly. 'Afraid so. My wife didn't settle back with me.'

'Oh.' Kate smiled in quick sympathy. 'I'm sorry.'

He nodded. 'Me too. I felt very strongly about joining my father but Caroline felt equally so about keeping her job in London. So now we're a statistic; one more marriage heading for the rocks.' He smiled ruefully. 'Sorry! That was more than you wanted to know.'

He was right there, thought Kate with a pang of guilt. Years ago she had refused to stay here with Jack for a not too different reason. She thrust the memory away and smiled warmly at Richard.

'Can I tempt you to more pudding?'

'No, thanks,' he said hastily, and took her empty plate. 'My turn. I'll fetch coffee.'

Kate moved behind a concealing fern, glad of a moment alone to get herself together. Just seeing Jack Logan again had been shock enough, but the news that he'd been divorced for years was shattering. No surprise in some ways; straight, attractive men of Jack's age—and Richard Forster's—were rarely just plain single. But Richard was clearly still affected by his break-up, while she doubted very much that Jack's recovery had taken long. Her eyes kindled. Lord knew it had taken him no time at all to find someone else after she'd left for London. Whereas she'd taken years to get over Jack Logan. She gazed out over the moonlit garden with nostalgia.

She'd been so young and so madly in love... She tensed, the hairs standing up on her neck when a voice spoke in her ear.

'Why are you hiding in here?'

She felt Jack's breath, warm on her skin, and turned sharply. 'Waiting for my coffee to arrive.' She looked past him, smiling brightly as Richard joined them.

'I was told you like yours black and sweet, Kate,' he informed her, handing her a cup. 'Can I bring some for you, Logan?'

'Good of you, but no thanks, I'm leaving,' said Jack. 'I just came to say goodnight.'

'Goodbye, then. So nice to see you again,' Kate said politely.

Jack nodded to them both and strolled off to find his hostess. Kate stared after his tall, commanding figure for a moment then turned to Richard with a smile. 'Jack and I were friends a long time ago.'

'So I gather,' he said wryly, well aware that there'd been a lot more than just friendship between them. And Jack Logan still wanted it.

Jack could have confirmed this. After leaving the party he'd felt a crazy impulse to head for Park Crescent to wait for Kate. But common sense warned that a brandy before bed was a better idea than hanging about outside her house in the small hours only to find that someone else had brought her home—Forster, probably. Or she could be staying the night with the Maitlands. His mouth twisted in sudden derision. It was unlikely she'd have fallen into his arms if he had lain in wait for her. But his body's reaction to even the thought of it made it plain that he still wanted her. He always had, from the moment he'd first set eyes on her.

Kate had been standing on the steps of the Guildhall, selling poppies for Remembrance Day. She'd accosted him with a smile, rattling her tin when he parked near her pitch. He'd bought the biggest poppy on her tray and on impulse presented it to her with a bow, and she'd blushed. Jack had never seen a girl blush so vividly before. He'd stared, fascinated by the tide of colour, but more people came up to buy poppies, he was late for an appointment, and when he returned to his car later she'd gone.

Back in the cold, dark present Jack Logan pressed a remote control and drove through tall iron gates along a winding drive to the stables he'd converted to a garage when he'd first started developing the property. At that turning point in his life, with a broken engagement, a hasty marriage and even hastier divorce under his belt, he'd made a conscious decision to steer clear of close relationships with women in future. From that day forward all his passions would be channelled into expanding the family building firm.

When he first bought the Mill House property his original plan had been to get rid of the house itself and use the land for one of the mixed housing projects that were rapidly winning Logan Development a respected name. But the almost derelict house, sleeping at the centre of wild overgrown grounds, cast such a spell on him he couldn't bring himself to demolish it. Instead he put the property on the back burner and concentrated on more pressing projects. When he eventually turned his attention to Mill House he'd planned to make it into a show house as an advertisement for the company's restoration skills before putting it up for sale. But the process of converting a virtual ruin into a dreamhouse backfired on him. While the house was slowly, carefully restored, and the land around it tamed and nurtured, he'd looked from tall windows at a seductive view of mill pond and chestnut trees and felt a sense of possession almost as fierce as the emotion once experienced for Kate. When the work was completed Mill House was so much his own creation it was impossible to let someone else live there.

Jack unlocked the boot room at the back of the house and

bent to pat the black retriever who came rushing in exuberant welcome to meet him. He let Bran out into the garden for a quick run and stood at the door, eyes absent on the moon's reflection in the water. After a few minutes he whistled and the dog shot back inside, getting underfoot in the kitchen as Jack made coffee in preference to fetching the brandy decanter. He sat down at the table to drink it and scratched Bran's ears, his smile wry as he looked down into the adoring eyes. Canine love was a lot easier to deal with than the human variety.

In bed later Jack gave up any pretence of trying to sleep. Normally he never allowed himself to dwell on the past, but one look at Kate tonight had opened a mental door that refused to slam shut.

Logan and Son had already won recognition as the town's premier building contractor when Jack's father sent him to make an estimate for a house extension. While Jack was making notes of the owner's requirements the kitchen door burst open and Kate had come running in, slender and coltish in T-shirt and jeans, bright hair flying.

She'd stopped dead at the sight of the visitor, colour high. 'Oh—sorry. Didn't know we had visitors.'

'It's all right, dear,' said Robert Sutton, and introduced the girl as his sister-in-law, Katherine Durant.

Jack held out his hand. 'I'm the son in Logan and Son,' he said, smiling, and Kate put her hand in his.

'I'm Kate,' she said breathlessly. 'I sold you a poppy the other day.'

'I remember.' Conscious that Robert Sutton was watching them like a hawk, Jack returned to facts and figures and Kate left them to it. To his intense disappointment she was nowhere to be seen when he left the house, but as he drove out into the road his heart leapt at the sight of Kate walking a little way ahead. He halted alongside and rolled the car window down. 'Can I give you a lift?'

She smiled demurely. 'How kind of you.'

On the way into town Jack learned that Kate had just celebrated her twentieth birthday. After a business course at the local college, she was currently temping with local firms while making applications for something permanent in London.

'Now you,' she ordered.

Jack told her he was four years her senior, with a degree in civil engineering, and had worked for a big name construction company during university vacations to gain experience. 'But my aim was always to join my father's firm once I had the education part out of the way,' he told her. 'Dad and I make a good team. Business is booming. Where shall I drop you?' he added, and from the corner of his eye saw familiar colour rise in her face.

'Confession time,' she admitted reluctantly. 'I wasn't going anywhere. I lurked in the road to—well, to ambush you. Just drop me anywhere convenient and I'll walk back.'

Bewitched by her honesty, Jack turned into the car park of the Rose and Crown. 'Have lunch with me first.'

She smiled at him radiantly. 'I'd love to!'

Their first meal together was a sandwich and a glass of lager, but to both of them it was nectar and ambrosia as they sat in a corner of the crowded bar, so absorbed in each other they could have been on a desert island. It was over an hour before Jack remembered to look at his watch.

'Hell, I must get back to work. But I'll drive you home first.'

'Absolutely not. I'll walk back.' Kate looked up at him anxiously as they reached the car. 'You probably think I had the most awful nerve, lying in wait for you like that.'

He'd smiled down into the dark eyes fastened on his as though his answer was a matter of life and death. 'I couldn't believe my luck,' he assured her huskily, and clenched his hands to stop them reaching for her. 'Are you free this evening?'

Later that night, after a session in the cinema more like hours of foreplay to Jack, he parked in a lane on the way back to Kate's home, ready to explode if he didn't kiss her, and almost before he could switch off the engine she was in his arms and his mouth was on hers. They devoured each other greedily, kissing and caressing until neither could breathe and the inside of the car was like a sauna.

'You're killing me,' groaned Jack. 'But I'll die a happy man—almost.'

Kate rubbed her cheek against his, threading her fingers through his thick black hair. 'What would it take to make you really happy?'

'Honestly?'

'Honestly!'

He cupped her face in fierce hands. 'To get you naked, kiss every inch of you and make love until we're both brainless.'

Shivering in delight at the thought, Kate licked the tip of her tongue round her parted lips and Jack growled and began kissing her again. At last he thrust her away with unsteady hands and fastened her seat belt.

'Does your sister know you're out with me?' he demanded.

'Of course,' she said breathlessly, and slanted a sparkling look at him. 'Elizabeth is looking forward to meeting you.'

Jack swallowed. 'Really?'

'Don't panic.' She gave a wicked chuckle. 'She only wants you to finish her extension quickly!'

From the first they saw as much of each other as Jack's workload allowed, and he made a point of visiting the Sutton house regularly once work was underway to make sure the extension was completed in good time. His aim was to impress Kate's family with his firm's work, and at the same time convince them that Jack Logan was a suitable husband for her. To his relief Elizabeth and Robert approved of both, and gave their blessing when he eventually asked permission to marry Kate.

Looking on her consent as a mere formality, Jack had proposed, supremely confident that Kate was so much in love with him she would forget her ambitions about a job in London.

What a fool! He flung out of bed to stand at his window, staring savagely at the night sky. Kate had been thrilled to wear his mother's engagement ring, and deliriously happy to make plans for a wedding.

'In the meantime,' she told him eagerly, 'you can apply for jobs in London. You could start with the construction company you worked for before—'

'Hey! Hold on, Kate,' he interrupted, frowning. 'I have no intention of working in London.'

'But Jack,' she said, taken aback, 'you'll have to when I get a job there.'

'Look, sweetheart,' he said, trying hard to be reasonable, 'Dad and I have big plans for Logan and Son. Even if I wanted to, which I most definitely do not, I couldn't desert him now, just when things are really starting to take off.'

Kate stared at him in blank dismay. 'But you've always known what I wanted to do.'

Jack held on to his temper with difficulty. 'I *thought* you wanted to marry me.'

'I do want to marry you! But I want a career in London at the same time. We could both have one, Jack.' She looked at him in pleading. 'I'm sure your father wouldn't hold you back if he knew how you feel.'

'You mean how *you* feel,' Jack told her shortly, then took her by the shoulders before laying it on the line. 'Listen, Kate, I couldn't stand being a little cog in some big company's machine. I want to build up my own outfit, not just for my father's sake, but for mine. I intend to run my own show one day. If you love me, stay and help me.'

But Kate was already sliding the ring from her finger, tears pouring down her face as she held it out. 'I do love you— I'm crazy about you. But you'd better hang on to the ring for a while because I really need to *do* something with my life before I settle down here for good. I'm not ready for that yet, Jack.'

Too proud and hurt to argue, Jack had put the ring away and driven Kate home, sure that parting without even a good-night kiss would make her so miserable she'd change her mind by morning. But the morning post had brought Kate requests for interviews from two London-based companies. Soon afterwards she was accepted by one of them as a management trainee, and rang Jack in excitement to tell him. He wished her good luck, but to her utter dismay refused to meet her to celebrate.

'I don't see the point,' he said tersely. 'You've made your choice, and I'm keeping to mine.'

'Shall I see you when I'm down next, then?'

But proud, obstinate and desperately hurt, Jack answered in a way that changed both their lives. 'No point in that either, in the circumstances.'

He heard her draw in a deep, unsteady breath, and waited, his tension mounting. 'I see,' she said in a dead little voice. 'If that's how you feel we'd better make it a clean break, then. Goodbye.'

Three months later Jack married Dawn Taylor, daughter of the landlord of the Rose and Crown.

CHAPTER TWO

IN ANNA'S guest room Kate lay equally sleepless, wishing she'd gone home. At least there she could have made tea, or gone on painting her sitting room. She sighed and thumped her pillow for the umpteenth time. It was Jack Logan's fault. Though to be fair, she reminded herself irritably, chance encounters with him were factors she'd dismissed as unimportant when she made the decision to return here. During her one visit home after leaving to start the new job she hadn't tried to contact him, and Robert and Elizabeth had moved to London soon afterwards. Kate's next visit had been years later, when the Maitlands bought a house in the area after Ben was head-hunted by a firm of local architects. There'd been occasional visits to Anna and Ben since, but from the day she'd given his ring back Kate had never laid eyes on Jack Logan again until tonight.

She stared into the darkness. He'd changed quite a bit. Which was no surprise. He'd packed a lot into his life in the years since their last meeting—not only the hard work which had brought him such meteoric success, but marriage and divorce along the way. Kate's eyes kindled. She was human enough to feel glad his marriage hadn't lasted. She'd never been able to think of it without a stab of pain. Jack had broken her heart in pieces when he married Dawn Taylor.

Kate was still thinking about this when she went downstairs next morning to make tea. The house was quiet and the kitchen immaculate, all traces of the party removed the night before by the catering firm. She looked up with a smile as Anna came in, yawning.

'I thought I heard you, Kate. Why so early?'

20

'I didn't get much sleep last night. Nothing to do with the bed,' Kate added hastily.

'But a lot to do with Jack Logan. Sorry, love, if I'd had the least idea that *he* was the secret lover—'

'Ex-lover.'

'Whatever. I'd have given you advance warning.'

'Did you know about his divorce?'

'No; I don't know much about him at all, other than his success with these restoration projects of his. Everything he touches seems to turn to gold. They call it Logan's luck hereabouts according to Ben.' Anna shook her head in wonder. 'To think it was Jack Logan's name that never sullied your lips!'

'What have you been reading lately?' said Kate, smiling, then pulled a face. 'Lord, I felt like such a fool when I asked about his wife. I wonder why the lovely Dawn left him.'

'No idea. Ask Jack.'

'As if!'

'Are you going to see him again?'

'I doubt it.' Kate sniffed. 'He was a touch pejorative about my track record in the romance department.'

'But engagements were your speciality. At least you never got married—and divorced—like him.' Anna looked speculative. 'There's no one significant in his life right now, though. According to Lucy Beresford—the fount of all knowledge—the eligible Jack Logan lives all by himself in that showplace of his.'

'Amazing. When I saw that article about it in the Sunday magazine I took it for granted Dawn lived there with him.'

'They must have split up before he developed the property.' Anna downed her tea at the sound of footsteps upstairs 'Stand by your beds! Ben's on the move at last.'

'I'll just wait to say hello and goodbye, then I'm off home,' said Kate, and smiled. 'Home. That sounds so good, Anna.'

'You owned the flat in Notting Hill.'

'True, but I never thought of it as anything but a temporary arrangement, somehow. But, thanks to darling Aunt Edith, I now have a home worthy of the name. And, most important of all, Jo loves it as much as I do.'

When Kate reached Park Crescent she stayed in the car for a moment, gazing in satisfaction at her inheritance. The house was a small gem of early Victorian architecture with white walls, bay windows and a dark blue door with a fanlight and stone pediment. Mine, all mine, gloated Kate as she locked her car and went inside. She scooped up the Sunday paper on the way to the room her aunt had always referred to as the parlour, and smiled, pleased, as she examined her handiwork. The wall she'd painted the day before was the exact shade she'd been aiming for now it was dry—somewhere between cream and muted pink—or Coral Porcelain as it said on the tin. A perfect background for the white-painted 1857 fire grate.

Interior decorating was new in Kate's life. Jo had helped choose furniture and pore over paint cards, Ben had given invaluable advice; Anna had been forthcoming, as usual, with her own opinions and Kate had been grateful to all of them. But the end result, she thought with satisfaction, was mostly her own.

She read a few pages of the Sunday paper over breakfast in the kitchen she'd had refitted before she moved in, then, rather lacking in enthusiasm after her sleepless night, went upstairs to change into jeans and sweatshirt ready for her daily session with a paintbrush. She checked her emails and then paused, as she always did, to look at the view of the lake. She jerked the curtain aside as she spotted a man running through the rain with long, ground-eating strides, a black dog loping beside him as they skirted the lake. Jack! Kate watched as he slowed down to a walk, the dog, a retriever, she noted enviously, padding obediently beside him. She dodged back in anticipation, sure Jack was making for Park Crescent. And felt like a complete fool when he unlocked a mud-splashed Cherokee Jeep near the park gate, loaded the wet dog inside and drove off. She was too busy for visitors anyway, she told herself irritably, and ran downstairs to open a tin of paint.

When Elizabeth and Robert Sutton moved to London Kate had lived with them at first. But after Joanna was born she eventually left the Sutton household to share a flat with Anna Travers. The two girls were kindred spirits from the moment Kate answered Anna's advertisement for a flatmate, and lived together in complete accord right up to the day Anna married Ben and then moved away, at which point Kate gave in to her current boyfriend's urging. Her feelings for David Houston were nothing like the passion she'd felt for Jack Logan, but Jack was long since married and she was long since over him, so she accepted David's proposal and moved in with him. But eventually their relationship wound down to an amicable end, and Kate exchanged the brick walls and leather and chrome of David's hip Thames-side loft for a small flat of her own at last in Notting Hill.

At that stage Kate's life was as close to ideal as she could make it. She moved swiftly up the ladder in her job, enjoyed a lively social life, spent her Sundays in her sister's household and remained on friendly terms with David. This well-ordered phase of her life went on until she met Rupert Chance, heir to a chain of supermarkets. He singled her out at a party and instantly began a relentless pursuit she was human enough to find flattering. He soon began persuading her to share his house in Chelsea, but Kate held back. She was attracted to the persuasive Rupert but caution prompted her to wait before burning her boats. Byronic good looks coupled with effortless charm had always won Rupert Chance anything he wanted the moment he wanted it, and he objected strongly when Kate insisted on keeping to her own flat. When they were married, he informed her, things would change.

Drastic changes came before that, in a way neither of them

could have foreseen. Edith Durant, elder sister of Kate's father, died at the age of ninety-one, and in her will left money to her niece Elizabeth and her house and contents to her younger niece, Katherine. Elizabeth and Robert Sutton celebrated their windfall with a luxury holiday during Joanna's autumn term, but died together when their hired car swerved off a mountain road during a storm.

Kate broke the news to Jo. She drove down to the school, held the child in her arms while she cried her heart out, and in her capacity as official guardian arranged for Joanna to take time off after the funeral. When the service was over Kate took Jo to stay overnight with Robert's elderly, grief-stricken parents, then on to Anna and Ben to recuperate. Their support was a great comfort while the child struggled to come to terms with her loss, and during their week's stay Kate took Joanna to see the house in Park Crescent. The child fell in love with it and, after much discussion, the decision was made to move from London. Instead of selling Aunt Edith's house they would live in it together, in the town where Joanna's mother and aunt had grown up.

The Notting Hill flat had been expensive to buy but with the improvements Kate had made over the years proved profitable to sell. The proceeds were enough to renovate and furnish the house in Park Crescent, and leave enough over for a respectable nest egg to cushion Kate's altered lifestyle. Joanna's education had been provided for since her birth, and her inheritance from her parents, along with the proceeds from the sale of their house, was carefully invested to provide for the future. Kate was determined to make life as happy and secure for the child as humanly possible.

Kate finished a tin of paint with a feeling of satisfaction for a job well done and called it a day. She soaked in scented hot water later with a heartfelt sigh of pleasure. Another wall had been painted and she'd taken it in her stride when Jack Logan drove off instead of calling in to see her. Her shrug rippled the water. No point in getting uptight. Casual sightings could be a fact of life from now on. She could run into Jack anywhere and any time. It was not a problem.

Anna rang later while Kate was getting dressed. 'Hi. How's it going?'

Kate reported on her painting progress, but Anna brushed that aside.

'How are you, really?'

'A bit tired, but I've had a long, lazy bath—'

'I meant after meeting the old flame!'

'Fine. Why shouldn't I be?'

'Not even a little bit singed round the edges?'

'Not in the slightest.'

'Thank goodness,' said Anna, relieved. 'Sleep well.'

Kate dried her hair, left it loose on her shoulders and took some coffee upstairs to the study at present doubling as both workplace and sitting room until her decorating was finished. She drew the curtains, switched on lamps and, with a sigh of satisfaction, curled up in the armchair to read the rest of the Sunday papers before supper. She frowned in surprise when the doorbell rang shortly afterwards. She got up to peer down from the window and saw a long, sleek car parked at the kerb and an all too familiar male figure standing under her exterior light. She went downstairs, fixed a polite smile on her face and opened the door to Jack Logan.

Her visitor loomed tall on her doorstep, looking very different from the night before in a battered leather windbreaker and jeans. He smiled, raking a hand through hair ruffled by the wind blowing along the street from the lake. 'Hello, Kate. I took a chance on finding you at home. May I come in?'

'Of course.' She led him along the hall to the kitchen and pulled out one of the kitchen chairs. 'Nowhere else to receive visitors yet, I'm afraid. Would you like coffee, or a drink?'

'Coffee would be good. Thank you.' Jack leaned against the counter, his eyes on the fall of burnished hair as he watched Kate get to work. 'I went for a run in the park with the dog this morning, intending to call on you afterwards, but Bran and I were so wet I decided against it.'

This information won him a warmer smile. 'Have you had the dog long?'

'Five years.' Jack slung his jacket on the back of a chair. 'He's a black retriever—great company. When I'm not around, Dad takes care of him.'

'How *is* your father?' Kate made the coffee, set the pot and a pair of mugs on the table and fetched sugar and milk, glad of homely occupation while she adjusted to Jack Logan's dominant presence in her kitchen.

'Dad's semi-retired, plays a lot of golf these days.' He smiled. 'I hoped he'd marry again, but I'm afraid he's a one-woman man.'

Which was more than could be said for his son, thought Kate with rancour. 'I was very fond of your father.'

'The feeling was mutual.'

She shot him a look. 'That can't have lasted once we split up.'

'You mean when you took off for London rather than marry me!' Their eyes clashed for a moment, then Jack shrugged. 'Actually my father was a lot more tolerant than me. He told me to give you time to spread your wings. But for me it was all or nothing.'

'You can't say you pined for long!'

'Actually, you're wrong about that.' Jack crossed his legs and sat back, surveying her thoughtfully. 'Maybe it's time you knew the truth.'

Kate shook her head as she poured coffee. 'No need, Jack. I chose to leave, and you married Dawn on the rebound. These things happen.'

'Not in the way you think.'

She gave him an assessing look, resentful that the lines on his face merely added character to the good looks of his youth. 'I don't think about it, Jack. It was a long time ago. No point in raking it all up again.'

'I look on it as setting the record straight.' He drank some of his coffee, then set down the mug. 'After you took off for London,' he said, with the air of a man determined to have his say, 'I began drowning my sorrows at the Rose and Crown most nights, and Dawn Taylor offered the kind of comfort I was fool enough to accept eventually, because I was so bloody miserable without you. But when she begged me to marry her because she was pregnant, I realised exactly what kind of a fool I'd been. Dawn was very popular with her father's punters, and Dad said I was an idiot to believe that the child was mine.' He gave her a straight look. 'Nevertheless, it could have been mine, Kate.'

She held his eyes. 'What happened to the baby?'

'Dawn miscarried soon after the wedding, eighteen weeks into the pregnancy.' His mouth twisted. 'My entire relationship with Dawn up to that point, including the marriage, added up to twelve weeks. You can do the maths.'

'So who *was* the father?'

'Someone else's husband.' Jack shrugged. 'So in a panic Dawn told me the baby was mine, hoping to pass it off on me as premature. When it all went horribly wrong she agreed to a quickie divorce and used my one-off settlement to visit her sister in Australia. I haven't seen her since.'

Kate digested this in silence for a while. 'She was a very pretty girl—spectacular figure,' she said at last, and looked at him very directly. 'It broke my heart when you married her so soon after we split up.'

His eyes hardened. 'You broke mine when you took off for London.'

'Oh, come on, Jack,' she retorted. 'London wasn't the moon. I could have come home to you every weekend right from the start, or you could have come to me, but not a chance. It had to be your way or nothing.'

'I changed my mind pretty quickly,' he said, startling her. 'I missed you like hell. I soon wanted you back on any terms. I was about to get in touch to tell you that, but Dawn got in first with her news.'

'You mean you expected me to rush back to you even though you slept with her the minute I left?' Kate eyed him coldly. 'I would have found out sooner or later. News travels fast in a small town like this.'

He shrugged. 'Not so very fast, apparently. You didn't know about the divorce.'

'I was living in London then, remember. And if they knew about it, Liz and Robert never told me.'

'Obviously not. But I'm surprised that the news hasn't filtered through to you since.' He smiled wryly. 'Talking of surprises, Anna Maitland looked thunderstruck last night when I gatecrashed her party.'

Kate nodded. 'Because you never go to parties, it didn't occur to her to invite you.'

'Does she know about our relationship?'

'As from last night she does. Anna knew I'd been engaged before I met her, but not the name of the lucky man. I couldn't believe my eyes when you strolled up at the party.' Kate smiled politely. 'But I'm glad you called in tonight, Jack. It gives me a chance to congratulate you on your success.'

'Thank you. We both achieved our aims, career-wise.' He eyed her quizzically. 'But I'm curious, Kate. I'm told you were on the point of marriage twice over the years. What made you back off?'

She hesitated for a moment, then decided it was fair return for Jack's explanation. 'The first fiancé—'

'Second,' he corrected.

She ground her teeth. 'All right, the *second* fiancé started talking about babies and a place in the country.'

'Ah!' Jack leaned back, eyes gleaming. 'The idea didn't appeal?'

'Not in the slightest. So we agreed—amicably—to call it a day, and I bought a flat in Notting Hill. I'd never lived alone up to that point, and enjoyed it so much that years later when I met the second—sorry, *third* fiancé, I insisted on keeping to my own place instead of moving in with him.' Kate looked away. 'A good decision, as it turned out—less complications when we split up.'

'Amicably again?'

'No. More coffee?'

'Thank you.'

Kate got up and filled the kettle again. 'Would you like something to eat? Anna gave me some leftovers.'

Jack shook his head. 'No, thanks, I had dinner with my father earlier. Tell me what happened to fiancé mark three.'

Her eyes shuttered. 'I'd rather not talk about that.'

'Then let's talk about your new job, instead. Will you be working in the town?'

She shook her head, smiling. 'Right here in my study upstairs.'

His eyebrows rose. 'You're writing a novel?'

'I wish! I'm a VA.' She chuckled at his blank look. 'A Virtual Assistant, Jack. Keep up! My computer skills are good, and I was a personal assistant for a while earlier on in my career. But this time I'll be working part-time at home for a handful of clients instead of full-time in an office for just one boss. I choose which people I take on and no coffee-making required for any of them.'

Jack looked sceptical. 'A pretty drastic career change! Are you sure you're cut out for it?'

'Absolutely. I started it up before I left London.' She described her enrolment on a VA Mastery Course the moment she gave in her notice. While she was selling her flat and organising the move, Kate completed the course, set up her personal website, named it KD Virtual Assistance, and asked Anna to advertise it in the local papers back home. Within weeks Kate had three clients, and by the time she'd moved into Park Crescent she had two more.

'I work for people who've set up their own businesses, but lack the time, or inclination, to spare for the administrative side. I meet each of them in person occasionally, of course, so it's not all virtual,' she told Jack. 'I do their invoicing, maintain databases, book appointments, make travel arrangements, or even just deal with household accounts. I won't earn anything like the salary I had before, obviously, but my services don't come cheap. Even working only twenty hours or so a week will give me enough income to live on and, most important of all, I'll be here all the time for Joanna when she gets home for the school holidays. She's boarding at the moment.'

'Twenty hours isn't much to someone of your calibre. What will you do with your spare time?'

'All the things I've never had time to do before—my own interior decorating, for one. Something new for me.' She smiled as she poured more coffee. 'I'm enjoying it. But if time begins to hang really heavy I'll take on more clients.'

The slate-grey eyes gleamed over the rim of the mug. 'So if I contacted your website I could ask you to work for me?'

She looked at him steadily. 'You could ask, but I'd refuse.'

'Why?'

'Oh, come on, Jack! You and I come with two much past history to make even a virtual partnership feasible.'

'You can't forgive my trespasses?'

'Surely we can forgive each other after all this time?' she countered. 'We're different people now.'

He eyed her in slow appraisal. 'You don't look different, Kate. With your hair down you look no older than the last time we met.'

'Flatterer!'

'Not at all.' He downed the last of his coffee and got up. 'Time I was off.'

'Thank you for coming, Jack.'

'My pleasure.' He shrugged on his windbreaker, sniffing the air as they went into the hall. 'Fresh paint?'

'In here.' Kate opened the door to the sitting room. 'Joanna's choice of colour and my handiwork. What do you think?'

Jack nodded in approval. 'It looks good. How about furniture?'

'Aunt Edith left me a houseful, but I auctioned some of it. I bought the rest locally, and asked for a delay in delivery until I finish painting. I sold my London furniture with the flat. It seemed the right time to make a fresh start.'

'Off with the old and on with the new?'

'Exactly.' She smiled coolly. 'We're both old hands at that, Jack.'

He shook his head, his eyes narrowed to an unsettling gleam. 'You're the one who gets through fiancés, Kate. I've only had one.'

'That doesn't count—you had a wife.'

He shook his head. 'Dawn doesn't count, either. I married her out of obligation, not love. Did you love the men in your life?'

'Not enough to marry them, obviously.' She brushed past him to the door and opened it. 'But I'm glad I know the truth at last. Thank you for making the effort to put me straight, Jack.'

'No effort involved, Kate,' he assured her and strolled across the pavement to his car. 'Thanks for the coffee. Goodnight.'

'Goodnight.' She waited politely until the car moved off, then went back to the kitchen to scowl at the assortment of party leftovers in the fridge. She put a selection on her plate, cut some bread and slumped down at the table, irritated because Jack had left without asking to see her again. Yet she'd been utterly convinced, right up to the last minute, that this had been the real purpose of his visit. She had wanted—craved—the glorious satisfaction of turning him down. More fool you, Kate, she thought scornfully, and doggedly munched through her supper without tasting a mouthful of it.

CHAPTER THREE

JACK LOGAN'S revelations gave Kate such a restless night she lingered longer than usual with the morning paper over breakfast next morning. She wrote a letter to Joanna afterwards, then finally got to work on reports for two of her clients and chased up late payments for another. She smiled in satisfaction as she shut down her computer. The great advantage of her new job was working at her own speed instead of to the hectic timetable of her former life. Like Jack, colleagues had asked what on earth she was going to do with herself. Work for half the day and then do as she liked, had been Kate's answer. She would take up tennis again, swim, go to a gym regularly instead of once in a blue moon, visit the local cinema and repertory theatre, enjoy Sunday lunch with the Maitlands, look up old friends, and gradually become part of the local scene again.

Anna rang before Kate started painting after lunch. 'Are you busy?'

'Why?'

'I need to see you. Could you possibly down whatever tools you're using and come over for tea?'

'Of course.'

When Anna let her in later Kate studied her friend closely. 'What's up?'

'I'll tell you in a minute. Thanks for coming, love.'

'Any time.' Kate followed her friend into the kitchen. 'It's the big plus of my new occupation. I can drop everything and run if necessary. Though Jack doesn't think much of my change of career,' she added casually.

'Jack?' said Anna instantly. 'You've seen him since the party?'

'He called in last night.'

'Surprise, surprise!' Anna nodded sagely as she made tea. 'Was the visit for old times' sake—or new ones?'

'Old. He came to tell me exactly why he married someone else in such a rush. Usual reason—Dawn was pregnant.'

'By him?'

'No, as it turned out, but it could have been. Jack was merely top of Dawn's sperm-donor list.'

Anna's eyes widened. 'She conned him!'

Kate explained about the miscarriage too far along into the pregnancy for Jack to be the father.

'So that explains the instant divorce. And,' added Anna thoughtfully, 'the lack of significant others in his life since, maybe.'

'There must have been some along the way. I can't see Jack leading the life of a monk!'

'You mean he's terrific in bed? Those dark, smouldering types usually are. Not,' Anna added hastily, 'that I speak from experience. At least not since I met Ben.' She shook her head in wonder as she filled teacups. 'Amazing! All those times I met Jack Logan at the functions Ben drags me to I never knew he was your mystery lover.'

'You adore going to functions with Ben!'

Anna nodded sheepishly. 'Of course I do. I love standing round with a drink making small talk—the sign of a trivial mind, I suppose.'

Kate laughed. 'The man you worked for didn't agree with that. He married you!'

'True. Ben said he was attracted to my razor-sharp mind before he noticed the packaging. Liar!' Anna giggled, then sobered abruptly, her eyes anxious. 'Are you really all right?'

'I'm fine.' Kate reached out a hand to touch Anna's. 'Jack just came round to set the record straight.'

'Did he ask to see you again?'

'No.' Kate grinned ruefully. 'Which really ticked me off. I was so looking forward to turning him down.'

'You still have feelings for him?'

Kate shrugged. 'If I do, I don't know what they are. But when I moved back here I knew I risked running into Jack some time. Though I didn't expect to in this house,' she added tartly.

'Tell me about it!' Anna made a face. 'Lucy Beresford thought it was such a coup for me, bringing him here, because normally he only graces the official functions I told you about, and corporate stuff. But Ben says he turns up at the occasional golf club dinner.'

'To please his father,' said Kate, nodding.

'I suppose that was his reason all those years ago when he wouldn't try for a job in London.'

'Not a bit of it. Jack was pleasing himself.'

'Do I detect an acid note?'

Kate's mouth turned down. 'I was so sure he loved me enough to come to London with me. Anyway,' she added briskly, 'that's all in the past. Now then, you asked me here for a reason. Spill the beans!'

'OK,' said Anna, with an odd little smile. 'I saw my doctor this morning.'

'Why? What's wrong?'

'Nothing, unless you count morning sickness—I'm officially pregnant!'

'Anna, how marvellous!' Kate gave a crow of triumph and hugged her friend affectionately. 'After all these years! How does Ben feel about it?'

'Thrilled to bits—so am I!'

'Me, too.' Kate patted her friend's cheek. 'I'm very happy for you. And so is Ben, by the display of flowers in the hall.'

'Actually,' said Anna, fluttering her eyelashes, 'those are not from my husband.'

'Don't tell me they're from someone else's!'

'Certainly not.' Anna grinned like the Cheshire cat. 'Mr Jack Logan sent them with his apologies and thanks.'

On the way back into town Kate felt oddly restless and wished she'd given in to Anna's coaxing to stay to dinner. There was no work to catch up on that couldn't be dealt with tomorrow.

For the rest of the week Kate's feeling of anticipation dwindled gradually as each day wore on with no word from Jack. By Thursday her sitting room was finished, along with her hopes of hearing from him again. Get over it, she ordered herself.

The chaise longue arrived next morning with perfect timing, just as Kate finished her daily stint at the computer, and tempted by the sunshine she decided to fit in a quick walk in the park before lunch. When she reached the lake path Kate's heart leapt as she spotted a tall figure with a black dog in the distance, but as she drew nearer saw that the man's hair was grey. As if Jack would be taking a stroll on a Friday morning, she told herself scornfully, then smiled in sudden delight as the man straightened from unfastening the dog's leash.

'Katherine!' said Tom Logan, with such obvious pleasure as he caught sight of her she felt her throat thicken.

'Mr Logan—how lovely to see you,' she said huskily, and ran into the arms thrown wide to embrace her.

'Jack told me you were back in town,' he informed her and held her at arms' length to look at her. 'How are you?'

'I'm very well.' She smiled at him affectionately. 'No need to ask how you are. You look marvellous.'

'Semi-retirement suits me,' he agreed. He whistled, and the dog raced back to sit obediently to have his leash attached. 'Good boy.' Tom Logan patted the gleaming black head. 'Are you in a hurry, Kate, or will you walk a little way with us?'

'I'd love to.' Kate bent to pat the dog. 'What a handsome lad.'

'Apple of Jack's eye.' Tom shot a look at her as they began walking. 'And good company for him. Other than Bran and me, Jack's cleaner is the only one to set foot in that house of his.'

'I thought someone in his position would need to entertain a lot.'

'He keeps to restaurants for that. But he's been in London all this week.' The keen eyes, so like his son's, surveyed Kate with interest.

'Has he?' she said casually.

'Didn't he say? Jack told me he called to see you the other night.'

'The conversation centred on past history.' She kept her eyes on the path. 'He told me about Dawn Taylor.'

'God, what a disaster that was,' said Tom grimly. 'But try not to blame Jack too much. After you left he was desperately unhappy, Kate. He missed you so much he worked himself into the ground all day and every day, with a couple of drinks in the Rose and Crown on the way home to help him sleep. Dawn was lying in wait for him every time of course, only too willing to console him, so the result was inevitable. I told him he was a fool to accept the child as his but, as you know better than anyone, Kate, my son can be as obstinate as a mule. So he married her.'

She gave him a questioning look. 'Do you blame me for that, Mr Logan?'

He stared at her, surprised. 'Good God, no, child. You were young, and it was only natural you wanted to see a bit of the world before you settled down. The two of you could have gone on meeting easily enough now and again.'

'It's all water under the bridge now.' Kate glanced at her watch. 'I must dash—pressing appointment in town after lunch with some curtains.' She smiled at him. 'After your next walk come to my place for coffee. Bring Bran with you. I live in Park Crescent, number thirty-four.'

'So Jack told me.' Tom Logan smiled reminiscently. 'Oddly enough, I know the house well. I did a lot of work for Miss Durant when I first started out on my own. She was one of the old school, a real tartar. But she knew her stuff when it came to maintaining her property. She approved of my work, so we got on well. You inherited a sound house, Kate.' He smiled and patted her cheek affectionately. 'It's so good to see you again, my dear.'

'Likewise, Mr L.'

'I think it's time you called me Tom!'

'Then I will. See you soon, Tom.' She hurried off to the park gate and turned to wave as she passed through to make for home.

Jack Logan felt so tired during the drive from London through heavy Friday evening traffic he rang his father from his hands free moible as he turned off the motorway and asked him to keep Bran for another night. But, after hearing about the encounter with Kate, Jack drove straight past the entrance to Mill House and headed into town, cursing himself for a fool as he parked near Kate's house. The lights were on. But that could mean time switches. The car he'd seen before was parked right outside her house again too, but even if it were hers it meant nothing. She could have taken a taxi into town, or someone—some man—could have picked her up to take her out.

He got out of the car, flexing his shoulders wearily. He rapped on the doorknocker instead of ringing the bell and waited, shivering, until light shone through the fanlight. After a moment Kate opened the door, her face guarded.

'Hello,' he said quietly. 'May I come in?'

Without a word she led the way into the sitting room and switched off the television, eyeing her visitor without visible warmth. 'You look tired, Jack.'

'The traffic was heavy. I rang my father during the journey

and heard he'd seen you today.' He gave her a wry, weary smile. 'So I took a chance on finding you in.'

Kate's feelings were mixed at the sight of him, her undeniable pleasure marred by anger with Jack for taking it for granted he could just turn up any time he fancied without ringing first. She knew that he'd made a note of her number last Sunday. He'd been leaning on the counter right next to the phone. When the phone call never happened she assumed Jack had no interest in reviving their relationship and had resigned herself to the idea so determinedly that she resented him now, for coming back to unsettle her again.

'Would you like a drink?' she asked politely.

'Could I possibly have some tea?'

'Certainly. Sit down and take a look at the room while I make it.' Kate went off to the kitchen, thankful that she hadn't changed from the tailored black trousers and sweater of the afternoon. Strands of hair were escaping from its coil, and her face could have done with attention, but Jack looked too tired to notice. He was probably hungry too, if he'd driven from London. But he was out of luck if he expected a meal. A visitor was no part of her plan for the evening. She'd hung her new curtains, stood back to admire, and then eaten supper early so she could settle down in her finished sitting room to watch the gardening programme Jack had interrupted.

Kate returned with a tray and put it on a small Pembroke table between a pair of cane-sided Louis chairs cushioned in faded russet velvet.

'I like the room,' Jack told her, standing tall in the middle of it.

'Milk?' she asked, though she knew exactly how he liked his tea—or had done, once.

'Thank you.'

'Do sit down,' she said, handing him a cup. 'Try the modern chaise. It's better suited to someone your size than the chairs. They belonged to Aunt Edith,' she added, 'which is why they look so much at home here.'

He smiled a little. 'So do you, Kate.'

She nodded. 'Surprising, really. Until I was handed the key I hadn't been inside since I was a small child. My aunt leased it out to pay her way when she installed herself in a retirement home. I used to drive down from London once a month to see her. Aunt Edith was quite a character—a bit deaf, but with faculties in good shape otherwise right to the end. We got on well together, but when I was told she'd left her house to me I couldn't believe my luck. And the moment I set foot in here again it was love at first sight.'

'I remember it well.'

She frowned. 'You knew my aunt?'

'I'm referring to emotion, not property.' Jack looked her in the eye. 'For me it was love at first sight when I bought that poppy.'

Her stomach gave a lurch she covered with a hard little smile. 'It was for me, too. Such a shame that kind of thing doesn't last.'

His answering smile set her teeth on edge. 'How long was it for you, Kate? Until you got off the train in London?'

'No,' she said, pretending to think it over. 'Surely that was about the time you started sleeping with Dawn. It ended for me when I heard you'd married her.'

His face darkened. 'I've explained that.'

'So you have. You were lonely, she was willing and I'd gone. All the way to London—a mere two hour drive in that car of yours! I was devastated when you wouldn't even meet me to say goodbye, Jack,' she added with sudden heat. 'I know I was the one who actually ended it, but I still couldn't accept that it was over between us. I missed you so much I was ready to pack in my job and find work at home instead. I came back, just before Liz and Robert moved, to tell you that. And heard you'd married Dawn.'

Jack's mouth twisted. 'With hindsight I realise I was a quixotic fool, but at the time I felt I had no option. She swore her father would throw her out in the street when he found she was pregnant, and she had no money other than the small wage he paid her. So because the child could have been mine, I did the "decent thing",' he added with bitterness.

'Past history now.'

His eyes met hers. 'Only where Dawn's concerned; not for you and me, Kate. Have dinner with me tomorrow.'

Kate shook her head. 'Not a good idea, Jack.'

'Sunday, then.'

'I meant any night.'

He put down his cup and leaned forward, his long hands clasped loosely between his knees. 'What harm would there be in two old friends sharing a meal?'

'Because we were never just friends.'

'True,' he agreed. 'That very first time, after lunch at the pub—'

'The establishment run by Dawn Taylor's father.'

'That's the one. You thought you'd been shameless.'

Kate fondly believed she'd kicked the habit of blushing, but with Jack's eyes holding hers she felt the annoying warmth rising in her face. 'I thought I'd had a terrible nerve,' she corrected, and felt the colour deepen at his look of triumph.

'You remember! I had to fight to keep my hands off you.'

She thawed a little. 'Did you?'

Jack nodded. 'We had something very special, Kate.'

'I don't deny it,' she agreed soberly. 'But the past tense says it all. We're different people now, older and hopefully wiser. Enough to know we can't go back.'

He looked sceptical. 'You came back here to live. You knew you risked running into me again.'

She shook her head. 'No risk to me, Jack. I thought you

were married, remember, and father of several children for all I knew.'

'And now you know I'm neither?'

Kate thought about it. 'I suppose the odd dinner would be pleasant. But nothing more than that, Jack. Relationships are altogether too much work.'

He nodded in grim agreement. 'I gave up on them the day my divorce came through.'

'So what do you do for—' She paused. 'Feminine solace?'

'You mean sex?' he said bluntly. 'I steer clear locally. But I spend regular time in London these days. I've got a flat near my offices there.'

'You mean you pay for your pleasures?' she said, equally blunt.

He looked affronted. 'Hell, no. I've never needed to. Besides, I have strong objections to sharing in that context. I just want your company over dinner, Kate,' he added. 'No strings.'

'No feminine solace involved?' she said lightly.

'Just the pleasure of your company would give me that, Kate.'

She looked at him thoughtfully. He'd asked to see her again, just as she'd wanted. If she was going to turn him down flat, now was the time to do it. Instead she found herself nodding in agreement. 'Why not?'

'Good,' said Jack briskly, and stood up. 'I'll call for you tomorrow. Seven-thirty?'

'Make it eight.' Kate went to the door with him. 'It was good to see your father again.'

'Dad thinks you've matured into a very beautiful woman.'

'How sweet of him! I like your dog, by the way.'

'I'll bring Bran to visit one day.'

'Please do. I thought your father looked great, Jack.'

He nodded. 'I hope I look half as good at his age.'

'The resemblance is so strong you're bound to.' Kate

smiled up at him, and Jack bent and kissed her lightly on the cheek.

'See you tomorrow. Thanks for the tea.'

Jack Logan drove home in triumphant mood. So Kate was willing to settle for friendship. He could wait until she was ready for more. He'd felt her stiffen slightly as he kissed her cheek, as though she'd been afraid he meant to do more than that, so the wait was unlikely to be long. She could say what she liked about relationships, but the chemistry between them still existed, alive and kicking, even after all these years apart.

His mouth tightened. The long parting would never have happened if he hadn't been such an idiot about Dawn. He should have questioned his paternity, or just offered to pay child support. But when Kate Durant preferred a London career to marriage with Jack Logan it wasn't only his heart that suffered. So he took what Dawn offered to massage his ego, and then paid for the privilege in the way he knew would hurt Kate most. It was years later before he realised how hard his marriage must have hit her when he heard that she was living with some banker in a pricey Dockside loft. But that was in the past. Now the banker was long gone, and so was the successor she wouldn't talk about. Jack Logan had developed patience over the years, and Katherine Durant was a woman worth waiting for.

Alone in her sitting room, Kate sat staring into space, sure she'd made a big mistake. Jack had finally asked to see her again and, instead of turning him down flat, she'd heard herself agreeing—just as she'd done the first time. But she had to eat. And it was only dinner, no bed and breakfast involved. Surely they could be friends again. Not that there was any 'again' about it. They'd never been just friends.

That first night in the cinema they'd sat together without even holding hands, yet by the time he'd stopped the car on the way home she'd been desperate for his kisses and anything else Jack Logan had to offer. She'd never been keen on the physical side of relationships up to that point, and frustrated, angry boyfriends had never stayed the course very long. With Jack it was so different she'd felt as though she'd die if he didn't take her to bed. And when he did she thought she'd died anyway, and gone to heaven. She smiled wistfully at the memory. Because they'd both lived at home with relatives the opportunities to repeat the experience had not been plentiful. But when either Tom Logan or the Suttons went out for the evening they'd dived into Jack's bed or hers the moment they were alone together.

That particular form of high-octane rapture happened only once apparently. She had never experienced it again.

When Jack Logan came for her, formal-suited and prompt at eight the following evening, Kate was ready in clinging wool crêpe the colour of vintage cognac. Long-sleeved and starkly plain, the dress relied on superb fit and a vertiginous neckline for its impact. And Jack's face told Kate that the dress, by no means new, was still worth every penny of the outrageous price she'd once paid for it.

'You look wonderful,' he told her.

Resisting the urge to tell him he did too, she thanked him politely. 'Would you like a drink before we go?'

'I'll wait until we get there.' Jack held her long black trench coat for her, and looked on in approval while she set her alarm and locked her door. 'I'm glad to see you're safety conscious.'

'Big city habits.' She smiled, impressed, when Jack opened the passenger door of his car. 'A Jensen, no less!'

'Classic cars are my hobby these days,' he told her, as he slid behind the wheel, 'and in common with Bran, a lot less trouble than humans.'

Kate laughed. 'You mean women.'

'If the cap fits,' he agreed, eyes crinkling.

Instead of making for the town centre as she'd expected,

Jack drove in the opposite direction. 'Country pub?' she asked.

'I've organised dinner at home. I thought you'd like to see my house.'

He was right about that! 'The one no woman sets foot in?' she asked lightly.

'Molly Carter sets foot in it regularly, twice a week when I'm away, more when I'm not.'

'I came across pictures of it in a magazine once, with a big article about you,' she told him, remembering her shock at finding his face in her Sunday paper. 'My colleagues were deeply impressed when I mentioned—very casually—that I knew you.'

'Did you say how well?'

'No. Not even Anna knew that.' She hesitated, then asked something she'd been burning to ask for years. 'Jack, did you pass your mother's ring on to Dawn?'

'No,' he said shortly, and turned down a narrow road towards a pair of handsome, wrought-iron gates. 'These are original,' he told her as he aimed a remote control.

Kate sat tense in anticipation as the car moved slowly along a narrow drive lined with trees. At the end of it Jack circled round a lawn to park in front of a long house with light blazing from rows of tall windows.

'Two hundred years ago it was a flax mill, but when I came on the scene it was practically a ruin,' Jack told her. 'At first I thought it was too far gone for restoration.'

'But you could see what it would become,' said Kate with respect. 'Or what it could go back to.'

'Exactly,' he said with satisfaction. As she got out of the car Kate's eyes lit up at the sight of a familiar figure in the open doorway.

'Tom!' she said in delight.

'I thought you wouldn't mind an extra guest, Kate,' said Jack dryly.

Tom Logan kissed her affectionately. 'I said he was mad to want his father along when he'd asked a beautiful woman to dinner, but Jack insisted.'

'Quite right, too,' she assured him, fleeting disappointment replaced by relief. Jack was obviously *not* expecting feminine solace in return for dinner.

CHAPTER FOUR

'WELCOME to my humble abode,' said Jack, the mockery in his smile telling Kate her relief was written on her face. 'I'll take your coat.'

'I'll do that,' said his father. 'You show her the house.'

Kate had pored greedily over the photographs in the magazine article but seeing the house with her own eyes was a different experience. A faded Persian carpet softened the granite flags of the entrance hall, but the main impression was light. The crystal-strung candles of twin chandeliers poured light down on walls and banisters painted pristine white. Kate stood utterly still for a moment then crossed the hall, drawn by the only painting on view, a portrait of a handsome, rakish man in Regency dress over a fireplace obviously original to the building.

'How very grand. He wasn't in the photographs. Is he an ancestor?' she asked, and Jack shook his head, grinning.

'Dad thought the chap looked a bit like me, so he bought it at auction.'

Jack led her across the hall into a long room with more white walls and rows of tall windows, but the light was softer here, from lamps shaded in neutral silk. An antique desk lived in harmony with large-scale modern furniture, but it was the dimension of the room that silenced Kate.

'Say something!' urged Jack.

'It's breathtaking. All this space!' She smiled as she waved a hand at the windows. 'You've got something against curtains?'

He shrugged. 'No neighbours, and the windows are draught-proof, made to my own specification to blend with the house. I had some blinds made for the bedrooms, but otherwise I let in as much light as possible.'

Kate gazed round her in awe. 'The photographs didn't do it justice. My place is a doll's house by comparison.'

'But equally attractive in its own way.' He took her arm. 'Let's join Dad. It's time I gave you a drink.'

The entire evening proved far more relaxed for Kate with Tom Logan there than if she'd spent it alone with Jack. The food was simple—a casserole of fork-tender beef slow-cooked with vegetables, herbs and wine and eaten at the kitchen table, with Bran casting a hopeful eye on the proceedings from his bed.

'It's cosier in here for just three of us.' Tom smiled affectionately at Kate. 'And it's not the first time we've eaten together round a kitchen table.'

'No, indeed. I used to love meals at your house.' She pulled a face. 'There was more formality at ours. My sister brought out the best china if Jack so much as ate a sandwich with us.'

'Which wasn't that often,' Jack reminded her caustically. 'Our relationship was cut painfully short.'

'Now then,' said his father sternly. 'You can't ask a girl to dinner, then throw the past in her face. You're not on firm ground there yourself.'

'How very true.' Jack gave Kate an ironic bow as he got up to take her plate. 'My apologies. How about organic ice cream straight from Addison's farm shop?'

'Perfect,' she said lightly.

After the meal Tom Logan took Kate into the living room while Jack made coffee. 'So, what do you think of the house that Jack built?' he asked as he put logs on the fire.

'Impressive,' she told him, gazing round the room. 'It's nothing like my preconceived idea of a mill house, much more of a home. But very definitely a man's home. Other than that muscular bit of sculpture on the desk, there are no ornaments, no photographs—just one solitary landscape and the art deco mirror over the fireplace.'

'It needs a woman's touch,' said Tom slyly, and laughed at the look she gave him. 'Just teasing!'

She grinned. 'I can just picture Jack's face if I suggested cushions and a flower arrangement.'

'I heard that,' said Jack, coming in with a tray. He set it down on the massive slab of rosewood used as a coffee table. 'You find my taste austere?'

'It suits the house.'

'Which doesn't answer my question.'

She began pouring coffee. 'My opinion doesn't matter. You're the one who lives here.' She smiled at him as he added a sugar lump to his father's cup. 'But actually I like your house very much, Jack.'

'It's a big place for one man,' observed Tom Logan, and looked round as Bran padded into the room. 'Is he allowed in here tonight?'

'Of course he is.' Jack bent to fondle the dog's head. 'I give him the run of the ground floor when I'm at home, but upstairs it's permanently off limits. To dogs, anyway,' he added, as Bran stretched out in front of the fire.

'Who cooked the dinner?' asked Kate. 'You, Jack?'

'Molly made it this morning, and I followed her instructions and put it in a slow oven at the required time.' He took a cup from the tray and sat down on the chair nearest to Kate's corner of the sofa. 'I forgot to ask if your tastes in food had changed.'

'What would you have done if I was a vegetarian these days? Opened a tin of baked beans?'

'We often shared one in the old days.'

Kate gave him a serene smile. 'But these are new days, Jack.' She turned to his father. 'Are you playing golf tomorrow, Tom?'

For the rest of the evening Jack was the perfect host. He

gave up sniping about the past, and even suggested that Kate came back to see the place in daylight one day and eat lunch on the terrace overlooking the mill pond. 'I keep a small boat if you fancy a row some time. It's a healthy way to keep fit.'

'Sounds good,' said Kate enviously. 'My rare bouts of exercise are in a gym. Rowing on water in fresh air sounds a lot more tempting.'

'Bring your niece in the school holidays,' said Jack. 'The garden in Park Crescent can't be very big. You could give her the run of the grounds here.'

'Poor little thing,' said Tom with compassion. 'It's been a big upheaval for her. How's she coping?'

Kate's eyes shadowed. 'Christmas was tricky—the first without her parents.'

'Did she come to you in London for it?' asked Jack.

Kate shook her head. 'Apart from a brief stay with her grandparents, Joanna spent the entire Christmas break in the Maitland household with me. Both sets of parents were there and neighbours came in for drinks, so there was a lot going on. One couple brought twin teenage sons along as company for Jo and she got on well with them, and spent quite a lot of time with them over the holiday. I took her shopping for furniture for her new bedroom, and we spent hours poring over paint charts together—everything I could think of to keep her in the loop over the move to Park Crescent. But neither of us enjoyed the day she went back to school,' she added bleakly.

'Half term can't be far away,' said Jack with sympathy, but she shook her head.

'There isn't one this term. Her school goes for the longer Easter holiday. But I'll drive down to take her out for lunch before then.'

Soon afterwards Tom Logan got up to go.

'You can't leave now, Dad,' protested his son.

'Early round of golf in the morning. Must get my beauty sleep.'

Kate got to her feet. 'Then maybe you'd give me a lift, Mr Logan. You pass near my place.'

'Don't go yet, Kate.' Jack put a hand on her arm.

'No, indeed. You stay, my dear,' said his father, kissing her cheek. 'Otherwise I'll feel guilty. Jack will run you home later.'

When Jack came back with the dog, Kate turned from the study of tree-fringed water in his painting. 'Where is this?'

'Right here in the grounds. It's the mill pond, complete with willows and chestnut trees.'

'You commissioned it?'

He nodded. 'Local artist. I was impressed by an exhibition of her work. She agreed to do it once she'd approved the location.'

'Would she have turned you down if she hadn't?'

'More than likely. But she took one look and named her price—which was steep. But I paid it willingly when I saw the finished work.'

Kate turned away, smiling wryly. 'How things have changed. When we were together I was just earning peanuts and you weren't much better off.'

'At the time Dad and I were ploughing most of the profits back into the business.' He bent to poke the fire. 'If he hadn't handed my mother's ring over I certainly couldn't have bought one for you right then. I had to borrow money from him for Dawn's settlement.'

Controlling her reaction to Dawn's name, Kate smiled brightly at Jack. 'But nowadays Logan Development is a roaring success and you can buy what you like.'

He straightened, and gave her a look which almost had her backing away. 'Is that your benchmark of success, Kate? To be able to buy what you like?'

Her eyes narrowed coldly. 'If it were would I have turned my back on a highly paid job?'

'I thought you did that to take care of your niece.'

'If it had been absolutely vital I kept the job Joanna could have shared my flat in Notting Hill, and I would have paid someone to look after her in the school holidays. But to me it seemed far more important to make a home for her here and look after her myself.'

'And you're right, Kate,' he said, with contrition. 'You obviously care very deeply for Joanna. I don't have a child in my life—one of the many things money can't buy.'

She turned away, looking at her watch. 'I should be going soon.'

'Why? I thought the great advantage of the new job was its flexibility.'

'I'm making a start on my bedroom. I'm sleeping in Jo's for the time being.'

'But there's time for a nightcap before you go, Kate. It's early,' he added, 'and you haven't seen the rest of the house.'

'I'll have some fruit juice, if you like, but I'll leave the rest of the tour, Jack.' The last thing she wanted at this stage was a visit to his bedroom, much as she'd like to see it. He might talk about being friends, but it wasn't easy. He'd been her lover for a brief, ecstatic time when they were young, but there had been long years after that when she'd thought of Jack Logan with no love at all.

'Sit down again,' said Jack. 'I'll bring your drink.'

Kate bent to fondle Bran instead. The dog half-closed his eyes in ecstasy as she found exactly the right spot behind his ear.

'You're a very handsome fellow,' she told him. 'I always wanted a dog like you.'

'You weren't allowed to have one?' asked Jack, and handed her a glass.

Kate shook her head. 'Elizabeth wouldn't allow it, and her

word was law. As you know, my mother died when I was born, and my father when I was ten, not long after Elizabeth got married. So Liz and Robert seemed like parents to me— and pretty strict ones at that. But it was good of them to take care of me,' she added hastily.

'You're repaying them by taking care of Joanna?'

'Absolutely not. I'm doing it because I love her.' She shivered. 'Let's talk about something else.'

'Come and sit down.' He switched off two of the lamps, stirred the fire into life and led her to the sofa. 'I never thought this would happen,' he said, sitting beside her.

Kate made no pretence of misunderstanding. 'You mean the two of us together like this in your amazing house?'

'Exactly.' Jack turned to smile at her, a glint in his eyes that had turned her knees to jelly when she was twenty.

But she wasn't twenty any more. 'I know what you mean. When I found those pictures in the magazine, I never imagined I'd see the place for myself.'

'It must have been quite a surprise to come across my face in your Sunday paper.'

Surprise didn't begin to cover it. 'Yes,' she said dryly, 'it certainly was.'

'Were you between fiancés at the time?'

'You sound as though I had a string of them!' she said tartly, and sipped some of her drink. 'I happened to be alone that morning, but I showed the article to Rupert later and mentioned that I knew you. I searched the piece for personal details about you, but the emphasis was on your professional life.'

'That was the deal with the journalist.'

Kate turned to look at him. 'Jack, where did you live when you were married?'

His eyes shuttered. 'Dad suggested we move into the block of flats the company was renovating on Gloucester Road at the time. I tried to make a go of the marriage, but Dawn and

I had so little in common it was obvious from the start that it was never going to work.' He drained his glass and turned to look at her. 'It's a part of my life I look back on with no pleasure at all—or pride.'

'You fulfilled your obligations, Jack.'

'But I did so for the wrong reasons,' he said savagely. 'I wanted to hurt you as much as I wanted to do the right thing for Dawn.'

She nodded sadly. 'You succeeded on both counts.'

'And soon realised my colossal mistake.' He was silent for a long interval, his eyes sombre as he stared into the fire. 'The surprise came when I learned that the baby wasn't mine. I found I'd actually wanted a child. My child, anyway. Does that sound mad to you?'

She shook her head mutely.

He smoothed his thumb over the back of her hand in silence for a while. 'So tell me,' he said, turning to look at her. 'Why did you send the third man packing? Was he another one wanting babies and a place in the country?'

'No. He didn't want children at all.' Her eyes kindled. 'I broke up with Rupert because he refused to take Joanna as part of the deal.'

Jack stared at her. 'What the devil did he expect you to do with her?'

'Hand her over to Robert's parents, who are lovely people, but far too elderly and frail to cope with a child of her age on a permanent basis. When I explained this he gave me an ultimatum. I had to choose between the child and him, right then and there. So I made it brutally clear that there was no question of choice, and never would be.' Her mouth tightened. 'Rupert took it badly—very badly.'

His fingers tightened on her hand. 'What happened?'

Kate eyes glittered icily at the thought of it. 'He flew into such a rage I thought he was going to beat me up. Dr Jekyll turned into Mr Hyde right there in front of me. But I was too furious on Jo's behalf to feel afraid. I just stood there, eye to eye, daring him to hit me. It was touch and go for a while, but like all bullies Rupert backed down in the end. At which point I threw the ring at him and told him to get out of my life.'

'Good God!' Jack stared at her, appalled. 'You took a hell of a risk, Kate.'

'I realised that the moment he'd gone. I shook in my shoes for ages afterwards.' She turned to look at him. 'Now you can see why I hate talking about it. I just can't believe I was such a bad judge of character.'

'Not entirely,' he reminded her. 'Instinct warned you not to move in with him.'

'True.' Kate's eyes darkened. 'He was in such a rush about everything, I felt uneasy. He bought the ring just days after our first meeting, but no matter how much he argued I insisted we had to know each other better before I actually wore it.'

'Did you love him?'

'I was attracted to him, certainly. He was charming, witty and very good company. But until that horrible night I'd never come up against the real Rupert Chance.' She shrugged. 'It clinched my decision to give up my job. I'd worked in Personnel for years and prided myself on my judgement when it came to people. If that was no longer working for me it was time to call it a day.'

'Did Joanna like him?'

'She never met him. He was abroad at the time of the funeral. My relationship with Rupert—if you could call it that— lasted less than a school term. Why?'

'Her reaction to him might have been interesting.' Jack gave her a crooked smile. 'I get a card from Sydney every Christmas, with the current snapshot of Dawn, husband and progeny—three sons at the last count. Her way of telling me she's a respectable matron these days.'

'Is she still gorgeous?' asked Kate, hoping Dawn had lost her looks by now.

'In a different, earth-mother kind of way I suppose she is.' Jack shrugged. 'She looks contented with her life, and who can ask more than that?'

'Are you contented with yours?'

He was silent for a moment, his eyes on the fire. 'I'm head of a very successful outfit,' he said slowly, 'with a beautiful house here and a flat in London, and I'm the proud owner of several classic cars and a great dog. So I must be contented.' He turned to look at her. 'Are you?'

'Yes,' said Kate firmly. 'I'm going to make a good life here for Joanna.'

'She's fortunate to have you to care for her.'

She shook her head. 'It's my good fortune to have Jo.'

'I'd like to meet her some time. You don't like the idea?' he added as she frowned.

'It's more a case of whether Jo likes it. I'd have to ask her first.'

Jack got up, clicking his fingers to the dog, who padded after him obediently. 'I'll just put him out for a moment.'

Kate sat very still when she was alone, staring, unseeing, into the fire.

'You're still frowning,' said Jack, coming back into the room.

Kate managed a smile. 'Just thinking. Where's Bran?'

'In bed.'

'Sensible chap. I should be making tracks for my own bed soon.'

'First tell me what's making you look so blue, Katie.'

Damn. She'd always turned to marshmallow when he called her that. 'You want the truth?'

He smiled crookedly. 'Probably not, but I promise I'll take it like a man.'

'To revert to the friendship issue—'

'You've changed your mind?' Jack sat down beside her and took her hand.

'No.'

'But you're thinking of Joanna. You chose her without hesitation over the objectionable Rufus—'

'Rupert.'

'Right. So it was obvious you'd make the same choice if she objected to me.'

'Exactly.' Kate smiled ruefully. 'So if I'm too much work as a friend I'll understand, Jack.'

'I've never been afraid of work.'

'I know that. Your father is very proud of you.'

His eyes softened. 'The funny thing is, Kate, that if you'd stayed with me I might not have achieved the same level of success. The all out concentration would have been impossible with you around to distract me.'

'Then maybe I did you a good turn by running off.'

'It didn't feel like it at the time,' he retorted.

'Nor to me.' Kate shook her head in wonder. 'I was such a *girl* when I met you, Jack. But I grew up pretty quickly after you dumped me.'

His eyes glittered dangerously. 'Your memory's at fault, Katherine Durant. It was you who dumped me.'

'Only technically!' She glared back. 'I had to salvage some remnant of pride! You wouldn't even meet me to say goodbye.'

'I was afraid I'd go down on my knees and beg you to stay.'

They stared at each other in silence broken suddenly by a log falling in the fireplace.

'That's an unlikely picture,' said Kate at last.

'The knees maybe,' he conceded. 'But not the begging.'

She shook her head. 'I can't imagine it.'

He shrugged. 'It belongs in the past, anyway, Kate. Far better to focus on the present.'

'You're right about that,' she said with a sigh. 'When Liz and Robert were killed, my own mortality hit me in the face. I even made a will.'

'Good move. Thinking in worst scenario terms,' he added, 'what provision is made for Joanna if anything happens to you, Kate?'

'Guardianship would go to her Sutton grandparents, with Anna and Ben named in the will as trustees.' She yawned suddenly. 'Sorry. It must be this fire. I really must go home now, Jack. Sorry to drag you out.'

He got up at once, and held out his hand to help her up. 'A gentleman—even the self-made variety like me—always sees a lady home, Miss Durant.'

'Another time I'll bring my car,' she told him, and flushed as she heard the promise implicit in her words. 'I'll just say goodnight to Bran before we go,' she said hastily.

'I hit on a good idea by asking Dad along,' said Jack on the drive back. 'You relaxed the moment you saw him, so you were obviously worried when I took you to my place for dinner.' He shot her a sidelong glance. 'Were you afraid that I'd fall on you with ravening lust before the meal or after it?'

Kate let out a snort of laughter. 'Neither, Jack. But you're right about your father. It was an inspired move to ask him along.'

'The idea was to convince you that my intentions were strictly honourable!'

'It succeeded. I enjoyed the evening very much.'

'In that case, come again soon.'

'The two of you must come to me next time,' she said impulsively, then bit her lip. 'But I'll have to paint my dining room first. Otherwise it's the kitchen table again.'

'As Dad said, it's something we've done often enough before.' Jack gave her a searching look as he parked outside her house. 'Tell me, Kate. Why are you doing all the painting yourself? Cash flow problem?'

Kate shook her head. 'It's just my way of putting my personal mark on the house—making it really mine.' She hesitated. 'Would you like some coffee?'

She unlocked her door and Jack followed her through the brightly lit house to the kitchen. He helped her off with her coat then turned her round into his arms.

'No coffee, not even ravening lust. Just this, Katie.' He bent his head and kissed her, and for a moment she stood ramrod stiff, fighting her own response. But as the kiss deepened, her lips parted to the irresistible familiarity and sheer rightness of it. With a sigh she surrendered to the arms which tightened round her, all her senses urging her to taste him, touch him, drink in the male, remembered scent of him as her body responded to the mounting urgency in his. *No,* reminded a voice in her head and she took in a sharp, shaky breath and pulled free. Jack raised his head and stepped back, eyes gleaming under narrowed lids.

'When a gentleman sees a lady home he deserves a goodnight kiss.'

She smiled brightly. 'What's a kiss between friends?'

'Do you kiss all your friends like that?'

'Only the men!'

Jack laughed. 'The girl I knew would have blushed when she said that.'

Kate shrugged. 'That girl grew up fast, Jack.'

'And I'm to blame.'

'Mostly,' she agreed, and went with him to the door.

'I must try to make amends. But before I leave I want something else.' He grinned as she backed away. 'Don't panic—just your mobile phone number.' He noted the number in his diary, then tore out a page, scribbled his own number and handed it over. 'Right then, Kate. If you need me, ring me any time. Goodnight.' Jack kissed her cheek and crossed the pavement to his car.

*   *   *

Mill House was the main topic of conversation over Sunday lunch next day at the Maitland house. Ben was as interested in Kate's description of the actual property as his wife, but he hooted at the look on Anna's face when she heard that Tom Logan had been present.

'Didn't Jack trust himself alone with you?' she demanded.

'Of course he did. But when the past rears its head between us the atmosphere tends to get a little tense. With Mr Logan there as peace-keeper it was a very pleasant evening.'

Anna sighed in disappointment. 'No red-hot sex then?'

'For God's sake, wife,' said her husband, laughing. 'You can't ask questions like that.'

Kate rolled her eyes. 'Oh, yes, she can, and frequently does. But, to satisfy your curiosity, Mrs Maitland, I made it very clear to Jack that the only thing on offer is friendship.'

'He was *happy* with that?' said Ben sceptically.

'He appears to be.'

'So when are you seeing him again?' asked Anna.

'We haven't set a date. But it's up to me, anyway. I'm giving Jack—and his father—supper at my place next time.'

'Is this going to be a regular kind of thing, then?'

'I hope so. I'm very fond of Mr Logan.'

Anna hooted. 'And what about Mr Logan Junior? How do you feel about him?'

'Ambivalent.' Kate smiled suddenly. 'Before I left London people kept asking me what on earth I'd find to do up here in the sticks. Time certainly hasn't hung heavy so far.'

CHAPTER FIVE

IN CONFIRMATION of this a message was waiting on Kate's telephone when she got home that evening.

'Richard Forster here, Kate. If you're an Oscar Wilde fan *The Importance of Being Earnest* is on at the Playhouse this week. I can get tickets for Wednesday or Thursday if you'd like to see it. We could eat somewhere first—or after. Let me know.'

When Kate rang him Richard sounded so delighted to hear from her she wouldn't have had the heart to say no even if she'd wanted to. Friendship with Jack Logan, she reminded herself stringently, needn't exclude all other men from her life.

'I love Oscar Wilde,' she told him. 'Thursday would be good. How are you?'

They chatted together for a while, arranged times and discussed eating places for their evening out, and Kate rang off at last, feeling rather pleased with life. Her good mood lasted for all of fifteen minutes, until Jack rang.

'You're hard to find,' he said irritably. 'You were out this morning, the line was engaged just now—and you've had your mobile switched off all day.'

'And hello to you, too.'

'Where were you?'

'Out,' she said baldly.

'I gathered that. I went for a run in the park with Bran and called at your house afterwards.'

'Apologise to Bran for me.'

'I told you I'd call in next time.'

'Surely you don't expect me to hang around on the off

61

chance! Anyway, now you're on the line it saves writing to thank you for last night.'

'The kiss was thanks enough,' said Jack, in a tone that curled her toes. 'Look, I'm tied up the first half of the week, but how about dinner on Thursday?'

'Sorry,' she said sweetly. 'I'm going to the theatre that night.'

'Pity,' he said, after a pause. 'Another time, then.'

'Lovely. Goodnight, Jack—'

'Hold it. Where were you today, Kate?'

She ground her teeth. 'Sunday lunch with the Maitlands. Satisfied now?'

'Not by any means. Goodnight.'

A slow smile spread across Kate's face as he disconnected. How lucky that Richard had asked her out first. Otherwise she might have been tempted to say yes to Jack. Instead he could just wait until she invited him to supper with his father. She liked Richard Forster's restful, unthreatening brand of charm, whereas there was something about Jack these days that made her uneasy. Not just the kiss last night, though that had been scary enough, if only because it made her crave more of the same. But she had a feeling that deep down, offers of friendship or not, he had some kind of hidden agenda. Kate's eyes narrowed darkly. If there were any grudges to be harboured she had far more right to them than Jack. She'd been so young and trusting back then. She'd never dreamed that he would refuse to see her again after she left for London. She'd fondly believed that they'd kiss and make up once she made the first overture. She kept on believing it—right up to the day she heard Jack had married Dawn Taylor.

The next few days were fully occupied. Kate got up early each morning to work on her computer, and in the afternoons went on with her decorating. By Thursday the evening with Richard Forster was a welcome change from wielding a paint roller. The acting was good and the small theatre full, and afterwards they discussed the play over supper at a new restaurant near the Guildhall.

'So how are you settling in?' asked Richard later, over coffee Kate had asked for very deliberately so he wouldn't expect any when he drove her home.

'I've just finished painting my bedroom. Tomorrow the new mattress arrives and with luck I'll have the room ready to sleep in by bedtime.' She smiled cheerfully. 'After that it's one more room to go, and then I start on the garden.'

'Do you like gardening?'

'I used to when I was growing up here, but I haven't done any for years. I've been watching TV gardening programmes lately to pick up tips.'

'You might want to find someone to do the rough work if the garden's been neglected,' advised Richard.

'It's been kept in pretty good nick, fortunately, and it's not big. I can easily manage it myself. I've invested in some spanking new garden tools, so once the weather gets warmer I'll make a start.'

On the journey back to Park Crescent Richard asked if Kate was free for dinner on Saturday, but she shook her head.

'Sorry. I'm off to the Cotswolds for the weekend to see my niece.'

'Some other time then. Enjoy your trip. I'll give you a ring when you get back.'

To Kate's relief Richard stayed in the car when they reached the house. 'I'll wait until you're safe inside,' he said, smiling.

Kate smiled back warmly, grateful to him for making it clear he didn't expect to be asked in. 'Thanks again, Richard. Goodnight.'

Kate felt very thoughtful as she locked up. Richard's request to see her again was rather worrying. She had no intention of seeing anyone on a regular basis right now, least of all a man she suspected of pining for his wife. Frowning abstractedly, she checked her messages and found a very short one from Jack.

'I hope you enjoyed the play, Katie.'

She pressed the replay button, sure she must have missed something, but the electronic voice said, 'End of message.'

Kate went to bed in pensive mood, wondering, not for the first time lately, whether she would have moved back here if she'd known about Jack's divorce. But it was done now. Jo loved it here, and Kate had Anna and Ben for support if—if what? If friendship with Jack Logan proved to be the slightest threat to her life with Jo, she would simply dispense with it.

Kate left town at mid morning the following Saturday and after a leisurely drive arrived at her Cotswold hotel in time to settle in and change her clothes. She ordered a lavish tea for later then set off in good time to have a word with the headmistress before collecting Jo at Manor House School, which was a typical Cotswold structure in honeyed stone with the steep-pitched roof and mullioned windows common to local architecture.

Kate was conducted straight to the headmistress's office, and once the greetings were over Dr Knight gave her the information she was anxious to hear.

'Joanna has done remarkably well since her return this term, Miss Durant. She is a mature child, and is coping bravely with her personal tragedy. There may well be tears when she's alone, but I have emphasized that she can come to me, or to Miss Hayes, my deputy, at any time. And Matron keeps a close eye on her, of course.'

'Thank you,' said Kate gratefully. 'It was very hard to part with her when I brought her back at the beginning of term. But during our weekly phone call she seems to be coping.'

'She's doing well, I assure you. And, in confidence,' added Dr Knight, 'Joanna told me she is very happy to be making her home with you, Miss Durant. She tells me you inherited a house.'

Kate gave a few details about it, then got up to leave. 'Thank you for seeing me, Dr Knight.'

The headmistress smiled as she shook hands. 'I'm always available if you have concerns. In the meantime, if you go down to the main hall and sign the book, Joanna will be there in a few minutes.'

Kate went downstairs to join a crowd of people on the same mission, and soon afterwards a bell rang and teachers ushered a stream of girls of various ages through the double doors.

Jo's bright hair was easy to spot among the tide of grey tweed overcoats. She said a word to a teacher, then came hurrying through the crowd, and Kate hugged her close for an instant.

'Love the pinstripes!' Jo cast approving dark eyes over Kate's trouser suit.

'Must get some mileage out of my old work clothes. I've signed the book. Should I be checking you out with someone?'

'I've already done that. Miss Hayes says I must be back by half past six.'

'Let's go, then.' They made their way through the chattering mêlée of girls and parents and went out to the car. 'I thought we'd have tea at my hotel,' said Kate as they drove off. 'Either in the lounge there, or you can sprawl on the bed in my room and watch television while you pig out on sandwiches and cake.'

'Guess which I prefer!' said Jo, with a giggle which did Kate's heart good.

'So how are you, Miss Niece?' she asked bluntly.

Jo sobered. 'I'm OK, sort of. I still have bad times, but not so often now.'

'Are they at night?'

'Sometimes. But the mornings are the worst when I wake up and realise I'll never see Mum and Dad any more.'

Kate swallowed a lump in her throat, unable to speak for a moment.

'I get over it by thinking of something else,' went on Joanna. 'You and the new house, Anna and Ben, even Josh and Leo, the terrible twins. Or I concentrate on a maths test or the prep I've got to get through later.' She straightened in her seat. 'Mummy wouldn't want me to be crying all the time.'

Listening in awe, Kate had to remind herself that Jo was only thirteen. 'You're absolutely right, darling. So what social events are delighting you this term?'

'There's a disco next Saturday night. Just girls, though.'

'I thought you socialised with the boys from King Edward's occasionally.'

'Not in the junior school, worse luck,' said Jo, pulling a face. 'Was it the same with you?'

'I went to an ordinary co-ed day school, with boys around all the time. At your age I was more interested in hockey and netball than any of that lot.'

Jo cast a mischievous glance at Kate's face. 'How about right now? Have you met anyone since you moved back home?'

'Yes,' said Kate with perfect truth. 'Lots of people. I told you about Anna's party, but since then I've had dinner with an old friend and I've been to the theatre with a new one. And here's some stop press news. Anna's going to have a baby!'

This information diverted Jo so effectively from Kate's social life that she talked of nothing else until they reached the hotel. Kate collected her key and asked to have tea sent up as soon as possible, then took Jo upstairs to a pleasant double room overlooking the grounds at the back of the building.

'Cool,' said Jo, impressed. 'Can I watch television?'

'You can do anything you like—within reason!'

Jo went off to explore the bathroom, exclaiming about the various products provided by the hotel, then came back to prop herself up on the bed and spend a happy few minutes with the remote control before finding a channel with a re-run of *Grease*.

'This is brilliant,' she said with smile of satisfaction. 'Can we have lunch here tomorrow, too?'

'If you like. Or would you prefer a scenic drive and a country pub somewhere?'

The smile faded. 'No, thank you. I'd rather come back here.'

Kate could have kicked herself. No child would fancy driving far after losing her parents in a road accident. 'Good choice. The receptionist told me they do a very good Sunday lunch here.'

Jo brightened. 'It's sure to beat school dinners!'

When a waiter arrived to deposit a laden tray on the small table Kate sent him on his way with a generous tip and pulled up two basket chairs. 'Right, then. Let's see what they found for us.'

Jo gazed in delight at the array of sandwiches, crumpets, cakes and scones, and two bowls of fresh fruit salad.

'Wow!' she said, and shook out a napkin to protect her grey uniform skirt. 'May I start?'

Using dinner later as her excuse, Kate ate very little, content just to drink tea and enjoy Jo's account of tests she'd done well in and others she hadn't, of goals she'd scored in netball, the dance session with her friends in front of *Top of the Pops* on television on Friday nights, and the wild, but much admired, exploits of Giles, the brother of her friend, Emma.

'How old is he?'

'Oh, quite old. He's in his first year at university.'

'That old!'

Jo grinned as she spread cream and jam on a scone. 'Jane's got a brother, too, but he's only fifteen.' She sighed. 'I would have liked a brother—or a sister.'

Kate's heart contracted. She put out a hand to touch a rather sticky little paw. 'I'm sure Anna will let you have a share in the baby.'

Jo's eyes lit up at the thought. 'I wonder what she'll have. Will Anna have a scan to find out?'

'I'll ask when I get home.'

After driving Jo back to school Kate felt at rather a loose end when she returned to the hotel. To pass the time until dinner she had a shower, fiddled a lot with her hair afterwards, and then rang Anna for a chat.

'Hi, Mumsie. How are you?'

'At this time of day fine. You do not, however, want anything to do with me in the mornings. How's Jo?'

'Doing well, thank God. She assures me she's coping and her headmistress confirmed it.'

'She's got grit, that niece of yours. Did you tell her about the baby?'

'Of course I did. She was thrilled to bits. She asked if you're going to find out what sex it is.'

'Good heavens no! Give her my love tomorrow, but say we'd rather wait until the baby's born. Oh, by the way— breaking news. Jack Logan has invited the Maitlands to dinner at Mill House next weekend. I trust you're suitably impressed.'

Kate blinked. 'I certainly am. Enormously. Is this pay back for gatecrashing your party?'

'Must be. Lucy will be livid.' Anna gave a little cough. 'Has he asked you, too?'

'No. The honour's all yours.'

'He only rang today. Maybe there'll be a message waiting for you when you get back. And report in the minute you arrive, please; the weather forecast's not great.'

Kate went down to the crowded, noisy bar in thoughtful mood. She ordered a glass of wine and sat down at the solitary vacant table to study the menu.

'The other tables are full. Would you mind if I shared?' said a pleasant male voice, and Kate looked up to see a man who looked vaguely familiar.

'Of course not. Do sit down.'

'I saw you at Manor House School this afternoon,' he said as he took the seat opposite. 'I'm Philip Brace. My daughter Leah is a pupil there.'

Kate smiled, enlightened. 'Ah, I see. I'm Kate Durant. I'm visiting my niece, Joanna Sutton.'

'In that case could I persuade you to join forces with me for dinner?' He gave her a rueful grin. 'I'd be grateful for company.'

'Was your wife unable to come?' asked Kate pointedly.

The smile vanished. 'We're recently divorced—very recently. It's my first turn to take Leah out this weekend.'

'Oh, I see,' said Kate, wishing she'd kept her mouth shut.

Philip Brace looked at her levelly. 'I can leave you in peace if you prefer.'

'Not at all. I'd be glad of company, too. Have you driven far?'

Having established that they lived less than thirty miles from each other, they discussed Jo and Leah, and exchanged opinions on the education the girls were receiving before breaking off to give their orders to the hovering waiter.

'I would have felt conspicuous as the only person on my own,' Kate admitted, once they were seated in the formal dining room later.

'I get more than enough of it on my travels for the firm.' He smiled hopefully. 'I'm driving Leah to Chipping Camden for lunch tomorrow. Would you and Jo care to join us?'

Kate explained about the tragedy which had turned Jo

against car journeys, and said something polite about joining forces some other time.

Philip shot her a look as he poured the wine he'd ordered. 'If I get too pushy just tell me to back off.'

'Oh, I will,' she assured him, smiling to take the edge off her words.

'One question,' he went on, once their first course was in front of them. 'If you are Jo's aunt, is there a matching uncle?'

'No. Other than me, her only relatives are a pair of elderly grandparents.'

'Poor little thing!' He smiled wryly. 'As you can probably tell, I was trying to find out whether I was trespassing on someone's preserves.'

'If you were I would have said no,' she assured him, and got on with her excellent dinner. The meal passed very pleasantly, they opted for coffee at the table afterwards, but when they left the dining room Kate stopped at the foot of the main staircase in the hall and held out her hand.

'I'll say goodnight now, Philip.'

'Shall I see you at breakfast in the morning?'

She shook her head smiling. 'I'm not a morning person. I'll probably see you at school later on.'

'I hope so. Goodnight, Kate.' He shook her hand very formally. 'Thank you for your company.'

Once she reached her room Kate rang reception to order breakfast there instead of in the dining room as she would have much preferred. Having dinner with a stranger was one thing, breakfast a different thing entirely. Philip Brace, she suspected, was another man finding it hard to adjust to single status.

Kate's phone rang when she was settled down in bed with a book. She checked the caller ID and smiled smugly. 'Hello, Jack.'

'Are you in your room?' he asked, 'or have I interrupted your dinner?'

'I've had dinner. I'm reading in bed.'

'Anna Maitland told me where you were this weekend. Why couldn't you have told me?'

'Last time we spoke you weren't exactly friendly.'

'I'd just heard you'd been to the theatre with Forster.'

'It's not against the law.'

'True. Why didn't you tell me where you were going this weekend?'

'To be honest, Jack, it never occurred to me.'

'God, you're a cruel woman!'

'Why did you want to speak to me tonight?'

'Must I have a reason?'

'It's a bit late for a chat,' she said tartly.

'I waited until now to avoid interrupting your dinner. Was it good?'

'Very good indeed.'

'Did you dine alone?'

Kate ground her teeth. 'As it happens, no. The father of one of the other pupils is staying here. He suggested we join forces.'

'Is he with you now?'

'No, Jack,' she snapped. 'I told you. I'm in bed.'

Jack chuckled. 'You're annoyed.'

'Such intuition! Is that why you rang? To annoy me?'

'No. I rang to invite you to dinner at Mill House next Saturday. With the Maitlands and the Beresfords.'

'Ah. Lucy won't be livid after all, then.'

'Run that past me again?'

'I spoke to Anna earlier. She didn't know you'd invited Mrs Beresford.'

'Were you offended because I hadn't asked you?'

'Not in the least. You're obviously repaying Anna's hospitality. You haven't had any from me.'

'No,' he agreed with a sigh, 'just hostility.'

'Nonsense. I've given you coffee.'

'Did you give Richard Forster coffee?'

'No. He left me very correctly on my doorstep.'

'Are you seeing him again?'

Kate bristled. 'As a matter of fact, he suggested dinner to-night, but Jo had a prior call on my time.'

'Good. If he suggests next Saturday, tell him *I* have a prior call on your time.'

'I most certainly will not. Besides, I haven't accepted your invitation yet, Jack.'

'You mean you've got some other man on a string as well?'

'I could be seeing Philip Brace.'

'Who the hell is he?'

'The man I had dinner with tonight. He lives in Worcester. It's not far to drive.'

'Do you intend seeing him again?'

'None of your business, Jack.'

Instead of hanging up on her as Kate half expected Jack laughed in her ear. 'It is, you know. Are you coming next Saturday or not?'

'I might as well.'

'I'll take that as a yes.' He paused. 'By the way, are you having breakfast with your new friend in the morning?'

'Yes,' lied Kate angrily, and disconnected, seething. Jack had absolutely no right to interfere in her social life. If she wanted to see other men she would, damn his eyes. But as she calmed down she was forced to admit the unpalatable truth. Compared with Jack Logan, all other men paled into insignificance.

Kate would have felt a whole lot better if she could have seen Jack pacing round his kitchen at Mill House at that very moment, cursing himself for behaving like a jealous school-boy. He was supposed to be patient, he reminded himself savagely. The plan was to win her back, not drive her away for good. He stopped dead so suddenly he stepped on Bran, who yelped in anguish. As he stroked the dog in apology Jack gave thanks for the second chance life had given him. This time he would make sure he took full advantage of it. He'd had no thought of marrying again, ever, until he'd met up with Kate again. He'd made work his life. But work was no longer enough. He wanted Kate back in his life for good this time, as his wife. When the time was right he'd tell her that and put his mother's ring back on her finger where it belonged.

There was no sign of Philip Brace when Kate arrived at the school next day and she drove Joanna back to lunch at the hotel with a light heart, prepared to savour every minute as her companion chattered happily throughout the deliberately careful journey.

The meal was a conventional roast, and Joanna ate hugely and then wandered with Kate in the hotel grounds in the pale winter sunshine afterwards.

'I've got another Sunday out before the end of term,' she informed Kate. 'But no Saturday.'

'Never mind. I'll drive over and back the same day, but you can still eat here if you like.'

'Is it very expensive?' asked Jo anxiously.

'No,' said Kate firmly. 'It's starting to rain. Let's watch television before tea.'

'I get tea as well?' said Jo rapturously.

'You bet.' Kate cast an eye at the slender, long-legged child, already as tall as her aunt. 'Where do you put it all?'

The afternoon passed far too quickly for Kate, but to her relief they arrived at the school just after Emma and Jane, Jo's bosom pals. In the flurry of introductions to parents and the comparisons the girls were making about their lunch, the dreaded parting was less painful than expected and Kate was halfway home before she remembered Philip Brace.

It was an unpleasant journey, with sleet slithering against the windscreen all the way. Her brightly lit house was a hugely welcome sight when Kate eventually turned into Park Crescent, and with a sigh of relief she locked the car, hurried into the house, deactivated the alarm, then locked her front door and threw the bolts. She'd turned off her mobile phone rather than have it ring while she was driving, and as half-expected there was a message waiting from Jack demanding a call when she got home.

She reported in to Anna first and then rang Jack.

'I'm back,' she said, in response to the barked 'Logan' in her ear.

'Thank God for that; I was worried. It's a hell of a night.'

'Tell me about it. Freezing fog added to driving sleet for the last few miles.'

'Do you have the right kind of phone in your car?'

'No.'

'Then get one, Kate. It's only common sense when you're driving long distances alone.'

'Yes, Dad.'

'I'm not your father!'

'True. You're my friend.'

He breathed in audibly. 'How was your day? Did your niece have a good time?'

'I think so. She certainly ate well. Jo must have a fantastic metabolism; she's as slender as a reed.'

'Takes after her aunt. By the way, did you manage to avoid your dinner partner today?'

'I forgot all about him when I took Jo back to school. I was too busy being bright and cheerful to give him a thought.'

'Good.'

'Why good, Jack?'

'Save your thoughts for me, Kate. I'll be in touch before Saturday. Sleep well.'

Kate woke next morning to the discovery that she'd slept very well indeed. During the week she had spent restless nights, worrying over what she would find when she saw Jo again. But reassurance over Joanna had combined with a tiring journey home and the gratifying chat with Jack to give Kate her best night's sleep for quite a while.

When the Suttons decided to send Joanna away to school Kate had been against the idea, convinced that the child would be miserable away from her family at the tender age of eight. But Jo had taken to boarding school life like a duck to water. And when Elizabeth and Robert were so cruelly removed from her young life the security of the familiar school background was a contributing factor in helping Jo to cope with her loss. And she still has me, thought Kate, as she wrote to Jo to tell her how much she'd enjoyed their weekend together. She made no mention of the extra care she'd taken on the drive back to ensure the safety of one of the few relatives Joanna Sutton had left in the world.

CHAPTER SIX

THE prospect of dinner at Mill House added a tinge of excitement to a week that was busier than usual. After Kate's weekend away she was obliged to labour hard and long to finish the dining room in the time left over from the work that brought in the money. She even refused an invitation to supper with Anna and Ben mid week, too tired by evening for anything more strenuous than a bath and an early night.

'I'll be seeing you on Saturday, anyway,' she said, when Anna objected.

'I was hoping you'd come shopping with me on Friday first, Kate. I need something new for Saturday.'

'You've got loads of clothes.'

'I can't get into the formal stuff. My waistline's expanding by the day. Lord knows what I'll be like by the time Junior actually arrives.'

In the end Kate agreed to an hour's shopping before the afternoon painting session. 'But one hour only,' she warned.

The hour expanded into an entire afternoon with a tea break incorporated into it, rather than afterwards in Park Crescent, due to Anna's aversion to paint smells.

'Can't cope in my condition,' said Anna, eyeing her reflection in a changing room. 'What do you think? The silk tunic and skirt, or the dress I tried on first.'

'That shade of blue looks great on you,' said Kate, and grinned. 'But so does the black dress. Buy both. Ben won't mind.'

Anna took the advice she wanted to hear, but no amount of coaxing persuaded Kate to buy something.

'I've got enough from my former life to last me for ages.

No point in wasting money on something new.' Kate patted Anna's hand. 'I promise I won't let you down again. No jeans this time.'

'You didn't let me down,' protested her friend. 'You made all the other women green with envy. Did you wear jeans when you had dinner with Jack?'

Kate shook her head. 'I thought we were eating out, so I honoured him with the dress intended for your party—the one I wore at your place at Christmas.'

'The drop-dead job with the cleavage?' Anna grinned. 'That must have got his juices flowing.'

'Is pregnancy to blame for this sudden earthiness of yours, Mrs Maitland?'

'No, just for my appetite. I need tea and cream cakes right now!'

By the time Anna dropped her off at home Kate had lost all enthusiasm for more painting. There was only one wall left to do and that, she decided, could wait. Now she had a sitting room worthy of the name she would spoil herself and stretch out on her new chaise to read instead of doing any one of a long list of things she should be doing instead. She enjoyed a whole hour deep in the intricacies of a courtroom thriller before the telephone rang to spoil her fun.

'Richard here, Kate. How are you?'

'I'm well. How are things with you?'

'Busy. Did you enjoy your weekend?'

'I did, very much. Nasty journey back, but it was worth it.'

'I'm sure it was. Look, Kate, I know this is short notice, but are you free tomorrow? A film, meal, anything you like.'

'Sorry, Richard. I'm already booked for dinner tomorrow.'

Kate could feel her face growing pink during a pause which lasted too long for comfort.

'Is that the truth?' he asked at last, 'or is it your way of letting me down lightly?'

'Richard,' said Kate on impulse. 'Are you going home about now?'

'Yes. I'm just locking up.'

'Would you like to call here for a drink first?'

'Of course I would. See you soon.'

Kate checked on the contents of the fridge and went back to the sitting room to her book. When she heard a car stop outside she put a marker in her page and got up to answer the door, then stared in dismay.

'You were expecting someone else?' Jack inquired sardonically.

'Yes, I am.' She shrugged. 'It's a bit awkward, but come in, if you like.'

'But you'd rather I made myself scarce.'

'Yes, please. I'll explain later.'

He threw her a flinty look, strode to the Jensen at the kerb and drove off with a growl of engine just as Richard Forster's car turned into the Crescent.

'Was that Logan?' he asked as he got out.

'Yes. Do come in.'

Kate showed him into the sitting room. 'I can offer you beer or a glass of wine. Or medicinal brandy,' she added as an afterthought, feeling rather in need of one herself.

'Beer would be good. Attractive house,' he added, looking round.

'Thank you. I won't be a moment.' Kate took a can of beer and a tonic from the fridge, filled two glasses and went back to the sitting room.

Richard took the beer and stood in front of the fireplace with the air of a man not expecting to stay long. 'You've asked me here for a reason, Kate,' he said without preamble. 'Will you tell me what it is?'

'It seemed better to talk to you face to face.' She drank some of her tonic. 'Firstly, I really am going out on Saturday night.' At least she hoped so.

'Firstly means a secondly coming up,' he said dryly.

She nodded. 'I have a question to ask. You don't have to answer it, of course.'

He looked at her with steady blue eyes. 'Ask away.'

'Are you still in love with your wife?'

Richard blinked, startled, as though this was the last thing he'd expected. He was silent for a long time, his face like a mask, then shrugged, his eyes hard. 'Yes,' he said bitterly. 'I am.'

Kate nodded. 'I thought so.'

'Because you're still in love with Logan?' he said, startling her in turn.

'I used to be, once,' she admitted.

'Is he taking you out on Saturday?'

'Not exactly. He's asked me to a dinner party at his house—with other guests,' she added.

Richard drank some of his beer, eyeing her over the rim of his glass. 'I've heard that entertaining at home isn't the Logan style.'

'So have I.'

Richard put the glass down on the table, and looked Kate in the eye. 'It's now established that you have a prior engagement on Saturday, but why, exactly, did you ask about my wife?'

'Look, Richard,' said Kate, taking the bull by the horns, 'I don't think casual dating is your kind of thing. If I've got a colossal nerve to think you'd want something less casual with me, I apologise, humbly. But I thought it best to say, face to face—'

'That a relationship of any kind between us is out of the question?'

'Yes, Richard. And not because I don't like you, because I do, very much. But my gut feeling tells me that the only relationship you really want is with your wife.'

For a moment Kate thought he would make a furious denial, but after a fraught silence Richard nodded grimly. 'Your instinct is right. I do want her back, for all the good it will do me.'

'Is she involved with someone else?'

'Not as far as I know. Caroline's a journalist and her sole passion is her job.'

'She might be finding it isn't enough by now. Have you asked her?'

'No.' His eyes hardened again. 'I refuse to go crawling. It's up to her to make the first move.'

Kate shook her head impatiently. 'Oh, come on! Forget all that macho nonsense. If you want her, make the first move yourself.'

Richard's jaw clenched, and for a moment Kate was afraid he was going to tell her to shut up and mind her own business. But eventually a wry smile dawned in his eyes and she breathed a sigh of relief. 'Maybe you're right, Kate,' he said at last. 'I'll go down to the flat on Sunday.'

'Why leave it until then? Go tomorrow.'

'She works on Saturdays.' His mouth twisted. 'The sky would fall in if Caroline knocked off before her beloved newspaper's ready for Sunday breakfast tables.'

'Insist that she does.'

'Carry her out over my shoulder?' he said, laughing, suddenly a different man from the wary lawyer of minutes earlier.

'Why not?'

'Why not, indeed!' Richard drained his glass and got up. 'OK, I'll give it a whirl. Have you ever considered a career in Relate?' he added.

She grimaced. 'Absolutely not. This is my first—and last—venture into marriage counselling!'

He shook her hand formally as she saw him to the door. 'Shall I let you know what happens?'

'Yes, please. Good luck!'

Kate waved him off, then rang Jack.

'What the blazes was all that about?' he demanded.

'Where are you?'

'I'm with Dad.'

'Can you come round for a minute?'

'You just threw me out.'

'If you want to know why, come back. Or not,' she added crossly. 'Up to you, Jack.'

'It had better be good,' he said ominously.

This time when Kate threw open the door Jack just stood there, waiting, tall and formidable and very much the head of Logan Development in a dark suit and long dark overcoat. 'Don't just stand there,' she said irritably. 'Come in.'

'If you're quite sure I'm not interrupting something,' he said with sarcasm.

'Oh, don't be difficult, Jack. Do you want a drink?' Kate turned her back on him and went along the hall to the kitchen.

Jack closed the door behind him and followed her. 'Have you got a beer?'

'Yes.' She handed him a can and fetched a glass. 'I've also got half a tonic waiting in the sitting room, so let's go in there.'

'You mean I'd better be sitting comfortably when you tell me what's up? I saw Forster arrive as I took off just now,' he added.

Kate threw him an exasperated look as they went back to the other room. She drew the curtains and switched on lamps and resumed her chair. Jack slung his coat on the end of the chaise and leaned back against the curved support, looking far more at ease than her previous visitor.

'Richard asked me out on Saturday night, Jack.'

'No surprise there.' He shot her a look. 'I hope you told him you were otherwise engaged.'

'Of course I did,' she said impatiently, and drank some tonic. 'But I suggested he came round on his way home so I could talk to him face to face.'

Jack leaned forward, his eyes suddenly intent. 'Why?'

'Richard had to be told that a relationship with me was never going to happen.'

The eyes narrowed. 'Anything to do with me?'

She shook her head. 'No, Jack, nothing at all. There's just no place in my life for any relationship of that kind right now, with you, Richard or anyone else. But that's irrelevant anyway, because he's still in love with his wife.'

Jack sat back, eyebrows raised, and drank some of his beer. 'Did he admit that?'

'Eventually, yes. At first he went all tight-lipped and said it was up to her to make the first move. But in the end he changed his mind and he's off to London tomorrow to make the move himself.'

'Because you told him to?'

'Because I advised him,' she corrected. 'He's a lawyer, remember.'

Jack raised an eyebrow. 'What happens if she shuts the door in his face? Will he come rushing back to cry on your shoulder?'

'If he does, all he'll get is sympathy. The situation remains unchanged.'

'The situation being?'

'That Joanna takes precedence over everything else in my life right now.'

Jack's mood changed abruptly. 'Of course. How is she, Kate? You said she enjoyed her time with you last weekend.'

'She seems to be coping remarkably well.'

He eyed her searchingly. 'But what happens at night, after lights out in her dormitory?'

Touched by his insight, Kate repeated the account given by Dr Knight. 'Jo's dealing with her loss far better than I ever imagined.'

'Having you as a guardian is a lot to do with it.'

'It's kind of you to say so, Jack.'

He grinned suddenly. 'Don't sound so surprised. I can be very kind when I put my mind to it.'

'I know that. So did Dawn Taylor.' Kate could have kicked herself when she saw Jack's smile vanish.

He abandoned his beer and got up. 'Time I was on my way. Thanks for the drink.'

Kate jumped up and put a hand on his arm. 'Do you have plans for this evening, Jack?'

He looked down at the hand. 'Why?'

'If you haven't, you could stay to supper. If you like,' she muttered, already regretting her impulse.

Jack's grin was back as he looked up. 'Thought you'd never ask.'

'You'll have to eat whatever I can find in the cupboard,' she warned, surprised to feel so relieved. 'Come into the kitchen while I forage.'

'I've got a better idea,' he said, sitting down again. 'Let's order in. You can impress me with your culinary skill next time.'

Kate returned to her chair, smiling gratefully. 'I won't say no. I've had a tiring afternoon.'

'Painting?'

'No, far more exhausting than that. I went on a shopping trip with Anna. She needed something to wear to your dinner party. Her current wardrobe doesn't fit.' Kate swirled the remains of her drink round her glass. 'Just between you and me, she's pregnant, and jubilant about it. So is Ben.'

'I can imagine he would be! Should I congratulate them?'

'I'm not sure if they've gone public on it, so maybe not yet.'

'My lips shall remain sealed. Would you have another beer?'

Kate went to fetch more drinks, and found Jack talking on his phone when she got back.

He closed it with a snap. 'That was Dad, worried something

was wrong. So I told him you'd asked me to supper and right now he's probably jumping joyfully to all the wrong conclusions.'

Kate handed him a beer, topped up her own glass and sat down. 'It's just supper, Jack.'

The black-lashed eyes gleamed as he pulled the tab on the can. 'But Dad will take it as a sign that you're thawing towards me. Are you?' he added.

'Yes.' Kate smiled at him cheerfully. 'I knew I'd upset you and wanted to show I was sorry.'

'In that case, let's see if we can manage the rest of the evening without coming to blows.' He gave her a sharp look. 'Not that I would ever, in any circumstances, raise a hand to you, Kate.'

'I know that,' she said impatiently. 'You can't have changed that much.'

His eyes held hers. 'I haven't changed at all when it comes to the important things in life.'

'Neither have I.' She grinned. 'As usual, I fancy some Chinese.'

He rolled his eyes. 'Let me guess—same old sweet and sour pork, spare ribs and spring rolls.'

'You remember!' She nodded with enthusiasm. 'With crispy seaweed on the side and masses of fried rice. I've got a menu in the kitchen. Shall I order now? I'm hungry.'

They sat at the kitchen table later, facing each other across a sea of foil dishes. Jack had discarded his jacket and rolled up his shirtsleeves when Kate provided large tea towels in lieu of napkins.

'Can't get grease on your bespoke suiting,' she said briskly.

'Amen to that. Next time I wear jeans. Because,' Jack added deliberately, 'there will be a next time, Kate.'

She shrugged. 'Why not? No harm in a takeaway now and then.'

They shunted dishes back and forth, emptying them with

hunger as Jack told her he'd called in to make sure she hadn't backed out of the dinner party. Assured that she was looking forward to it with bated breath, he grinned and began to talk about his latest restoration venture. Kate listened with keen interest as he described the transformation of a disused factory into affordable flats.

'No pricey loft apartments like the one you shared with fiancé mark two,' he told her, and nodded wryly at her startled look. 'Oh yes, news filtered through to me eventually. Unlike your banker a lot of people can't afford that kind of thing, but they still want comfort and style. This project will provide both. The building's user-friendly, and will include smaller apartments for first time buyers and a children's nursery school.'

'Convenient for shopping and schools for older children?' Kate asked, breaking open a fortune cookie.

'Only ten minutes from both. The wasteland around it will be landscaped into gardens to provide as green an environment as possible.'

'It sounds wonderful, Jack.'

'When it's nearer completion I'll take you over it.' He leaned over to read her fortune. 'New horizons are opening for you,' he intoned solemnly.

'Pretty general sort of forecast,' said Kate, and handed him a cookie.

Jack broke it open. 'You are about to receive your heart's desire!' he read.

'You're kidding!'

'Alas, yes,' he said, grinning. 'Mine's the same as yours.'

Kate bundled the debris into a waste sack and ran hot water and detergent into the kitchen sink. 'You go up to the bathroom and wash—last door on the landing at the back,' she told Jack. 'I'll scrub my grease off down here.'

He returned a few minutes later. 'I resisted the temptation to explore,' he said self-righteously.

'You can take a look if you like.'

'I'd rather you showed me round.'

Kate felt like a proud parent showing off its child as she led the way upstairs.

'This is where I work,' she said, at the threshold of her study. 'Jo is next door, in the blue and yellow room. And I'm through here.' She led him across the landing to her newly painted bedroom, then opened the door on the bathroom with the tub Ben had found for her in a reclamation yard. 'That's the lot. If you were a prospective buyer, how would it strike you?'

'Any smart young couple would go mad for it,' Jack assured her. 'But you don't intend to sell, surely?'

'No. I just wanted an objective opinion. I've never done any decorating before.' She pulled a face. 'The preparation is the hardest part. Once I get to the actual painting, it's easy.' She held out her hands ruefully. 'They'll never be the same again.'

'Wear gloves!'

'I do, most of the time. But you can't wear them for everything.'

'True,' said Jack, and turned to look at the mahogany sleigh bed visible through the open doorway to Kate's room. 'I assume that belonged to the famous Aunt Edith?'

She nodded. 'Impressive, isn't it! They make good copies these days, but this is the real McCoy. The auctioneer who came here to value the other furniture salivated when he saw it and offered me a good price, but I refused to part with it.'

'Very wise. If he was salivating, the price was probably half of what it should have been.'

'Cynic!'

'Realist,' he contradicted, and took her hands in his. 'Shall I kiss them better?'

Kate stood very still, suddenly aware that the door to her

bedroom stood open in invitation. She looked up into Jack's eyes and felt her knees tremble.

'Shall I?' he repeated, his voice deepening.

Kate watched mutely as he lifted each hand to his lips in turn, the touch of his open mouth on her skin sending her pulse into overdrive. 'Thank you,' she said hoarsely. 'Much better—'

The rest of her words were smothered against his mouth as Jack pulled her into his arms and kissed her hungrily, his lips and tongue so irresistible she melted against him, her heart pounding as his hands slid beneath her sweater. She felt a familiar, liquid rush of hot response as his kiss deepened and, without taking his lips from hers, Jack picked her up and carried her through the door of her room. But when he laid her down on the bed Kate rolled to the far side and stood up, shaking her head in vehement rejection.

Jack stood breathing heavily, his eyes hard as flint. 'Why not?' he demanded harshly.

Kate brushed past him out of the room and hurried down the steep staircase, her knees trembling. It was her fault. Jack Logan was a man, after all, and a man who had once been her lover. She didn't blame him for wanting to make love to her, but she couldn't let that happen. She wasn't laying herself open to that kind of pain again.

Jack came into the kitchen behind her and picked up his jacket. 'Kate,' he said harshly, 'all you had to do was say no.'

She turned on him, eyes flashing. 'I know that.'

He raked a hand through his hair, his eyes angry. 'Then why in God's name make me feel like a rapist?'

She let out a deep, unsteady sigh. 'I told you that friendship with me would be hard work, Jack.'

'So you did.'

Kate eyed him uncertainly as he shrugged into his jacket. 'If you'd rather I didn't turn up tomorrow, I quite understand.'

He stared at her in disbelief. 'And what reason will you give your friends for staying away?'

She bit her lip. 'Migraine, stomach bug, whatever.'

'And when Anna Maitland comes rushing here to check up on you?'

'I don't let her in because she's pregnant and I might be contagious.'

Jack slid into his overcoat, looking at her steadily. 'Kate, I vote we delete the past few minutes and go back to the supper we shared. I enjoyed the evening up to that point and, unless you were putting on an act, you did too.'

'Of course I did.'

'So stop behaving like an idiot and come to Mill House tomorrow as you promised.' Jack's lips twitched. 'You know you want to see Lucy Beresford's reaction to the house.'

Kate laughed unwillingly. 'True. All right, Jack,' she said, resigned, and looked at him squarely. 'I apologise.'

'For what, exactly?'

'For being late with my no. It won't happen again.'

'Next time you'll say yes?'

'There's never going to be a yes, Jack,' she said with such emphasis his eyes narrowed.

They stared into hers for a long, tense interval, then he shrugged. 'Never say never, Kate.' He smiled suddenly.

'What now?'

'Did your aunt sleep alone in that erotic bed?'

'As far as I know, she did.' Kate grinned. 'Though, somehow, I never thought of her as my *maiden* aunt.'

'You think she had lovers?'

'She was in the army in the Second World War, so she probably had more than one. And she worked in London as some tycoon's right hand for years afterwards. She bought this house with money he left her in his will, so maybe their relationship was closer than she let on. Apparently my father was surprised that she chose to come back here to live.'

'Obviously a family trait,' said Jack dryly, and took Kate's hand with the care of someone handling a stick of gelignite. 'Are we on track again? If friendship's the only thing on offer, I'll settle for it. But I won't lie to you, Kate. I want more than that.'

'That's all there is, Jack,' she said flatly.

'The chemistry's still there,' he pointed out, and released her hand. 'You felt it just as much as I did before something put on the brakes. So I repeat. Never say never.'

CHAPTER SEVEN

KATE had fully intended taking Saturday off to get in the mood for Jack's dinner party. Instead she went on with her painting with the radio turned up high, trying to drag her mind away from the few brief, heated moments that had given her such a frustrated, restless night. She was the guilty one—or the stupid one. It was herself she'd been fighting, not Jack. For one desperate moment she'd wanted to pull him down on the bed and make love with him until the world went away.

Her face set in determined lines as she put her painting paraphernalia away later. The solution was simple. If she was never alone with Jack again it couldn't happen. But that would mean no more impromptu suppers. Her shoulders sagged. It had been so good to spend time with him again and just talk. Quite apart from the unique physical chemistry between them, Jack had once been the best friend she'd ever had. She'd been madly in love with him, but she'd also liked him better than any man she'd met before or since. The loss of friend as well as lover had made the pain and disillusion even harder to bear when it all ended in tears.

The doorbell rang just as Kate was about to go upstairs for a bath. She opened the door to find a young woman proffering a flower arrangement.

'Kate Durant?' she asked. 'These are for you.'

'Thank you,' said Kate, surprised, and hurried inside to read the card attached to the basket.

'For Katie,' said the message.

Kate blinked hard as she looked at the delicate blend of freesias and miniature tulips. She set the basket of flowers on the table in the sitting room and stood back to admire, her new resolution wavering already. The subtle colours blended so perfectly with the room—Jack had obviously chosen them personally. Afraid to trust her voice she thanked him via a text message.

'We were going to offer to come and pick you up tonight,' Anna rang later to inform her. 'But it occurred to me that you'd rather drive yourself. You might—' cough '—want to stay on for a bit after we've gone home.'

'I very much doubt that, but there's no point in coming miles out of your way to collect me,' said Kate tartly. 'I'll drive myself.'

'You sound a bit snappy!'

'Sorry, sorry. I've just finished the last wall in the dining room and I'm a bit tired.'

'For heaven's sake, Kate,' said Anna in exasperation, 'surely you could have taken the day off today of all days! No wonder you sound on edge.'

'Why should I be on edge?'

'I assume that it's dinner for six tonight?'

'I think so.'

'Then Lucy Beresford—the biggest gossip in town—will take it for granted that you and Jack are, or are intending to be, a couple too.'

'Oh, God! I hadn't thought of that.'

'Well, I had. Have you seen Jack lately?'

'We shared a Chinese here last night.'

'Does this mean you're getting back with him, then?' Anna demanded.

'No. At least not in the way you mean.'

'Pity. Now tell me what you're wearing so we don't clash.'

Kate had signed on with a doctor, and even with Anna's dentist, but had never made it to a hairdresser. She wished she had, later, when her hair refused to behave. Her intention had been a sleek, sophisticated knot to wear with her sleek, sophisticated suit, but her slippery hair refused to stay up, and after a while she gave in and left it loose. But when she viewed the overall effect with the suit she wasn't unhappy. No cleavage or anything clinging tonight, not even jewellery, other than her gold watch. The mannish tailoring of her black velvet trousers and jacket was softened only by the gleam of a white silk camisole. And, because the weather was no more in party mood than she was, Kate pulled knee-length black boots over the velvet trousers to protect them from the pouring rain, belted on her trench coat, switched on the burglar alarm, locked the door behind her and stood under the shelter of the door pediment to aim the remote at her little two-seater.

When Kate reached Mill House the door was standing open and Jack, wearing a more casual suit than usual, came to meet her with a golf umbrella.

'Hi,' she said brightly. 'What a night! Am I the first?'

'Yes. Come and talk to Bran before I banish him to the boot room.'

'Hold on, I'm just collecting my shoes.'

When she slid from the car Jack shouted, 'Sit,' to the retriever as he came bounding towards her in welcome, and Kate bent to scratch Bran's ear, full of admiration when he obeyed his master instead of jumping all over her as he obviously wanted to.

'You are so gorgeous,' she told him, and Jack laughed.

'Just like his master.'

'You wish!'

The dog trotted happily beside them as they went inside. In the small outer hall Kate exchanged her boots for the silver-heeled black silk shoes and handed her coat to Jack, her eyebrows raised when he stood looking at her in silence.

'You don't approve?' she demanded. 'Should I have worn a dress?'

'You look sensational and you know it,' he said gruffly. 'Your hair looks hellish sexy like that with the tailored suit.'

'I wasn't aiming for sexy,' she protested.

'Then God help me when you do!'

'Did you get my message about the flowers, Jack?' she said hastily. 'They were lovely. Thank you.'

'I aim to please.' He clicked his fingers to the dog. 'I'll hang your coat in the boot room. Come and meet Molly.'

Two women turned round from the range, smiling, as Jack led Kate into the kitchen.

'Ladies, this is my friend, Kate Durant,' he announced.

'I'm Molly Carter,' said the young one, surprising Kate. 'This is my mum, Hazel. She's helping out tonight.'

'Nice to meet you,' said Hazel, a neat figure in a white lawn apron over a black dress. 'I'm just the help. Molly does the cooking.'

'And it's wonderful,' Kate assured her. 'I tasted some of it the other night!'

Molly smiled, pleased. Small and sturdy in jeans and vast white apron, with blonde hair in a braid down her back, she was much younger than Kate had expected. 'I hope you like the menu for tonight. It's simple because the boss thought it best not to be too adventurous, but I hope it will suit everybody.'

'No doubt about that,' Kate assured her, as Jack came back from exiling Bran.

'Right then, Kate,' he said briskly. 'Let's have a drink before the others arrive. Any bits and pieces, Molly?'

'Cold ones on the coffee table, Boss, hot ones to follow when the others arrive,' she informed him, and went back to stirring something in a saucepan.

Kate followed Jack to the main room and stopped in her tracks. Spring flowers in a shallow creamware bowl sat between the promised dishes of canapés on the big rosewood table, but the sight that brought a smile to her face was the pile of large suede cushions stacked either end of the sofa.

Jack's lips twitched. 'Forster isn't the only one who can

take advice,' he said smugly. 'You mentioned something about cushions and a flower arrangement, I believe?'

She gave a snort of laughter. 'I wasn't *serious*, Jack!'

'Now she tells me. What do you think? The official colours, I was informed, are caramel and mocha.'

'You bought them here in town?'

He nodded as he removed the cork from a bottle of champagne. 'And I ordered the flowers the same time as yours, but Molly did the arranging.'

'Your Molly's quite a star, isn't she? But she looks so young!'

'After catering college she couldn't find a job which paid enough, so she answered my advertisement. She's saving to open a place of her own one day.' Jack filled two glasses and handed one to Kate.

'Then I hope you pay her well!'

'I do. And will pay more like a shot if someone tries to steal her from me.' He touched his glass to hers. 'Let's drink a toast to my first dinner party.'

'I've eaten dinner here before,' she reminded him.

'That was just family supper with Dad. Tonight's entertainment is more ambitious—a first at Mill House.'

'Why now?'

Jack shrugged. 'I decided it was time to repay hospitality at home.'

'You may regret it,' Kate said ruefully. 'After tonight, according to Anna, Lucy Beresford will be convinced we're a couple.'

'Don't worry,' he said casually. 'At the Maitland party I told her that we'd known each other in the past. As far as she's concerned, I've merely invited an old friend to make up the numbers.'

'Thanks a lot!' Kate chuckled. 'More flattery like that and I'll get above myself.'

Jack grinned and offered her the canapés. 'Lucy needn't know your support was vital to calm my nerves.'

'Nerves, my foot!' Kate bit into a delicious combination of shrimp and meltingly light pastry. 'Yum, these are delicious! Molly made them herself, of course?'

'As you say, she's a star—and, don't worry, I'm paying her a bonus; Hazel, too.' Jack looked at his watch. 'The others should be here any minute.'

'Let's wander into the hall, then. My sole reason for being here is to see the reaction when your guests arrive.'

'Is that true, Kate?'

She sipped some of her drink and threw a smile at him over her shoulder as she strolled across the hall to the fireplace to look up at the portrait. 'No, of course not.'

He followed her and stood so close she felt his breath on her neck. 'Am I forgiven for last night, Katie?'

'No forgiveness necessary or required, Jack.' She turned to smile at him as tyres crunched wetly outside. 'Show time.'

A peal on the doorbell brought muffled barking from Bran in the boot room as Jack went to admit his remaining guests, Hazel following to collect umbrellas and raincoats. 'Good evening, everyone,' Kate heard him say. 'Welcome to Mill House.'

The Beresfords came in first, George balding and fifty-something with twinkling eyes, his wife forty going on eighteen in a pink prom dress. Lucy's eyes widened as she took in her surroundings, then narrowed in swift speculation when she saw Kate standing near the fireplace.

'How nice to see you again,' she said, rushing to join her. 'Isn't this the most marvellous house? What a romantic drive-way, Jack.'

Kate said the appropriate things and turned to kiss Anna. 'You look ravishing in your new blue, Mrs Maitland.'

'Thanks, friend. Clever of you to wear black with this background,' Anna murmured. 'What a place!'

Ben came to kiss Kate and Jack ushered them all into the main room, avoiding Kate's eyes as Lucy went into more high-decibel raptures. Jack provided champagne; Hazel came in with a platter of hot canapés and Kate stood with George near the fireplace, answering questions about the house she'd inherited.

'I've been dying to see *your* house.' Anna smiled demurely at Jack. 'Kate's told me so much about it.'

Lucy glanced across at Kate, sharp-eyed. 'You've been here before?'

'My father knew Kate when she lived here in the town as a child,' said Jack blandly. 'He insisted I invited her to kitchen supper to talk about old times.'

Anna choked on a mouthful of pastry and Ben proffered a napkin.

'Steady the buffs,' he murmured, smiling at Kate.

Conversation grew general with the second glass of champagne, and by the time Hazel returned to announce dinner Jack Logan's first guests at Mill House were in mellow mood.

The dining room was smaller and more intimate than the main room, but Jack had kept to his white theme for the walls, with a large pencil drawing of Bran as the only artwork. The furniture was modern and very plain, the table set with white porcelain and gleaming crystal, which reflected flames from thick white candles in heavy glass holders. Once everyone was seated, Hazel came in to offer a choice of lobster ravioli or pears with Stilton for the first course.

'Molly thought the lobster might not suit everyone,' said Jack, smiling. 'Being a mere male such things never occurred to me.'

'You need a woman in your life, Jack,' said Lucy, and gazed at her husband in wide-eyed innocence when he frowned at her.

'Anna says you've finished your decorating, Kate,' said Ben swiftly.

'I certainly have.' She smiled at him. 'My garden's the next thing on the agenda.'

'You're so self-sufficient!' exclaimed Lucy. 'Anna tells me you've painted your entire house yourself. Amazing. I wouldn't know where to start. Did you go on a course?'

'No, I just cheated a bit. I had the ceilings, cornices and gloss paint done by a professional before I moved from London. He relined the walls too, ready for me to start painting. I finished the last room this very afternoon,' said Kate.

Anna smiled at her affectionately. 'Thank goodness for that. I hate the smell of paint.'

'No wonder, in your condition—' Lucy bit her lip, eyeing Ben in contrition. 'Sorry. My big mouth.'

'Not to worry,' said Ben easily, and smiled across the table at his wife. 'This is as good a time as any to make the announcement. We're expecting our first child in the autumn.'

Jack sprang up to shake Ben by the hand, careful to avoid Kate's eyes as he asked permission to kiss the mother-to-be. 'Congratulations. Let me give you some more champagne.'

Anna shook her head regretfully. 'I've had my quota for tonight. Mineral water from now on, please.'

It was a very animated gathering who went on to eat hot glazed ham with spinach soufflé, followed by simple, perfect apple pie and local cheese served with Molly's savoury biscuits. When they went back to the main room the fire had been replenished and a dish of *petit fours* placed beside a coffee tray.

'Marvellous meal,' said Anna, sitting by Kate with a sigh. 'My compliments to the chef, Jack.'

'I'll pass them on to her.' He smiled at Kate. 'If you'll pour the coffee, I'll pass the cups round. Hazel's helping Molly clear up.'

Having diligently avoided the slightest suggestion of acting as hostess up to that point, Kate had to give in about the coffee, conscious of Lucy Beresford's eyes boring into her as she filled the cups. Jack could do what he liked with the cakes, she decided, and leaned against a suede cushion beside Anna, out of range of Lucy's eagle eye. But Lucy wasn't done with her.

'I hear you have the most extraordinary job, Kate,' she said, leaning forward in her chair. 'Anna says you work from home as a virtual assistant. What on earth does that mean?'

Kate gave a brief, succinct explanation.

'She works with five clients, and doesn't make coffee for any of them,' put in Jack, picking up the plate of cakes. 'Can I tempt you, Anna?'

'Unfortunately, yes.' She sighed and chose a morsel smothered in chocolate.

Lucy did the same, but Kate shook her head, also refusing the brandy the men accepted.

'I'm driving, Jack.'

'So are you, dear,' George told his wife, who pouted girlishly, but made no protest.

'I wouldn't mind a nice little job like Kate's,' she declared, 'but George won't let me work.'

From the look on his face, Kate took it this was news to him.

'I never minded making coffee for my boss. In my opinion you just can't beat the personal touch,' Lucy went on relentlessly. 'The man I worked for was utterly devastated when I left to get married.'

'How about you, Kate?' said Ben, taking the chair nearest to her. 'Did your boss tear his hair when you resigned?'

She grinned at him. 'She paid far too much to her hairdresser to do that.'

'I'd hate to work for a woman,' said Lucy promptly.

'Kate worked *with* one, not for one,' said Anna, licking her fingers. 'She was Deputy Director of Human Resources by the time she resigned her London job.'

Lucy was silenced for a split second. 'Goodness, life must

be very different for you in a quiet town like this,' she said, regrouping.

Anna got up. 'If Kate will direct me, I need to find the ladies',' she announced.

'You'll have to ask Jack,' said Kate, smiling at her. 'I don't know where it is.'

'Really?' said Lucy, brightening. 'I'll come with you then, Anna.' She took Jack's arm, smiling up at him coquettishly as they left the room.

'You mustn't mind my wife, Kate,' said George kindly. 'She's got this boundless curiosity. She's probably nagging Jack to show her round the entire house right now.'

Kate gave him a friendly smile, and got up to take the coffee pot. 'I think I'll ask Molly for a refill. I do know where the kitchen is,' she told Ben as he opened the door for her.

Kate met Jack in the hall. 'I'm on my way to ask Molly for more coffee.'

'Good idea.' He grinned conspiratorially. 'How are you, Katie?'

'Bearing up,' she returned, rolling her eyes, and he laughed, smoothing a hand down her hair as she went on her way.

The kitchen was already tidy and the redoubtable Molly had a thermos of fresh coffee waiting to refill the silver pot.

'Mum can take it in.'

'Thank you,' said Kate gratefully. 'It was a fabulous meal, Molly,' she said as Hazel went off with the coffee. 'I hear you want to open a place of your own one day. When you do I'll be your first customer.'

'First dinner on the house then,' Molly assured her, beaming. 'You think the meal went down well tonight? I hope it wasn't too boring.'

'It was perfect. You must have seen the empty plates coming back! Mr Maitland had two helpings of everything. He said the apple pie was even better than his mother's.' Kate smiled at the sound of an imperious bark from the boot room.

'I think someone wants to say hello,' said Molly, and handed over a small dish of titbits. 'You can give Bran his treat, if you like—only mind that velvet.'

Kate received an enthusiastic greeting from Bran, who fussed over her in delight for a while, then wolfed down his goodies and went to stand pointedly at the outer door.

'You go back, Miss Durant. I'll let him out,' said Molly. 'The downstairs cloakroom is second on the right across the hall, by the way.'

Kate spent a few minutes there to marshal her forces, then went back to join the others.

'You've been a very long time,' commented Jack.

'I had a chat with Bran.'

'You were so long I poured the coffee,' said Lucy sweetly. 'Who's Bran?'

'My dog,' said Jack, and smiled as he took hairs from Kate's sleeve. 'You've been cuddling him.'

'Guilty as charged,' she said, and resumed her seat by Anna. 'How do you feel?' she said in an undertone, as Lucy fluttered round the men with the coffee pot.

'Fat,' said Anna ruefully. 'I shouldn't have eaten so much, but the food was so gorgeous I couldn't resist.'

'I relayed the praise to Molly.'

'Is Hazel her daughter?'

'Hazel is Molly's mother,' said Kate. 'How old is Molly, Jack? She looks like a schoolgirl.'

'Twenty-two and born old, according to her mother. There's a mature brain under that mane of blonde hair.'

Kate could practically see Lucy's brain ticking over. Blonde? Twenty-two?

'They say the way to a man's heart is through his stomach,' warned Lucy sharply. 'You'd better be careful, Jack. Maybe your Molly has designs on you.'

'You bet she has,' he said, unperturbed. 'She wants my backing when she opens her own restaurant.'

For the rest of the evening Jack did his best as host to keep the conversation general, but Lucy aimed barbs at Kate so often that at last George Beresford turned a look on his wife that plainly said 'enough' and she pouted and turned all her attention on Jack. Eventually Ben decided his wife looked tired and asked Lucy if she was ready to drive them home. Jack kept Kate firmly at his side while he received thanks for his hospitality. Anna and Ben kissed her goodnight, and George did the same, winning a sharp look from his wife, who kept her kissing strictly for her host. Jack stood in the open doorway as his guests hurried to the car under umbrellas, then went back inside to Kate with a sigh of relief.

'Thank you,' he said simply, running a hand through his hair.

'What for?'

'Just for being here.' He grimaced. 'I'll make sure I have a previous engagement when Lucy Beresford invites me to dinner again. I had a meal there once, purely because she wouldn't take no when I drove George home from a meeting.'

'She insisted you came to Anna's party as well,' Kate reminded him as they went back to the living room.

'For that alone I'm grateful to her,' admitted Jack, and put more logs on the fire. 'What can I give you to drink, Kate?'

'I should be going home.'

'Let's unwind for a bit first. Lucy gave you a hard time tonight. What got into the woman?'

'She resents me.' Kate kicked off her shoes to curl up in a corner of the sofa among the new cushions. 'Before Anna's party the Beresford dinner table was the only one in town you'd graced with your presence, so Lucy feels possessive where you're concerned. I'm afraid she took one look at me when she arrived tonight and jumped to the obvious conclusion. She was jealous.'

Jack groaned. 'Dammit, Kate, the woman's married to

someone I do business with, and has a couple of teenage children. Besides, I don't find her remotely attractive.'

'Maybe not, but Lucy lusts after you, Jack.'

'God!' He rubbed a hand over his chin, his eyes eloquent with distaste. 'Next time George needs a lift home I'll get him a taxi.'

'In the meantime I'll take you up on that offer of a drink. I'd like some tea.'

'You sit by the fire and I'll make it,' he said promptly.

'No, I'll come with you. I need a chat with Bran.'

'A fine thing,' said Jack as they crossed the hall, 'when a man is jealous of his own dog.'

Kate chuckled. 'He's a very handsome chap.'

Bran was wildly delighted to see them and after an interval of greeting and patting Kate perched on the table, swinging her feet, and Bran sat as near as he could get, gazing up at her in adoration.

'Just a teabag in a mug will do,' she told Jack as he filled the kettle. 'Make it strong. I need it.'

'I need something stronger than tea,' he said with feeling. 'I enjoyed my first shot at home entertaining, but next time I'll ask a different pair to make up the six.'

'You like Anna and Ben, then?'

'I do, very much. Though I get the feeling that Anna would cut my liver out with a blunt spoon if I hurt you in any way. I assume she knows our past history?'

'Afraid so.'

'Including Dawn?'

'Yes, but she won't broadcast it.'

'She doesn't have to. The story of my marriage and divorce is well known.'

'Do you mind?'

'I was young enough to mind quite at lot at first, but I got over it.' Jack turned to look at her. 'Getting over you, Kate, was a damn sight harder. And my way of coping was a hard work no play lifestyle that did wonders for the company but nothing for me socially. At least,' he added candidly, 'not until we opened the London office. But that's all in the past. From now on I'll do more entertaining at home.' He touched a hand to her cheek as he handed her the tea. 'It felt so right to see you at the other end of my table, Katie.'

She sipped carefully, trying to bypass the lump in her throat.

'Did it feel right to you?' he asked quietly.

Kate looked up into his intent eyes. 'Yes, Jack it did. But you can't expect me to play hostess every time you entertain.'

'Why not?'

'I'm not getting into that kind of arrangement with you.'

'You're afraid of what people might think?'

'I'm more concerned with what you might think, Jack.' Kate put down her half empty mug and slid off the table. 'Time I went home.'

Jack caught her by the elbow, his touch burning through the velvet. 'Stay.'

'No,' she said flatly.

'I meant long enough to drink your tea,' he said impatiently. 'Come and sit by the fire for a few minutes. Bran can come as chaperon if you like.'

'Jack, I want to go home,' she said with such vehemence that he released her and went from the room. She pushed a hand through her hair, blinking hard, and crossed the room to tear a sheet from a roll of paper kitchen towel.

'Katie!' said Jack behind her.

She buried her face in the paper towel, but he took her by the shoulders and turned her round until her face was against his shirt. Jack smoothed a hand over her hair and held her until the tears stopped He left her for a moment, then put his arms round her again.

At last she drew away and scrubbed the sodden paper over her face. 'Sorry,' she said thickly.

'So am I. I can't handle it when you cry.' Jack smoothed a strand of damp hair from her forehead. 'I've brought your things if you really must go now.'

'Right.' She sniffed inelegantly. 'Where's Bran?'

'He couldn't handle it either. I put him in the boot room.'

Kate looked up at Jack in remorse. 'Poor Bran.'

'Not poor Jack?'

'That, too—sorry about your shirt,' she added hoarsely, eyeing the mascara streaks and sodden patches on his chest.

'The shirt will wash.' Jack took her hand. 'Stay until you feel better, Kate. I'll make more tea, and we'll take Bran in by the fire until you're in good enough shape to drive home.'

'All right,' she said listlessly. 'But I'll just wash my face first.'

A few minutes later, curled up in a corner of the sofa with Bran at her feet and a fresh mug of tea steaming at her elbow, Kate felt a little better. Jack settled beside her to finish his brandy, long legs stretched out in front of him.

'I can guess why you cried,' he said quietly.

She gave him a narrowed, sidelong glance. 'Can you?'

'I could have cried myself. This was how it should have been all along, the two of us as a couple, entertaining friends to dinner. And it's how it would have been if I hadn't made such a hellish mess of things.' He turned to her in sudden urgency. 'But it could be like that in future. I want you back, Kate. I've tried to be patient, not rush things, but we've wasted so much of our lives already.'

'No!' Kate tore her eyes away from the demand in Jack's, and shook her head. 'One can't go back.'

'But you did *come* back,' he said quickly, his eyes triumphant. 'And you knew from the magazine article that I was still here.'

'Also still married, as far as I knew,' she reminded him. 'But the fact that you're single again doesn't change anything. It would be disastrous for us to get back together.'

'Why?' he demanded.

'First and last and most important, I have responsibility for Joanna.' Kate turned her head and met his eyes. 'And secondly, Jack, I'm not the girl who was so hopelessly in love with you all those years ago. We're both responsible adults now, so if you want me as a friend, fine. But I don't want you as a lover.'

Jack's eyes turned to steel. 'I don't believe that. Last night your body responded to me just the way it used to—until your mind slammed on the brakes.'

'That was chemistry. It doesn't mean anything. You could always make me respond, Jack.' Her mouth tightened. 'You obviously had the same effect on Dawn.'

'Which is the real obstacle,' he said harshly.

'Only one of the many.' Kate stood up. 'Time I went home. Where did you put my boots?'

'In the kitchen. I'll fetch them.'

Kate bent to stroke the dog, blinking when she felt tears threaten again. She was tired, that was all. She'd been a fool to finish painting today after a virtually sleepless night. And, though she'd enjoyed the evening in some ways, in others it had been a strain, due partly to Lucy Beresford and her sniping, but not entirely. Jack was right. At the dinner table she *had* felt regret for what might have been. She sighed, and as though tuned in to her mood, Bran got up to push his head against her thigh in comfort.

When Jack returned he waited in silence while she changed her shoes, then held her raincoat for her and went through the hall to open the main door. He frowned at the sheeting rain, but before he could put up the golf umbrella his phone rang, and he closed the door on the deluge to answer it.

'No, Ben, she was just leaving.' He listened intently for a moment, looking at Kate. 'Sounds bad. I'll hand you over. You'd better tell her yourself.'

Kate snatched the phone from him. 'Ben! Is something wrong with Anna?'

'No, love, nothing like that. She's worried to death about *you*. Thank God you haven't left yet. The roads are flooded pretty much all the way from Mill House into town. We only just made it home in George's Range Rover, so you wouldn't have a hope in your car—' He broke off. 'Hang on, Kate, Anna wants a word.'

'Tell Jack either he must drive you or you stay the night,' said Anna fiercely. 'Don't even think of trying to drive yourself. Lucy had hysterics when we hit the first flood water, so I had to take over.'

'But you're pregnant!'

'There were loads of police about and the men were over the limit, so there was no choice. It was a slow journey, but with Ben as co-driver I was fine. But that was in a four wheel drive, Kate. Let me talk to Jack.'

'Anna—'

'No arguing; hand the phone back.'

Kate gave Jack the phone and stood watching his face as he spoke to Anna. At last he said goodnight and snapped the phone shut.

'I'm sorry, Kate. I can't drive you as I'm already over the limit.' He gave a wry shrug. 'No help for it, I'm afraid. You'll have to spend the night in my guest room.'

CHAPTER EIGHT

KATE'S first instinct was to refuse point blank. Then common sense kicked in. It was her only option. 'Thank you,' she said reluctantly. 'Sorry to be a nuisance.'

'Not at all,' said Jack politely. 'I'll show you where to sleep.' He ordered Bran to his bed, and opened the door into the hall.

In silence Kate followed him up the white-painted staircase to a room no bigger than her bedroom in Park Crescent. The furniture was plain and contemporary, and the curtains and bedcovers were white but, unlike the rest of the house, the room was painted a creamy shade of yellow.

'Attractive,' said Kate, so tired by this time she could hardly stand straight.

'Sherbet,' said Jack.

She stared at him blankly.

'You're up on paint colours, Kate. This is Sherbet.'

'Oh, right.'

'The bathroom—a very small one, is behind the door over there,' he informed her. 'I hope you sleep well.'

'Thank you.'

Jack said goodnight and closed the door and, with a sigh Kate collected some hangers from the wardrobe and went into the bathroom. It was small, as Jack warned, but wonderfully warm and fully equipped with everything a guest could need, best of all a towelling dressing gown. She undressed hurriedly and got into it, then hung her suit and camisole on the shower rail, rinsed out her underwear and arranged it on the radiator. She was squeezing toothpaste on to a brand-new toothbrush when Jack knocked on the bedroom door.

Kate opened it to find him holding out one of his white T-shirts.

'I thought you might need this.'

'Thank you. I borrowed the dressing gown,' she added unnecessarily.

'So I see. Goodnight again.'

'Goodnight, Jack.'

Kate brushed her teeth, washed her face again, and did what she could with her hair. At last, almost dizzy with nervous strain and fatigue, she turned back the bedcovers, took off the dressing gown and laid it on a chair. She pulled the big T-shirt over her head and turned off the bedside lamps, then slid thankfully into bed. Bed and breakfast after all, was her last waking thought.

She woke with a start, face wet and heart pounding at the sound of Jack's frantic voice as he shook her gently. Her eyes widened in horror as she took in her surroundings. She was downstairs in the hall and Bran was barking frantically somewhere. Oh, God, she thought. Not now, not here!

'I'm so s-sorry,' she said through chattering teeth.

Jack slid out of his dressing gown, his face haggard as he wrapped it round her. 'Put that on while I sort the dog out. Don't move an inch until I get back.'

Kate tied the cord with shaking hands and found a handkerchief in one of the dressing gown pockets. She mopped her face and had composed herself slightly by the time Jack came back.

'I left my bedroom door ajar, which is why I heard you crying,' he said grimly. 'You scared the hell out of me when I found you halfway down the stairs. But when you looked right through me my hair really stood on end. Tears were streaming down your face but your eyes were totally blank. Once I realised you were sleepwalking I was afraid to wake you, so I went down beside you, step by step, ready to grab you if you fell.'

'I never fall,' she said hoarsely.

Jack's eyes narrowed. 'You do this often?'

'Occasionally, in times of stress.' She shrugged. 'It's my own fault. I hardly slept last night after—after you left, and then I worked all day to finish painting. I was tired even before I arrived. Lucy was bitchy, and I got uptight with you over times past and on top of that I couldn't go home because of the floods and—' She hesitated, biting her lip.

'And the final straw was spending the night in Bluebeard's castle. So in your subconscious you tried to escape,' said Jack grimly.

She shook her head. 'It's nothing to do with this house, Jack, or escape.'

'When did the sleepwalking start?'

'Ages ago. But by the time I moved in with Anna I was more or less over it.'

His face hardened into bitter lines. 'But one hour in bed in *my* house and you wanted out.'

Kate's teeth began to chatter, and Jack's eyes darkened with contrition. 'You're freezing. I'll get you back to bed, then make you some more tea. Give me your hand.'

She let him lead her up the stairs, feeling contrite herself when she realised that Jack's only garment was a pair of boxers. 'You must be cold, too.'

'Only with fright.' He took in a deep breath. 'Once my pulse rate drops below a hundred again I'll be fine.'

When they reached the spare room Jack switched on the light and stared at the bed. The quilt and pillows were on the floor, the fitted bottom sheets snarled in a crumpled heap, and he swore under his breath when he picked up the pillows.

'When you cry you really cry. These are damp.' He turned to her and undid the dressing gown to touch the T-shirt. 'Hell, this is, too. I'll bring you another one with the clean sheets—' He stopped suddenly and shot her a look. 'Are you likely to do this again tonight?'

'I don't *know*,' she said miserably.

'Have you done any sleepwalking in Park Crescent?'

'No.' Not yet.

He looked at her searchingly. 'Did it start when we broke up? Is that why you won't let me get close again?'

'Part of it.' She shrugged. 'Stress acts in different ways on different people—migraine, anxiety attacks and so on. In my case it's sleepwalking. But I hadn't done it for years until Liz and Robert were killed. Then I had the row with Rupert and it happened again.'

'And I caused this tonight by pestering you to come back to me,' Jack said harshly. He picked up the towelling dressing gown and held it out. 'Go in the bathroom and put this on while I strip the bed. You need sleep.'

Kate splashed cold water on her swollen eyes, then went back into the bedroom.

Jack looked up from the linen he was bundling together, his eyes strained. 'I hope to God you don't go walkabout again.'

'If I could promise not to, I would,' she said unhappily. 'I hate doing it, Jack. Waking up somewhere else is pretty scary, believe me.'

'I do.' He stood very still, every muscle in his bare chest taut, then pulled on the dressing gown and tied the cord with unnecessary force. 'There's a remedy. For tonight, at least.'

'Knockout drops?' she said, trying to smile.

'No.' Jack eyed her in appeal. 'Look, Kate, I make this offer with the best of intentions, so don't panic. Come and sleep in my room. That way we might both get some sleep. At least I'd know if you took off again.' He smiled a little. 'I promise faithfully to keep to my side of the bed. It's big enough to sleep four at a pinch, so no problem with over-crowding.'

Not trusting her voice, she nodded slowly in assent.

The master bedroom was at the other end of the upper

corridor and the bed was vast, as Jack had promised. He turned back the covers on the far side, told her to get in, then searched in a chest between the tall windows. He tossed a thick white sweatshirt on the bed for her, then made for the door.

'Where are you going?' she demanded.

'To make you that tea. You're shivering, Kate. For God's sake, get into bed and try to get warm.'

Kate took off the dressing gown, pulled on the warm fleecy shirt, and slid under the covers, teeth chattering. This was probably a big mistake, but it was better than waking up in some other part of the house again, scaring Jack and waking Bran into the bargain.

Jack came back with a tray and put it on the chest. He ordered Kate to sit up, propped pillows behind her and then brought her a mug of tea. 'I added a spoonful of something medicinal,' he told her. 'We need it.'

'Thank you,' she said, subdued, and sipped gratefully, feeling the warmth spread through her as the brandy and scalding tea did their work. When Jack slid in beside her with his own drink she shot him a rueful glance. 'One way and another, you won't forget your first official dinner party.'

'True.' He grinned suddenly. 'If Lucy Beresford could only see us now!'

'She'd be wild with jealousy.'

'But certainly wouldn't picture us drinking tea together! You'd better look out, Kate. I think she's also jealous of your relationship with Anna Maitland,' he warned.

She pulled a face. 'I'll watch my back on two counts, then.'

'If she gives you any trouble, let me know,' said Jack grimly. 'I'll get George to sort her out. He may look easy-going but there's steel underneath that sense of humour.'

'I saw that for myself. I like him.'

'You like Ben Maitland, too.'

'I do. From the first day Anna introduced me to him I felt

I'd known him all my life,' Kate explained. 'And he's great with Joanna. She adores them both, and she's thrilled to bits about the baby.'

'Ben's a lucky man,' said Jack, and took her mug away. 'Time you went to sleep, Kate.'

'It seems hardly worth it.'

'A couple of hours' rest would do you good, so I'm putting out the light.'

'Goodnight then, Jack. And thank you.'

'No thanks necessary. Now give me your hand and try to relax.'

Kate did as he said and slid down in the bed, smiling when she found there was almost a foot of space between them. But the hard, warm grasp of Jack's outstretched hand gave her such a sense of security she felt herself relax, muscle by muscle, as she slid into mercifully dreamless sleep.

CHAPTER NINE

KATE woke slowly to pale daylight filtering below the Roman blinds and the discovery that Jack was close against her, his arm heavy on her waist. At some point in the night he'd moved close, holding her spoon fashion. She could feel his breath on her neck and kept perfectly still until a slight movement told her Jack was awake. She smiled to herself. It was a new experience to wake up with him like this. In their youth their sessions in bed had been all too brief, and never overnight.

'I know you're not asleep,' he whispered, and moved away to leave space between them. She turned over, smiling as she faced him, and he brushed a stray lock of hair back from her forehead. 'We've never woken up together before, Katie.'

'I was just thinking that.'

His eyes held hers. Seen at this range in the morning light, she could make out little flecks of silver in the dark-rimmed grey irises. 'I've never done this with anyone else, either,' he said casually.

Kate's eyebrows shot up. 'You must have done!'

He shook his head. 'During various encounters over the years I never stayed the night.'

'You're forgetting Dawn.'

'As if either of us could ever do that!' he retorted. 'Just for the record, when we were married Dawn and I didn't sleep together.'

Kate stared in disbelief. 'If she was expecting your child you must have done some time!'

'Before the wedding our few encounters were brief and to the point,' he said with brutal frankness. 'Dawn's room was

113

over the garage block at the pub. It had a separate entrance via a fire escape. She began asking me up there for coffee after her shift at the bar, but at first I politely declined. Then one night I felt so damn miserable I caved in. But I never stayed until her father closed the pub, let alone the night.'

Kate eyed him curiously. 'And after you were married?'

Jack's mouth turned down. 'The bride felt so ill at the register office she couldn't cope with the meal her mother had organised. Only Dad and her parents were there, so as soon as the knot was tied the newlyweds went straight to the flat in Gloucester Road and Dawn went to bed. I spent the afternoon doing paperwork, and my wedding night watching television on the sofa in the sitting room. Next day I bought a bed for the spare room and slept there from then on.'

'Was she unwell all the time then?'

'Pretty much. Her mother was a godsend. She came in every day, did laundry and housework and left meals for me. I went back to the flat in time for dinner every evening, but I ate alone because Dawn couldn't stand the sight of food. I sat with her afterwards, but—' He paused, rubbing his chin. 'To be blunt, conversation was an uphill struggle at the best of times, so we just sat staring at the television, or I made paperwork an excuse and escaped to the spare room. Then one night she woke in pain, and I rushed her off to hospital. You know the rest.' Jack kissed Kate's nose and slid out of bed. 'I'm hungry. Stay there and I'll bring you some breakfast.'

'Certainly not, I'll come down!'

Jack pushed her gently against the pillows. 'Rest for a bit, you look tired. I'll throw Bran out and then bring up a tray. Humour me, Kate.' He pulled up the blinds, collected some clothes and went into the bathroom. When he emerged in a heavy sweater and workmanlike cords, he was a little heavy around the eyes but otherwise looked none the worse for his disturbed night.

'Ten minutes,' he promised.

When the door closed behind him Kate made a dash for the bathroom. Longing to take a shower, she contented herself with washing her face and rubbing toothpaste over her teeth with her finger. She rinsed with cold water, borrowed Jack's comb then tidied the bed. She got into it and leaned back against stacked pillows as she noted every detail of the masculine room, which held no clutter of any kind other than a few books on the bedside tables. Except for the two antique chests, Jack had obviously bought his bedroom furniture from the same source as everything else in the house.

Jack arrived soon afterwards with a tray he set down on the low chest at the foot of the bed. He handed her a glass of orange juice, then gave her a fork and a linen napkin and put a large serving plate between them on the bed.

'Heavens, Jack,' she said, eyeing the pile of toast surrounding a big mound of scrambled eggs. 'I can't eat all this.'

'Good, because half of it is for me. No room for individual plates on the tray. Don't worry,' he said, grinning. 'I've got my own fork.'

Kate chuckled, and asked about the furniture when Jack sat beside her with the plate between them.

'The firm concentrates on quality rather than mass production and made everything individually to my specifications. After their coverage in the article the orders came flooding in, so we're all happy,' said Jack. 'I believe in patronising local tradesmen. Come on, eat up,' he added, 'you're lagging behind.'

When the plate was empty Jack got up and filled two mugs, then returned to his place on the bed.

'I made the coffee while Bran was out doing the necessary, then decanted it into Molly's insulated jug. I like my coffee red-hot.'

'I remember,' said Kate, sipping cautiously.

Jack leaned back at the foot of the bed, eyeing her in wry

amusement. 'I've thought of having you in this bed right from the moment we met up again, Kate, but never in quite these circumstances.'

'I bet,' she said dryly, and smiled. 'But this is nice, just the same, Jack.'

'It is,' he agreed. 'Friendship with you isn't really such hard work.'

'Even after the fright I gave you last night?'

He frowned. 'What happens when you sleepwalk in Park Crescent?'

'I haven't so far.'

'How do you know?'

Kate drank some of her coffee. 'For obvious reasons I'm always barefoot when I wander. If my feet are clean when I wake up I'm in the clear. And, contrary to belief, sleepwalkers don't drift round like ghosts; they knock things over and bump into furniture. So if everything's in its place I know I've stayed in bed all night. Besides,' she added, 'even if I found the key and unbolted the front door in my sleep I'd wake up pretty quickly when the alarm went off.'

'True.' Jack looked relieved. 'You've had that kind of se-curity everywhere you've lived?'

Kate nodded soberly. 'Robert installed it in their place, and I had it done in Anna's flat when I moved there. David's loft was already like a fortress, so no problem, but I did the nec-essary when I went to live alone in Notting Hill, and again before I moved into Park Crescent.'

Jack looked thoughtful as he finished his coffee. 'You might not get out of the actual house there, but those stairs are hellish steep. You could fall and break something—like your neck.'

Kate shook her head. 'There were stairs in the Sutton household, but I stayed in one piece.'

'How often did it happen there?'

Her eyes dropped. 'More than I liked. As you can appreciate, it was a bad time for me when I was first living with them in London. But it only happened once after I moved into Anna's flat.'

'Did she know about it beforehand?'

'Of course. I had to tell her that when I applied to share. But Anna wasn't fazed. Her brother was captain of the first eleven at his school and used to walk in his sleep before important cricket matches. He'd get out of bed in the dormitory with his bat, and shape up to an invisible wicket.'

Jack grinned. 'That must have been fun for his mates.'

'Apparently they just bowled a few balls to him and he went back to bed.'

'You're making that up!'

'I'm not. Nick Travers told me that himself.'

Jack chuckled as he put their mugs on the tray, then shot her a questioning look. 'Are you having lunch with the Maitlands today?'

Kate shook her head. 'I'm having supper with them during the week instead.'

He looked at her speculatively. 'And you've finished your painting, so what are you going to do today?'

She shrugged. 'Nothing much.'

'Then you can do that here with me, Kate.'

'I'll have to if the floodwater hasn't gone down,' she reminded him.

'So you will,' he said with satisfaction. 'Until I'm sure it's safe for you to drive, you're my captive. We can share leftovers for lunch.' He smiled. 'It's a fine day, so we could take Bran for a walk first to work up an appetite.'

'All right, you've persuaded me.' Kate had intended to say yes right from the start, but Jack didn't have to know that. 'May I have a shower, please?'

'Of course. I'll make more coffee when you come down.'

Kate hurried to the pretty spare room, gathered up the sheets and removed the covers from the duvet and pillows and folded everything into a neat pile. After her shower she put on Jack's sweatshirt in preference to her thin camisole, pulled on her boots, used a lipstick, dragged a comb through her hair and hurried down to the kitchen with the bundle of laundry.

Bran came to meet her in such joyous welcome she scratched his ears and dropped a kiss on his head.

'How about me?' asked Jack.

Kate grinned. 'You want me to scratch *your* ears?'

'I meant the kiss.'

'OK. Bend down, then.'

Jack bent his head and Kate stood on tiptoe to kiss his cheek.

'Is that the best you can do?' he demanded.

'Bran didn't complain.'

Jack snatched the bundle from her, dumped it on the floor and pulled her into his arms to kiss her squarely on her protesting mouth, while the dog frisked round them, obviously thinking it was some kind of game. 'I like *that* kind of kiss,' Jack informed her as he let her go.

'I'll make a note of it,' Kate said breathlessly, and tore a sheet from the roll of kitchen paper. 'Here, lose the lipstick. That shade just isn't you.'

Jack grinned and scrubbed at his mouth. 'Come and sit down. I've made coffee.'

'I'll deal with this lot first. Where's your washing machine?'

'Leave it. Molly will do it.'

'Certainly not, I will,' Kate said firmly. 'And if you show me where you keep your spare bed linen I'll make the bed, too.'

'You never used to be so bossy,' he complained, and took the laundry into the boot room, which was fitted with every conceivable aid for washing, drying and ironing, along with a refrigerator and vast freezer, and floor to ceiling cupboards for food storage.

Kate smiled as she saw the small folding stepladder near the tall cupboards. 'That's for Molly, I assume. This is very impressive, Jack, but why a boot room?'

'This end of the house contained the actual living quarters for the mill owner, with a scullery here where the boots were cleaned by the boy employed for the job.'

Once the washing machine was in action Jack insisted Kate had some coffee before she put clean linen on the spare bed.

He perched on the corner of the table, one foot swinging. 'In fact, I've got a better idea. I've started the fire in the living room and even tidied up a bit, so you can lie on the sofa there and read the Sunday papers with Bran while *I* do the bed.'

She smiled warmly. 'An offer I can't refuse! Thank you, Jack.'

In the morning sunshine, with flames leaping in the fire-place and two brand-new paperback novels placed beside the Sunday papers on the rosewood table, the living room looked very inviting. Bran deserted Kate instantly to lie on the rug in front of the fire, and she added more logs, bent to stroke the dog, and then curled up in a corner of the sofa. She read a few headlines in the papers but, unable to resist any longer, picked up one of the books, a thriller she'd intended to buy the moment it was out in the bookshops.

The story was riveting from the first page. But almost at once the warmth of the fire combined with her disturbed night to add weight to her eyelids and soon she put the book down and lay back against the new cushions. She stirred to the touch of familiar lips on hers and her mouth curved in response as her eyes opened on a look in Jack's which turned her heart over. He stretched out beside her and caught her close, and Kate felt his heart hammer against her as his mouth crushed hers in a kiss that went on and on until neither could breathe and his lips left hers to cover her face and throat with kisses as he slid his hands up her ribs. He pushed the sweatshirt up until his lips found her breasts and she gave a low, gasping moan as he held her in an embrace that threatened to crush her ribs.

'When I woke up this morning,' he said hoarsely, 'I wanted this so much I could barely breathe.'

'I wanted it too,' she said huskily, and buried her face against his neck.

'I wish I'd known that.' He turned her face up to his. 'Tell me about your dream last night. What sent you running head-long down the stairs?'

'As usual I was looking for you, but never finding you.' She put a hand to his cheek. 'I didn't need much persuasion to sleep in your bed. I wanted to break my dream.'

Jack sat up and pulled her up with him in the crook of his arm. 'If I helped with that I think I deserve a reward.'

'You want me to put on lunch?'

'I'm hungry for you, not lunch. Come back to bed with me.'

'How about Bran?'

'He can stay in his own bed.' Jack got up and held out his hand, a look of such blazing relief in his eyes when she grasped it, she hugged him close when he pulled her to her feet.

I want this so much, Kate thought as they went upstairs together. I need it to make up for all those times when I searched for Jack in my dreams and could never find him.

'If I were the hero in a romance,' Jack said huskily, 'I would have swept you up and carried you up to bed, but it's a fair trip from the living room up the stairs. But,' he added, picking her up once they reached the top corridor, 'I can man-age it from here.'

Kate gave a breathless laugh as he strode the short distance to his room. Once inside he kicked the door shut, kissed her until she was even more breathless, and laid her on the bed.

'I've never stopped loving you, Kate,' he said, leaning over her. 'You may find that hard to believe, but it's the truth.'

'Is it, Jack?' she said quietly. 'There were long years when my feelings for you were more like hate.'

'I don't blame you.' He stretched out beside her and held her close, his cheek on her hair. 'I don't blame Elizabeth, either.'

Kate stiffened and turned in his arms. 'Liz? What do you mean?'

'She never told you, then.'

'Told me what?'

'I went to London to see you the minute my divorce was final. Your sister had already moved to a different house by then, but I persuaded the new owners to let me have the Suttons' forwarding address and went straight there.' Jack laid his forehead against hers, eyes closed.

'What happened, Jack?'

'Elizabeth wouldn't let me through the door. She said you had a new job and had moved out to share a flat.' His mouth twisted. 'No matter how hard I pleaded she wouldn't give me your telephone number or tell me where you lived. She said you wanted nothing more to do with me, ever, and slammed the door in my face.'

Kate burrowed closer. 'Oh, *Jack*—she never told me.'

'It was at that point I gave up on relationships. Eventually I heard you were living with some banker in Docklands.' Jack kissed her fiercely. 'I wanted to kill him.'

Kate's eyes flashed. 'Now you know how I felt about Dawn—and you.'

'You wanted to kill me?'

'Yes. Very slowly.'

'Do you still want to kill me?' he asked, and took her ear-lobe between his teeth. 'Because if you don't let me make love to you very soon you'll get your wish.'

Kate gave a smothered laugh. 'That's the last thing I want, Jack.'

He pulled her closer. 'What do you want then, my darling?'

Instead of words Kate gave him a slow, explicit smile which won her a kiss she responded to with such fervour he lifted her from the bed and stood her on her feet to undress her with unsteady hands, fighting to go slowly rather than tear off her clothes. When she was naked to the waist he began kissing his way down her throat to her breasts, lingering on nipples that rose erect and hard in response to his lips and tongue. But when he reached for her zip she shook her head.

'You too,' she ordered, and Jack began pulling off his clothes. But, before he could get naked, Kate had undressed herself and burrowed under the covers. She turned them back a little and held out her arms. 'Hold me, please.'

Jack dived under the quilt, exerting every iota of will-power he possessed to keep from pulling her beneath him and taking swift, desperate possession of her in the way he'd wanted since he first set eyes on her again. He drew in a deep, shuddering breath and closed his eyes as he kissed her gently, teasing her tongue with his and nibbling gently on her bottom lip. He pressed kisses all over her face while his hands stroked and smoothed, and gained his reward when he felt the tense, slender body begin to relax.

'No rush,' he whispered in her ear. 'I want to enjoy every little inch of you.'

Kate felt as though every bone in her body was slowly melting as Jack kissed her and caressed her with a languorous lack of haste that made her impatient at last for the heat and hunger she'd seen in his eyes before she dived into bed. But at last his caresses grew more urgent, his lips and tongue and grazing teeth sending fiery sensation from the tips of her breasts to the part which melted in hot liquid response deep down inside her. She thrust her hips against him and felt a surge of triumph as his breath caught and his muscles grew taught under the hands she dug into his shoulders. She gave a husky little moan as his caressing fingers slid between her thighs to find the small, hidden bud that rose, tumescent, to the caresses which sent her wild with almost unbearable pleasure, and in answer to her gasped, broken pleading he nudged her thighs apart with his knee. He raised his head and their eyes met and held as he took slow, sure possession of her at last. They stayed as still as their rapid breathing allowed for a moment, then began to move together, savouring every last nuance of sensation as he slid home and withdrew, then repeated the process a little faster and harder each time, their mutual fire stoked higher and higher with every stroke until the rhythm of their loving rose to frenzy and at last the climax engulfed them in heart-stopping release.

'We never achieved that in the past,' Kate whispered a long time later.

Jack raised the face he'd buried in her hair and lifted an eyebrow. 'That?' he inquired. 'A small word for a mind altering experience.'

She chuckled. 'I meant the timing. We were sometimes out of step back then.'

'You mean I was so hot for you I sometimes lost control,' he said wryly. 'I felt the same this time. It took every scrap of will-power I possessed to keep from ravishing you the moment I laid you on the bed.'

'Ravishing is good,' she assured him. 'A woman likes to know she's desirable.' Kate's eyes clouded. 'It was a long time before I felt even passably attractive after you left me for Dawn.'

He winced, and moved away a fraction. 'I suppose this banker of yours helped with that.'

'Yes, he did. But it was never like this with David.' Kate looked at him steadily. 'Nor with anyone else, Jack.'

He pulled her back into his arms and kissed her. 'God, I've missed you, Katie.'

They lay in each other's arms for a long, quiet interval, but at last Jack kissed her again and slid out of bed.

'Let's eat,' he said, getting dressed.

'You go on down. I'll follow you in a minute.'

He grinned as he collected her clothes. 'I've watched you dress before.'

'But not lately and not today.' Kate pulled the quilt up to her chin.

Jack gave her a threatening look as he strolled to the door. 'Ten minutes or I come and get you.'

Once the door closed behind him Kate slid out of bed, picked up her clothes and raced into the bathroom. Ten minutes later she met Jack in the hall.

'I was just coming to look for you.'

Kate patted her midriff. 'I'm hungry. I didn't think I would be after that huge breakfast, but I am.'

Jack grinned. 'Making love always did give you an appetite. You were so skinny in those days it always amazed me that you ate as much as I did—more sometimes.'

'Lucky metabolism.'

Bran came wagging in joyful greeting as they went into the kitchen. Kate made a big fuss of him, then inspected the kitchen table with approval. Jack had put out the remains of the ham with a bowl of ripe red tomatoes, a loaf of Molly's wholemeal bread and the platter of cheese from the night before.

'I gave Bran one of his treats to celebrate,' said Jack as he began to carve the ham.

'Celebrate what?' said Kate innocently.

He gave her a look which curled her toes. 'You know damn well!'

Kate enjoyed the meal far more than the dinner of the evening before. They brought each other up to date on their taste in books, Jack reported on the progress of his current project and Kate talked about her clients and the trip she was making the following weekend to see Joanna.

When her phone rang Kate touched a finger to her lips and showed Jack the identity of her caller as she went out into the hall. 'Hi, Anna.'

'Did Jack drive you home last night?'

'No. I stayed the night in his guest room.'

'Thank goodness for that. I was worried sick. Look, I must apologise for Lucy. She was an absolute cow to you last night.'

'Not your fault. She's obviously got a great big crush on Jack.'

'I didn't realise just how great big it was. She was so cock-a-hoop about being invited, but then she found you in possession, stunning in your black velvet against all that whiteness, and Lucy was jealous as hell.'

'You looked stunning yourself. But did Lucy borrow her dress from her daughter by any chance?'

'No way—Rose wouldn't be seen dead in something like that.' Anna chuckled. 'Lucy was—and is—a fan of *Sex and the City*, hence the dress and matching toenails. She owns the entire series on DVD and watches for hours when George is away.'

'That explains a lot. But I don't remember her looking like that at your party.'

'You were too stunned by meeting Jack again to notice.'

'True. But never mind Lucy; is everything all right with baby after your epic drive home last night?'

'Absolutely fine. Anxious Daddy cooked lunch today and I'm putting my feet up this afternoon.'

'Good. Keep doing that. I'll talk to you tomorrow.'

Kate turned to see Jack laughing in the doorway. 'Did you eavesdrop?'

'Every word. You were discussing Lucy Beresford's dress, I take it.'

'Guilty! Girls will be girls.' She explained about the television series which Jack, as expected, had never seen, so wasn't much the wiser.

'Are you saying she got herself up like that purely on my account?'

Kate grinned. 'It certainly wasn't on mine!'

Jack's mouth twisted in distaste. 'Even if I were fool enough to play around with the wife of a friend I like and respect, it would not be Lucy Beresford.'

'Sensible man!'

He sighed. 'But somehow I have to make that clear to the lady, and at the same time keep George as a friend.'

'Tricky,' agreed Kate.

Jack's patience suddenly ran out. 'You could help me with that.'

'How?' she said, eyes narrowed.

He took her hands in his. 'Darling, I meant to wait a while before I brought it up, but surely you can see what I'm getting at?'

'No, I can't.'

'The best way out of the dilemma is to acquire a wife of my own—you, Kate.'

She stared at him. 'Are you serious?'

'It's not the sort of thing one says as a joke! We've wasted too much of our lives apart already, so for God's sake let's get married, Kate.' He waited, his eyes darkening at her lack of response. 'I see. You obviously don't care for the idea. Should I have gone down on one knee?'

'The answer would still have been no, Jack.'

He dropped her hands, turned his back and strode into the living room to stand at the far windows, his back turned.

Kate followed as far as the fireplace. She waited quietly until he faced her, and forced herself to meet the ice in his eyes.

'Did you plan this?' he asked, in a voice so quiet and cutting she winced.

'What do you mean?'

'When you met me again, and found I was divorced,' he went on in that same deadly quiet voice, 'did you see a golden opportunity for revenge?'

'Unlike you to be melodramatic, Jack,' she said with distaste. 'Anyway, you're wrong.'

'I don't think so.' He thrust his hands in his pockets and strolled towards her, lover transformed into menacing stranger. 'The more I think about it, the more I'm convinced that you've had this in mind from the moment we met up again. String him along, play hard to get, and then show him what he's been missing. And put the cherry on top by turning him down flat when he proposes. Did that feel good, Kate?' he demanded.

She shook her head silently.

'So now what? Don't tell me you want us to be good friends!' He gave a mirthless bark of laughter. 'At this moment in time, Kate Durant, I don't feel friendly at all.'

'I can see that, and I'm sorry for it.' She turned away, unable to hold that hard, implacable gaze a moment longer. 'It's my fault. I shared your room last night because after the sleepwalking episode I was scared to stay on my own.'

'That was last night,' said Jack grimly. 'But it was broad daylight when we made love this morning. You were wide awake when we walked all the way upstairs to my bedroom, Kate. You had ample opportunity to say no along the way. So why the hell didn't you?'

She eyed him in surprise. 'Surely it's obvious. I wanted to make love with you—simple as that.'

'Why?'

'Curiosity, nostalgia, lust—take your pick. I wanted to find out if it would still be good with you.'

'And was it?' he asked casually, as though her answer was unimportant.

But Kate knew it wasn't. She could see a telltale pulse throbbing at the corner of his clenched mouth. 'It was miraculous, Jack. I told you that. Better than with anyone else. But it makes no difference. Even if you're still of the same mind…and, by the look on your face, I doubt that—I can't marry you.' She hesitated. 'We could be lovers again, though, surely?'

Jack gave her a flaying look, then bent to put more logs on the fire. 'You mean you love the sex, but you don't want me as a husband?'

'Something like that.'

He turned expressionless eyes on her. 'Did it give you a buzz to tell me that, Kate? Did it make up for your hurt when I married Dawn?'

'You have no idea how much you hurt me,' she said with sudden passion. 'One of my reasons for turning you down is to avoid similar hurt in future.'

His mouth twisted. 'A pity you didn't let me know that sooner.'

'A great pity,' she agreed.

'What are the other reasons?'

'Pretty obvious ones. When I inherited the house I found a new job, made a home here for Joanna and me—'

'And there's no room for a husband in your tidy little life,' Jack said harshly. He looked at her objectively, as though seeing her for the first time. 'When we met up again I thought you'd hardly changed at all. I was wrong. You've grown hard, Kate.'

'I prefer to think of it as mature. But I agree I'm not the malleable little girl you once knew.'

'Malleable!' He laughed again. 'That's a joke. Nothing I could do or say back then changed your mind about a job in London.'

'True. But marrying someone else by way of retaliation was a bit extreme, even for you, Jack,' she flung at him.

They looked at each other in hostile silence for a while, then Jack took the phone from his pocket, excused himself politely and went out. Kate stayed by the fire, staring down into the flames as her heartbeat gradually slowed to normal. The odd, abrupt proposal had taken her by surprise. She just hadn't seen it coming. If she had, maybe she could have deflected it somehow without alienating Jack so completely.

Jack came back into the room with Bran padding after him, and Kate bent to fondle the dog's ears to hide the sudden tears of bitter regret in her eyes.

'I rang up to check on the roads,' Jack told her, making the fire safe. 'Apparently there's a lot of surface water in places, so I'll drive you back in the Jeep. I'll have your car sent to Park Crescent in the morning.'

Kate eyed him militantly. This was the last thing she wanted. 'I'm perfectly capable of driving through a few puddles.'

'The river's broken its banks at one place. Your car is too small to cope,' he said in a tone that warned her not to argue.

'I don't want to put you out—'

'You're not. I was driving into town to see Dad, anyway. If you'll get your things I'll bring the Jeep round.'

Feeling well and truly put in her place, Kate went up to the guest room. She removed the sweatshirt, folded it neatly and left it on the bed, put on her camisole and suit jacket and went downstairs. Jack was waiting with her raincoat over his arm. He held it out, and in silence Kate put it on and belted it tightly.

'I'll just say goodbye to Bran before I go.'

'No need. He's coming with us.'

The sunshine had gone, leaving an overcast afternoon as dark as Kate's mood as Jack helped her up into the Jeep, her only consolation the welcome from Bran behind his wire screen.

When they reached the main road there were large stretches of surface water in some places. As they drew nearer the river, the water grew deeper and Kate realised that Jack had been right. Only a four wheel drive could have made the journey in safety.

'If you can't get my car back tomorrow it doesn't matter,' she told Jack. 'I can walk into town if I need anything.'

'Fine.'

And that was the sum total of their conversation until they arrived in Park Crescent. Instead of getting out right away, Jack looked at her for a long moment and she waited in foreboding, sure she wouldn't like what he had to say.

'I made a big mistake when I asked you to share my bed last night,' he said at last.

'And I made an even bigger one in agreeing.' Kate gave him a mirthless smile. 'I realise now that there was a much better solution to the sleepwalking problem. Instead of sharing your bed I should have taken Bran up to the guest room to share mine.'

'Dogs aren't allowed upstairs in Mill House,' Jack said after a pause, and got out. He came round to lift her down, and then waited while she unlocked her door and de-activated her alarm.

'Thank you for driving me home,' Kate said politely.

'My pleasure,' he said with sarcasm.

'Goodbye, Jack.' She closed the door, turned the key in the lock and rammed the bolts home hard enough for him to hear.

It was only after the Jeep moved off that she conceded that Jack had every right to be angry. Even hurt. This was the second time she'd rejected him.

As she went upstairs to change her clothes Kate felt a deep, mounting sense of guilt. For the first time in her life she had let her hormones take control. She had known, in her heart of hearts, that if she let Jack make love to her he would take it as a sign of something far more significant than mere sex. Last night, when he was smiling at her down the length of his dinner table, it was obvious that he'd taken it for granted they were back together again in every sense of the word. But she'd assumed he just wanted them to be lovers again. The idea of marriage had never occurred to her.

If only it hadn't rained so much.

Kate pulled on thick socks and jeans and a heavy sweater and tied her hair back from her tired face. She eyed her reflection with distaste. The way she looked now it was pretty amazing that Jack had wanted her at all. But their relationship had never been about looks. It was about the kind of rapport they'd shared over lunch today as much as the heat and rapture of their lovemaking earlier on. And there was no use blaming the rain. Without the flooding she wouldn't have stayed the night, it was true. But even after the upset about the sleepwalking she should still have had the strength to control her own libido in broad daylight. She scowled at herself. Normally she never noticed that she had a libido. With Jack it was different. Just one look from those silver-flecked grey eyes and every clamouring hormone she possessed ran riot.

CHAPTER TEN

THAT weekend marked a downward turn in Kate's 'tidy little life'. Her painting and decorating was finished, it was too cold to start gardening, and it was so hard to fill her free time she accepted another client. When she found her keys posted through the door and her car parked outside she wrote a polite letter of thanks to Jack, but after that had no further contact with him of any kind. And felt the lack of his forceful presence in her life just as painfully second time round as the first.

Over supper mid week Anna was agog to hear details of the sleepover at Mill House. Armed against this in advance, Kate reported that she'd slept in a guest bed and stayed for lunch next day, after which Jack had driven her home in the Jeep.

Anna sighed, disappointed. 'We thought there might have been more to it than that.'

'You did, not me,' protested Ben. 'Leave the girl alone.'

Kate blew him a kiss. 'Thanks for the "girl" bit.'

'Pity though,' said Anna with regret. 'I hoped that spending the night together would do the trick.'

'We didn't spend the night together,' Kate reminded her. At least, not all of it.

Kate was heartily glad when the weekend arrived at last and she could make for Manor House School to spend a few happy hours with Joanna. The time with her passed far too quickly, as always, and Kate was in melancholy mood after taking Jo back to school that evening. When Philip Brace intercepted her in the car park she was pleased to see him and this time, with nothing in the world to hurry home for, she accepted his offer of a drink or coffee in the nearest pub before the drive back. Philip was an interesting companion and the interlude was pleasant, but when he saw her to her car afterwards Kate thanked him rather formally for the coffee and his company.

'No doubt we'll see each other at school again some time.'

'I'll look forward to it,' he assured her, his wry smile telling her he knew exactly where she was coming from.

Kate's mood deteriorated on the journey home. There was no point in encouraging Philip Brace—or anyone else. The only man she wanted in her life was Jack Logan. And fat chance there was of that that now. She would just have to make the best of life without him. Again. Easy to decide, she thought morosely, but hard to put into practice, even though Jack could have been on another planet for all she knew until she met his father in the park one Saturday afternoon with Bran.

'What the devil happened between you two, Kate?' Tom Logan asked bluntly when the greetings were over.

Kate fondled the dog instead of meeting his eyes. 'What do you mean?'

'You know perfectly well, my girl. Jack is like a bear with a sore head these days. When I see him, that is. He's either working all the hours that God sends on several projects at once, or driving to London—sometimes there and back the same day.'

And Kate, stabbed by jealousy, could well imagine why. 'I haven't seen him, Tom.'

'Which accounts for his permanent black mood!' He sighed. 'I was so sure you two would get back together. What went wrong, Kate?'

Kate smiled into the striking Logan eyes. 'How about I tell you over coffee at my place? You never did bring Bran to visit me.'

While Bran explored the garden Kate showed her visitor

over her house, anxious for his opinion. 'What do you think of it?'

'You've done a very good job,' he assured her. 'Your aunt would be pleased. The house would sell like the proverbial hot cake if you put it on the market.'

Kate shook her head. 'Not for sale. It's mine.'

'Just like Jack and that great house of his.' Tom followed her into the kitchen to call Bran inside and sat down at the table with the dog at his feet while Kate made coffee. 'But I'll say the same to you as I said to him; bricks and mortar are poor substitutes for a loving relationship.'

'True, but they cause a lot less pain.'

Tom nodded slowly. 'I grant you that.'

'You know Jack asked me to marry him?'

'Just the bare facts. He said you refused, but he wouldn't say another word.'

Kate heaved a sigh as she brought the tray over to the table. 'I hoped we could stay friends but Jack isn't having any.'

Tom looked her in the eye. 'This is the second time you've turned Jack down, remember.'

'I know.' She looked at him in appeal. 'I hope it doesn't change things between you and me.'

'Not in the slightest, love.'

To prove it, Tom Logan stayed with Kate until Bran grew restless. 'I'd better take this chap home. Shall I give Jack a message?'

Kate shook her head sadly. 'I doubt that he'd want one.'

Later that afternoon she thought for a brief, hopeful minute or two that she was wrong when a familiar florist's van drew up outside her house. Her spirits soared when she was given a basket of spring flowers but took an instant nosedive when she read the card. The flowers were from Richard Forster. Not Jack.

'Kate, your strategy worked like a charm. With heartfelt thanks, RF.'

Too bad she couldn't think of a strategy to improve her own life, she thought grimly.

A few days later Kate drove to collect Joanna for the Easter vacation.

'I'm dying to get out of my uniform,' said Jo, as they left the school car park. 'Are we having lunch on the way?'

'Would I expect you to survive if we didn't?' Kate teased. 'But not the posh hotel today; you can make do with a burger somewhere.'

'Cool! We don't get burgers in school.'

'At those fees I should hope not.' Kate glanced sideways to see a worried frown on Jo's face. 'What's up?'

The dark eyes gazed at her anxiously. 'I know it's terribly expensive to keep me there. Can you really afford it?'

'I don't have to, love. When you were a baby Robert took out an education insurance which covered your fees right up until you leave the place.' Kate patted her hand. 'There may be a few extras along the way due to cost of living and school trips and so on, but I can cope with that.'

'Can't you take the extras out of my money?'

'If it was absolutely necessary I could, but it's not, so chill, OK?'

Joanna Sutton was at the stage where she was an adult one minute and a child the next, but the child predominated as she raced through the rooms in Park Crescent, exclaiming in delight as she went.

'My room looks great! And I love the sitting room now it's furnished. Is that the paint colour I picked?'

'It certainly is. Your Coral Porcelain turned out well.'

Jo gazed round the room in approval, then turned a determined glance on Kate. 'I've got something to say.' She paused and took a deep breath. 'The thing is, I should have said it ages ago.'

'Spit it out, then,' said Kate in alarm. 'What's wrong?'

'Nothing. I just want to say thank you,' blurted Jo. 'For taking me on, I mean.'

'Oh, Joanna! No thanks necessary,' Kate assured her, weak with relief. 'I'm only too happy to "take you on".'

'You really mean that? I've been worried. You know, because you gave up your job and sold your flat and—'

'Hey! Let's get something straight here. I was about to resign from my job anyway. And I sold the flat because I inherited this house.'

'But you only came to live in it because I didn't want to stay in London after Mum and Dad died,' Jo reminded her.

'True,' Kate agreed and smiled into the anxious elfin face. 'But it was no sacrifice. I love the house and, though I'm sorry for the tragic circumstances that made it necessary, it's a great big bonus to have you sharing it with me. OK?'

'OK.' Joanna heaved a heartfelt sigh of relief.

'Right. Now you've got that off your chest ring Grandma and tell her you're home.'

Jo made her call, and reported that her grandparents were looking forward to her visit. 'I'll try not to wear them out,' she added, grinning.

'Good. We're having supper with Anna and Ben tonight, by the way.'

Jo beamed. 'Great! Is Anna OK?'

'Blooming. She's dying to see you. Pop upstairs for a bath while I unpack for you.'

'I'm supposed to do it myself,' Jo said, pulling a face.

Kate tapped her nose. 'I won't tell if you won't! Now go.'

A minute later there was a scream of delight from upstairs and Jo came hurtling into the kitchen in her briefs and the unnecessary minuscule bra she'd asked for because all her friends had one.

'The cropped jeans and stripy top in the wardrobe,' she panted, 'I just love them, Kate—thanks. Can I wear them tonight?'

'That was my plan. Now scoot.'

Jo tore back upstairs and returned later, the gleaming hair brushed, her slender, long-legged body graceful in denims and pink and lavender top. 'Well?' she demanded, doing a twirl. 'Do I look cool or what?'

Kate blinked at the transformation from schoolgirl into something else entirely. 'I don't know about cool, but you certainly look grown up,' she said with misgiving.

Jo punched the air in delight, then stopped, the joy suddenly draining from her face.

'What now?'

'I forgot for a minute,' she whispered guiltily.

'And so you should,' said Kate with emphasis. 'Your mother and father would want that.'

'I hope so. Because I'm much better lately. I hardly cry at all. Do you?'

Kate shook her head. 'Elizabeth disapproved of tears.'

'I know! When I fell down when I was little she used to dust me off and tell me to stop making a fuss.' Jo's mouth drooped. 'But I wouldn't like her to think I didn't grieve for her—and for Daddy.'

'Darling, you'll never forget them, and you're bound to miss both of them terribly at times, but they would want you to stop grieving now and get on with your life.' Kate took her hand. 'They made me your official guardian, remember, so you know they trusted me to take care of you. And I will.'

'I know that, Kate.' Jo smiled valiantly. 'What time are we due at Anna's?'

Joanna slept late next morning, and Kate, awake early as she always seemed to be lately, got up quietly and had finished her morning's work before Jo appeared in the study doorway, yawning widely.

'Sorry I slept so long, Kate.'

'Did you enjoy your lie in?'

Jo nodded with enthusiasm, pushing the hair out of her eyes. 'But if you want me to get up earlier I will. Mum would never let me stay in bed after nine.'

Kate switched off her computer and got up. 'Let's have some brunch.'

'The thing is, Jo,' she said, when they were tucking into bacon and eggs, 'in my opinion you get enough rules and regulations in school. That doesn't mean you've got *carte blanche* to run wild at home now you've only got me to answer to, but you're definitely entitled to a lie in on your first morning.'

'Thanks, Kate. I had such a great time with Anna and Ben, but I was really tired by the time we came home,' said Jo. 'But you didn't have a long sleep, and you've been working all morning.'

'Which means we can now go out to play,' said Kate promptly. 'Anna is meeting us at two to go shopping.'

'I enjoyed that enormously,' said Anna later, while they were waiting for tea and cakes in her favourite coffee shop. 'I adore spending other people's money.'

'You spent some of your own, too,' Kate reminded her.

'Anna just had to buy the baby something,' said Jo, and smiled in satisfaction. 'We did, too.'

'Hard to resist,' agreed Kate. 'If I were any sort of god-mother-to-be I'd be knitting those cute little white things instead of buying them, but I know my limitations.'

Anna chuckled. 'You're off the hook—both grandmothers are knitting furiously as we speak. Oops, I almost forgot.' She fished an envelope out of her handbag and handed it to Joanna. 'This is for you.'

Jo's eyes lit up like lamps when she took out a party invitation. 'Josh and Leo's birthday—it's a disco!' she added in excitement. 'I can wear some of my new stuff. What do you think—denim mini-skirt or white jeans?'

'Jeans!' said Kate and Anna in unison.

'The Careys are transforming their barn into a nightclub for the party, brave souls that they are,' said Anna. 'Ben's volunteered his services as extra doorman, and you can spend the evening with me, Auntie.'

With Joanna at home, life was no longer flat for Kate. The days took on an agreeable pattern, with a walk in the park every day as soon as Kate switched off the computer, and some kind of outing in the afternoon. On the first Sunday Kate put a chicken in to roast before the usual walk with Joanna in the park, and waved, smiling, as she saw Tom Logan coming along the lake path towards them with Bran.

Kate made the introductions as they met up with him, eyeing Tom in alarm. At close quarters he looked pale and drawn, in such contrast to his usual health and vitality that she took his hand to feel his pulse surreptitiously as he kissed her cheek. But his smile was warm as he turned to Joanna.

'I'm very glad to meet you, my dear. This handsome fellow is Bran, my son's dog.'

'How do you do, Mr Logan?' said Jo, and bent towards the dog in yearning. 'Will he let me stroke him?'

'As much as you like, pet. He laps it up.' Tom turned to Kate. 'Joanna's with you for the Easter holiday?'

'Most of it. I'm driving her to Worcester to stay with her grandparents later this afternoon, but only for a couple of days. She's invited to a party on Saturday.'

'It's a disco,' Joanna informed him.

He smiled indulgently. 'I'm sure you'll have a really good time, sweetheart. Are you going along as chaperon, Kate?'

She laughed. 'And spoil the fun? No way; I'm just the

chauffeur. Come back and have some coffee with us, Tom. Or better still, stay and share our roast chicken.'

He shook his head, his eyes on Joanna as she yearned over the dog. 'That's very kind of you, but Jack's due back from London in time for supper and I'm chef.'

'Are you sure you won't come back and just rest for a moment first?' asked Kate in an undertone. 'You don't look at all well.'

'I overdid it on the golf course yesterday, that's all, love. If you like dogs, Joanna,' he added, 'I'll bring Bran to see you another time.'

'I could walk him in the park for you,' she offered eagerly.

'I may take you up on that.' He turned to Kate and, to her surprise, hugged her close again as he said goodbye.

'Come and see us soon and, in the meantime, go easy on the golf.' She kissed his cheek affectionately.

'Goodbye, Mr Logan.' Jo bent to stroke the wagging dog one last time. 'See you later, Bran.'

Kate sent Joanna upstairs to pack while she checked on the vegetables roasting in the oven with the chicken, and then stood gazing out of the window.

'What's the matter?' said Jo, returning with a holdall.

'I'm really quite worried about Mr Logan. He looked very unwell—and normally he's as fit as a fiddle.'

'I hope he's not ill. I liked him—and I just adored Bran.' Joanna sighed. 'I love dogs, but Mum didn't, so I couldn't have one.'

'Neither could I, same reason,' said Kate, and got up briskly. 'Right then, let's get this lunch on the table. And no seconds today,' she warned. 'Grandma will probably have an enormous tea waiting for you.'

The drive to Worcester through the afternoon sunshine was pleasant, and the Suttons so welcoming that Kate gave in to their urging and spent an hour with them before leaving. And was glad she had when she got home. Without Jo the house seemed deadly quiet. Kate rang her to report in then stretched out on the chaise with a book and the Sunday papers. And wondered how Jack had spent his weekend.

At that precise moment Jack Logan was on his way home from London in determined mood. He'd spent the previous evening with a woman who was attractive, intelligent and very good company when their various commitments allowed them to spend time together. Hester Morris was a high-flyer with a successful career in advertising, and outspoken about having no desire for marriage and children. He liked her very much, and enjoyed their no-strings relationship. But their first evening together since Kate's reappearance had been oddly unsatisfactory and, cursing himself for a fool, Jack had pleaded an oncoming migraine after dinner and rung for a taxi. Hester had taken it in her stride and Jack had kissed her cheek, promised to get in touch soon, and went back to his own bed to avoid sharing Hester's. He'd never had a migraine in his life, but on the spur of the moment it had been the only excuse he could think of to avoid hurting someone he valued as a friend.

As he turned off the motorway to make for home Jack looked truth in the face. Life with Kate for a friend was a hell of a sight more bearable than life without her. He'd call round tonight and tell her that, and hope to God she hadn't changed her mind since he saw her last. Her niece would be home for the Easter vacation by now, of course, but the little girl would surely be in bed if he left it late enough. He smiled sardonically. After forcing himself to keep away from Kate for weeks, his welcome was unlikely to be warm whatever time it was. After supper he would ask his father to keep Bran until tomorrow so he could stay with Kate long enough to make his peace—if she let him through the door.

Kate had just laid a tray with a chicken sandwich and a cup of coffee when the bell rang. Her heart took a flying leap against her ribs as she went into the hall. Jack Logan was the only man tall enough to identify through the fanlight over the front door. She clamped down on a rush of delight and smiled coolly as she opened the door.

'Why, hello, Jack. This is a surprise.'

'Let me in, please,' he said brusquely.

'Why?' she demanded, angered by his peremptory tone.

'I have something to show you.'

'You're interrupting my supper.'

'Are you alone?'

'Yes.'

'Good, because we need to talk. This is important, Kate.'

'It had better be. Close the door behind you.'

Jack followed her into the sitting room, eyeing the tray on the Pembroke table. 'One sandwich? Not much of a supper.'

'Big lunch.' Kate stood with arms folded. 'But you didn't come here to discuss my eating habits, so show me whatever you want to show me—'

'And get out,' he finished for her.

'I hope I wouldn't be as rude as that.' She looked up at him, wishing she felt as indifferent to him as she was trying to make out. He obviously hadn't had time for a haircut lately and, in a battered trench coat over a crew neck sweater and cords, Jack looked so much like the young man she'd once fallen in love with it was hard to maintain her distance. But something in his demeanour was deeply disquieting.

'I had dinner with Dad before I came here. He asked me to show you these.' He handed her an envelope. 'Look inside.'

Kate looked at him questioningly, but Jack's expression gave nothing away. She withdrew two photographs from the envelope and sat down with a bump, feeling the colour drain from her face. Both studies were of the same girl, the first at Joanna's age, the second as a radiant, smiling bride in her twenties.

Jack tossed his raincoat on a chair and put a hand on her shoulder. 'Kate, are you all right?'

'No, I'm not all right,' she snapped, her eyes glued to the photographs. The girl in them had dark, curling hair, but otherwise the likeness to Joanna was unmistakeable. 'Who is this?' Though there was only one woman it could be.

'My mother. My father met her when the first photograph was taken. They were in school together.' Jack breathed in deeply. 'He thought he was seeing things when he met Joanna in the park this morning.'

Kate nodded slowly, her eyes on the photographs shaking in her unsteady hand. 'So that's why he looked so ill.'

'He idolised my mother. We both did.' Jack's deep, authoritative voice grew husky. 'You know she died when I was fifteen. It took me years to get over losing her. But Dad never has. Coming face to face with Joanna today was a hell of a shock to him.' He sat on the end of the chaise and put an ungentle finger under Kate's chin to tilt her face up to his. 'When were you going to tell me that we had a daughter?'

CHAPTER ELEVEN

'I WASN'T going to—ever.' Kate pushed his hand away and looked up at him with hostility. 'Because in the eyes of the world she's not our daughter, she's my *niece*, Jack. All the time she was growing up I had to stand back and look on from the sidelines while my child called someone else Mummy.'

His fists clenched. 'Why in God's name didn't you tell me you were pregnant?' he demanded, glaring at her.

She glared back in hot resentment. 'I didn't realise I was for a while! There was a lot going on in my life at the time: the move to London, getting to grips with the new job, living alone in digs.' She wrenched her eyes away. 'And pining for you, Jack.'

Kate had put her sickness and weariness down to the changes in her life at first, but eventually she bought a test kit that confirmed her fears. At the time the Suttons had been packing up, ready for the move to London. Kate went home that weekend, officially to give them a helping hand, in reality desperate to contact Jack and tell him about the baby. But Elizabeth met her at the bus station with the shattering news that Jack Logan had married Dawn Taylor the previous weekend, and Kate's life fell apart.

'Dear God!' Jack seized her hand again. 'If I'd known in time I would have paid Dawn off and married you right away, Kate.'

She snatched her hand away. 'Not the ideal way to start a marriage, Jack.'

'Better than letting you go it alone!'

She gave a mirthless little laugh. 'Ah, but I didn't go it

alone. Far from it. Liz guessed my little secret right away and
seized her chance to acquire the child she couldn't have herself because, she informed me, she'd had to look after me
instead of having a child of her own. This was payback time.'

Jack sat back, his face haggard. 'No wonder she slammed
the door in my face when I came looking for you. She was
afraid to let me see the baby.'

Elizabeth's plans were cut and dried before Kate returned
to London that terrible weekend. The Suttons would bring
Kate's baby up as their own on condition that she obeyed
their rules.

Jack looked sick. 'Don't tell me they sent you off to some
kind of home!'

Kate shook her head. 'Nothing so dramatic. Elizabeth
merely insisted I live with them in the new house in London.
She wanted to make sure I took vitamins and received regular
medical attention so that ''her'' baby would be a perfect,
healthy specimen. She had no qualms about the father. She
went off you big time when you married someone else, of
course, but from a breeding point of view the Logan genes
were perfectly acceptable.'

'I'm so glad my pedigree came up to scratch,' said Jack
savagely. 'Did you manage to keep working?'

'Yes, thank God.'

Kate had always been slender. And, because morning sickness and misery over her situation killed her appetite, her
shape altered so little her condition went unnoticed at work.
She was passionately grateful for it. Her job was the only
thing that kept her sane. She worked well into her sixth
month, and by buying clothes a size or two larger than usual
managed to disguise her not very considerable weight gain
and keep her secret.

'I managed to carry on keeping my secret,' Kate told Jack,
'because at that stage I developed a kidney infection and had

to take time off. I also suffered from depression, and sank into such depths of hormonal despair Liz and Robert decided to move to another part of London where no one knew us.'

Jack frowned. 'Surely neighbours must have noticed you were pregnant?'

'I never met Elizabeth's neighbours. Or wanted to. Besides, I was ill for quite a while, and even when I got better I never went out except to the antenatal clinic and for a daily walk in some park Liz drove me to, as far from home as possible. I felt like the skeleton in the closet!' Kate smiled grimly. 'It was around then that the sleepwalking started. Eventually Liz was so afraid I'd fall and harm the baby that Robert put a bed in the dining room on the ground floor, and I slept there until Jo was born.'

Jack closed his eyes for a moment. 'God, what a life! You must have hated my guts.'

She shook her head. 'No, Jack, I missed you and grieved for you, but I didn't hate you. After all, I was the one who left you and opted for a clean break. I could hardly object when you found someone else. Anyway the sleepwalking phase didn't last long because I went into labour a month early.' Kate looked away. 'I had a Caesarean section, which is why I wouldn't let you undress me that day. I didn't want you to see my scar.'

Jack grasped her hand so tightly she protested, and he lifted it to his lips in apology. 'Go on, darling. Tell me the rest.'

Kate faltered slightly at the endearment, but went doggedly on to talk about the deal with Liz, which meant handing the baby over the moment it was born. But when Kate went into labour both Suttons had such heavy colds they were barred from the maternity ward.

Kate sighed deeply. 'So I was the first to see her, and I loved her so much, Jack. I used to stand gazing at her for ages in the baby unit. She had to stay there for a while because she came early, and I had to go home without her. It was such a terrible wrench to leave her behind that I told Liz the deal was off. I wanted to keep my baby after all.'

'What changed your mind?' asked Jack with compassion.

'Liz was the only mother I ever knew, remember, and a pretty forceful personality. She played on the guilt angle that responsibility for me had kept her from having a child of her own, and this was a perfect way to repay the debt.'

Kate tried to sound dispassionate as she told Jack how her sister kept hammering on that to support a child Kate would have to work full-time and pay a child-minder. If she did that, Liz threatened to wash her hands of her. Kate would be forced to bring up her baby on her own in some poky bedsitter and farm her out to strangers so she could keep working. At that point post-natal depression hit Kate so hard she was in a terrible state by the time Joanna was discharged and Elizabeth took full advantage of it.

'I was in no condition to look after a child, physically, mentally or financially, she told me. She, on the other hand, could give my baby a good home, constant care and attention, and when the time came Robert would pay for a good school.' Kate took in a deep breath. 'In desperation I finally caved in, totally brainwashed about the good of my child, but I had to stick to Sutton rules. I was forbidden to give my baby her bottle, or bathe and change her, or even pick her up when she was crying in case she bonded to me and not Liz. But I dug my heels in and made two rules of my own. I insisted that I was made Jo's legal guardian, and that I chose her name. But I had no say in it when they sent her to boarding school at the age of eight,' Kate added bitterly.

Jack got up and paced round the room like a restless tiger. 'Did they keep you shut up in a downstairs room again after the baby was born?'

'No, of course not. But I went back to work far sooner than I should have because it was such torture to watch Liz do all the things I should have been doing for my baby girl. And, in the end, even though it broke my heart to leave her, I answered Anna's advertisement for a flat share.'

He frowned. 'Does Anna know about any of this?'

'No. I told her I was recovering from a broken engagement, which was no lie, Jack. And Anna finds it quite natural that I'm so attached to my "niece", because she is, too.'

He looked at her questioningly. 'What do I tell my father?'

'The truth, what else?'

Jack sat on the end of the chaise and took her hand again. 'Once Dad told me about meeting Joanna I realised why you won't marry me. But what I don't understand,' he added, 'is why you brought her here to live. You must have known I'd meet her one day.'

Kate shrugged. 'I thought it didn't matter if you did. I never saw a photograph of your mother, remember, and Jo doesn't resemble you or me in any way, except for my kind of body shape. I had no intention of turning up on your doorstep and confronting you with your love child, I assure you.' She looked down at their clasped hands. 'Personally, I wasn't keen on coming back here. Even after all these years I didn't relish the idea of seeing you play happy families with Dawn. But Joanna was desperate to get away from London after Liz and Robert died, and there was this house, just waiting for us to move into it. Jo fell in love with it, so here we are.'

Jack was silent for a while, then got up and stood over Kate, his eyes implacable. 'Right. This is what we do. Now I know the truth, you and I simply get married and—'

'Live happily ever after?' She shook her head. 'There's nothing simple about it. You're not thinking straight.'

He sat down again, his eyes boring into hers. 'One thing I do have straight. We *must* tell Joanna.'

Kate's eyes blazed. 'And just what are "we" going to tell her, Jack? That her Daddy married someone else the minute my back was turned, and I gave my baby away like a pound of tea because I couldn't face life as a single mother?

Something,' she added with bitterness, 'I've regretted every single day of my life since.'

'Then it's time to change things.' Jack's hand tightened on hers. 'Surely Joanna could cope with the facts if you explained them to her?'

She gazed at him in anguish. 'How can I do that to her, Jack? She's just lost the people she knew as parents. It would be like taking them away from her all over again.'

'She has two real live parents to take their place.'

'I can't take the risk.' Kate shivered. 'If I tell her the truth she might hate me. I won't do it, Jack.'

'Better than having her find out by accident.'

'I don't know. Maybe you're right. But Jo's so vulnerable right now.'

'Does she know anything about me?'

'Only that I've been seeing an old friend.'

He shrugged. 'Then she'll think it perfectly natural if you keep on seeing me.'

'So she can get used to having you around?'

'I want a whole lot more than that!' He touched a hand to her cheek. 'These past few weeks I've tried to prove to myself that I can live without you, Kate, but only proved that I can't. On the way home from London today, hours before I knew the truth about Joanna, I decided to play it your way, as your friend or anything you want. But you know damn well that *I* want to be husband—and your friend. The two are not mutually exclusive. For God's sake, Kate, I love you. And, in spite of my past sins, I know you still love me.' He pulled her up out of her chair and held her by the shoulders. 'Are you going to tell me I'm wrong?'

She stared up into the compelling eyes for a long moment, then shook her head wearily. 'No. You're not wrong, Jack.' She leaned into him, her cheek against the soft wool of his sweater. 'But Joanna comes first.'

'Then I'll do my best to make her like me.'

'She likes your father.' Kate looked up at him with a wry little smile. 'And she fell madly in love with Bran.'

'Ah!' Jack's eyes gleamed. 'Does she know he's mine?'

'Yes.'

'Good. I'll use him as my trump card. When do I meet her?'

'I'm fetching her from Worcester on Tuesday, so come to supper on Wednesday, if you like. It would help pass the time for her until Saturday.'

'What's happening on Saturday?'

Kate told him about the disco and, to her amusement, Jack scowled in disapproval.

'You're letting her loose among teenage boys?'

'She's thirteen, Jack. And Ben will be on hand to help Jim Carey fend off gatecrashers, so she won't come to any harm.'

'I'll ring Jim and offer my help—'

'No, you will not, Jack! Get to know Joanna first before you start acting the heavy parent.'

He smiled reluctantly. 'All right. You win—this time.' He picked her up and sat down on the chaise with her on his lap. 'You do realise what this means?' he said, his eyes inches from hers.

'What does what mean?' she said unevenly.

'If you refuse to tell Joanna I'm her father I'll just have to marry her aunt and become her uncle.'

'No way. Living a lie isn't easy, Jack—I speak from experience.'

'I thought you'd say that,' he said with satisfaction. 'Then we revert to Plan A and get Joanna so used to having me around she'll probably start asking my intentions.'

'You haven't been around at all lately,' she reminded him tartly.

His eyes smouldered. 'Do you blame me? You turned me down for the second time, Kate.'

'Don't tell me you were heartbroken, Jack Logan,' she retorted. 'I happen to know you went back to your haunts in London!'

'Yes. For all the good it did me.' He held her closer, smiling ruefully as he told her about the unsuccessful evening with Hester Morris. 'You can laugh if you like.'

She shook her head, secretly so delighted she wanted to hug him until his ribs cracked. 'I didn't *want* to turn you down, Jack. You can see, now, why I did. Besides, I didn't turn you down flat the first time either. I just wanted to work in London for a while before getting married.' Kate sighed. 'I took it for granted I'd see you every weekend once you realised you couldn't live without me.'

'Which is exactly what happened,' he said grimly. 'Only fate—in the shape of Dawn—intervened.'

'And what a shape it was,' Kate retorted. 'No wonder you couldn't resist.'

Jack kissed her suddenly, holding her still when she tried to protest, and after a moment or two Kate gave up protesting and kissed him back. He raised his head, his eyes gleaming as he smoothed a lock of hair back from her face. 'It was nothing to do with her shape,' he said huskily. 'I was like a kid wanting comfort, and Dawn provided it as bait to hook a husband. Not that I'm blaming her—it was my mistake.'

'You paid through the nose for it, Jack!'

'You paid a far higher price than me. But we can't go on paying, Kate.' He kissed her again, his hands sliding into her hair to hold her still. She leaned into him and he smoothed a hand down her face, his forehead against hers. 'I want you so much,' he said hoarsely, and she clutched him closer, aroused by the note of desperation in his voice.

'Have you left Bran outside in the car?'

'No.' He put her away from him to look into her face. 'He's staying with Dad again tonight. Why?'

'I just wondered.' Kate relaxed against him again. 'I'm so

glad you know everything, Jack. It's been desperately hard to keep the truth from you.'

'You've never told anyone else? Not even the banker you were engaged to?'

'Not even David. While Elizabeth and Robert were alive I couldn't tell anyone.' She paused. 'Besides, you're the only one I ever wanted to tell, Jack.' And right now she also wanted him to pick her up and carry her upstairs to bed. She was trying to find a way to tell him that when Jack set her on her feet and stood up.

'I should be going. You look tired, Katie.'

She pulled a face. 'You mean I look like a hag.'

Jack smiled. 'You look so much the opposite of a hag I'd better go before I do something you'll regret.'

Kate looked him in the eye. 'Do you want to stay the night?' she said baldly.

With a groan of pure relief Jack picked her up and sat down with her on the chaise. 'Of course I want to stay the night!' he said roughly and rubbed his cheek against hers. 'Not just to make love, though God knows I want that so much I ache for you, Katie. But I need to hold you in my arms all night most of all, to make up for all those other nights when you weren't there.'

'My thoughts exactly.' She grinned as Jack stood up with her and set her on her feet. 'Only my version had you carrying me up to bed. But don't try it. The stairs here are too narrow.'

'No romance in getting you black and blue,' he agreed. 'You go up first so I can enjoy your back view.' He gave her a tap on the bottom and Kate gave him a smile of such radiance his eyes blazed in response.

'I've missed you, Jack.'

'I've missed you too.'

'Then why did you keep away?'

He smiled crookedly. 'Because I'm a stubborn idiot. I had to prove that I could, I suppose. But I'm here now.'

'Only because you wanted to show me your mother's photographs,' she reminded him as she started up the stairs.

'I had other reasons.' He followed her up so closely she could feel his breath on her neck. 'Some of them very pressing,' he added huskily as he picked her up on the landing. 'Even shorter journey this time,' he said with satisfaction, and carried her into the bedroom. 'In college a girl told me that carrying a woman to bed was the best foreplay of the lot.'

'So that's why you do it!' Kate chuckled as he sat down with her on the bed, holding her on his lap. 'And did it work with the lady in question?'

Jack shook his head regretfully. 'I never tried it. She was a gorgeous Amazon, built on generous lines. Think of the damage to my ego—and other parts—if I'd dropped her halfway!'

Kate let out a snort of laughter as she hugged him close. 'She was right, though. It does appeal to the female in a woman.'

'It helps when the female is a featherweight. Like you.'

'You mean skinny,' she said, resigned.

He undid the buttons on her shirt and peeled it off, then turned her away from him to unclasp her bra. 'Definitely not skinny—just fine, delicate bones covered with silky skin,' he said unevenly, and kissed the back of her neck as he caressed her breasts, taking deep satisfaction in her hurried breathing. Kate endured the exquisite torture for a moment, then twisted round and flung her arms round his neck and, with a relishing sound, he kissed her fiercely. Her hands slid under his sweater, tugging at it until he yanked it over his head and pulled her against his chest.

'Wait,' said Kate hoarsely, and stood up to kick off her suede boots and undo the zip of the tailored trousers she'd worn for the trip to Worcester. Holding his eyes, she slid them off, removing the strip of lace beneath at the same time, and Jack went down on his knees to kiss her scar. She stood as still as she could under the gentle caress, but the hurried frantic rhythm of her breathing gave her away as his lips moved lower and lower until his tongue penetrated moist heat to find the tiny secret part of her that quivered, erect in its hiding place, so exquisitely sensitive that when his caresses homed in on it she gasped and stiffened, her hands fisted in his hair as waves of sensation swept over her.

Jack got to his feet and laid her on the bed, looking down at her in such triumphant possession Kate felt a throb of fiery response in the place where he'd just caused such havoc. He stripped off the rest of his clothes and joined her, uttering a visceral groan of pure pleasure as their bodies came into full naked contact.

'Firstly, I've now seen—and kissed—the famous scar,' he said against her mouth.

'Not only the scar!' She thrust herself closer, her eyes gleaming in triumph as she felt his erection nudge against her.

'Secondly, and maybe thirdly and fourthly, I want to do this—and this.' He slid his hands down her spine, then up to her breasts, cupping them as he bent his head to take a nipple into his mouth, his fingers teasing its twin. She made a sound he stifled with a kiss, and then moved his lips over her face as his hands continued such subtle torment she felt she'd die if he didn't take her soon and, just as she was about to pummel him in desperate demand, he sheathed himself inside her to the hilt and she gave a moan of passionate relief.

'I love you so much, Katie,' he said, his voice gruff with the raw need he was fighting to keep in check.

'I love you, too,' she said breathlessly, the last word swallowed in a gasp as he began to move and her body responded ardently as he thrust harder and deeper. Her hips rose to meet him, flesh meeting flesh as the relentless rhythm accelerated to a wild crescendo that sent her gasping into orbit seconds before his own release engulfed him and she held his face to her breasts in fierce possession as his body poured its tribute into hers before collapsing on top of her, taking away what little breath she had left.

When he found the will to move, Jack turned over on his back, rolling her with him and Kate drew in a deep, reviving breath as she settled in the crook of his arm.

'This is how it should have been all along,' he said, a lazy note of contentment in his voice.

'If we had been together all along—fourteen years to be precise—we would be an old married couple, and "this" as you put it, would surely be less frenetic by now,' Kate pointed out.

'I meant just being here together, in bed in each other's arms instead of all the nights we spent alone. At least I did,' he added, and put her away a fraction to look into her eyes. 'You shared a bed with this banker of yours.'

'You make that sound like a rude word,' she protested. 'His name was David, and I was engaged to him. Of course we shared a bed. But he had a television in the bedroom so I often fell asleep while he was watching England play cricket on the other side of the world, or whatever.'

'No wonder you packed him in.' He pulled her closer, his cheek against hers. 'When you come to live at Mill House you sleep—or not sleep—with me. No television in my bedroom.'

'I noticed,' she said absently, and pulled back a little, frowning. 'Jack, if we manage to sort things out with Joanna, and we do move in with you at Mill House one day, what will I do with this one? I hate the thought of selling it.'

'Make it over to Joanna,' he said promptly. 'It can be leased out until she's old enough to decide what happens to it.'

Kate sighed. 'It sounds so easy when you talk about it like that, Jack, but first we've got to get over this great big hurdle of telling her she's ours.'

'At least you said "ours" not "mine",' he said, kissing her.

Kate kissed him back, then turned to look at her alarm

clock. 'It's after midnight,' she said with regret. 'Time you were going, Jack.'

He pulled her close again. 'Why?'

'You work long hours and need your sleep. Besides,' she added, batting her eyelashes at him, 'I'm not sure I want that Jensen of yours parked outside my house all night.'

'I came in the Jeep.' Jack smiled triumphantly. 'And I left it near the park gates, well away from your smart front door.'

'Did you now!' Kate's eyes narrowed speculatively. '*And* you left Bran with your father.'

'I certainly did.'

'So you intended to stay from the start.'

'While I was driving from London I decided to come here after seeing Dad and tell you I was ready to do any damn thing you wanted as long as we were part of each other's lives again. I left Bran with him so I could spend time persuading you after Jo was in bed.' He smiled crookedly. 'I thought she was much younger than she actually is, Kate. When Dad mentioned the photographs the truth hit me in the face.'

Kate looked at him in entreaty. 'Were you angry with me, Jack?'

'I was euphoric!' He pulled her close, his cheek against hers. 'I'm still trying to come to terms with the miraculous fact that we've got a daughter. All I have to do now is persuade you to let her know she's got a real live father—and a mother I want to marry as soon as I can get the ring on her finger.'

Kate stirred next morning, afraid she was dreaming again when she felt the touch of coaxing lips and hands. But she opened her eyes to find Jack was there in the flesh, real and warm and already aroused as he caressed her awake. He kissed her in tender possession as he slid slowly home inside her, waking all her senses one by one, the subtle seduction so perfect she never wanted it to end and held him close to experience every last nuance of pleasure as the throbbing died away.

'Good morning,' he said against her mouth.

'It certainly is,' she agreed breathlessly and winced as she looked at the clock. 'A very early good morning, Jack!'

'Some people go out to work,' he told her and slid from the bed to pull on his clothes. 'And, much as I'd like to stay all day with you in that bed, I must dash home to shower and dress. I'll scribble a note to Molly to leave us something for dinner, and pick you up tonight about seven. Unless,' he added, looking down at her, 'you have something better to do?'

'I haven't got my diary with me, but offhand I can't think of anything,' she said flippantly, then smiled at him. 'What could possibly be better?'

'Exactly. What are you going to do after I've gone?'

'My usual shift at the computer.' She looked at him questioningly. 'I thought I'd ask your father round to lunch later and tell him my story. Or would you rather do that yourself?'

Jack leaned over to kiss her. 'No, my darling. You tell him—it's your story.

'It's yours too!'

'But you're the heroine; I'm just the villain of the piece.'

She shook her head. 'Not to me, Jack.'

He pulled her up into his arms. 'Then from now on I'll do my damnedest to be the hero.' He kissed her again and, with a deep sigh of regret, let her go. 'I'll see you later.'

Kate forged through her morning's work, then rang the Suttons in Worcester to talk to Joanna and, once assured that her child was well and happy, Kate rang Tom Logan and suggested he come round for a sandwich lunch.

When he arrived, looking rested and with his colour back, she threw her arms round him in relief. 'Thank goodness, you look yourself again! You had me really worried yesterday.'

'No wonder. When I saw Joanna I swear my heart stopped for a moment. I couldn't believe my eyes. She was my Margaret to the life!' Tom kissed her cheek. 'Jack rang earlier to check on me. He sounded happy, Kate.'

She smiled radiantly, then bit her lip. 'I'm happy too, except for one thing. I have to tell Joanna the truth, and I'm such a coward about it, Tom.' Kate led him into the kitchen and took the cover from a platter of chicken sandwiches. 'Help yourself; I'll eat and talk at the same time.'

She told her story again briefly and succinctly, editing out the parts that would cause him unnecessary pain.

'My dear girl,' he said, shaken. 'To think you've had to keep this to yourself all these years.' He reached across the table to take her hand. 'But now, my love, you've got to bite the bullet and tell Joanna.'

Kate nodded reluctantly. 'But not until after the party. I want her to enjoy that before I hit her with the truth.'

Tom Logan's grasp tightened. 'In my opinion you and Jack should tell her together.'

'She needn't hear about Dawn and the baby. I'll tell her I broke up with Jack—which is true—and he married someone else on the rebound before I knew I was expecting his child.'

Tom shook his head. 'Even at first glance Joanna strikes me as mature for her age. I think she deserves the truth, warts and all. I'll make that clear to Jack when he comes to collect the dog.'

'I can't say I agree with Dad,' said Jack later, as Kate received a warm welcome from Bran in the Jeep. 'I haven't even met her yet, but I don't relish telling my daughter I was such a fool over Dawn.'

'Then don't,' said Kate firmly. 'We'll play it my way, and give Jo the abridged version.'

'Thank you, darling. I've never thought of myself as a coward until now. But then,' he added, 'I didn't know I was a father until now, either.'

When they got to Mill House they went for a walk in the gardens with the dog before dinner, arms around each other like teenagers as they circled the millpond. Afterwards Jack went up for a shower while Kate sat in front of the fire in the living room with Bran to wait for him, her eyes thoughtful as she gazed into the flames.

'What at you thinking about?' asked Jack, as he joined her.

'Would you mind if we told Joanna our story here?' Kate curled up against him. 'No matter how she takes it, she still has to live with me afterwards, so I'd rather we didn't have the showdown in Park Crescent.'

'You'd rather my house was ruined for her than yours,' said Jack ruefully.

She nodded. 'I tend to think in worst scenario terms.'

'In which you've had some experience,' he said grimly.

'So have you. But let's not spoil our evening by worrying about it. What did Molly leave us for dinner?'

By mutual consent there was no more talk of the coming confession. Instead Kate told Jack everything she could about his daughter as they enjoyed fillet of lamb cooked with garlic, thyme and cannelloni beans. They spent an hour in front of the fire afterwards and then took Bran out for a walk, but when they'd settled him down for the night Jack took Kate's hand and led her straight upstairs.

'I've got some lonely nights in front of me, so let's go to bed,' he said firmly, and she rubbed her face against his sleeve.

'Yes, please!'

Jack drove Kate home early the following morning and kissed her goodbye with tension she felt as keenly as he did.

'I'll leave you in peace with Joanna tonight,' he said, holding her tightly.

'Come to supper tomorrow, then,' said Kate.

'I've got a board meeting that day,' he said wryly. 'It's going to be hard to keep my mind on the job, when all I can think of is meeting my daughter for the first time.'

CHAPTER TWELVE

'IT WAS lovely to see Grandma and Grandpa,' said Joanna, on the journey from Worcester, 'but I'm glad to be going home. I missed you, Kate.'

'I missed you, too.'

'What did you do while I was away?'

'I worked, as usual, and I had dinner with Jack Logan—'

'The old friend with the great dog,' said Jo promptly, and slanted a cheeky grin at her. 'Did you have a nice time?'

'Very nice, thank you,' said Kate primly. 'I thought you might like to meet him too, so I asked him to supper tomorrow. We'll stop in town on the way home and buy some food.'

'Is he bringing Bran with him?'

'No. But if you play your cards right Jack might ask you round to his place to play with Bran in the garden there. It's huge, with a millpond.'

'Is he rich then?'

'He's well off, certainly, but only because he's worked very hard to achieve it.'

'Will I like him?'

'I don't know. I hope so, Jo, because I like him a lot.'

'Then I expect I will, too.'

'I'm glad we've got a guest for supper,' said Jo the next day, as she took a tray of cupcakes out of the oven. 'It takes my mind off the party.' She smiled sheepishly. 'I keep thinking about it all the time.'

Praying that the party would live up to her expectations,

Kate handed her the icing sugar. 'How are you going to decorate the cakes?'

Jo eyed them with satisfaction. 'I thought white icing with a chocolate mini Easter egg to finish them off. They came out well, didn't they? I hope Mr Logan likes cake.'

'He'll love those,' said Kate with absolute certainty. 'But I think you'd better call him Jack, to avoid confusion with his father.'

As seven-thirty approached Kate wondered if Jack was in an equal state of tension. To avoid formality they were eating in the kitchen and the dress code was jeans and sweaters. Blissfully unaware of the emotion almost choking Kate, Jo laid the small kitchen table with a checked cloth, put red candles on white saucers, and then went into the sitting room to set out nuts and savoury biscuits. Kate did some deep breathing exercises, checked on her tomato sauce, fiddled with her hair, put some lipstick on, then tensed at the sound of a car and went into the hall.

'That sounds like Jack's beloved Jensen,' she said, amazed that her voice sounded so normal.

'Shall I go?' asked Jo when the bell rang, and Kate nodded, rigid with stage fright as she watched Jo open the door to her tall father, who stood equally still as he set eyes on his daughter for the first time.

'Hello,' he said at last, and smiled down into the dark eyes surveying him with frank interest. 'I'm Jack Logan.'

'Hi, I'm Joanna.' She smiled warmly. 'You look like your father—I met him on Sunday with your gorgeous dog.'

'Thank you, I'll take that as a big compliment. I hope you like these.' Jack handed her a brightly wrapped package, then held out an armful of pink and white lilies to Kate and kissed her very deliberately on the mouth. 'You look very beautiful tonight.'

'Thank you, these are lovely,' Kate said breathlessly, her

colour high. 'Go into the sitting room with Jo while I put these in water. What did you get, love?'

'Chocolates!' said Jo with relish and turned to Jack. 'Thank you—' She hesitated. 'Kate said I should call you Jack. Is that OK?'

'Absolutely,' he assured her and exchanged a look with Kate that spoke volumes.

'How about a beer?' she said huskily. 'Back in a moment.'

Kate put the lilies into a jug of water, poured beer into a glass and went back to the sitting room, relaxing slightly when she found Jo curled up in a chair, chatting easily with Jack about her stay with her grandparents.

'I forgot to tell you, Kate,' she said. 'When I had tea in a café in Worcester with Grandma I saw Leah Brace from school. She was with her father. He sent you his regards.'

'How nice of him.' Kate avoided Jack's eyes as she handed him his beer. 'Let's sit down. Supper's not quite ready yet.'

He took the foot of the chaise, smiling at Jo. 'Kate tells me you're going to a party on Saturday.'

She nodded, eyes sparkling. 'The Carey twins invited me. Do you know them?'

'I know their father.' He smiled wryly. 'I didn't realise Jim's twins were old enough for disco parties.'

'It's their fourteenth birthday,' Jo informed him. 'The party sounds like fun, it's in a barn.'

Kate sat with them for a while, content to sit in silence while the two people she loved best in the world got to know each other, but after a while she excused herself to see to the meal.

'Shall I help?' said Jo, jumping up.

'Stay and entertain our guest,' said Kate. 'Just kitchen supper tonight, Jack,' she told him. 'I shan't be long.'

He smiled at her then turned to his daughter as he accepted the nuts she offered him. 'Tell me about school, Joanna. What subjects do you like best?'

Finding it hard to tear herself away, Kate went back to the kitchen to grill bacon to crispness while water heated for the pasta. She put bowls in the oven to warm, set out dishes of grated cheese on the table, filled wineglasses and cut thick slices from a loaf of Italian bread, checked on her sauce, plunged the pasta into the pot and went to fetch the others.

Joanna talked with complete ease as she helped serve the meal, laughing when Jack told her that the last time he'd had supper with Kate she hadn't honoured him with her culinary skill.

'We sent out for Chinese,' he said, grinning at Kate. 'But this is much better. Great sauce.'

'We had great roast chicken on Sunday too, with herb stuffing and bread sauce,' Jo informed him. 'Kate's a good cook. But I expect you know that,' she added, twirling pasta round her fork.

'We hadn't seen each other for years until recently,' Jack said regretfully, 'so I'm not as familiar with her cooking skills as you, Jo. But I hope to be in future,' he added, his eyes spearing Kate's.

Jack insisted on helping to clear the table after the first course, which resulted in much bumping into each other as the three of them got in each other's way in the small kitchen.

'For heaven's sake, sit down, Jack,' laughed Kate at last. 'Leave the rest to us.' She shot him a meaningful glance as Jo put her cupcakes on the table.

'Those look good,' he said promptly. 'Did you make them yourself, Kate?'

She shook her head. 'Jo's work, not mine.'

'I won't mind if you don't like cake,' Jo assured him shyly. 'Kate's got some cheese.'

Jack took a cake, pronouncing it so delicious he asked for another. 'Best I've tasted in a long time,' he told her, and Joanna flushed with pleasure as she ate hers.

'Thank you. I like baking.'

'Just as well,' said Kate dryly. 'My culinary skills don't extend that far.'

They stayed at the table to drink coffee, Jo completely at ease with her new acquaintance as she asked questions about Bran.

'Come round to my house at the weekend to see him,' said Jack casually. 'I'll get Molly to organise a special Easter Sunday lunch.'

'Who's Molly?'

'She's the good fairy who cleans my house and leaves me delicious meals.'

'She's very young to be such a fabulous cook,' said Kate. 'I've sampled some of her food, Jo. It's delicious.'

'No more delicious than the meal I had tonight,' said Jack emphatically. 'So is that a date, Jo? Or will you be too tired after your party?'

She shook her head, smiling. 'I'd love to come.'

'I'll expect you about twelve, then. We can have a stroll with Bran in the garden before lunch.'

'Great,' said Jo, and got up. 'Past my bedtime,' she announced and leaned down to kiss Kate's cheek.

'Goodnight, darling, sleep well.'

Jo smiled as Jack got to his feet. 'It was nice to meet you. Thank you again for the chocolates. I'll look forward to Sunday.'

'So shall I,' he assured her.

Jo hesitated, then held up her face and Jack touched his lips to the smooth cheek, his voice husky as he bade his daughter goodnight.

When they were alone Kate exchanged a long look with Jack, then went into his arms with a shaky sigh.

'Well?' she said, tipping back her face. 'What do you think of our daughter?'

'She's a darling.' Jack leaned his forehead against hers. 'I can't believe she's ours. I hope to God we can tell her the truth without turning her against me.'

'And me,' she reminded him, but Jack shook his head.

'She very obviously thinks the world of you, so that won't happen, Kate. As I said before, I'm the villain of the piece.'

'We needn't tell her about Dawn—'

'But we will.' Jack raised his head. 'Meeting her tonight clarified that for me. If we have any hope of life together as a family, Jo must know everything.'

'I just wish we could tell her in a way that wouldn't hurt her—or you.' Kate took his hand. 'It's not late. Stay for a while, Jack. I need you.'

'I need you too,' he said with feeling, and drew her down on the chaise with him. 'Would our daughter be shocked if she saw me cuddling you?'

'She's thirteen, not three, Jack! She'd probably think it strange if we weren't.'

He laughed and rubbed his chin over her hair. 'Do you think she liked me?'

'Of course she did. Otherwise she wouldn't have been chatting away so happily.'

'I'll ask Dad round to lunch on Sunday, too. He can always take off later if he can't face the showdown.'

Kate nodded thoughtfully. 'Good idea. Jo liked him and, after all, he is her grandfather.'

'He knew that the moment he saw her, which is why he was knocked for six.' Jack sighed. 'I suppose I'd better be on my way. Shall I call in tomorrow?'

'Not tomorrow. Ben's away so we're sharing pizza and a video with Anna in the evening, but we're in on Friday. Come for a drink on your way home.'

'I'll finish early for once. I need to make the most of her while I can.' He stood up with Kate and set her on her feet. 'After Sunday's revelations she may never want to set eyes on me again.'

*   *   *

Jack's words stayed with Kate as she got ready for bed. It was hours before a dream-troubled sleep overtook her, but she woke early and got up feeling tired and heavy-eyed, in direct contrast to Joanna, who came bounding into the kitchen, full of the joys of spring.

'I like Jack,' she announced. 'He's easy to talk to, like Ben. Only better looking,' she added with a grin, and poured herself some orange juice. 'He's quite a hunk!'

'I'm glad you approve,' said Kate dryly. 'How about scrambled eggs?'

'No thanks. I'll just have yoghurt and toast.' Jo applied herself to her breakfast while Kate drank a cup of tea. 'Aren't you going to eat anything?'

'In a minute.'

'You look a bit pale.'

'I'll be fine after more tea.'

Joanna gave her a questioning look. 'When you knew him before, was Jack your boyfriend?'

'Yes.' Kate braced herself. 'In fact we were engaged briefly, but it didn't work out.'

'What happened?'

Kate busied herself with pouring tea. 'I was determined to work in London; Jack was equally determined to stay here, so we decided on a clean break.'

Jo frowned and reached for more toast. 'I bet you were both sorry afterwards.'

'Yes, we were.' Which was an understatement. Feeling like someone on the edge of a precipice, Kate changed the subject to Jo's choice of birthday present for the twins. 'We'd better pop into town this afternoon and find something.'

Jack rang before they went out, to ask if his daughter approved of him, and laughed, relieved, when Kate told him he was not only easy to talk to but better looking than Ben Maitland.

'You can't get higher praise than that,' Kate assured him.

'Thank God for it. I'll sleep a lot easier tonight than I did last night!'

'So what do you think of Kate's friend, Jo?' asked Anna that evening.

'I think he's lovely. Much better looking than David,' said Jo, startling Kate.

'You remember David, then?'

'Of course I do.' Jo pulled a face. 'He used to come to Sunday lunch sometimes when you were together. He talked down to me. You know, as if I was a baby—which I suppose I was then. But Ben and Jack treat me like an adult.'

'As they should,' said Anna, trying not to laugh. 'So you approve of Jack?'

Jo nodded, and flashed Kate an impudent smile. 'I think he wants to get back with you.'

'Do you, indeed!'

'Why do you think I went to bed so tactfully last night? I could tell he was dying to be alone with you.'

Kate stared at her, speechless, and Anna dissolved into helpless laughter.

'What do they teach you at that all girl establishment of yours?'

'It's a school, not a convent,' Jo pointed out. 'And some girls have boyfriends back home and bore you rigid about what they get up to with them. Not me, of course,' she said regretfully.

'Not yet,' murmured Anna, and helped Jo to more pizza. 'How would you feel if Jack Logan did get back with Auntie?' she asked bluntly, ignoring Kate's glare.

Jo thought about it as she munched. 'I wouldn't mind at all. He's cool. And he's potty about Kate.'

'Why do you think that?' demanded Kate, her colour high.

Jo gave her a pitying look. 'It was pretty obvious! Besides,' she said thoughtfully, 'you sort of look right together.'

When they got home Kate waited until Jo was in bed, then rang Jack to report on the topic of conversation over pizza at the Maitland house.

'Anna just asked her straight out?' said Jack, laughing. 'What did you do?'

'Blush,' said Kate succinctly. 'Trust Anna to ask the question I wouldn't dare to. Anyway, we're in the clear. She seems quite happy about you as the current man in my life.'

'The only man in your life! Was marriage mentioned?'

'Even Anna didn't go that far!'

'Pity. Jo's opinion would have been interesting.'

'She thinks we look sort of right together, if that's any comfort.'

'Damn right it is! Dad's very happy about Sunday, by the way. Last I heard he was off to buy the biggest Easter egg in town.'

'How sweet!' Kate took in a deep, unsteady breath. 'Oh, God, Jack, I do hope there's a happy ending to all this.'

'Amen to that. In the meantime I'll call in tomorrow evening to make the most of my daughter while I can.'

Jack's second visit was as much a success as the first. Joanna opened the door to him again and greeted him with such open pleasure that Kate could tell he wanted to hug her. He stayed for an hour, admired the sweatshirts purchased as birthday presents for the twins, and approved the white jeans and jade-green top Joanna fetched to show him.

'I was going to wear my mini-skirt to the party,' she told him, 'but Kate and Anna said the jeans would be better.'

'Try them on and show Jack how you'll look tomorrow, if you like,' said Kate, and Joanna rushed off immediately.

Jack groaned. 'Mini-skirt with those long legs?'

'My sentiments exactly,' said Kate, grinning. 'Anna's, too.'

Joanna came back into the room in her party gear, her eyes sparkling as she did a twirl. 'What do you think?' she asked Jack.

'Absolutely gorgeous,' he said without hesitation.

Kate and Joanna saw him to the door when he left soon afterwards, and Jack kissed Jo's cheek and Kate's mouth before getting into his car.

'You really like him, don't you?' said Jo as they waved him off.

'Yes, darling, I really do. Now, take the new things off and climb into your pyjamas. You need an early night tonight if you're partying tomorrow.'

It was hard to know who was the more tense when Kate delivered Joanna to the Carey house the following evening. Music was thumping from a barn decorated with fairy lights and a large streamer wishing Josh and Leo a happy birthday, and Jo took in a deep breath as the two boys raced towards her, their eyes snapping with excitement as she handed them the parcels she'd taken ages to pack earlier.

'Hi,' they said in unison as they tore away the paper. 'Great! Just what we wanted—thanks a lot.' They handed the presents to their mother and grabbed Jo's arm. 'Leave your coat with Mum and come *on*, it's party time!'

With anxious eyes Kate watched her ewe lamb run with the twins towards the lights and music, then turned to smile ruefully at their mother.

Megan Carey patted her hand. 'She'll have a great time. Don't worry; the others are a nice crowd of kids and Jim and Ben are on hand to keep a discreet eye on things.'

Kate thanked her warmly, told her she was at the Maitland house if needed and, with a last glance towards the barn, waved at Ben at his post on the door and went to join Anna.

As usual Anna's company was a calming influence as Kate reported on the previous evening.

'He seems to be calling in quite a lot lately. Are you still just good friends?'

'Jack wants more than that.'

'Of course he does—he's a man!' Anna looked at her curiously. 'Does he want to marry you?'

'Yes.'

'Do you want to marry *him*?'

'Yes.'

'Then what's stopping you—?' Anna breathed in sharply and put a hand on her stomach, her eyes wide.

Kate jumped to her feet in alarm. 'What's wrong?'

'Nothing at all.' A beatific smile spread over Anna's face. 'I think my baby just said hello for the first time.'

Kate hugged her. 'How lovely! Isn't it the most wonderful feeling—?' She bit her lip and stood back, colour rushing into her face as Anna stared at her in silent, wide-eyed question. Kate sat down abruptly and took in a deep breath. 'It's all going to come out tomorrow, anyway, so I'll tell you first, Anna. I remember exactly how it feels to be pregnant because, although she doesn't know it yet, Joanna is my daughter, not my niece.'

Anna gave a screech and pulled Kate into her arms, tears pouring down her face as she held her close for a long, emotional interval. 'Sorry, sorry!' she said at last. 'It's hormones. But you must know about that. For heaven's sake don't leave me in suspense, love—' She stopped dead and moved back to peer into Kate's face, swallowing hard. 'Oh, my God, it's Jack, isn't it? He's her father.'

Kate sat with her on the sofa and told her story with as little drama as possible, but by the end of it both of them were in tears again. 'So tomorrow, after Easter Sunday lunch at Mill House,' Kate finished thickly, 'Jack and I are going to make a clean breast of it and throw ourselves on our daughter's mercy. Funny, really,' she added, sniffing, 'I've kept my secret all these years, and now I've told my story three times in one week.'

'Three times?'

'Jack's father.'

'Oh, of *course*.' Anna blew out her cheeks. 'Poor man. He must have thought he was seeing a ghost if Jo looks that much like his wife.'

'She does. Margaret Logan had dark curling hair like Jack's, but otherwise it could have been Jo in the photograph. When I saw it the hairs stood up on the back of my neck.'

'I bet they did.' Anna let out a deep breath. 'It's a pity you're driving Jo home. You could do with a stiff drink. I know I could. But, since neither of us can indulge, let's have some coffee.'

In the end Kate made the coffee because Anna was in such a daze after the revelations that she couldn't concentrate enough to operate the machine. She was still talking about Jo when Kate's phone interrupted the flow.

'Joanna!' Kate spilt some coffee as she grabbed the phone, then blew out her cheeks in relief. 'Oh, Jack, thank God. I thought something was wrong with Jo.'

'Why?' he demanded. 'Didn't she want to go to the party?'

'She wanted to so much I just hope she isn't disappointed.'

'She won't be. She's probably having the time of her life. How did she look?'

'To quote you, Jack, she looked absolutely gorgeous.'

'In that case she's probably beating off dance partners with a stick. If they have dance partners these days. Tell her I want chapter and verse tomorrow.' Jack took in an audible breath. 'How the hell are we supposed to get any sleep tonight, Katie?'

'Beats me.' Kate glanced at her watch. 'Only half an hour to go and I pick her up.'

'Next time I'll do that—I hope.'

'I hope so too, Jack.'

'That was Daddy, worrying about his daughter, I assume,' said Anna, handing Kate a fresh cup of coffee.

'About tomorrow too, like me!'

'Try not to worry, love. Knowing Jo as I do, I'm sure she'll take it well.'

'I just keep thinking she'll hate me for giving her away.'

Anna put her arm round her. 'Jo loves you far too much to do that. She's also mature enough to understand why you felt you had to.'

When Kate arrived back at the Carey house the party had transferred to the kitchen where all the flushed, excited guests were consuming mugs of hot chocolate while they waited to be picked up. Jo was in the middle of an animated group in loud discussion over some pop band, totally unaware she was being watched, and Megan Carey laughed softly as she showed Kate into the room.

'Someone had a really great time, by the sound of it.'

Kate grinned. 'Not only Jo. Everyone else too.'

'Kate!' Jo's eyes lit up as she turned round.

'Hi. Did you have a good time?'

'The best,' said Jo simply, and with unaffected good manners thanked Megan and Jim Carey, then said her goodbyes to the group, who followed her outside to Kate's car to wave her off.

'Thanks again for the presents. See you Tuesday,' shouted Leo and Josh in unison.

Jo nodded vigorously and waved until the car reached a bend which took it out of sight of the house. 'That was such a cool party,' she told Kate with satisfaction. 'Great music, with a DJ, and there was a real bar. We had cocktails! Non-alcoholic,' she added hastily.

'I'm glad you enjoyed it, love,' said Kate with relief.

'Did you have a nice time with Anna? Silly question,' added Jo with a giggle. 'I expect you talked and drank coffee all night. Is she OK?'

'She's euphoric. She felt the baby move for the first time while I was there.'

'Wow!' said Jo, awed. 'Did she cry?'

'Yes, a bit,' admitted Kate. 'I even shed a godmotherly tear myself. Are you tired, darling?' she asked as they arrived home.

'I wasn't until now,' Jo admitted.

'Straight up to bed then. You need some sleep.'

'You do too, Kate; we're partying again tomorrow,' said Jo happily.

Kate woke up downstairs in the middle of the night, to find Joanna patting her hand.

'Oh, darling,' she said, shivering. 'I'm so sorry. Did I frighten you to death?'

'A bit. You came into my room, then sort of glided out again, so I got up to see if you were all right. You didn't answer me so I realised you were sleepwalking. A girl in my dorm does that.' Jo pulled a face. 'It's creepy, but Miss Hayes said sleepwalkers mustn't be shocked awake, so I followed you down here before I woke you. I'll get your dressing gown,' she added as Kate's teeth chattered. 'Then I'll make you some tea, or something.'

'You get the dressing gown, I'll make the tea,' said Kate. 'Sorry about this. It's a stupid habit.'

'I know. Mummy told me—shan't be long.' Joanna raced upstairs, and Kate pulled herself together and made for the kitchen to fill the kettle, glad to get into her dressing gown when Jo ran back with it.

'You should go back to bed,' she said sternly, holding it out.

Kate hugged her and promised that once she'd made their drinks she would do as she was told. Back in bed she drank her tea, then slid down under the covers, glad to get warm again while she waited for morning, knowing of old that she'd get no more sleep that night. But, to her delight, Jack rang before she got up.

'How are you, my darling?'

'All the better for hearing your voice, Jack,' she assured him.

'And how's our daughter? God, that gives me such a kick to say that. Did Jo enjoy the party?'

'She certainly did. I'll leave it to her to tell you the details.' Kate sighed. 'Time to get up, I suppose. What are you doing right now?'

'I'm in bed, waiting impatiently to see my two girls again.' His voice dropped a tone. 'I wish I had you here with me.'

Kate laughed, told him she loved him and ordered him to behave himself until she got to Mill House.

'Does that mean I don't have to once you come?'

'Certainly not,' she said primly. 'Thank you for ringing, Jack. I was feeling pretty tense.'

'I thought you might be. Do you feel better now?'

'Yes. I love you, Jack.'

She heard a quick intake of breath. 'I love you too, my darling. See you soon, and don't be late.'

Feeling a lot more prepared to face the day, Kate got up and had a bath, then came out to find Jo on the landing, her eyes anxious.

'Are you all right, Kate?'

'I'm fine. Sorry I gave you such a fright. I'd promise not to do it again, if I could.'

'I don't mind! I was just worried you might fall on the stairs.'

'It's never happened yet,' Kate assured her briskly. 'Right then, your turn in the bath.'

There was much discussion as to the appropriate wear for lunch at Mill House but knowing that Jo would inevitably spend time with Bran in the garden, Kate advised jeans and sweaters again for both of them and for Jo a chunky navy fleece with a hood in case it was chilly later on. Jo spent the morning making more cakes for Jack and, once these were iced and carefully packed in a plastic box, she begged to take off for Mill House.

'Jack won't mind if we're a bit early, will he?'

'You just want to see Bran,' accused Kate, laughing.

'True.' Jo's eyes danced. 'But you want to see Jack!'

When Kate turned down the drive to Mill House Jo's eyes were like saucers.

'Gosh, you were right,' she breathed in awe. 'It is a big garden.' She bit her lip, frowning.

'What's up now?'

Jo's knuckles were white as she gripped the box of cakes. 'If Jack is this rich I can't give him cakes as a present.'

'I can assure you,' said Kate with conviction, 'that he would like nothing better. Anyone can go out and buy something—like me. But you made him something with your own fair hands. Mega Brownie points for that, believe me.'

Jo relaxed, then said 'Wow!' as the house came into view. 'What a place—oh, and look, there's Mr Logan with Bran.' She put the box on the floor and was out of the car almost before Kate switched off the ignition. 'Hi, Mr Logan, hello Bran.'

Tom helped Kate from the car, smiling as he watched his granddaughter frolicking with the excited dog. 'How are you, my love?'

'As well as can be expected,' she said wryly, kissing him, then smiled radiantly as Jack came out of the house, a look in his eyes that warmed her right down to her toes. 'Good morning. How are you?'

'All the better for seeing you,' he assured her, and put his arm round her as he kissed her.

Joanna abandoned the dog to run to him. 'Hello, Jack. Happy Easter.'

'Likewise. Do I get a kiss too?'

Joanna promptly obliged, then turned to Tom Logan and reached up to kiss his cheek. 'Happy Easter, Mr Logan.'

'And a Happy Easter to you, sweetheart,' he said, clearing his throat. 'Let's go inside. Molly wants to meet you. It's all right, Jo,' he added, eyes twinkling. 'Bran can come too.'

'I've got to get something from the car first,' she said and ran to get her box of cakes. 'It's a little Easter present for you, Jack,' she said diffidently, taking off the lid.

He stood very still for a moment as he saw the cakes. Then he handed the box to his father and hugged Jo close. 'Thank you, pet. That's the nicest present I've ever had.'

'It certainly puts mine in the shade,' said Kate, resigned, and handed him one of the carrier bags she took out of the car. 'I've got one for you too, Tom.'

There was much laughter as the men received large chocolate Easter eggs with *Tom* written on one in white icing, and *Jack* on the other.

'But you have to share with me,' warned Kate. 'I love chocolate.'

'She certainly does,' said Jo as they went into the house. 'Kate ate more than half the box you gave me, Jack.'

'It's amazing she stays so slim,' he said, shaking his head, and smiled as he went into the kitchen. 'Molly, you've met Kate of course, but this is Joanna.'

'Hello, Miss Durant.' Molly wiped her hand on her apron and held it out, smiling. 'Hi, Joanna. I hear you went to a party last night. Did you have a good time?'

'I certainly did. Nice to meet you, Molly.' Jo shook the hand and sniffed the air. 'Wow! Something smells wonderful.'

'I hope you like turkey.' Molly turned to Kate. 'I've laid the table in here because the boss said it would be easier for you. Everything's ready. The turkey's in the warming oven with the vegetables, but the gravy should be heated through before you dish up.'

Kate handed her a carrier bag. 'Thank you, Molly. This is for you—just a little joke present to mark the occasion.'

The girl flushed with pleasure, stammering her thanks as

she received a chocolate egg inscribed *Molly* and, after instructions about ice cream in the freezer and a plate of treats for Bran in the refrigerator, the young cook wished them all a happy day and went home to her family.

'I'll show you the rest of the house after lunch, Jo,' said Jack, 'but I think we'd better eat now if the meal's ready.'

'You pour the wine, and I'll carve,' said his father, as Kate turned the heat up under the gravy. He took the turkey from the warming oven and put it on the table, then handed the oven gloves to Joanna. 'You can put the vegetable dishes on the table, love.'

Kate had been utterly convinced beforehand that she wouldn't be able to eat a thing, but in Jack's large, welcoming kitchen, with Jo so obviously enjoying herself, she relaxed and tucked into turkey and stuffing and roast potatoes with as much gusto as her child, who obviously considered Bran's presence in his bed the crowning touch to the meal.

'So tell us about the party,' said Jack, when Jo was into a second helping.

'It was just brilliant! In London I always felt like the odd one out at neighbours' parties because I'm away at school. But Josh and Leo made sure I knew everyone right from the start and they were all friendly so I had a really good time.'

'Did you dance a lot?' asked Tom.

'They don't dance, Dad,' teased Jack. 'They just prance around together.'

'We do dance,' said Jo indignantly, and smiled at him sweetly. 'It's just different from the minuets and things they did in your day.'

'*Touché*,' chuckled Tom Logan as Jack threw back his head and laughed, utterly delighted with his daughter.

'Cheeky!' said Kate, grinning.

'Josh and Leo asked if I could go to the cinema with them on Tuesday,' announced Jo, with a sideways look at Kate.

'Mrs Carey will bring them in and their dad will collect them from Park Crescent afterwards. If that's all right with you?'

Not daring to meet Jack's eyes, Kate agreed that it would be perfectly all right.

'Thanks, Kate. I met lots of people last night but I like Josh and Leo best,' added Jo. 'Because they're adopted, like me, I suppose. Did you know Mrs Carey was a twin?' she asked Jack.

'No—no, I didn't,' he said, and swallowed the rest of his wine.

'They prefer one of the parents to be a twin if they want to adopt twins,' Joanna informed the company at large.

Kate exchanged a wild look with Jack. 'When did Elizabeth tell you that you were adopted, Jo?'

'A long time ago, when I was in nursery school. She said other mothers had to take whatever baby God gave them, but she'd chosen me because I was special.' Joanna eyed her in surprise. 'You must have known about it.'

'Yes,' managed Kate. 'I knew. But Elizabeth never mentioned that she'd told you.'

Tom Logan shifted uneasily in his seat, and Kate smiled at him reassuringly. 'You look tired.'

'I didn't sleep much last night. Overdid the golf again,' he said unconvincingly.

'Jo didn't sleep enough last night, either,' said Kate as she got up to clear away plates. 'She found me walking in my sleep, so we had tea and hot chocolate in the middle of the night to recover.'

'It was all right,' said Jo, picking up a vegetable dish. 'Mummy told me that Kate did that sometimes, so I knew what was happening.'

'Pretty scary for you, just the same,' said Jack, meeting Kate's eyes.

'I've got something for you, Joanna,' said Tom, getting up. 'Come with me—yes, Bran, you can come too.'

Jo went with him eagerly, the dog padding after her, and Jack got up and caught Kate to him.

'I'll send Dad home and then we sit down with Jo. If she knows she's adopted she might as well know the rest of it.'

Kate put her head on his shoulder. 'You're right. I'll just load the dishwasher and clear up, then maybe we can walk in the garden. It might be easier outside.'

'It won't be easy anywhere,' said Jack heavily, 'but it has to be done.'

Between them they managed to make the kitchen tidy by the time Jo came back with Tom, carrying a huge Easter egg. She put it on the table and went straight to Kate to throw her arms round her, burrowing her face into her shoulder.

'I showed Joanna some photographs,' said Tom, his eyes meeting his son's. 'But I left the explanations to you.'

'*Dad*—' began Jack wrathfully, but Kate shook her head.

'I'm glad you did, Tom.' She put Jo away from her and looked into the dazed elfin face searchingly. 'Jack and I need to tell you a story, darling, to explain why you look just like the girl in the photograph.' Kate looked up. 'You needn't stay, Tom.'

'I started it, so of course I'll stay.'

'Then let's take Bran out into the garden,' suggested Jack. 'We'll make our confessions in the sunshine.'

'Confessions?' said Jo fearfully, looking from his face to Kate's.

Once outside the four of them paced along the gravel paths and around the millpond while Kate told Joanna her story. When she came to the part where she heard that Jack had married someone else, he took over and told his daughter how he'd been a fool to even look at another woman, let alone get into a situation where he felt he had to marry her.

'But you had to take responsibility for the baby,' said Jo, going straight to the heart of the matter.

'Exactly. But not only was the baby born too soon to survive, it turned out that I couldn't have been the father, so Dawn agreed to a divorce.'

'But what happened to your baby, Kate?' asked Jo. Then, seeing the look in Kate's eyes, she breathed in sharply, an incredulous look dawning in her own. 'Oh. You mean—' She swallowed hard. 'I'm the baby?'

'Yes, darling. Elizabeth persuaded me to let her bring you up because I was on my own and was quite ill for a while after you were born. Also I had to work and she could look after you better than I could.' Kate took in a deep, shaky breath. 'But it broke my heart to part with you.'

'And you look like the girl in the photograph because she's my mother,' said Jack with such obvious difficulty that Jo's lip trembled in sympathy. 'I've only just found out that I have the incredible luck to have a daughter, but Kate couldn't bear to tell you the truth because you're still grieving for the only parents you ever knew.'

Joanna stopped by a carved stone bench. 'I need to sit down.'

'Me, too,' said Tom, and took her hand to draw her down beside him.

Joanna fondled Bran as she looked up at Kate and Jack, who were leaning against each other for support. 'You know, I was going to look for my real mother one day, as long as you didn't mind, Kate.'

'Now you don't have to,' said her grandfather.

'No, I don't.' Jo was silent for a long time, but at last she stood up and flung her arms round Kate. 'Now I know why I've always felt so close to you. But I used to try and hide it so Mum wouldn't be hurt.'

'And I tried my best just to be Auntie,' said Kate unsteadily, 'but it was so *hard*. I could hardly bear it sometimes. I hated it when they sent you away to school. The day they took you off to Manor House I cried my eyes out.'

Jack had been very silent during this exchange, but Kate

could feel the tension in his body. She was about to put him out of his misery and ask Joanna how she felt about him when her child detached herself and held out her hand to him.

'I've only just met you so this is pretty weird.' She smiled shakily. 'But I'm sure I'll get used to you as my father pretty quickly now I know.'

'If this was a film,' said Kate, trying to introduce a lighter note into the situation since Jack was near to tears as he grasped his daughter's hand, 'you would run into his arms and cry "Daddy!"'

To her relief Jo chuckled. 'You've been watching too many TV movies.'

'I'd like it very much, just the same,' said Jack huskily.

'OK then,' said Jo, smiling at him, and stood on tiptoe to kiss his cheek as he put his arms round her and hugged her close. 'So what do I call you now?' she asked.

'Jack works for me,' he said promptly.

Jo nodded. 'Me, too.' She turned to Kate questioningly.

'I'm still the same old Kate, darling.'

'But I,' said Tom Logan, getting up from his seat, 'will only answer to Grandpa. OK?'

'OK,' agreed Jo, looked dazed. 'Gosh, this is all a lot to take in.'

'Let's go inside,' said Jack. 'Bran needs his dinner.'

'And I need some tea,' said Kate, suddenly weak at the knees from excess of emotion. 'While I enjoy a cup or two with Grandpa in front of the fire, perhaps you'd like to show Jo round the house, Jack.'

He assured her he was only too delighted and, after Jo had the pleasure of giving Bran his meal she went off with Jack. Kate watched them go with eyes which suddenly filled with tears. Tom Logan put his arms round her.

'There, there, darling, no need to cry. I was quite right, you know. Joanna is a mature enough child to understand.'

'And to forgive?'

'She doesn't see any need for forgiveness, Kate.'

Kate drew away to blow her nose and smiled up at him, comforted. 'I hope you're right.'

'Of course I am. Now, you make the tea and I'll carry the tray.'

When Jack and Joanna joined them in the living room Tom Logan smiled at them.

'Sorry, but I couldn't wait for you; I started on the cakes.'

'Then I'd better get stuck in before they vanish,' said Jack, filling a plate.

'What did you think of the house, Jo?' asked Kate.

Jo looked up from stroking Bran. 'It's fantastic. Jack said he did it all himself.'

'I had some help,' he admitted, grinning, and sat down by Kate. 'But the concept, the design and the interior décor is all my own work. I used to haunt the place while it was being restored. Some of the brickies and carpenters thought I was a pain in the neck.'

'But you had to see it was done properly,' said Jo in approval. 'Just like Kate and her house.'

Jack nodded. 'Talking of which, Jo, I think you ought to know that I want to marry Kate as soon as possible.'

'I have to agree because I've already turned him down twice,' Kate explained. 'He might never ask me again.' She smiled at Jo. 'Are you going to congratulate us?'

'Pretty weird, congratulating my own parents!' Jo smiled and bent to kiss Kate and Jack in turn. 'But I do—' She frowned suddenly. 'Does this mean you're going to sell your house, Kate, and come to live here?'

'Close,' said Kate. 'We're both coming to live here, if that's all right with you, Jo, and I'm going to make Aunt Edith's house over to you. If you're agreeable we'll let it out and you can have the rent money for your college fund. Do you want some tea?'

'No, thanks,' said Jo, stunned, and looked at Jack. 'Do you have a Coke or something?'

'Molly stocked me up, so I'm sure she thought of it. Go and forage in the kitchen, help yourself.'

'I'll come with you, Jo,' said Tom, and laughed. 'Look, Bran's coming too. You've made a hit there, love.'

When they were alone Kate turned to Jack anxiously. 'How do you feel?'

'Fantastic.' He let out a deep breath. 'I just want to sit here with you and fall apart with relief. She took it so well, didn't she?'

'Amazingly well.'

Jack rubbed his cheek against her hair. 'How do you think she'll react if I suggest adopting her officially?'

'I've no idea. If she wants to stay Joanna Sutton, you may have to live with that.'

'I can do it. At this moment in time I can do anything,' he said, and turned her face up to his to kiss her.

'Oops, don't look, Bran!' said Joanna, interrupting them. 'Be careful, Grandpa,' she warned, turning to Tom. 'Make sure you knock on doors from now on.'

He laughed and ruffled her hair. 'I had plenty of practice at that when they were young, believe me!'

'Right,' said Jack, getting up. 'Now we are all present again I have a certain omission to make good. Everyone received a present today except Kate.' He took a box from his pocket and went down on one knee in front of her. 'Here we go again. For the third time of asking, Katherine Margaret Durant, will you be my wife?'

'Oh, yes, please,' she said, so fervently Joanna giggled.

'Don't try to give it back again,' said Jack sternly as he slid his mother's ring on Kate's finger.

'No chance,' she assured him and waggled her fingers at Jo as she bent to examine the ring. 'This belonged to your grandmother—the girl in the photograph.'

'It's so pretty! I don't know how you could bear to part with it last time,' said Jo, examining the posy of diamonds, and smiled at Jack. 'My name's Margaret, too.'

His eyes flew to Kate who nodded. 'I told you I laid down the law about the names. So she is Joanna, which is the nearest I could get to your baptismal name of John, and Margaret after your mother.'

Seeing that his son was momentarily deprived of words, Tom Logan blew his nose loudly. 'Right then. Now Joanna knows the truth, when are you two going to tie the knot?'

'I hadn't thought that far,' said Kate, eying her daughter uneasily.

'I had,' said Jack with feeling.

'If you get a special licence,' said Jo matter-of-factly, 'you could get married just before I go back to school, then you wouldn't have to worry about me while you were away on your honeymoon.' She grinned broadly as her parents stared at her open-mouthed. 'You're not getting any younger, so why hang about?'

'My sentiments exactly,' said her grandfather in approval.

'Besides, Bran and I want to be bridesmaids,' said Jo, hugging the dog.

On a sunny, brisk April day there was a big turnout for the marriage of John Logan to Katherine Durant. Due to the hole-and-corner misery of his first marriage, Jack had insisted on celebrating in style as he finally married the love of his life. Miss Joanna Sutton, soon to be officially Joanna Logan, was chief bridesmaid, Mrs Ben Maitland having regretfully declined the office of matron of honour due to her rapidly increasing girth.

Tall and elegant in formal morning coat, Jack turned at the altar with Ben Maitland as the organist began the wedding march, and smiled, a lump in his throat, as he saw his bride, in a narrow dress of champagne slipper satin, enter the church on his father's arm, with their daughter close behind in a matching chiffon which, she told Anna, made her look like the fairy off the Christmas tree, but which secretly was exactly the kind of dress she'd always yearned for. She winked at the Carey twins as she passed and beamed at Anna. But when she smiled reassuringly at her father as she took the bride's bouquet, Jack smiled back so proudly she felt warm inside.

The sun shone on the wedding group as the photographers dodged about, with much laughter from the assembled guests when the bridesmaid insisted on the inclusion of a handsome black retriever in all the shots, complete with brand-new leash and a rose thrust through his collar. The reception in the hall of Mill House was a very animated affair with an array of Molly's delicious food that had all the guests demanding the name of the caterer, and after Ben had made a witty, entertaining speech and proposed the health of the enchanting bridesmaid and her canine escort, Jack waited for silence, then smiled down at his wife and across the hall at the daughter standing between the Carey twins with Bran.

'Today I've finally been united with the beautiful woman I wanted to marry years ago, the moment I first set eyes on her. And, to add to my incredible good fortune in doing so, I also gained a beautiful daughter.'

'Logan's luck,' shouted someone, above the applause. The Carey twins cheered as Jack beckoned Joanna over to stand beside him and he grinned at them, then kissed Kate and Jo in turn and raised his glass. 'Ladies and gentlemen, please join me in a toast to Kate and Joanna, for making me the happiest—*and* luckiest—man on the planet.'

THE MILLIONAIRE'S REWARD

BY
ANGIE RAY

A RITA® Award winning author for her first novel, **Angie Ray** has written historical and paranormal novels, as well as romance. The mind of this native Southern Californian is buzzing with ideas for stories and she loves brainstorming while taking walks. Her husband and two children also provide plenty of distraction, but sooner or later she's always drawn back to the computer for 'just one more scene'– which invariably leads to another book!

Chapter One

The necklace was the gaudiest, ugliest piece of jewelry Garek Wisnewski had ever seen.

Rubies and emeralds vied for glittering supremacy in a bright yellow-gold setting decorated with enough curlicues and whorls to make a Russian czar blink. Any woman wearing this necklace risked blinding innocent bystanders—or being mistaken for a Christmas tree. This bauble had nothing to do with beauty or elegance—it was about money, pure and simple.

"It's perfect," he told the chignoned blonde behind the counter who'd been batting her eyelashes at him ever since he entered the store. "I'll take it."

"An excellent choice," she congratulated him. "You have exquisite taste, Mr. Wisnewski."

"Thank you."

The young woman didn't appear to notice the irony in his voice. Placing the necklace in a satin-lined case and ringing up the sale, she chatted vivaciously. "Women adore rubies and emeralds. They're so much more interesting than diamonds, don't you think? I'm sure your girlfriend will love the necklace."

She paused to check his reaction to her comment, and he recognized the look in her eyes. In the last hellish month, he'd been forced to deal with numerous women, all with similar predatory expressions. He'd devised several strategies to deal with them: attack, retreat and play dead.

He used the attack method only in extreme situations; the blond salesclerk didn't qualify—at least not yet. Retreat was impossible until he got his credit card back. Which left only one option.

He didn't offer either a confirmation or a denial of her guess about the necklace's recipient.

She wasn't deterred by his lack of response, however. Finishing the transaction, she slid the jewelry case across the glass counter—along with a business card.

"My home phone number's on the back. If you ever want a private viewing of our…inventory, please call me."

Garek shoved the box into his pocket, but left the card on the counter. "That won't be necessary," he growled.

He strode to the door, almost bumping into another customer who blew into the shop, along with a freezing gust of wind. Short and round, the man stood in the doorway, nose dripping, as he stared up at Garek.

"Hey, I know you!" The man's Neanderthal forehead cleared and he winked at Garek. "I saw your picture in the *Chicago Trumpeter* this morning. Hank, right? Heh, heh, heh—"

"Excuse me," Garek said icily. "You're blocking the door."

The man stopped sniggering and quickly stepped aside. Garek exited, shutting the shop door with a bang. He stood on the cold, dark sidewalk, sleet stinging his face and hands.

He yanked on his gloves and wrapped his muffler around the lower half of his face. Annoyance making his steps brisker than usual, he headed down the sidewalk, cursing himself for ever agreeing to talk to that damn reporter.

He'd broken his usual no-interview rule because she'd said she was doing an article on how business-men had contributed to the revitalization of the city by providing jobs for displaced workers. If he'd known what she really intended, he would have shown her out of his office immediately. Now, because of lowering his guard for one moment, his life had become a liv-ing hell. Oh, he'd been mildly amused at first. The rib-ald jokes from the men. The fluttering glances from the women. But then, he'd started getting letters. Sacks of them. And women started showing up at his office. And his apartment. At restaurants where he was dining...

Lengthening his stride, he stepped over a puddle. Last night had been the final straw. He'd been about to close a deal with a prospective client over smoked pork tenderloin and Yukon Gold mashed potatoes when an enterprising young woman named Lilly Lade had shown up professing to be a singing-telegram girl—but she'd seemed more interested in stripping than singing. While horrified matrons looked on, he'd had to bun-dle the woman up and forcibly escort her from the restaurant.

Unfortunately, once outside, she'd thrown her arms

around his neck and planted a kiss on his mouth. He'd thrust Lilly away, but not before a tabloid photographer had snapped several shots.

Trying to ignore the freezing wind, Garek hunched his shoulders and turned the corner to where his limousine waited. The situation was no longer amusing. In fact, he was damn well fed up—

"Oof!"

A woman made the small sound as she ran into him at full speed. The packages in her arms went flying. And so did she. She landed on her rear in the snow.

Instinctively, he crouched by her side. "Are you all right?"

Her blue eyes, framed by long black lashes, looked slightly dazed, but she nodded. "I'm fine…."

His gaze dropped to her mouth, watching her lips form the words. Her upper lip was long and perfectly straight, with no indentation at all, curling up slightly at the corners. The lower lip was shorter, and fuller, but not much. The effect was amazingly sensual.

He bent closer to hear her over the whistling wind.

"I'm so sorry—"

"It was my fault," he interrupted, dragging his gaze away from her mouth. "I wasn't looking where I was going."

"No, no. I was running, trying to catch my train— oh, my things!"

With only slight support from his steadying arm, she scrambled to her feet and grabbed a box that had fallen onto the ground. A turquoise scarf and tissue paper peeping out from under the crushed lid, she stuffed the box back into her bag.

"Are you sure you're all right?" He picked up her hat

and she crammed it onto her head, the bright red yarn concealing all but a few short black curls.

"Yes, I'm sure." She smiled ruefully, her teeth very white against the golden hue of her skin, a dimple appearing in her cheek. "My packages have suffered the most, I think."

"Let me help you," he said, capturing a bag on the verge of blowing away. He swept several small boxes into it, his attention focused more on her than his task. She didn't seem to recognize him—a rarity these days. He couldn't see her figure, wrapped up as it was in a slightly shabby coat that was several sizes too big. But she was small, perhaps an inch or two over five feet, and he'd felt the fine bones of her hand through her mitten when he'd helped her up.

He picked up a tiny pair of pink, yellow and blue tennis shoes. He glanced at the woman again. Young—but not too young to have a child. "There's mud on these shoes. I'll replace them and anything else that's damaged."

"Oh, no!" she protested immediately. "It'll wash off. And if it doesn't, my niece won't notice a few spots… oh!"

She hurried off to retrieve a baseball rolling slowly down the gutter toward a storm drain. He saw a magazine, its pages fluttering in the wind. "Is this yours?" he called to her as he bent to pick it up.

She glanced over her shoulder and nodded, before reaching for the baseball.

Garek picked up the magazine, then froze as he saw his own face staring up at him from the cover.

His jaw tightened. Ramming the tabloid into the sack, he stalked over to where she crouched in the gutter. As she stood up, he shoved the bag into her arms.

"Here," he said curtly. "Watch where you're going next time."

He stomped away, only to step directly into a puddle. Icy water splashed into the top of his shoe. Cursing under his breath, he squelched down the street to the waiting limo and climbed inside. "Home, Hardeep."

"Yes, sir," the chauffeur replied.

The car purring down the street, Garek looked out the window. He saw the woman still standing in the gutter, clutching her bags and staring at the limo. She wore an expression of profound bewilderment.

Anger swept through him. She must have been lurking on the corner, waiting for him. If the magazine hadn't given her away, he would've believed their collision was an accident. He'd even been about to offer her a ride home.

Oh, she was good, better than most. Innocent-looking—except for her mouth. He should have been warned by that mouth....

He sat in brooding silence until the chauffeur stopped in front of his apartment building. Not until he went inside and reached into his pocket did he realize that something was missing.

The emerald-and-ruby necklace was gone.

Cold, wet and tired, Ellie entered her apartment and dumped her bags on the small kitchenette table with a sigh of relief. "Hi, Martina," she said to her cousin who was checking a large pot on the stove. "How'd you do on your final?"

"Fine. It was easier than I expected." Martina lifted a steamer, laden with tamales, from the pot and set them on the counter. She glanced over her shoulder, her long, dark hair swinging. Her already well-arched brows rose. "What happened to you, *chica?*"

Ellie shook her head as she pulled off her coat and wet mittens and walked over to hold her cold hands next to the ancient but blessedly warm furnace. "It's a long story. Suffice it to say I bumped into Mr. Grinch and missed my train." She sniffed the air appreciatively. "Those tamales smell awfully good. Can I have one?"

"Well...okay, but just one. They're for the party tomorrow night. Who's this Mr. Grinch?"

"Nobody," Ellie dismissed the unpleasant man. Although in truth, with his sleek leather gloves and expensive limo he'd obviously been *somebody*. Somebody rich and spoiled who'd suddenly decided she wasn't worth the time and effort it took to be polite. Sinking into a chair, she peeled back the hot corn husk and bit into the tamale. The spiced meat inside burned her mouth, but she was too hungry to care. "Mmm, this is fantastic, Martina. Better than your father's. You should sell these. You'd make a fortune."

"I like cooking...but not that much." Briskly, Martina piled the tamales into a glass dish. "How was business at the gallery today?"

"Not bad. A lot of people came in. I talked one couple into taking a painting home to try it out. And I sold a sculpture." Carefully, Ellie broke a piece off the tamale and watched a thin wisp of steam rise into the air. "The woman loved it. She said it reminded her of the feeling she had when she first fell in love. She didn't even look at the price tag. But when I told her how much it was, she said she couldn't afford that much, and could I please give her a discount. I told her maybe a small one, but she said she could only pay half the price and so—"

"And so you ended up practically giving it away," Martina finished for her, shaking her head. "You never could bargain worth a dime. A Hernandez without the haggle gene—it's unnatural."

Ellie made a face at her cousin. "I'm getting better."

"Yeah, right. I thought you said Mr. Vogel was going to have to close the gallery if it didn't start making a profit."

Ellie bit her lip. She *had* said that—and it was the truth. The thought scared her. She'd worked hard, but the gallery had failed to meet its expenses the last three months in a row. If she didn't figure something out soon, Mr. Vogel wouldn't be able to afford to keep it open. And then what would Tom and Bertrice and all the other artists who showed their works at the gallery do? What would *she* do? She loved her job.

Okay, so occasionally she had to clean houses on the side to make ends meet—what was a little drudgery when she had the gallery to look forward to? At Vogel's, a hundred exciting, unexpected things could happen. A sculptor could come in, eager to debate the merits of his latest creation. A scruffy college student could walk through the door, carrying a portfolio of the most amazing sketches she'd ever seen. Or a customer could come in, someone eager to escape their narrow existence and view the world through a different perspective—a perspective of shape and form and color....

"Sales will pick up," she told Martina with more confidence than she felt.

"You need to advertise. Business is all about advertising." Martina, majoring in marketing at a nearby college, considered herself—at age twenty-one—an expert in all things related to business. "And contacts. You need to cultivate the right people."

Ellie grimaced. "You mean suck up to some rich business executives and their spouses?"

"It's called networking. You're such a snob, Ellie."

"I am not!"

"When it comes to art, you are. My heart bleeds for that poor woman who came to the gallery yesterday—"

"Martina! I told you what she said—"

"Oh, yes, she wanted to know if the painting would be a good investment. It's not a crime, Ellie, to want to make money."

"If she wants to make money, she should invest in real estate." Ellie glanced over her shoulder at the worn leather sofa in the living room—and the multihued artworks that covered every square inch of the wall above. "Art shouldn't be about money."

Martina rolled her eyes. "You're missing the point, Ellie. It *is* about money—at least for now. You should have found something to sell that woman, not suggested she try another gallery. You need to think like a businessman." Martina put the tamales in the refrigerator, then approached the bags on the table. "Did you get my magazine?"

"Yes, it's in there somewhere." Ellie nibbled her tamale absently. Was Martina right? Was she a snob when it came to art? Maybe. Well, okay, probably. An artist poured so much of himself into a piece, spent so much time and effort to get the composition, the colors, the textures and a thousand other details just exactly right. It seemed wrong somehow to let someone who cared nothing about the artist's creative endeavor take a piece home.

Unfortunately, she couldn't worry about right and wrong anymore.

She swallowed a bite of tamale with difficulty. She

couldn't allow the gallery to close because she didn't like the fact that someone saw dollar signs instead of art when they looked at a painting. She couldn't afford to demand that people appreciate a painting or a sculpture the way it deserved to be appreciated. "Okay, Martina. From now on, I'll act like a businessman. I'll be cold, hard, ruthless—"

"Maybe you can just be practical…what's this?" Martina let out a low whistle.

Ellie glanced up to see her cousin staring down at the contents of a flat jeweler's box.

"What'd you do, Ellie? Make a withdrawal at the bank?"

Brushing the soft *masa* crumbs off her fingers, Ellie got up to look in the box. She gasped when she saw its contents.

Emeralds and rubies flashed in the apartment's dim light, their sparkle silent testimony to their authenticity.

"Good heavens," Ellie said faintly. "It must belong to that man—Mr. Grinch."

"He's not going to be happy when he finds it missing," Martina observed.

"No, I don't think so," Ellie agreed, wondering who on earth he'd bought such a hideous necklace for. His wife? She couldn't imagine a snooty society maven ever wearing something so garish. A girlfriend on the side? Much more likely, she thought, wrinkling her nose.

She looked at the name of the jeweler on the white satin under the lid. "I guess I'll have to take it to the jeweler's tomorrow." She sighed. Tomorrow was Christmas Eve—she had two houses to clean and her aunt's and uncle's party afterward. She really didn't have time to make another trip up to Michigan Avenue.

It would serve him right if I didn't return it until *after* Christmas, she thought, feeling just a little bit grinchy herself.

"This guy must be really rich." Martina glanced sideways at Ellie. "I wonder who he is."

"I have no idea." And she didn't *want* to know.

"Mmm." Martina was still eyeing her. "Some old guy, I suppose."

"Not really. Thirty, maybe."

"Thirty! That's not bad at all. Good-looking?"

"I didn't think so," Ellie lied. In fact, her first impression had been that he was very attractive. When she'd first looked up into his concerned face, her heart had given an odd little thump. He'd seemed so friendly, his greenish eyes smiling down at her...until suddenly, for no reason at all, they'd turned a frosty gray.

She'd fumed over his rudeness all the way home. She'd apologized automatically—but really, the collision had been his fault as much as hers. He hadn't been looking where he was going and he'd been walking very fast. He'd knocked her off her feet, caused her to drop and damage some of her gifts and made her miss her train, as well. He could have at least offered her a ride. Not that she would have accepted, but still... He'd probably been worried that she'd get his fancy limo dirty.

No, he hadn't been attractive at all, she realized now. "He was big with mean eyes," she told her cousin.

"Fat?"

Actually, he'd felt like solid steel when she bumped into him. "I couldn't tell—he had on an overcoat. But he had a Van Gogh sort of face."

"What's that supposed to mean?" Martina asked. "He only had one ear?"

Ellie laughed and shook her head, but didn't say any more. It was too hard to explain. In her mind's eye, she could see the man clearly, the heavy eyebrows, the penetrating eyes, the angular features just slightly asymmetrical....

"Hmmph. I don't know why rich men all have to be ugly as dirt." With a sigh, Martina reached into the bag again and pulled out the magazine she'd asked Ellie to buy. "Well, maybe not *all* rich men," she amended, holding up the magazine to show Ellie the cover. "Garek Wisnewski is a doll, don't you think?"

Ellie had grabbed the magazine at the store with barely a glance at the cover. Looking at it now, she stiffened.

Dominating the page was a picture of a half-dressed redhead and a man staring angrily at the camera—a man with familiar cold gray eyes below slashing black brows.

The expression on his face had been exactly the same a few hours ago when he'd left her standing in the gutter.

Ellie looked at the headline above the picture.

Main Course: Hanky Panky, it screamed in eye-popping red print. *Dessert: Chicago's Most Eligible Bachelor.*

Chapter Two

Getting in to see Garek Wisnewski was like trying to get in to see the pope.

Ellie had been worried that the office building might be closed on Christmas Eve, but it wasn't. Employees filled the marble foyer—at least the part Ellie could see from the security desk near the entrance while the guard inspected her ID. He looked at her license closely, as though he suspected it might be a forgery, before demanding to know her business. She told him, then waited, shivering every time someone opened the door and let a blast of cold air in, while the guard made a telephone call, casting suspicious glances at her the whole time.

As ten minutes stretched into twenty, Ellie began to be annoyed. She'd come straight here from cleaning the second house on her schedule and she felt grimy and sweaty. She needed to go home and wash and change for the party. She wanted to be at her uncle's, not standing in this cold foyer waiting on Garek Wisnewski. She wished she hadn't let Martina talk her into trying to contact him directly.

"Don't you see, Ellie?" Martina had said. "This is your chance. Return the necklace and ask him if he needs any art for his office. Maybe he'll buy something. And if you're lucky, maybe he'll ask you out on a date."

Ellie rolled her eyes. "I doubt he would appreciate anything at Vogel's. And if he asked me for a date—which he wouldn't!—there's no way *I* would agree to go anywhere with him. I told you how rude he was. Besides, what kind of man gets featured on the cover of tabloids with his 'exotic dancer' girlfriend?"

"Maybe that's why he was rude—because he was embarrassed about the picture."

Ellie glanced at the scowling face on the magazine cover—and at the redhead wearing a big smile and not much else. The caption identified her as Miss Lilly Lade and stated her occupation.

Embarrassed? Ellie didn't think so. There'd been too much hard self-assurance in his bearing. Even if he had been, that still didn't excuse his rudeness. Nor his execrable taste in women—and jewelry. Now the necklace made perfect sense.

But in the end, she hadn't been able to outargue Martina or her own conscience, which told her that if she really wanted to help everyone who relied on the gallery, she would swallow her pride and go see Garek Wisnewski.

It was the logical thing to do. No matter how rude he'd been, he'd be grateful when she returned his tacky necklace.

After looking up Wisnewski Industries in the phone book and discovering its ritzy address on the Loop, she took the train from her last job into town. When she first saw the skyscraper, it reminded her of a fortress—all gray stone with narrow, impenetrable windows.

The overzealous security guard reinforced the impression.

He finally hung up the phone and turned to her, a clipboard in his hand, his eyes still suspicious. "Fill in your name and address, and I'll give you a pass to go up. Leave your coat and things here."

Did he think she had a weapon hidden in a pocket? Ellie shed her wet coat and took the clipboard, filling in the gallery's address rather than her own. She clipped the plastic pass to the strap of her purse.

Upstairs, she had to run another gauntlet—of navy-suited, gimlet-eyed assistants. At the final desk sat a woman with shiny silver-gray hair cut like a helmet and piercing blue eyes who gazed disapprovingly at Ellie's jeans and yellow sweater. She made a brief phone call, then escorted Ellie into the inner office.

Wood paneling, plush carpet and heavy furniture met Ellie's gaze. Trite, but obviously expensive oil landscapes hung on the walls. Directly ahead, seated behind a carved mahogany desk in a thronelike chair, was Mr. Eligible Bachelor himself.

Dressed in a gray pinstripe suit, white shirt and black tie, he looked as conservative as his office, although not quite as elegant. His tie skewed slightly to one side as if he'd tugged at it, and his jacket looked a little tight across the shoulders. His clothes didn't really suit his blunt features and muscular build.

"So you tracked me down," he said.

Ellie stared into eyes as cold as the storm outside. "I beg your pardon?"

The cynical lines around his eyes and mouth deepened. "Do you think you're the first woman to engineer a meeting and come chasing after me?"

She stiffened. He thought she'd bumped into him on purpose in order to meet "Chicago's Most Eligible Bachelor?" Was *that* why he'd so abruptly abandoned her on the sidewalk yesterday?

What an ego!

Trying to control her temper, she walked forward and held out the jewelry case. "I came to return this."

He took the case and flipped up the lid. He stared at the necklace a moment, his expression inscrutable, then closed the box. Leaning back in his chair, he looked at her.

She expected him to thank her, express his gratitude, perhaps even apologize for his rudeness. But he did none of these things.

"I suppose you expect a reward," he said.

In that instant, Ellie realized she would prefer to scrub Mrs. Petrie's toilets every day for the rest of her life rather than sell anything from the gallery to this man. He sat there, making no effort to stand or invite her to sit, offering her money instead of thanks, his every action, his every word an insult. She knew this kind of man—one who cared nothing about people or their feelings, one who cared only about money and what it could buy. He would never spend his cold hard cash on something as frivolous as art. Contemporary art especially would be incomprehensible to him.

Ellie clenched her fists. Her first impulse was to refuse with icy politeness, then turn and walk out. But just yesterday she'd promised herself she would think like a businessman. Businessmen weren't polite—as Garek Wisnewski had just so unpleasantly demonstrated—and they weren't squeamish about money.

"Yes, I do expect a reward," she said with all the poise she could muster. She met his gaze directly, calmly, not blinking even when his eyebrows rose.

The corner of his mouth curled upward. "At least you're honest about it." He pulled a checkbook from his coat pocket. "How much?"

"Five thousand." She named the first figure that came into her head.

He stared at her for a long, silent moment.

Putting up her chin, she waited.

She didn't have to wait very long. With a shrug, he picked up a pen, wrote a check and held it out to her.

Taken off guard, she stared at the slip of paper. She might not have inherited the Hernandez haggle gene, but she'd thought *he* would know how to negotiate. What kind of businessman handed over five thousand dollars so easily?

"Well?"

Glancing up, she saw him watching her, his eyes narrowed. Quickly, she stepped forward and took the check. She glanced at it, seeing a five followed by the requisite number of zeros. She hesitated again, struggling with her conscience. She was about to give him the check back, when the phone rang.

Garek Wisnewski pressed a button and his assistant's voice came over the line.

"There's a delivery here from marketing," she said.

"Send it in." His gaze flickered toward Ellie.

Clearly, she was dismissed. His rudeness made her spine stiffen—and subverted her conscience. "Thanks for the check," she said airily. Stuffing the slip of paper in her purse, she headed for the door.

It opened before she reached it, and a skinny young man—a boy, really—entered, carrying a large, flat, cloth-covered rectangle. Setting it on a cherrywood table, he mumbled, "Mr. Johnson told me to bring this straight up," then bolted from the room, slamming the door behind him.

Ellie blinked at the boy's behavior. But probably all of Garek Wisnewski's employees were terrified of him, she decided, moving toward the door again.

A flutter caught her eye as the cloth slipped from the rectangle. She stopped, her eyes widening at the revealed portrait.

Or rather, at the revealing portrait.

Lilly Lade, in full-breasted, bare-buttocked, dimple-thighed glory, rose from a large white clamshell, her red hair contrasting vividly with the bright blue ocean behind her. Two leering "wind gods" hovered at one side, their expressions as crude as the artist's brushwork.

"Was there something else?"

Ellie jumped at the sound of his harsh voice. "No, not at all." But she couldn't resist adding, "I was just thinking this is exactly the kind of painting I would expect you to have." She smiled sweetly.

His stony gaze dropped to her mouth, then lifted. "You object to nude portraits?"

"No, I object to bad art."

"Ah. An expert."

The sarcasm in his voice annoyed her almost as much as his rude stare. "I work in a gallery."

"The poster store at the mall?"

"Vogel's in Pilsen," she snapped. "Specializing in

contemporary art. Feel free to stop by if you ever want to buy something with a little higher concept." Turning on her heel, she grabbed the doorknob and twisted it.

A large hand reached over her shoulder and rested against the door, preventing it from opening. Scowling, she glared over her shoulder. A broad expanse of male chest met her gaze. Quickly she looked up—a long way up. He was bigger than she remembered. How had he managed to cross the room so quickly and silently?

He loomed over her, staring down at her with narrowed eyes. "I've already paid—I'm not paying any more. Anything else you want to offer me will have to be for free."

Outrage stiffened her spine. "There's nothing I want to offer you," she said, yanking at the doorknob. It didn't budge. "Will you please take your hand off the door?"

His gaze wandered over her, lingering on her mouth. "If you change your mind, contact me—but first use that money to buy some clothes that have a little 'higher concept.'"

He released the door, and she yanked it open, angry enough to spit paint, and stormed out.

When she arrived home at her apartment, she went inside and slammed the door.

Martina came out of the bedroom, dressed in velvet pants and a red sweater, her head tilted as she put a dangling earring in her ear.

"You're back!" she said. "I was beginning to worry. How'd it go?"

"Fine." Ellie thrust her coat and boots into the closet, then stalked into the kitchen. "Although I'm thinking of writing a letter to the *Chicago Trumpeter*."

Martina, following her into the kitchen, blinked. "You are?"

"Yes, to tell them they made a mistake about Garek Wisnewski." Ellie took the five-thousand-dollar check from her purse, shoved it in the junk drawer and slammed it shut. "They should have named him Chicago's Most *Obnoxious* Bachelor."

It might have been Christmas Eve with most of the country in festive spirits, but Garek wasn't sharing their happy mood. As far as he was concerned, the day was the culmination of a perfectly rotten month.

The painting of Lilly Lade—Ted Johnson in marketing's infantile idea of a joke—had been annoying. The Hernandez woman witnessing the delivery, on top of taking him for five thousand dollars, had been galling. But neither of those compared with the torture that he now endured—Christmas Eve with his sister, Doreen.

"I went to a gala at the country club," she commented as a maid poured wine in Garek's glass. "All the right people were there. The Mitchells, the Branwells. Even the Palermos. Their nephew Anthony asked Karen to dance."

"Anthony Palermo is a total geek," Karen said, the first words she'd spoken during the meal. "He has hands like wet gym socks and breath like week-old dog food."

"Karen!" her mother exclaimed. "You mustn't talk about Anthony like that. The Palermos are one of the most wealthy and distinguished families in Chicago. You should remember that."

Karen lapsed back into a sullen silence that lasted until the unappetizing meal was finished and Doreen led the way to the living room, where a mountain of presents was piled under a twenty-foot gold-and-silver tree. Karen fell to her knees and started ripping open packages. Garek retrieved a slim, flat case from under the tree and handed it to his sister.

Doreen seated herself in a red-brocaded wing chair and unwrapped the gift with admirable restraint, unsealing each taped seam carefully, without any visible excitement. But when she saw the contents of the jeweler's case, a spark lit up her usually cold gray eyes. "Ahh," she said.

On the other side of the room, the sound of ripping paper stopped. Karen came and peeked over her mother's shoulder.

"Good Lord!" she exclaimed, staring at the emerald-and-ruby necklace. "You must have spent a fortune, Uncle Garek!"

Doreen's mouth pursed. "Karen, don't be crass."

Her shoulders hunching, the girl returned to the tree. She opened another present—a notebook computer from Garek. Her face completely expressionless, she set it aside.

Doreen, whose gaze had followed her daughter, barked, "Karen...what do you say to your uncle?"

"Thank you, Uncle Garek." Karen's monotone had as much enthusiasm as a zombie's. Surrounded by the presents she'd opened—piles of clothes, tennis gear, skis, jewelry, purses, shoes—she looked under the now-empty tree. "Is that all?" she whined.

Doreen glared at her daughter. "Karen, I don't like your tone. Or the expression on your face. If you can't look and sound more pleasant, then go to your room."

"Fine." Tucking the computer under her arm, Karen headed for the door.

"I don't know what's the matter with that girl," Doreen said in a loud voice before her daughter had even left the room. "I've told her over and over again that she must be polite to you. Although I can't blame her for being disappointed. Whatever possessed you to buy a computer?"

Frowning, Garek watched his niece leave the room. "At Thanksgiving I heard her say she wanted one."

"I wish you would have spoken to me first. We already have a computer. Girls her age prefer feminine things—like jewelry."

Garek thought of the conversation he'd overheard on his last visit. Karen had been talking on the phone, telling some unseen person that she *desperately* wanted a new computer. "I think you underestimate Karen."

Doreen stiffened. "I believe I'm better acquainted with my own daughter's likes and dislikes than you. You barely know her."

That was true. He'd been close to Karen when she was younger—she'd been bright and funny and interested in everything. But since becoming a teenager, she'd changed. She'd grown about ten inches into a tall, lanky brunette with a pale complexion and hostile brown eyes. Only rarely did he catch a glimpse of the curious, affectionate child she'd been.

"I'm afraid those terrible friends of hers are having a bad influence on her," Doreen continued. "One girl's father is a truck driver! If only I could send her to a decent school, instead of that horrible one she's attending now."

"You can afford it." Garek walked over to the tree, looking at the jumble of gifts Karen had left behind. "If you want to."

Doreen almost dropped the necklace. She snapped the box closed and glared at him. "You don't know what

it's like to have your beloved husband die and be reduced to living in poverty—"

"Come off it, Doreen." Garek nudged the tennis
racket with his toe, then bent down and picked it up. He
took a practice swing. Lightweight, perfectly balanced,
the racket sliced through the air. "Grant divorced you
long before he died. And he paid through the nose to get
rid of you. If he'd been smart, he would've made you
sign a prenuptial agreement."

"I would never sign something like that—I would be
grossly insulted if he'd even asked. Besides, I deserved
every penny I got in the settlement. It wasn't my fault
he fell for that little slut. I should have gotten more. But
I never get my fair share. Just look at Wisnewski Industries. It's not right that Father left the company to you
and…and for heaven's sake, must you swing that
racket? Those ornaments are all Lennox crystal and
they cost a fortune. If you break one, I'm going to be
very upset—"

"The company was bankrupt."

His comment successfully diverted her from the
safety of her ornaments. "A temporary setback, nothing
more. The company is making millions now."

"Of which you, as a major stockholder, receive a
very large portion. I know, since I sign the checks."

She sniffed. "I can barely maintain my position with
those paltry dividends. I'll never get my name into the
Social Register at this rate."

"What the hell is the Social Register?"

"It's a book listing the names of an elite group of people. The right kind of people. Like the Palermos. Ones
that have a certain background—"

Garek couldn't believe his ears. "Our grandparents

were peasant Polish immigrants. Is that the kind of background you're talking about?"

Doreen's nostrils quivered. "Ancestry is only one of the considerations. There are other ways to qualify— like founding a charity for some worthy cause. Ethel started a foundation for the symphony."

"You hate the symphony."

Doreen gripped the arms of her chair. "Just because you have no appreciation for music, don't assume no one else does—"

"Okay, okay." He shrugged. "If you want to give money to the symphony, fine. Just don't ask me to make a donation."

A flush mottled her cheeks. "I shouldn't have to ask you. It's the least you could do. That disgusting picture of you and that...that dancer person has undoubtedly hurt my standing with the Social Register committee—"

"I said no, Doreen."

"Very well." Lines radiated from her pinched lips. "I'm not going to argue with you. If you won't help me set up a foundation, I'll just stick to my regular activities with the Women's League. Did I tell you Nina Lachland is on a fund-raising committee with me? She tells me a lot about her husband's business. She told me Wisnewski Industries is trying to buy out the Lachland Company, which was news to me."

He kept his stance relaxed, but inwardly he tensed. "So?"

"So, did you know there's another company interested in buying Lachland? Her husband doesn't like this Ogremark very much—"

"Agramark."

"Ogremark, Agramark, whatever. But he might

change his mind if he found out that you're having trouble finding financing for the purchase."

Garek stopped swinging the racket. "Are you trying to blackmail me, Doreen?" he asked very softly.

She smiled. "Of course not. I don't know why you would say that."

Garek didn't smile back. Acquiring Lachland was key to his plan for expanding Wisnewski Industries. Unfortunately, Agramark Inc., a subsidiary of the Calvin G. Hibbert conglomerate, was also pursuing the small shipping company. The conglomerate had all the advantages: financial resources far beyond his own, connections to key players, high-powered lawyers to deal with the legalities. In spite of all this, Garek was determined to make the acquisition and was close to succeeding.

If Doreen didn't sour the deal.

How the hell had she found out about his difficulty with the financing? He gave her a long, hard look. "I warn you, Doreen, don't interfere with my business."

"Business, business, business. That's all you think about. It's time you did something for your family. Is that so much to ask for? I don't want much—all you need to do is sponsor a foundation for me."

"Is that all?" he asked ironically.

"Actually, now that you mention it, no. I also want an assistant from Wisnewski Industries to handle all the details—I can't because of my delicate health."

Doreen was as healthy as a draft horse. She had a similar bone structure to his, with big hands and feet. When she was younger, she'd had a plump, curvaceous figure, appealing in an earthy sort of way. After she married Grant Tarrington, however, she'd lost every spare ounce of fat in an effort to look more "delicate." Unfortunately, the weight loss only made her look harsh and angular.

"I also want you to stop sabotaging my efforts to be included in the Social Register," she continued, warming to her subject. "Stop dating disreputable women and find a nice, respectable girl. Someone like Amber Bellair. I talked to her yesterday and we agreed…"

"You agreed what?" Garek asked very quietly.

"You needn't sound so nasty. We just agreed that you seem…lonely."

His grip tightened on the tennis racket as he thought of all the plans he'd made and the hours he'd put in to make the Lachland acquisition happen. Once he signed this deal, he could…well, not relax, exactly. But maybe the pressure would ease up some.

He didn't want to risk losing this deal. But he sure as hell wasn't going to let Doreen think she could get away with this kind of manipulation every time she wanted something.

"The only problem is that Ethel may not like me setting up a competing foundation," Doreen said, drumming her manicured nails on the arm of her chair. "She can be a little spiteful. She might even block my Social Register nomination. Perhaps I should find something else to support. Something cultural. Like the ballet. Or art. Art would be very classy. We could open a gallery on Michigan Avenue. Or better yet, River North—"

"A gallery?"

"To exhibit the work of the artists we sponsor. Some up-and-coming young people recommended by the Institute. Not any of those trashy modern artists, but young men and women with real talent…"

She went on, but Garek was no longer listening. He was remembering the woman who'd returned the necklace—Eleanor Hernandez. What was it she'd said? *I work at a gallery...specializing in contemporary art... feel free to stop by if you ever want to buy something with a little higher concept.*

A greedy little witch—as greedy as Doreen—only with a pair of bright blue eyes and the sexiest mouth he'd ever seen....

"I don't think I'm being unreasonable, Garek. You can afford it. It wouldn't hurt you to show a little generosity, you know. I am your only sister—"

"Very well."

Doreen gaped, her jaw sagging in a way that counteracted the most recent efforts of her plastic surgeon. "You'll do it?"

"Do I have a choice?"

"No. For once, you're going to have to do what I want."

Any of the businessmen who'd dealt with Garek Wisnewski would have been highly suspicious—if not downright skeptical—of his sudden acquiescence. But Doreen only smiled smugly, visions of how her name would look printed in the Social Register dancing in her head.

She didn't even notice the way her brother adjusted his grip on the tennis racket and executed a neat and deadly backhand.

Chapter Three

"It's your best work ever."

Tom Scarlatti's brown eyes lit up behind the thick, round lenses of his glasses. "You think so, Ellie? My roommate said it looked like a two-year-old painted it."

Ellie studied the canvas propped against the gallery counter. Although he'd used her as a model, the final result bore no discernable resemblance to her. But the free-flowing curves and vivid colors created a sense of space and harmony that was arresting.

"Your roommate is an engineer," she pointed out. "He knows nothing about art."

"That's true." Tom's narrow chest expanded a bit. "Actually, I do think *Woman in Blue* turned out well. I really hate to sell it."

"If you want, I can put a Not for Sale sticker on it," she offered. "Although I'm sure you could get an excellent price for it."

Tom reached out and touched the edge of the canvas with the very tips of his fingers, gently, tenderly. But then his hand dropped limply to his side. "I've got to sell it," he said with a sigh. "My landlord is threatening to evict me. He's a very unpleasant man. He doesn't understand about art at all—"

The bell jangled as someone entered Vogel's. Tom stopped talking, looking toward the door. Ellie turned, a smile forming, only to freeze when she recognized the man walking toward her.

Garek Wisnewski.

What on earth was *he* doing here? It had been a week since the ugly scene in his office, and she'd done her best to put him out of her mind. But she couldn't help thinking about him every once in a while—like when she'd gone to her cousin Vincente's house last weekend and saw his daughter wearing the tiny tennis shoes she'd bought her for Christmas. Or when she'd seen the towering gray walls of Wisnewski Industries through the train window on her way to a job a few days ago. Or when she'd looked in the junk drawer this morning and seen the crumpled five-thousand-dollar check shoved in the back that she hadn't quite been able to bring herself to cash, ruthless businesswoman or not.

Every time she thought of him, she remembered the ugly necklace and his rudeness when she'd returned it, and she grew angry all over again.

She clutched the gallery keys lying on the counter, wishing she'd locked the door. Had he come here to make another crude proposition?

"Excuse me," she muttered to Tom, moving out from behind the counter.

Tom sidled toward the door. "I'd b-better go," he murmured.

Ellie restrained an urge to grab his arm and cling to him—she didn't want to be left alone with Garek Wisnewski. But she couldn't do that to Tom. Tom was painfully shy around most people, and well-dressed, high-powered businessmen were the type he most dreaded.

Did Garek Wisnewski always wear a suit? she wondered as she approached him. His clothes made a valiant effort to give him a civilized veneer. They couldn't disguise, however, the grainy texture of imminent five-o'clock shadow on his jaw—evidence of barely restrained, more primitive male tendencies.

Like predation. Intimidation. Domination.

"Good evening, Mr. Wisnewski." She kept her tone polite, but cool. Not an easy feat considering the way her senses were humming on full defensive alert. She was conscious of her own clothes—a red cashmere sweater with a tendency to pill, a short black skirt, black tights and chunky black platforms. "May I help you?"

He eyed her consideringly—probably planning to give her some more wardrobe advice, she thought angrily.

"I'm just looking." He turned his gaze to a flat glass case filled with dirt and trash. "So this is 'high-concept' art. Very impressive."

She bristled at his sardonic tone. Few of the general public recognized or appreciated the skill and creativity that went into contemporary art. A lot of people snickered or looked scornful when they first came in. Usually, though, after she explained a little about the piece and the artist's concept, most viewed the work with more respect.

She didn't bother to explain anything to Garek Wisnewski, however. Why waste her time? He'd obviously come to mock her. Didn't he have better things to do?

Apparently not. He moved on and she followed closely behind, glaring at his big hands clasped behind his broad back—he was so bulky, she didn't trust him not to knock something over. Although he did walk gracefully, she admitted grudgingly to herself, his shoes making almost no sound on the polished wooden floor.

He gazed at an antique water pump resting on a square glass case filled with lightbulbs. Another lightbulb sprouted from the spigot. His eyebrows rose halfway to his dark combed-back hair.

His expression infuriated her. "It's time for me to close." She struggled to keep her tone polite. "Perhaps you could come back some other day."

"I'll only be a few more minutes," he told her, then proceeded to stroll around the gallery as if he had all the time in the world. He eyed the various pieces, his mouth curling in the same sardonic smile she'd noticed in his office. He even laughed at Bertrice's recycled-trash sculpture of a giant cockroach, although he tried to cover the sound by coughing.

He stopped in front of the counter, looking at the painting Tom had just left.

"I'll take this one."

She blinked, wondering if she'd misunderstood. "You want to buy *Woman in Blue*?"

"Yes." He arched an eyebrow at her. "Is there a problem?"

"No, no. I'm just surprised." Stunned might be a more accurate description. "*Why* do you want to buy it?"

"Do you question all your customers on why they're purchasing an item?"

"Not usually. But most of my customers like contemporary art."

"You think I don't? You shouldn't be so quick to judge me." He pulled his wallet from inside his coat pocket and produced a platinum credit card. "Can you have the painting delivered to my office?"

She didn't take the card. "*Woman in Blue* won't fit with the decor of your office. Are you sure you wouldn't like something else—something that would suit your personality better?" Her gaze rested a moment on the giant cockroach.

His gaze followed hers, and his eyes gleamed, whether with laughter or anger, she couldn't tell. Anger, she hoped. But he didn't withdraw the credit card. "I prefer this one."

She didn't believe he'd come here just to buy a painting, but even if he had, she wished he would have chosen something else. She didn't want him to have *Woman in Blue*. He would never appreciate it, she was sure. She opened her mouth to refuse to sell the painting to him, then paused.

Hadn't she just recently vowed to think like a businesswoman? To sell to anyone who came through the door? Could she in good conscience refuse the sale when the gallery—and Tom—needed it so much?

The answer was unpalatable but obvious.

With the very tips of her fingers, she took the credit card and rang up the sale. "Thank you, Mr. Wisnewski," she forced herself to say. "It will be delivered first thing tomorrow."

"Excellent." He glanced at his watch, then at her.

"Ms. Hernandez, I need to discuss something with you, but I know you're anxious to close. Will you have dinner with me so we can talk?"

She stiffened. So he *had* come here to proposition her again! "No."

"It's important," he said, not even blinking at her refusal. "It concerns the gallery."

"What about the gallery?" she asked.

"Come to dinner with me, and I'll tell you."

"Why can't you tell me here?"

"I never discuss business on an empty stomach."

His smile made her even more suspicious. It was the kind of smile that made a woman want to smile back, that made her want to do whatever its owner asked—and oh, didn't he know it!

"If you're not interested," he said when she didn't respond, "I can always find another gallery." He took a step toward the door.

"Wait!"

He paused and she bit her lip. She knew he was manipulating her—but her curiosity was too great to resist. "Let me get my hat and coat and lock up," she muttered.

He didn't have the limousine tonight. Instead, he had a big black Mercedes with soft leather interior. She paid little attention to the luxury, however.

"What about the gallery?" she asked again when they were driving down the street. "Do you want to buy another painting?"

"Not exactly." He turned a corner, avoiding a snowdrift that had spilled out into the street. "Do you own the gallery?"

"No, Mr. Vogel does."

"Ah, then perhaps I should be talking to him."

"Not really. He hasn't been active in managing the gallery since his wife died. He's elderly, and his health is frail, so he lets me run the gallery for him. He trusts me completely."

"Does he? Then obviously I needn't have any qualms."

The dry note in his voice made her bristle, but before she could respond he spoke again. "I'm sorry, but I need to concentrate on my driving. I'll explain everything over dinner."

The request was a reasonable one. The road was treacherous, covered with ice and full of potholes, and the pounding sleet made the visibility poor. But in spite of the conditions, Ellie didn't quite believe him.

At the restaurant, they were quickly seated at a table with white linen tablecloths, china and crystal.

"Have you been here before?" he asked.

"No. Look, what's this all about?"

He picked up the wine list, his eyebrows rising. "Are you always so impatient?"

"Only when someone is being extremely evasive."

His eyes gleamed again in that odd manner. For a moment, she thought he was going to put her off once more, but then he said bluntly, "I'm starting an art foundation and I'm looking for artists to sponsor and a gallery to exhibit their work. I think Vogel's might be perfect."

Ellie leaned back against the cushioned seat and stared at him. Her heart started to pound. A foundation—it could make a world of difference to the gallery. She could hire art photographers, place ads in expensive magazines, attract the notice of critics and collectors who could transform an unknown artist like Tom into an overnight sensation. She could replace the lighting, fix the elevator and install a sculpture garden on the roof the way she'd dreamed....

The waiter came to the table. While he explained the prix fixe menu for the day, Ellie tried to rein in her excitement. There were a thousand galleries in Chicago, and after speaking with them, what were the chances Wisnewski would choose Vogel's? Not very high. She needed to convince him that Vogel's would be the best choice for his foundation to sponsor.

After the waiter left, she leaned forward again. "Vogel's would be ideal," she said earnestly. "Our goal is to encourage a climate of excitement, inquiry and dialogue for progressive art. We look for unconventional pieces that are conceptual and theoretically based. You won't see similar works at other galleries. Everything we handle is unique. The artists are all extraordinarily creative and innovative. Tom Scarlatti, for example, the man at the showroom when you came in earlier. He painted the canvas you bought. I'm sorry I didn't introduce you. He's a little shy. But I can arrange for you to meet him another time—"

The sommelier approached the table. Ellie tried to contain her impatience while he discussed with Garek the appropriate vintage to complement their meal. Finally the wine had been decided, the bottle brought and the ritual of pouring and tasting finished, and she was able to continue. "With the right kind of support, I believe Tom could become an important new force in the art world—"

"You appear to think very highly of this Tom Scarlatti," Garek interrupted.

"Yes, I do." She picked up her wineglass. "He's brilliant, a genius in his own way—"

"Is he your boyfriend?"

The wine halfway to her mouth, Ellie paused. She stared at the man sitting across from her.

Cool gray eyes stared back.

"No," she said slowly. "Why do you ask?"

"Just curious. Surely you must have a man in your life?"

"Not that it's any of your business, but no, I don't." She set the wine down and gave him a direct look. "I'm not interested in having a relationship right now."

The corners of his mouth twitched at her thinly veiled rebuff. "You want to concentrate on your career? I'm surprised."

"Why?"

"Because most women, no matter how much they deny it, are still more interested in finding husbands than in building their careers."

She didn't like his cynical tone or the implied criticism of women. "Really? I've experienced exactly the opposite. Most of the men I meet are desperate to get married. Especially the older ones—the ones your age."

He straightened a little. "I'm twenty-nine," he said curtly.

"Oh?" Lowering her eyes to conceal her smile, she picked up the wine again and sipped it.

There was a small silence as she drank. "Only a year or two older than you, surely," he said.

She set down her glass abruptly.

The waiter returned and placed a dish on the table. "Baby leeks cooked in their own juices," he announced.

"Just what we needed," Garek said blandly.

Ellie couldn't help laughing. "I'm twenty-four," she admitted. Then, vexed with herself for revealing even this small piece of personal information, she returned to business. "About the gallery—"

He shook his head. "You don't need to tell me any more about it. I've already made up my mind. And I've decided on Vogel's."

For a second, she thought she must have misheard him. But at the same time, she knew she hadn't. Joy burst inside her. Vogel's was saved! She wanted to dance on the table, sing at the top of her lungs, reach across the table and kiss Garek Wisnewski right on the mouth….

Almost as if he could read her mind, his gaze dropped to her lips.

Her mental celebrations came to a screeching halt. He'd looked at her mouth that way in his office. Right before he told her to contact him if she wanted to "offer" him something.

She leaned back in her seat, her smile fading.

What was going on here? This was Garek Wisnewski, the obnoxious jerk who'd knocked her over in the street and grossly insulted her when she came to his office. Garek Wisnewski, the arrogant, money-grubbing businessman who did nothing without calculating the profit. What was the catch?

Judging from the way he was looking at her mouth, she suspected she knew exactly what the catch was.

The waiter returned with more food. Ellie waited until he left before she asked quietly, "And what do you want in return?"

Garek took a bite of the Iowa lamb loin and chewed for what seemed like an awfully long time. "That's an odd question," he finally said. "Why does anyone start an art foundation?"

"Because they love art."

"And you don't think I do?" He offered her some of the braised legumes, but she shook her head. "I told you not to judge me too quickly," he said.

He was being evasive. Why? "Why *my* gallery? You don't even like me."

His eyebrows rose. "What gave you that idea?"

"You weren't exactly polite when I returned the necklace."

"I apologize for that. Women who seek me out tend to have an ulterior motive."

"They want to get their picture in the paper?" Ellie guessed.

"They want to get married."

Ellie choked on her goat cheese and bleeding-heart radishes. The poor man obviously suffered from a serious medical condition—paranoia conceititus. "I have no desire to marry you, I promise."

He smiled, but with a slight cynical lift to his lip. "That's why I chose your gallery—you're honest enough to admit that it's the money you care about."

She opened her mouth, then paused. She doubted she could make him change his mind about her—and if she tried, he'd probably accuse her of trying to make him fall in love with her or something else equally ridiculous. "What exactly will this foundation do?" she asked instead.

"The usual. Exhibits—shows, I believe you call them?—featuring the gallery artists. I'll send an assistant to the gallery tomorrow. She'll report to you, and you can tell her whatever needs to be done. I also want you to work with her to arrange a special pre-opening event, a silent auction, to be held at my sister's home. I would expect you to choose the art, naturally."

Ellie took a sip of the heady wine, considering which of the artists she should feature. Tom, without a doubt, and Bertrice. And maybe Carlo Bustamente—

"I would expect you to attend the silent auction, of course," Garek continued. "And I'll need to take you to the symphony this Saturday—"

"The symphony!" She set down her wine. "I understand the silent auction. But why the symphony?"

"I'm going to have to introduce you to art collectors. There will be quite a few at the concert."

"Why can't you bring them to the gallery?"

"I run a business. I don't have time to run a shuttle service."

What he said made sense—almost. She suspected the whole art foundation was a ploy of some kind. To get her to go to bed with him? That seemed pretty far-fetched. He was rich—and not completely unattractive. Surely he could find some woman to overlook his warped personality without going to so much trouble. More likely he needed a tax write-off. Or maybe he was a frustrated artist and needed a place to exhibit his paint-by-number masterpieces….

Her hand jerked as a terrifying thought occurred to her, causing her almost to knock over her wine.

"That portrait I saw in your office…" She tried to sound casual, although everything inside her was recoiling with horror. "The one of Lilly Lade—did you paint that?"

He looked startled. "Good God, no. Why do you ask?"

"No reason," she lied, leaning back to allow the waiter to take her plate. She rested against the cushioned chair, her terror receding—although not completely. She knew Martina would tell her to plaster the gallery walls with hundreds of portraits of Lilly Lade if that's what it took to get him to agree to use Vogel's for his foundation, but Ellie couldn't do it. She couldn't allow someone like Garek Wisnewski to distort the gallery into something unrecognizable.

"If I agreed to this," she told him, "I would have a few conditions."

"What conditions?"

"First, I must have complete control over the direction and focus of Vogel's. I have the final say in all decisions. Nothing is exhibited unless I agree."

"That's fine. I don't want to change anything about the gallery. It's perfect the way it is."

She searched his expression but couldn't detect any sarcasm in either his voice or face. "Second, this is business, nothing else."

"Naturally. What else would it be?"

She frowned, but all she said was, "You accept the conditions, then?"

"That's all? You don't want me to get your name in the Social Register?"

She stared at him. "I beg your pardon?"

"Never mind. Yes, I accept your conditions."

"Then I accept your offer," she said solemnly.

"Thank you."

She couldn't help smiling at his slightly ironic tone. He smiled back, and she felt the same pleasant jolt she'd felt the first time she'd met him.

She squashed the feeling immediately. This was Garek Wisnewski, she reminded herself. Sure, he could be charming when he wanted, but that didn't change the fact that he personified arrogance and conceit. And in spite of his agreement to her conditions, she didn't really trust him. She couldn't shake the sense that he had some hidden agenda, some secret purpose that he wasn't telling her. He was up to something.

But what?

Chapter Four

Garek detested the symphony. When he felt compelled to attend for one reason or another, he usually escorted Doreen or Amber, but they enjoyed it as little as he did. Amber pretended to like the music but always seemed more interested in looking around the theater from their balcony seats to see who was there than in anything happening onstage. Doreen, whom he suspected of being tone deaf, usually fell asleep about halfway through, her head lolling in time to the flutes. During the intermission, neither Doreen nor Amber ever mentioned the concert. Instead, they estimated the cost of Buffy Vanderhorn's designer gown and speculated as to whether Tritia Mitchell's jewelry was real or fake.

Therefore, it was something of a shock to discover that Eleanor not only listened to the music—she listened with intense concentration.

He stared at her, frowning slightly. Seated next to him

in the darkened theater, she seemed very small, the top of her head barely reaching his chin. She appeared as fragile and breakable as the strings of the violins being played onstage—and yet, her back was as straight as the conductor's baton.

The evening wasn't turning out the way he'd expected. When he'd picked her up earlier, he'd been stunned by her appearance. From the top of her carefully arranged curls, to the beaded silver sheath that hugged her curves, she looked utterly gorgeous.

He'd told her so, but to his annoyance, his voice was husky, like a teenager's on his first date.

"Thank you," she'd responded coolly. Distantly. *Regally.*

She'd kept up her air of nonchalance until they were actually in their seats and the music started. Then her indifference disappeared.

The light from the stage illuminating her expression, he watched as her eyes glistened with each blare of the French horns and her lips trembled with each screech of the violins. The notes and chords, meaningless to him, obviously enthralled her in some way that he couldn't begin to fathom.

By the time the curtain went down for intermission, her face was glowing—until she caught him looking at her. Then her expression cooled again. "I've always liked that particular conductor," she said as he escorted her out to the lobby. "He can elicit music from an orchestra like no one else."

"You sound like an expert."

"Do I?" She shrugged, the movement drawing his attention to her creamy shoulders covered only by a gauze wrap. "Actually, it's been a long time since I've been to a symphony. I listen on the radio sometimes. Do you come very often?"

"Occasionally." The light from the chandelier caused her silver dress to gleam, making it difficult not to stare at her—as he noticed several other men blatantly doing. He put his hand on her elbow and directed her toward the bar. "Some of the people I do business with sponsor the symphony. I have to make an appearance once in a while. Would you like some champagne?"

She gazed at him searchingly. "Do you ever do anything just for fun?"

She sounded half disapproving, half curious. "There's no time for fun if you want to succeed in business," he told her. "You're competing to stay alive in a ruthless environment. But the reward is huge."

She accepted a glass of champagne from him but didn't drink. "Money, you mean?"

He nodded.

Her mouth formed a little moue of distaste, drawing his gaze to her pursed lips, but before she could say anything, a booming voice called his name. Turning, he saw Ethel Palermo bulldozing her way through the crowd, her meek little husband, George, trailing behind. With an inward sigh, he introduced Eleanor, but Ethel paid little attention.

"Is your sister here?" she demanded.

"I haven't seen her."

"Hmmph." Ethel's snort was full of disapproval. "I talked to her this afternoon. She said she was leaving on a cruise tomorrow and had to finish packing. I reminded her how important it is to support the symphony, and she said she would try to come."

"Maybe Doreen succumbed to one of her headaches," Garek said. "She has them frequently, you know." Most frequently when faced with the thought of spending three hours at the symphony.

"Hmmph." Ethel adjusted the diamond tiara nestled in her silver, beehive hairdo, then inspected Eleanor with sharp eyes. "Eleanor Hernandez? I've never heard of you."

With an easy smile, Eleanor responded, "There's no reason you should have."

To Garek's surprise, she continued, conversing pleasantly with the older woman. After just a few minutes, Ethel was telling "Ellie" about her three sons—all of them ungrateful slobs—her daughter—a constant source of disappointment—and her ten grandchildren—all amazingly beautiful, intelligent and talented. When Ethel revealed that the oldest showed a remarkable talent for art, Ellie mentioned her gallery experience and talked about ways to encourage the child.

"Although talent is often inherited, it must be nurtured," she said seriously. "Are you or your husband creative?"

Ethel nodded. "I've always liked art. And George plays the violin."

Ellie turned to George, a smile lighting her face. "You do? My father also played. What did you think of the soloist?"

"I thought his improvisation was weak. It lacked passion."

"Oh, no! The passion was there. It was just very restrained—very subtle."

"Subtle?" A spark lit up George's normally glazed blue eyes and his nasal twang grew more pronounced. "Nonexistent, I thought…"

Perhaps it was just a fluke, Garek thought as he listened to George happily dissecting the performances of the whole orchestra, that Ellie had managed to charm the most difficult couple in Chicago.

But the same thing happened with the Branwells, the biggest snobs west of the Mississippi, and again with the Mitchells, a couple whose doomsday conversation would scare even the most determined optimist.

"You seem to be enjoying yourself," he said in a neutral tone of voice when they were alone for a moment.

"Yes, I am."

"You certainly handled the Palermos well. I've seen veteran society hostesses tottering off in a daze after an encounter with them."

"Oh?" She rearranged her shawl over her arms. "I found them very interesting."

"Interesting?" He couldn't keep the disbelief from his tone. "George and Ethel Palermo?"

She tilted her chin a little. "Yes—why not? George is virtually an expert on the symphony, and Ethel had a lot of interesting insights on her family."

"And the Branwells and the Mitchells? Did you find them *interesting,* as well?"

She nodded, then looked at someone behind him. He turned to see Jack Phillips, an old business acquaintance, approaching—along with a tall, thin blonde dressed in black satin.

"Garek, darling!" Amber Bellair cooed. "Where have you been? I haven't seen you in ages!"

Garek shrugged and performed the introductions.

Amber looked Ellie up and down dismissively, then turned back to Garek. "Why don't you ever call me anymore? I've been terribly lonely."

"You told me you never wanted to see my face again."

"*Darling*...I was *joking*. You can always call me." She drew a French-manicured fingernail down his chest. "Anytime."

"Sorry, Amber, that won't be possible." From the corner of his eye, Garek watched Eleanor smile at something Jack said to her. "I'm very busy."

"Busy with Ms. Hernandez, I suppose."

He turned his gaze back to Amber's narrow, aristocratic features. "I'm sponsoring an art foundation through the gallery where she works," he said evenly. "Our relationship is purely professional."

Her mouth curled in a sneer for the blink of an eye, then disappeared, leaving her face smooth and blank. "I understand."

What she understood was questionable, but the bell sounded, cutting off their conversation. The crowd started moving toward the theater doors.

"It was a pleasure meeting you, Jack." Ellie's warm smile faded only slightly when she turned to Amber. "And you, too, Ms. Bellair."

Amber waved her hand carelessly, barely glancing away from Garek. "Darling, when you get tired of... working so hard, give me a call."

She strolled off, and Garek escorted Eleanor toward the theater doors.

"Ms. Bellair is a good friend of yours?" Ellie's voice was almost as cool as Amber's had been.

"Not exactly." He tried to increase their pace, but the crowd made it impossible. "We dated for a while."

"But you broke up?"

"She was getting a little too...serious."

"I understand," she said, in much the same tone as Amber had a few minutes ago. He looked at her sharply.

Her expression was bland. "You don't want to give up being Chicago's Most Eligible Bachelor."

He flinched as she said the stupid title out loud. "Hardly," he snapped.

She made a slight choking noise. She didn't smile, but her eyes gave her away, and he scowled. "It's not funny," he told her.

"No, of course not," she agreed, coughing.

"That idiotic newspaper article has caused me more grief than you can possibly imagine." He stepped back to allow her to precede him into the row.

She didn't move, the laughter in her gaze gone. In its place glimmered a different emotion, a softness…sympathy?

She touched his arm lightly. "Money must be an awful burden in your relationships."

The muscles in his forearm contracted at the brush of her fingertips, even as he blinked at her words. He'd always found money to be a great advantage. "Why would you say that?"

"Because…oh, I'm so sorry, ma'am!" Ellie stepped forward into the row of seats to allow a woman with sharp elbows to pass.

Garek followed Ellie, turning sideways, to shuffle past the patrons already seated. He waited until they reached their own seats before asking again, "Why would you say that?"

"What? Oh," she whispered as the lights dimmed and the curtain rose, "just that it must be terrible to have women interested in you only because of your money."

The music started, and she turned her attention to the stage.

Ignoring the opening strains, Garek stared down at her.

Amber obviously hadn't believed him when he said his relationship with Ellie was purely professional, but it was true. He would never be interested in someone as venal as Eleanor Hernandez—she was merely a means to an end.

Still, he couldn't help feeling a niggling annoyance, as he sat through the second half of the concert, that she would assume that women were interested in him *only* because of his money.

Chapter Five

Garek took Ellie to a French restaurant the following week. The tuxedoed waiter seated them in the atrium, a secluded area lit by candles, decorated with flowers and featuring a magnificent view of the city skyline. The decor was elegant, the clientele exclusive and the prices exorbitant.

Naturally, Ellie thought wryly as she ate wild Atlantic salmon and Alsace-style cabbage and listened to Garek explain a few details of the art foundation. He was obviously used to the best. Which boded well for the foundation. He would make it a success, she was positive. She should be deliriously happy. And she would be, if it weren't for one thing. Him.

She looked at the hard angles of his face, listened to the authority in his voice as he recited facts and figures. He had the kind of self-confidence that came from knowing he could make his own way in the world without help from anybody. She might have admired the trait, envied it, even—if she hadn't met his ex-girlfriend. It was hard to envy a man who'd been involved with a woman whose eyes were as cold and calculating as Amber Bellair's.

"Any questions?" he asked as the waiter set plates of chocolate-raspberry torte in front of them.

A million, she thought, glancing away from his strong features. Were all the women he knew like Amber Bellair? Did they all look at him like an investor assessing a potentially profitable enterprise? Were they all like painted photographs, flat and artificial?

"No," she said, fiddling with her fork.

"I received the assistant's report. She said you've been extremely busy this last week."

Ellie nodded. Preparing for the silent auction and the show took a lot of time. She'd been able to quit her housecleaning jobs since Garek was paying her a generous salary—almost too generous. She couldn't quite shake the suspicion that he had some ulterior motive. But although she'd tried several times to question him, he remained evasive. He wasn't one to reveal a lot about himself.

"Would you like to go over the budget figures?" he asked.

"No, thank you."

His eyebrows rose.

"I've always preferred art and music to math," she felt compelled to say. "Balance sheets give me a headache."

"Didn't you say Martina was studying business?" he asked. "Perhaps she could go over the numbers for you."

He'd met her cousin when he'd picked Ellie up earlier that evening, and they'd seemed to hit it off immediately. Martina had tossed her mane of long dark hair and smiled flirtatiously at Garek while Ellie got her coat. "You better snap him up quick, El," Martina had whispered in her ear before they left, "or someone else will. If only I didn't have a boyfriend!"

Ellie picked up her fork. "That's really not necessary," she murmured to Garek before taking a bite of the torte.

"You think she won't be able to understand it?"

Ellie bristled immediately. "I'm sure she would. She's graduating in June, a year early. She's absolutely brilliant."

"Is that so?" His mouth curved upward at her defense of Martina, but he didn't pursue the subject of the budget. "Martina said you're from Philadelphia," he said instead.

"Did she?" What else had her cousin said? Ellie wondered uneasily.

"Do your parents still live there?"

"They died in a car accident when I was thirteen."

She said it matter-of-factly, but the long-ago loss still had the power to cause a dull ache in her heart.

"I'm sorry," he said quietly. "That must have been difficult for you."

She turned away from his steady gaze and looked out the window at the city lights sparkling in the cold, dark night. She didn't want him to be sympathetic. "Fortunately, I had relatives who took me in." She looked back at Garek and forced herself to smile. "What about your family?"

"My father died of a heart attack eight years ago. My mother remarried and moved to Florida a few years later. I rarely see her. There's just my sister and me. And my fifteen-year-old niece."

Her breath caught. Even less did she want to feel sympathy for *him*. But it was impossible not to. He recited the facts as unemotionally as she had, but she knew only too well how pain could be hidden under a facade.

"Are you close to your niece and sister?" she asked, resisting a foolish urge to reach across the table and touch his hand.

He shrugged. "I don't have a lot of time. Work keeps me busy."

His response should have banished all sympathy for him, but it didn't. After her parents died, she'd lived with her grandfather, but she'd called her aunt and uncle and cousins almost every day and stayed with them every summer. They'd filled a terrible void in her life. Apparently Garek's business had performed that function for him.

But that was his choice, she reminded herself. He could have chosen to reach out to his sister and niece. "You should make time," she said quietly.

He sipped his coffee. "Thinking of starting an advice column?"

She ignored his gentle mockery. "I think it's a mistake to put work before family."

"But what if your family depends on you to work to make money?"

She frowned. "Your sister and niece depend on you financially?"

"Not exactly. I'm speaking more hypothetically."

"Every situation is different. Everyone must make their own choice." She twirled a bite of torte in raspberry sauce. "I just think sometimes people end up regretting their choices."

"Hmm," he murmured noncommittally. "Tell me more about your family."

She doubted he was really interested, and she didn't want to get drawn into talking about her grandfather and the messy details of their estrangement, but she went ahead and told him about her uncle Rodrigo and aunt Alma and their six children. The three older were all married with children of their own.

"Then comes Martina, then Roberto, then Alyssa," she continued. "Alyssa is about the same age as your niece—she'll be fourteen in March."

"How long have you shared an apartment with Martina?"

"About a year. Ever since I moved to Chicago. I was broke and there aren't a lot of high-paying jobs for art history majors—"

"You have a college degree?"

"Yes, a master's. Why do you look so surprised?"

"No reason. Is your cousin Roberto still in high school?"

"No, he graduated last year." Just in time to get himself thrown in jail. But she wasn't going to tell Garek that. "He's very sweet. Sometimes he takes his machismo a little too seriously, but he has the kindest heart of anyone I know. He'll play cards with Grandma Pilar for hours, even though she cheats and can't always remember his name. He can be a little impulsive sometimes, but he always means well. He's very protective of me."

"Do you need protecting?"

"No, of course not. Although Robbie thinks so. Probably because of…" She paused, vexed with herself for talking too much.

"Because of Rafe?"

She straightened. "How do you know about him?"

"Martina said I was a 'vast improvement over Rafe.' Your ex-boyfriend, I take it?"

"Mmm." She was definitely going to have to have a talk with Martina. "I brought him to Chicago to meet everyone. Martina and Robbie didn't like him. And it turned out they were right."

"Rafe broke your heart?"

"No, he just toughened it up a bit." She felt his gaze on her face. Afraid he would ask her more questions, she added lightly, "Everyone has to have at least one failed love affair. Even you, I'll bet."

He had to think for a while. Either he'd had so many, he couldn't remember, or he'd never been in love. She wondered which it was.

"There was Monica Alexander," he finally said. "I was madly in love with her."

"What happened?"

"She dumped me when my father died and his business declared bankruptcy. I had to leave college to sort out the mess."

She grew still, watching him from wide eyes. "How terrible."

Garek looked amused. "It wasn't a huge tragedy. In fact, it was probably the best thing that could have happened to me. I was able to focus all my attention on the business."

"But you must have been terribly hurt—and at a time when you needed her the most."

He shrugged. "I survived."

Obviously. But at what cost? Was that when he'd acquired the air of cynicism that marked his features so strongly now? Was that when he'd begun to have so little faith in people—especially women?

The meal finished, he drove her home and walked behind her up the outside stairs to her apartment. "The Institute of Art is having a private opening of their new exhibit tomorrow night," he said. "I've arranged for tickets. I'll pick you up at seven."

More networking, Ellie thought, stopping in front of her door. And more time spent with Garek Wisnewski. "Wasn't the symphony enough?"

"I thought you would like going to the art show."

She would *love* to go, despite a slight lingering doubt about his motives. Once again, how could she refuse? "Okay. Thanks." She smiled at him.

His gaze narrowed a bit and drifted over her.

"What?" she asked, her smile faltering.

"You've got salt on your coat. Hold still."

Glancing down, she saw him brushing at a gray mess on her side. She must have grazed against the spray of salt and ice on his car, she realized.

She swayed a little, and he put his hand on her shoulder, holding her firmly as his gloved fingers swept along her hip, removing the last traces of dirty salt, his touch brisk, efficient, impersonal. When he finished, he released her, said good-night and left.

She watched him until he got in his car and drove off.

An uneasy feeling curling in her stomach, she went inside.

Chapter Six

Stacy Hatfield, the assistant Garek had assigned to work on the foundation, was bright, enthusiastic and very young—barely eighteen. Ellie would have enjoyed working with her if it weren't for one thing—the girl had a huge crush on Garek Wisnewski.

Ellie's own feelings were growing more and more confused. During the last week and a half, he'd taken her to the art show, several dinners, a play and a basketball game. She kept reminding herself that their relationship was purely business, but sometimes, for a moment or two, she would forget. She'd lain awake all night thinking about him, her thoughts going round and round in circles, until she swore she wasn't going to think about him at all. But that was difficult to do when Stacy talked about him constantly.

At the gallery, Ellie tried to escape the girl's chatter by going upstairs to the framing studio, but Stacy merely packed up her laptop and followed.

"Mr. Wisnewski's the best employer I've ever had," Stacy said, her fingers flying over the keyboard. "Actually, he's the only employer I've ever had, unless you count Mrs. Bussey, whose kids I baby-sat when I was fourteen—she had a nervous breakdown after she had her fourth child in six years—but everyone at the company agrees that Mr. Wisnewski is the best. He is so generous. I told him he was paying you way too little, and he said to double your salary."

Startled, Ellie looked up from the long, thin piece of oak she was pretending to inspect. "Stacy! I can't accept that!"

"Of course you can. You deserve it. You've been working like a dog."

It was true—she *had* been working long hours. But accepting a raise didn't feel right. If Mr. Vogel had given it to her, she wouldn't have objected. But Garek…

"Did you have a good time at the game?" Stacy asked. She had an amazing ability to talk and type at the same time at a combined speed of approximately eight hundred wpm.

Ellie sat down at the miter box with the piece of oak molding. "It was very nice. We had courtside seats, we ate catered food in a private box at half time, and the Bulls won." She'd enjoyed herself at the game. Afterward, though—

"Are you going out with him on Saturday?" Stacy asked, her fingers flying across the keyboard. "It's his birthday, you know. He's going to be thirty. Kind of old, but he's so gorgeous, I almost don't care."

Ellie hadn't known. Why hadn't he told her?

"How is the catalog for the silent auction coming along?" she asked, hoping to divert the girl.

"Fantastic. The pictures the new photographer took of the art turned out great. He also took a picture of Mr. Wisnewski and Mrs. Tarrington, Mr. Wisnewski's sister, to send to the newspapers to help publicize the event. I was surprised Mr. Wisnewski agreed to that. He hates any kind of publicity."

Ellie usually subdued any impulse to question Stacy about Garek, and she tried to restrain her curiosity now. But somehow, she couldn't stop herself from saying, "Oh?"

Stacy needed no further encouragement. "Ever since being named Most Eligible Bachelor he's been hounded by women," the girl said. "I read in the *Chicago Trumpeter* that a woman waited for him in a parking garage, then jumped on the hood of his car and started kissing the windshield. She left red-lipstick imprints all over the glass before he could get her off. Another woman broke into his house and stole all his underwear and put it up for sale on eBay. The police caught her and arrested her, but not before she'd sold a pair of boxer shorts to a woman living in a Florida retirement community. He threatened to sue the *Chicago Trumpeter* and they've backed off for the last month or so, but we still get women calling or coming to the office on some pretext, hoping to meet him."

Ellie bent over the miter box, the whine of the saw ringing in her ears as she remembered Garek's surliness when she'd bumped into him on the sidewalk. What had he said in his office the next day? *So you managed to track me down.*

She still couldn't really excuse his rudeness to her. But she could understand it. She even sympathized with him in a way—she hated the press, also.

She didn't want to like him. She didn't want to be *aware* of him. But it was hard not to be. At the art show, she'd been conscious of his hand at the small of her back as he guided her from painting to painting, his bulk protecting her from being jostled by the crowd. When he took her to dinner, she was conscious of his hands on her shoulders as he helped her off and on with her coat. At the play, a comedy, she'd been distracted several times by his deep, rather rusty-sounding laugh; that had been bad enough, but then afterward, she'd neglected to button her coat before they went outside. Greeted by a blast of icy cold wind, she'd started to tug off her gloves, but he'd grabbed her hands and pulled her into a sheltered doorway. "I'll do your coat up for you," he'd said, and proceeded to fasten each button from her throat to her hemline.

She'd tried not to let his closeness affect her. She'd tried to ignore the increasingly familiar curling sensation low in the pit of her stomach. Just as she'd tried, a few days later, at the basketball game, not to notice the way his hair grew to a point at the nape of his neck; the way he listened silently, intently, to what she said; the masculine scents of wool and leather that clung to him; and the amusing contrast of the floral scent of his hair.

A gift of shampoo from his niece, he'd said when she impulsively asked about it last night after inviting him into her apartment for coffee. Sitting next to her on the couch, he'd immediately put down his cup and leaned over to sniff her hair.

"Mmm, strawberry, I think." He lifted a strand of her hair and ran it through his fingers.

Her entire scalp prickled at his touch. He continued to stroke her hair, his fingers gradually weaving their way deeper and deeper into its thickness until he was cradling her head, holding her completely still as he stared down at her mouth with a dark, intense look in his eyes.

Her heart pounded against the wall of her chest as if trying to get out. She knew she should pull away. She knew letting him kiss her was opening the door to all kinds of trouble. But the feeling inside her didn't respond to arguments. The feeling wasn't logical. It wasn't sensible. It was just there. Hot and needy and demanding. One kiss, it told her rational self. Just one kiss....

"Ellie? Ellie? Is something wrong with the frame?"

She came out of her trance to find Stacy staring at her. "The frame?" Ellie repeated stupidly before she remembered. She looked at the angle she'd cut into the oak. "Oh, yes. I mean no. It's fine. I'm sorry, I wandered off for a moment there."

A knowing smile appeared on Stacy's face. "I understand. I'd be in a daze too if Garek Wisnewski was in love with me."

"Stacy, please!" Ellie felt her cheeks heating up. The girl was too romantic...and too naive. "Garek Wisnewski isn't in love with me. He and I are just friends."

She bent over the miter box again, with another piece of molding. Friends...she tested the word in her head. How else to describe their relationship? It wasn't just business, anymore, she couldn't deny that. But they weren't really dating, either. If they had been, surely he would have kissed her last night when she'd made no move to stop him.

But instead, he'd released her and headed for the door. She'd felt bereft, confused. Had she misread the look in his eyes when he looked at her mouth? She'd never liked her mouth. In school, the other kids had teased that her lips were "upside down." Maybe he stared only because of their odd shape....

He'd paused by the door and looked down at her, frowning. "I'll pick you up at seven on Saturday." Then, as suddenly as he'd abandoned her, he'd pulled her to him and had pressed a hard, swift kiss against her mouth, before striding out the door.

That kiss...it had been so brief, over almost before she realized what he was doing. Even so, she couldn't stop thinking about it. Rafe's most passionate embraces had never affected her the way Garek's fleeting kiss had.

"I didn't even know about his birthday," she said out loud to Stacy. "I don't really know him that well. And he doesn't know me."

"He knows enough," Stacy said. "And what else do you need to know about him except that he's a hunk?"

What he was thinking. Feeling. What he thought about *her.* "This is a ridiculous conversation," she told Stacy.

"I heard him tell his sister on the phone that he wanted to introduce you to her soon—"

Ellie's heart skipped a beat. "You shouldn't repeat things you overhear," she reprimanded the girl, but not with as much conviction as she should have.

Stacy ignored her. "Garek's sister is very important to him. I heard that the necklace he bought her for Christmas cost a fortune. Emeralds and rubies are very expensive."

The girl nodded in a knowledgeable manner, but Ellie barely noticed. He'd bought that necklace for his *sister?* He hadn't talked about Doreen Tarrington much, but he must care for her to buy her such an expensive piece of jewelry. Granted, he had terrible taste, but still, it had been kind of him.

Garek Wisnewski, *kind*?

"Technically, his sister is in charge of this art foundation," Stacy continued. "But her health isn't too good, so he won't let her do any work. She loves art. He started the foundation for her."

The piece of wood in Ellie's hands splintered. "He did?"

"Yes, Mr. Wisnewski's secretary, Mrs. Grist, told me all about it," Stacy said. "His sister told him she wanted to start an art foundation and Mr. Wisnewski agreed to finance it for her."

Ellie remembered her suspicion when Garek had proposed investing in the gallery. Why hadn't he admitted it was for his sister?

She remembered something he'd said. *You shouldn't be so quick to judge me.*

Ellie picked up a fresh piece of wood. "That was very...kind of him," she said slowly.

Garek was hard at work late Friday afternoon when the phone rang. Impatiently, he glanced up, his eyes burning from reading the small, tight print of a contract. He had a stack of documents he needed to go through and sign in order to finalize the terms for financing the prospective buyout of Lachland, and he wanted to finish today.

"Yes?" he said curtly into the phone.

"Mrs. Tarrington's here to see you," his assistant told him.

Ah, Doreen. He looked down at the contract he'd just signed. The deal with Lachland hadn't closed yet, but the financing was in place. Doreen didn't know it yet, but her ace had been trumped.

Garek smiled. "Send her in, Mrs. Grist."

Doreen came in, wearing a black designer dress with a black-and-white scarf pinned at her shoulder that had the unfortunate effect of making her look sallower than usual. She carried a flat, rectangular box in her black-gloved hands.

"Happy birthday, Garek," she said, kissing the air by his cheek, then settling herself into the leather chair opposite him.

He sat back down and opened the box. "A tie," he said. Mustard yellow, emblazoned with a coat of arms, it was uglier than the muddy green one embroidered with a well-known designer's initials that she'd given him last year. It was even uglier than the putrid maroon-and-gold one she'd given him the year before that, the one she'd accidentally left the half-price sticker on.

"I traced our family tree back to Polish royalty," Doreen said. "This is our ancestral crest."

Garek almost laughed. The Wisnewskis were descended from pure peasant stock and Doreen knew it. But he allowed no trace of his thoughts to appear in his expression. "Thank you, Doreen. How was your cruise?"

She coughed a little and her normal foghorn voice weakened. "The cruise was horrible. We sailed through a hurricane and I was sick the whole time. Karen was heartless—she reminds me of you. She had no sympathy for my illness. She lounged around the pool the whole time, flirting with the crewmen. I complained to the captain about allowing employees to fraternize with the guests…but never mind about that." Her gaze sharpened on him. "I spoke to Ethel this morning. She said she saw you at the symphony with some woman. And at the art exhibit. And at the Cape Cod Room."

"Ethel ought to be a reporter for the *Chicago Trumpeter*." Garek half rose from his chair. "If that's all, Doreen—"

"No, that's not all, Garek Wisnewski! Who is this woman?"

Garek reseated himself, biting back a smile. "Her name is Eleanor Hernandez."

"Hernandez—that sounds Mexican."

"So it does."

Silence fell in the office.

Garek leaned back, waiting for the explosion. Doreen had complained frequently about the influx of Mexican immigrants, ignoring him when he pointed out their own grandparents' parallel circumstances.

Finally, Doreen broke the silence. "I'm glad to see you're keeping up your end of our bargain."

He frowned. "I beg your pardon?"

"Our bargain," she repeated. "To start dating a nice girl. Ethel told me she is a perfectly charming young woman."

Garek made no response. At that particular moment, he was incapable of one.

"Ethel also said that she received an invitation to the silent auction for the art foundation. She told me—confidentially, of course—that her friend on the Social Register committee is very impressed by the foundation. He made a note when Ethel mentioned it to him. It's possible I'll be listed in the summer edition. Ethel said it's going to press in a few weeks—"

"Doreen," Garek cut her off. "I have to get back to work." Ignoring her indignant sniffs, he escorted her out of his office, then returned to his desk and sat down, frowning. His plan to teach Doreen a lesson had gone crazily awry. But then, a lot of things hadn't gone the way he'd expected in the last few weeks. Ever since he'd met Eleanor Hernandez.

His gaze drifted to the canvas hanging on the wall opposite his desk.

Woman in Blue.

He'd intended to give the painting to Ted Johnson—payback for the Lilly Lade painting—but instead, on some incomprehensible impulse, he'd ordered it hung on his office wall.

The painting had an oddly compelling quality. He stared at it, trying to comprehend its appeal, but without success. The random daubs of color, the splotches and squiggles didn't make any sense—just like Ellie.

He couldn't quite figure out what she wanted. He'd thought at first it was money, pure and simple, but she wasn't very consistent about it. When he'd taken her to the art show and she'd admired a small ceramic vase, he'd offered to buy it for her, but she'd refused. Even more surprising, when he'd given her a raise, she'd tried to refuse that also. He'd disregarded her protests, but still, he found her actions odd. She must be after something else. But what? Publicity for the gallery? Definitely. But there had to be more than that. Something just for her. Fame?

Maybe. Although it was hard to believe that someone who could smile the way she did could be so calculating. When Ellie smiled, her eyes smiled also, and her whole face glowed. Warmth practically radiated from her. Sometimes when she smiled, he found himself liking her…like a friend. Although friendship wasn't what he'd felt a few nights ago when he'd stood at her apartment door, looking down at that siren mouth of hers. He'd wanted to rip off her clothes, throw her down on the floor and make hard, sweaty love to her until neither one of them could move....

Hell.

He frowned at the painting on the wall, then bent back over the contracts on his desk. Going out with Ellie was business, an extreme measure undertaken to protect Wisnewski Industries. Once he'd closed the Lachland deal and his sister found out he'd tricked her, he wouldn't need to spend any more time with Ellie. No more froufrou art shows or la-di-da symphonies. He planned to make a quick, clean break with Eleanor Hernandez, and he had no intention of complicating the matter by getting involved with her.

No intention at all, he told himself again later that evening as he rang her doorbell.

Martina, dressed in boots, a denim skirt and an emerald blouse that flattered her dark hair and eyes, let him in.

"Big date tonight?" he asked her.

She flashed a bright smile. "My boyfriend is coming to get me and we're driving up to Madison."

"Madison? That's a long trip in this weather."

"Yeah, we're going to spend a couple of nights with some friends of his. Go ahead and sit down. Ellie's not quite ready yet."

He sat on the sofa, talking casually with Martina while some part of his brain filed away the information that there would be no one in the apartment when he brought Ellie home tonight; it would be completely empty. Quiet. Private.

Not that it mattered.

He forced himself to focus on Martina. She had a flirtatious, sensual manner—except when she talked about business. Then she was as coolheaded as any of his vice presidents. He'd had a chance to talk to her several times in the last couple of weeks, and he liked her.

"What do you think of Ellie's new acquisition?" Martina asked, waving a hand at the artwork resting on the coffee table.

It looked like a lump of mud. "Very unusual."

Martina snorted. "It's a piece of crap, that's what it is."

Eyeing the brown mass, Garek wondered if she meant the remark literally.

"But half the stuff she brings home is crap," Martina continued. "Just let some crackpot wander into the gallery and tell her some sob story and she immediately opens up her purse. Just because her father was an artist and could never sell any of his work, she feels compelled to buy something from everyone."

Garek frowned, but before Martina could say anything more about Ellie's father, he heard footsteps behind him. Standing, he turned to see her coming from the bedroom. For a moment, all he could think of was how gorgeous she looked. A scrap of blue velvet clung to her breasts, waist, hips and thighs, emphasizing her smooth curves.

"Happy birthday!" She smiled up at him and held out a box that he hadn't even noticed she was holding.

A flat, rectangular box.

Her smile made accepting the box a bit less painful. He opened it and stared down at the tie within.

Green musical notes floated down the length of it. The widest part featured miniature newsprint with a headline: PUKE ON NUKES. The whole thing appeared to have been splattered with a rainbow of paint.

"How…colorful," he said.

"It's a bit outrageous," she admitted, glancing at his face a trifle anxiously. "But I thought you ought to loosen up and try something a little less conservative than the ties you usually wear."

"Did an artist from your gallery design it?" he asked.

"Not exactly. I haven't displayed any of his work. But he came into the gallery last week and he's trying very hard to get established…"

He looked at her, then at Martina, who rolled her eyes before discreetly disappearing into her bedroom.

Suddenly, Garek wanted to laugh. Struggling to keep a straight face, he looked back at Ellie. "Then you'll have to help me put it on, won't you?"

Her radiant smile made the sacrifice worthwhile.

He pulled off his old tie, and bent his head so she could put the new one around his neck. His movement brought his face into close proximity with her bare shoulders and he inhaled the scent of the light perfume she wore. All desire to laugh disappeared. Straightening back up, he put his hands on her waist to steady her—or perhaps himself, he wasn't sure.

Her waist felt tiny within the grasp of his hands. The tips of her breasts were only inches away from his chest. The slightest tug would pull her up against him….

"There you go." She stepped back abruptly.

His hands fell to his sides and he looked down at the knot she'd tied with amazing speed and skill. "You've done this before."

"I always tied my grandfather's for him." She sounded a little tense. "Let me get my coat and we can go."

The club he took her to was small and dark and intimate. On the dance floor, she moved with a sensual Latin grace that sent his temperature soaring. He couldn't take his eyes off her. The clinging blue dress made him want to run his hands from her shoulders down to her hips. He managed to restrain himself for at least an hour—until the band finally decreased the tempo and played a slow dance. He pulled her into his arms.

She hesitated; then, her arms lifted around his neck and she moved closer, her breasts pressing against his chest.

Missing a step, he steered her into another couple. He recovered quickly, however, and tightened his arms around her. His hands slid down over her hips. She made no objection, just squirmed closer.

He groaned. He was in heaven. And hell. He wanted to get the hell out of there, take her back to her apartment and—

"Garek," she murmured.

"Hmm?"

"I know why you started the art foundation."

He stiffened slightly. "You do?"

"Yes. I know you're doing it for your sister." She leaned back to smile at him. "Why didn't you tell me? I think it was a very kind and generous thing to do."

Garek stared into her shining eyes. "I'm a businessman," he said. "I'm never kind or generous."

Still smiling, she shook her head and rested her cheek against his shoulder. He looked down at her soft hair, a whirl of thoughts in his head. She didn't believe him, obviously. What would she say, he wondered, if he told her that he had started the foundation only to annoy his sister, not to please her? What would she say if he told her he didn't care at all about pleasing his sister; but that the idea of pleasing *her* was becoming more and more appealing?

Involuntarily, he tightened his arms around her. He'd

drunk too much wine. That was why he was having these puerile thoughts....

A sudden, bright flash nearly blinded him. Blinking as his vision slowly cleared, Garek saw a man with a camera hurrying toward the door.

Annoyance raced through him, but then he sighed. Actually, he was surprised it hadn't happened sooner.

"Hope you don't mind having your picture in the paper," he said lightly, glancing down at her.

Shock and dismay fluttered across her face. "Aren't you going to try to stop him?"

"I can if you want me to."

She nodded mutely.

He caught the man just as he was climbing into a car. After a brief scuffle, Garek managed to get the camera. As he stripped out the film, the photographer said, "Aw, give a guy a break. My editor said she'd give me a bonus if I got this picture."

"Get the hell out of here," Garek snapped. "Before I decide to take you apart, as well."

The reporter gave Garek an appraising glance, then got in his car, apparently deciding retreat was in order. "Can't blame a guy for trying," he yelled out the window before driving off.

Garek made his way back into the restaurant.

"Did you catch him?" Ellie asked anxiously when he was close enough to hear.

"All taken care of." He looked at her pale face and put his arm around her. "C'mon. Let me take you home."

Driving down the dark, icy streets, they didn't talk much. Garek thought about the incident in the club and Ellie's reaction. She should have been delighted about that picture. She could have parlayed it into publicity for the gallery and thus for herself. What kind of sane person turned down such a golden opportunity?

He stopped the car in front of her apartment building and looked at her.

"You didn't introduce me to any clients tonight," she said.

"No," he said.

There was a slight pause.

"Would you like to come in for some coffee?" she asked.

The streetlight haloed her face, emphasizing her wide, clear eyes and sweetly smiling lips. Maybe she was as honest and genuine as she appeared. The only problem was—he didn't want her to be. He didn't want to be attracted to her. He didn't need to complicate this situation any more. If he had any sense at all, he would let her go up to her apartment alone....

He looked at her, all soft-eyed and dewy-lipped.

That mouth.

"I'd love to come in," he said.

Chapter Seven

As they stepped into the apartment, Ellie pulled off her glove and reached out to turn on the light. Before she could do so, however, Garek's hand closed over hers. He'd taken off his gloves, too, and his fingers were warm. He shut the door, cutting off the glow from the porch light and casting the apartment into complete darkness. Ellie stood perfectly still, the blackness pressing against her, the scent of damp wool, icy wind and male musk filling her nostrils. Outside the apartment, the savage sleet and wind howled; inside, all was quiet—except for the wild beating of her heart.

His arms came around her, he pushed her against the door, and he kissed her.

The darkness whirled around her. His mouth was hard against hers, the intensity of its demand shocking.

She put her hands on his chest to push him away, but then the kiss changed. It became gentle, tender.

She hesitated. She'd wanted him to kiss her. *Really* kiss her. She'd been curious ever since that frustrating half kiss he'd given her the night of the basketball game. And now she knew. She knew…oh, dear heaven! She knew it felt wonderful to be kissed by Garek Wisnewski. He was so big, she would have thought he would crush her, but he held her so lightly, so gently, it was like being cradled in a cocoon. But at the same time, there was nothing soft about him. His body felt hard and muscled, his lips firm against hers. Rippling sensations flowed over, around and all the way through her. She liked being kissed by him. She liked the way his mouth felt on her lips and her chin and her neck….

She felt his fingers undoing the buttons of her coat; his hands burrowed underneath, stroking her sides. That felt good, too. She reached up, entwining her fingers in his hair, pressing herself closer to him.

His hands slipped down the velvet of her dress to her waist, then up to the undercurve of her breasts, then down to the tops of her hips. And then back up again until his thumbs were resting against the sides of her breasts.

She was aware, suddenly, that she was on the verge of breaking some tenuous thread of restraint, of allowing herself to go beyond what she'd intended. She'd only wanted to know what it was like to kiss him. She hadn't intended it to go any further than that. She hadn't expected to feel like this. To want him so intensely…

But she did. She didn't care about anything else. She only wanted the kiss to go on and on…she wanted him to touch her breasts. She wanted him to touch her all over—to make love to her….

The door suddenly pushed against her back, thrusting her forward. Garek held on to her, stepping backward, pulling her with him. The light flashed on, blinding her as a familiar voice said, "Something's blocking the door...oh!"

Ellie blinked at Martina, who stood openmouthed in the doorway, her boyfriend behind her.

"Martina! What are you doing here?" Aware, suddenly, of Garek's arms around her, Ellie stepped away from him.

Martina's wide-eyed gaze flickered back and forth between Ellie and Garek. "The road was snowed under...we're going to drive up tomorrow afternoon instead...I'm really sorry, I didn't mean to interrupt!"

"You're not interrupting." Ellie wondered if she looked as self-conscious as she felt. "Hi, Billy. Come sit down."

"Uh, thanks, but I have to go," he muttered with an uneasy glance at Garek's stony face. "See ya tomorrow, Martina."

"Bye, Billy." Once Billy left, Martina started sidling toward her room. "Uh, I'm really tired." She faked a yawn. "I better go to bed now. Good night!" She scuttled the last few steps into her bedroom.

Garek turned back to Ellie, his eyes dark and intense. "Come to my apartment with me." His voice was low and husky.

"No." She glanced away from his compelling gaze.

He cupped her face in his hands, forcing her to look at him. "Have dinner with me tomorrow night, then. At my apartment."

The expression in his eyes made her tremble. She knew she should say no. She had to say no. She opened her mouth to say no.

"Yes," she whispered.

A light blazed in his eyes and he gave her a quick hard kiss. "Until tomorrow."

And then he was gone.

Chapter Eight

Ellie found it difficult to concentrate on work the next day. She hung a painting, moved a sculpture and worked on balancing the accounts. Unfortunately, she hung the painting upside down, dropped the sculpture—the head broke off—and could not get the accounts to balance no matter how many times she checked the numbers.

Finally, she gave up all pretense of working and sank onto the flat, leather bench that sat in the middle of the gallery so people could sit and look at the art. Coincidentally, it also gave her an excellent view of the clock. Three fifty-eight. Three fifty-nine. Four o'clock….

In one hour she could go home and get ready to go to dinner at Garek's.

And to make love.

The words had been unspoken, but she'd heard them loud and clear all the same.

Was she insane?

She must be.

How else could Garek Wisnewski have affected her like this? Last night, she'd felt hot inside and out, she'd yearned for his touch, she'd forgotten all caution, all logic, all common sense....

How had he done that to her?

After he'd left last night, she'd sat in a daze on the couch in the living room, not moving until she heard the creak of a door hinge. Glancing over, she'd seen her cousin cautiously stick her head out. "Is he gone?" Martina had whispered.

Ellie had nodded.

Martina had opened the door all the way and come out into the living room. Clad in a long flannel nightgown with pink bunnies on it and a fuzzy bathrobe, she'd sat cross-legged on the couch next to Ellie.

"Wow," she'd said. "You look like you've died and gone to heaven. He must be one heckuva kisser."

"Martina..."

"Oh, come on, El...fess up. I can't believe what I just saw. You haven't so much as looked at a man since you came to Chicago. I was beginning to think I was going to have to send your name to the nearest convent."

Ellie had frowned. "Just because I don't jump into bed with every guy I meet doesn't mean I want to be a nun."

"Yeah, yeah." Martina hadn't been put off by Ellie's discouraging tone. "Garek Wisnewski, of all people! I thought you hated him."

Ellie had thought so too. But something had changed in the last few weeks. "He's not as bad as I thought," she'd admitted. "He makes me laugh. He can be really kind. He cares a lot about his sister—"

"Ellie…" Martina had stared at her, a frown knitting her forehead. "Are you in love with him?"

The question had rasped on Ellie's skin like an ice scraper. "No, of course not," she'd said automatically.

"Yeah, right," Martina had said. "I believe that one."

"It's true," Ellie had insisted. "I'm not in love with him."

"Well, you should be. You should forget about that loser, Rafe—he never cared about you. He was only out for what he could get. Garek is different. I've seen the way he looks at you. I think he's in love with you. Or if he's not, he will be soon." Martina had yawned. "I've got to get up early. Good night."

Ellie had gone to bed soon after Martina, but she hadn't slept well.

Are you in love with him?

Fourteen hours later and the question was *still* echoing inside her head.

Ellie closed her eyes, blocking out her view of the ridiculously slow-moving clock. Was she in love with Garek? She didn't think so. And yet, she'd never felt like this before, not even with Rafe. With Rafe, she'd felt an odd mix of excitement, curiosity and rebellion. With Garek, she felt excitement, too, but it was fueled more by a genuine liking of him as a person. Rafe had talked a lot, but rarely backed up his speeches with action. Garek, on the other hand, spoke very little, but he accomplished everything he set out to do. Rafe had ridiculed her interest in art and music. Garek wasn't necessarily a devotee of either, but he obviously recognized the importance of both and shared her deep commitment to supporting artists and the arts. Rafe hadn't cared about his disabled father and ailing mother—she

hadn't even known of their existence until he broke up
with her. Garek obviously cared deeply about his family—he supported his sister and gave her loving,
thoughtful gifts. Like the necklace. And the art foundation…

If she let the relationship continue on its natural
course, if she went to his apartment and had sex with
him, she would probably fall in love with him. But
would he love her in return?

Martina seemed to think so. But Ellie wasn't so sure.
She thought about how badly Rafe had hurt her. She
didn't want to go through that again.

And yet, in more ways than one, she'd been hiding
ever since she came to Chicago. She couldn't live the
rest of her life this way. At some point she was going to
have to take a risk on someone.

Maybe it was time to take that risk….

She looked at the clock.

Four fifty-seven. Four fifty-eight. Only two more
minutes….

The door opened and a woman entered. She wore a
royal-blue designer suit, her hair fresh-from-the-salon
styled and tinted, a large diamond on her finger. She had
that too-perfect look of plastic surgery and could have
been anywhere from thirty to fifty years old.

Usually Ellie would have been delighted at the arrival
of a customer, no matter how close to closing time. But
today she only wanted to hurry home and get ready to
go to Garek's.

With an effort, she hid her impatience. "May I help
you?"

"I am Doreen Tarrington," the woman announced.

Doreen Tarrington…Garek's sister?

Ellie smiled, warmth curling inside her. Had he sent his sister to meet her? "Mrs. Tarrington! How nice to finally meet you. I'm Ellie Hernandez, and *this* is Vogel's Gallery."

Doreen did not smile back. Nor did she take Ellie's outstretched hand. Haughty gray eyes gazed disdainfully around the room, and as she looked at several of Ellie's newest purchases, a horrified expression settled on the woman's features. "I *knew* it. I *knew* it!" she said bitterly.

Ellie's hand dropped to her side. The warmth inside her faded. "Is something wrong?"

"I would certainly say so—this place is ghastly! This isn't *real* art! What will the Palermos and the Branwells think? He did this on purpose. I know he did!"

"Who?" Ellie asked.

"Garek." Loathing filled Doreen's voice. "My brother. He picked this gallery to humiliate me. The wretch. The terrible wretch!"

Ellie's stomach knotted. "Mrs. Tarrington, you don't know what you're saying. Garek did this for you—"

Doreen laughed cynically. "Is that what he told you? You obviously don't know him very well. Or do you?" The piercing gray gaze, suddenly looking very much like Garek's, swept over her. "He's sleeping with you, isn't he? A common sales clerk! I can't believe Ethel was taken in by you—or Garek, either. But of course he wasn't. I see it all now. I make a perfectly reasonable request that he start an art foundation for me, and what does he do? He seeks out the trashiest gallery he can find just to annoy me. How like him. How very like him!"

Ellie opened her mouth to say something—anything—but Doreen continued, her anger as biting and unstoppable as the wind over Lake Michigan.

"And you—I suppose you're the 'suitable girl' I asked him to find." Doreen's hard gaze swept over her again. "How much did he pay you to play this horrible trick on me? Or did you do it for free, thinking he really cared about you? I hope you weren't that naive. The only thing my brother cares about is himself. And money, of course."

Without another word, Doreen turned on her heel and left the gallery. Ellie, feeling dazed, went into her little office and sat down. She stared at the canvas over her desk. It showed an artist drawing the barren landscape outside his window—only in his rendition everything was green and in flower.

Ellie had always liked the painting. It reminded her to look on the bright side. But now it seemed to have a totally different meaning.

Had she been looking at everything through rose-colored glasses—seeing only what she wanted to see?

She picked up a pitcher of water, but her hands were shaking so badly, she put it back down.

That woman—that horrible woman was Garek's sister? She obviously didn't think too highly of her brother. Could what she'd said be true? Had Garek chosen Vogel's and gone out with Ellie to *humiliate* his sister?

Ellie clasped her hands together tightly. She didn't want to believe it. But it all rang true. All the little inconsistencies that had puzzled her, that she'd ignored, now made terrible, sickening sense. His seeking her out for his art foundation after insulting her in his office. His quick decision to choose Vogel's without even speaking to any other galleries. His insistence on taking her to the symphony, to dinner, the art show and the basketball game....

Ellie felt cold inside. She'd thought he was a kind and generous man who loved his family. But now with that facade stripped away, she saw the same man who'd left her standing in the gutter—cold, selfish, heartless. Did he care about anyone or anything other than himself?

Money, according to his sister.

Ellie folded her arms on the desk and put her head down on them.

She should have questioned him more closely instead of allowing herself to believe the best. But that was what she'd *wanted* to believe. If Doreen hadn't come in, Ellie would probably be on her way over to his apartment right now, planning to spend the night with him….

Air burned inside her lungs, stinging her throat and nose and eyes. She'd thought she might be falling in love with him. She'd thought he might learn to love her. How could she have been so stupid?

"Ellie?"

Startled, she lifted her head. "Robbie?" Blinking back her tears, she looked at her handsome cousin standing in the doorway of her office. "What are you doing here? I thought you were still in jail."

He hunkered down next to her. "I got out early for good behavior. I only have to report to my parole officer once a week."

"That…that's great." With an effort, Ellie tried to put aside her emotional turmoil and concentrate on Robbie. He looked thinner than she remembered, and his skin had a slightly sallow cast—but his hands twitched with the same restless energy, and when she sniffled, she caught the scent of Old Spice, the cologne he'd always favored. "Have you seen Aunt Alma and Uncle Rodrigo yet?"

"Not yet. I'm not so sure they'll want to see me."

"Of course they will," she said automatically, although, secretly, she wasn't so sure about Uncle Rodrigo—he'd been extremely angry when his son got arrested. "How are you doing, Robbie?"

"Good. I've been clean for the last six months."

"That's great. I'm so proud of you."

"Thanks, El. But never mind about me. Why were you crying?" His big brown eyes, so like Martina's, were full of concern.

Ellie's shaky composure threatened to crumple under his inquiring look. She tried to smile. "Nothing, really. I was just upset about…something to do with the gallery."

"Are you crying over that Wisnewski guy?"

Ellie straightened abruptly. "Where'd you hear about him?"

"Martina said you're in love with him."

"Martina told you that!"

"Yeah. I called your apartment this morning and talked to her awhile. She told me all about you and Wisnewski."

Ellie wished they would have talked about something else. Didn't Martina know by now not to say anything about Ellie's love life to Robbie? "Well, it's not true."

He looked as though he didn't believe her.

"Really," she insisted, wiping the tears from her face. "Oh, maybe I thought I was for a minute or two, but now I know I was mistaken."

He was still staring at her, a frown on his face. "I've never seen you cry over a man before—not even that jerk Rafe."

"Robbie, this is ridiculous." She stood up. "I don't want to talk about Garek Wisnewski anymore."

Cracking his knuckles, Robbie stood also. "He hurt you."

"Yes…I mean, no, not really," she said, alarmed. She remembered what had happened the last time Robbie got that look in his eyes. He'd always been way too protective. "Don't worry. I can handle my love life. Hadn't you better go see your parents?"

The bloodlust died out of his eyes and he shuffled his feet. "Ellie, I hate to bother you when your heart is broken and all—"

"It's *not* broken!"

"—but I don't know if my father will let me in the house," Robbie said, ignoring her interruption. "I have a friend who's going out of town and he said I could stay at his place starting tomorrow. But tonight…"

"You're welcome to stay with me," she said. "Martina's going to be gone—I'm sure she won't mind if you use her room."

"Thanks, El—you're the best. Oh, and one more thing. I have a friend—another friend. He wants to be an artist. He's really talented…."

Ellie's heart sank a little. "Did you meet this friend in prison?"

"Yeah, he got busted for some pyramid scheme. But he's completely reformed—he's a real smart guy. He's taken every mail-order course there is. If you ever need an undertaker, a minister or a lawyer, he's your man."

"Uh, exactly how long has he been in prison?"

"Not that long. The thing is, he's decided he really wants to be an artist. You think you could take a look at his stuff?"

"Sure," she said listlessly. "Have him bring by some samples of his work tomorrow."

"Thanks, El. I owe you one. Say, could you give me the key to your apartment?"

She handed over the key, and he gave her a casual hug. "Thanks again, El. Oh, and listen. If you need any help, if you want me to punch your boyfriend's lights out or something, you let me know."

"I will," she told him, touched in spite of herself.

Once he was gone, she sank slowly back into her chair, imagining a confrontation between the two men—Garek getting beat up and Robbie being hauled back to jail.

She hoped she never saw Garek again. But even more, she hoped he and Robbie never met.

Ellie was sitting on her couch that evening, across from Robbie and his friend Caspar, when the phone rang. Trying to ignore it, she pretended to study Caspar's painting.

Caspar hadn't been able to wait until tomorrow to show Ellie his work, so Robbie had invited him to come over. Caspar seemed nice enough—he was a tall, thin young man with lank brown hair and a skittish gaze— but Ellie hadn't been too thrilled to find him in her apartment when she arrived home. His paintings held even less to thrill her. His bland landscapes did little to distract her from the shrill ringing of the telephone. Was it her imagination or did the phone actually sound *angry?*

"Ellie? Ellie? Are you there?" The harsh voice coming from the answering machine definitely sounded angry. "Pick up the phone, Ellie, or I'm coming over...."

Becoming angry herself, Ellie stalked over to the phone on the kitchen wall and snatched up the receiver. "I can't talk right now," she snapped. "What do you want?"

"What do you think I want?" he snarled. "I want an explanation of that message you left on my phone."

"I don't care what you want—" Seeing Robbie and

Caspar eavesdropping with blatant interest, she hunched her shoulders and turned her back to them. "I don't want to go out with you anymore, you snake," she hissed, adding a few improvements to the calm, cool message she'd left earlier. "I don't ever want to see you again, you miserable excuse for a human being. Which part don't you understand?"

"Oh, I understand you're upset about something. I just don't understand what."

"I had a little visit from your sister today. Let's just say that she opened my eyes as to your true character."

There was a long silence. Then, his voice grim, he said, "I'm coming up."

"Coming up? What do you mean?" She ran over to the window and saw him getting out of his car, cell phone in hand. "No! You can't—"

The line went dead. She saw him put the phone in his pocket and start up the stairs.

Panic assailed her. She didn't want to see him. She didn't want to talk to him. She wanted to hide. She'd get Robbie to tell him to go away....

Robbie!

Oh, dear heaven. There was no predicting how Robbie would behave.

The doorbell rang.

She wondered if there was any chance Garek would just leave if she ignored it.

The bell rang again—a long, extended ring, as if someone was holding his finger on the button.

"Robbie," Ellie said. "Could you and Caspar please go into Martina's room for a few minutes?"

Robbie frowned. "Who's at the door? That guy you're in love with?"

"I'm not in love with him!" she snapped, her patience fraying badly. "I just need to talk to him—privately."

Robbie didn't move, his frown deepening. "You're sure acting strangely, Ellie. Crying over this guy one minute and snapping at me the next—"

"She's probably pregnant, man," Caspar said. "That's how my sister was when her old man knocked her up."

"Pregnant!" A murderous rage lighting his brown eyes, Robbie took an impulsive step toward the front door.

Ellie caught his arm. "Robbie, I'm *not* pregnant!"

"My sister denied it too," Caspar said. "But five months later she had little Willard. Cute kid. Except his head was kind of pointy—"

"Oh, for heaven's sake!" Ellie couldn't take any more. "Robbie and Caspar, in the bedroom—*now!*"

Robbie looked as though he was going to refuse, but she gave him a stern look, and reluctantly he allowed her to push him toward the bedroom. "If you need any help," he said, cracking his knuckles, "just call out and I'll be glad to—"

Ellie slammed the door closed.

Taking a deep breath, she wiped her damp palms on her skirt, smoothed her hair, then marched over to the door and opened it.

Garek immediately shoved his way past her. "We need to talk."

"About what?" she said as coolly as she could. "About the art foundation you started for your sister? Doreen told me how much she appreciates your efforts on her behalf."

He gave her an unreadable look. "So?"

"So! So!" She stared at him in disbelief. "May I ask you one question? And please be honest. Did you know your sister would hate Vogel's?"

He hesitated, then answered bluntly. "Yes."

Pain lanced through Ellie's heart. She wanted to creep into the bedroom and hide. But she couldn't let herself hide from the truth any longer. She needed to know it all. "Did you deliberately choose Vogel's to annoy her?"

He met her gaze, his own level. "Yes."

The pain grew worse. "And did you go out with me for the same reason?"

"Yes."

That was it, then. Her throat was so tight, she could barely speak. "Then there's nothing more to say." Afraid she was going to start crying, she turned away.

He caught her arm, and she blinked back her tears. She couldn't cry—she *wouldn't*. Not in front of him. She yanked free of his grasp and folded her arms across her chest, glaring. "Will you please leave? You accomplished everything you set out to do."

Garek stepped back. He shoved his hands in his pockets, making no effort to defend himself. How could he? Everything she'd said was true. But somehow, at the same time it *wasn't* true. He'd certainly started out the way she said. But nothing had turned out as he'd expected. He'd wanted to spite his sister—but it had been a long time since he'd even thought of that. He disliked contemporary art—but he enjoyed listening to Ellie's enthusiasm for it. He'd gone out with her to teach Doreen a lesson—but somehow, when he was with Ellie, he forgot about his sister. He looked at her flushed cheeks and pursed lips. His gaze flickered down to her rounded breasts pushed up by her folded arms, then back up to meet her angry eyes head-on. He wanted her with an intensity he'd never experienced before. He wanted her—and he wasn't willing to give her up.

"Whatever I intended at the start of our relationship doesn't really matter anymore. Everything has changed. I didn't expect it to. I didn't want it to. But there's something between us, Ellie, something I can't deny and neither can you. Come on," he said, his voice low and seductive. "Admit it. You want me as much as I want you."

"You're crazy." Ellie glared at him, hating the arrogant certainty in his tone. "How could I want you? Everything I thought I liked about you was a lie. You don't like your family, you don't like art or music. You don't even like *me*."

"You're wrong, Ellie." His hard gaze turned dark and sensual. "I do like you."

Before she could move, he took her in his arms and kissed her. For a second, everything inside her went limp. He was right. She did want him. She did want to find out what was between them....

But she wasn't completely stupid.

With every ounce of willpower she could summon, she pulled away from him. "No, Garek. I—"

"Hey, El," a voice interrupted her. "You need some help getting rid of this jerk?"

As one, Garek and Ellie turned toward the bedroom.

Garek's eyes narrowed when he saw the stranger standing in the doorway. Pierced and tattooed, the young man had the wiry build and mean eyes of a street kid, and he smelled of too much cologne. Who the hell was he and what was he doing in Ellie's apartment?

Ellie didn't appear too pleased at the stranger's appearance either. "Robbie, I told you I can handle this myself."

"Robbie?" Garek looked sharply at her. "Your cousin, I take it?"

She didn't answer his question, all her attention focused on Robbie. "Please go back into Martina's room."

"In a minute, *prima*." The mean eyes met Garek's. "First I want to find out what this *perro's* intentions are."

"And you wonder why I prefer to keep some distance between myself and family members?" Garek drawled.

Ellie didn't look amused. "Garek, please be quiet—"

"Don't worry, El, I'll shut him up." Robbie rushed at Garek.

Garek waited until the other man was almost on him, then quickly sidestepped.

Robbie went barreling past, crashing into the coffee table and shattering the lump of mud sculpture into a thousand pieces.

"Robbie! Garek! Stop this at once!"

Robbie didn't appear to hear Ellie. A snarl on his face, he got up and hurtled back toward Garek. Garek met him with a punch to the gut, causing Robbie to double over. Garek grabbed him by the shoulders and followed with an uppercut to the jaw. Robbie collapsed to the floor.

With a shriek, Ellie rushed to her cousin's side. "Robbie! Robbie! Are you all right?"

Wincing, Robbie sat up. "I think so," he said thickly, rubbing his jaw. He glared at Garek. "Think you're pretty tough, huh? This isn't over. Not by a long shot. You're not getting away with what you did to Ellie. You're going to have to do right by her—"

"Caspar!" Ellie called out hastily, cutting her cousin off. "Come help me with Robbie!"

Garek, leaning against the door to catch his breath, watched as another man came out of Martina's room and helped Ellie support Robbie into the bedroom. Pieces of the lump-of-mud sculpture made crunching noises as the trio stepped on them, pulverizing them into dust.

"Don't worry, man," Garek heard Caspar mumble to Robbie. "We'll figure something out—"

Ellie shut the door and came back into the living room.

"Charming cousin you have," Garek said.

She glared at him. "Did you have to hit him?" she asked indignantly.

Garek folded his arms across his chest. "He attacked me."

"Well, you didn't need to be so...so violent."

Garek, recognizing a woman's illogic when he saw it, forbore to respond. Instead, he asked, "What was he talking about? What have I done to you?"

Her gaze slid away and she hunched her shoulders irritably. "Nothing. Would you please leave now? I think you've caused enough trouble for one night."

"I'm not leaving until we get this mess straightened out between us—"

The bedroom door flew open again.

Ellie turned. "What is it now—" She stopped.

Once again, Robbie stood in the doorway. Only this time, he held a gun.

Chapter Nine

"Robbie!" Ellie cried. "What are you doing? Put that gun away!"

Garek looked at the gun, then at Robbie. "Don't be a fool, Hernandez," he said coldly.

Ellie moved in front of Garek. "Robbie," she pleaded. "Remember what happened last time you shot someone."

"Rafe was an ass, Ellie. He deserved to be shot in the rear end."

Garek, tense and watchful, frowned at the name. Rafe…Ellie's ex-boyfriend?

He tried to pull her behind him, but she yanked away. "Get out of the way," he growled at her, "before your idiot cousin shoots you."

Ellie didn't budge. "Garek will leave, Robbie. You don't need a gun."

"Who said I want him to leave? Caspar and I came up with a better idea." His gaze on Garek, Robbie ground a dirt clod from the sculpture under his heel. "My aim has improved since the business with Rafe, *perro*. You better do what I tell you, or you'll be sorry."

"What is it you want?"

"You're going to marry Ellie," Robbie said deliberately. "My friend Caspar here is an ordained minister."

Caspar gave a little wave from the bedroom.

"Robbie!" Ellie was horrified. "Are you insane?" She sniffed the air, then looked at him suspiciously. "Were you smoking something while you were in the bedroom?"

"No way," Robbie said. "I'm clean. I just want your baby to have a daddy."

Ellie felt, rather than saw, Garek turn to stare at her. Her cheeks burned, but she didn't look away from her cousin. "Robbie, I told you before I'm *not* pregnant. Put that gun down right now—" She started forward, only to stop when Garek put his arm around her shoulders. She glanced up at him and received a shock. In spite of his cool facade, a muscle ticced in his jaw, and fury blazed in his eyes. A sick feeling of dread rose inside her.

"Very well," he said to Robbie. "Let's hurry up and get this over with, then."

Triumph flashed in Robbie's eyes. Keeping the gun trained on Garek, he stepped aside so Caspar could emerge from the room. The tall thin man approached the happy couple and opened a white leather prayer book.

"Dearly beloved..." he proclaimed.

Ellie's body jerked in silent protest. The arm around her shoulders tightened.

"Better to play along," Garek said to her under cover of Caspar's booming voice, "than to risk someone getting hurt. We can deal with it afterward."

"No," she said stubbornly. "Robbie, I refuse to go

through with this ceremony. What are you going to do about it? Shoot me?"

His big brown eyes took on a wounded look. "You know I would never hurt you, Ellie," he said indignantly. "I would just have to shoot your boyfriend."

"That's not funny, Robbie." She knew he didn't really mean it. But then he hadn't really meant to shoot Rafe, either. Could she ever forgive herself if he accidentally hurt Garek?

When she didn't say anything for a few seconds, Caspar cleared his throat. "Do you, Garek, take this woman…"

"This is ridiculous!" she burst out. "It's completely illegal. Don't we have to have blood tests or something?"

Caspar shook his head. "The law is much more lenient nowadays. Blood tests aren't required."

"But what about a license? We have to have a license!"

"Don't worry," Caspar informed her. "I can print a blank one off the Internet. They're good in any state."

As Caspar proceeded with the ceremony, Ellie glanced despairingly at Garek, hoping for some help.

He was watching her with a cynical twist to his mouth that made her stiffen. How dare he look at her like that? As if…as if he thought she *wanted* to marry him.

Garek made his responses in a calm, cool voice that caused her to grit her teeth. She had to choke out the words.

"I now pronounce you husband and wife," Caspar said.

"Congratulations," Robbie said, beaming at the two of them over the top of his gun.

"Thanks," Garek said, his voice full of sarcasm. "We appreciate your…good wishes. You two can leave now. My…*wife* and I would like to be alone."

Robbie shook his head. "No way. We've got to make sure this marriage starts off right."

Ellie didn't know what he was talking about and at this point she didn't care. She felt completely drained. This night that she'd so looked forward to had turned into a nightmare. The only good thing about it was that it couldn't possibly get any worse….

"You two need a wedding night." Robbie sat down on a chair and used the gun to motion the couple toward Ellie's bedroom. "And I'm going to make sure you get it."

Inside the bedroom, the newlyweds stared at each other for a long moment.

Ellie broke the silence first. "So what do we do now?"

He shrugged. "Go to bed." He sat down on the mattress and lay back, watching her. "I hope you don't snore."

She stared at him. "You've got to be joking."

"No, I'm not. I'm a light sleeper and snoring keeps me awake—"

"Not about *that*." She waved her hand impatiently. "I mean about spending the night here. Together."

He put his hands behind his head. "I don't see that we have much choice."

"Are you crazy? We do have a choice. We can wait until Robbie falls asleep. Or we can try to go through the window—"

"Too dangerous. I have no desire to risk waking your trigger-happy cousin, or to get shot in the rear as I try to shimmy out the window." He dismissed her plans with a yawn, then patted the mattress beside him. "Come to bed…*wife*."

Ellie couldn't stop staring at him. Was he insane? She

knew he was angry. Why wasn't he yelling at her? Why was he pretending this marriage was real? "Garek, stop fooling around."

"Who's fooling?" In one swift, graceful motion, he rose to his feet and crossed the room to where she still stood by the door. He put his hands on the wooden panel on either side of her head and bent down to touch his mouth lightly to hers. "We have all night—let's make the most of it."

His mouth closed over hers, and she forgot to think. The attraction that she'd tried to deny flared up immediately, swamping her brain with Technicolor emotions, flooding her body with fluorescent sensations.

She responded blindly, instinctively. His arms came around her, hers curled around his neck. His grip on her tightened; then suddenly, he lifted her and carried her across the room.

He laid her gently on the bed, still kissing her, pulling off his coat and shirt and quickly unbuttoning her blouse. His warm hand cupped the curve of her breast.

Air grated in her lungs. She felt as though she were on fire. His kiss wasn't gentle. It wasn't tentative or kind or respectful. Instead, it was hungry, carnal, overwhelming, unstoppable. His mouth pulled on hers, as if trying to suck the very soul out of her, so he could take possession of it, take possession of her....

She broke away, gasping for air. "Stop," she panted. "We can't do this…"

He kissed the line of her throat, down to the curves of her lace-covered breasts. His fingers undid the button of her skirt, and eased down the zipper, spreading the fabric to expose a scrap of silk and a line of lace.

"Why not? You got what you wanted, didn't you? Marriage to Chicago's Most Eligible Bachelor…"

The sarcasm in his voice broke through the haze threatening to envelope her. What was he talking about? Did the conceited jerk really think she wanted this? That she wanted to marry *him*, a man who was using her to punish his sister?

She pushed at his shoulders.

He resisted. His fingers teased under the line of lace, pausing to splay across the indentation between her hip and abdomen, before drifting lower still…

Flattening her palms against his chest, she shoved harder.

With a curse, he rolled away. She scrambled onto her knees, ready to flee the bed if he made any move toward her. But he didn't. He lay there, his breathing harsh, his arm thrown over his eyes. His whole aspect was one of pain.

The frantic racing of her heart slowed. Uncertainty trickled through her. She touched his arm tentatively. "Garek?"

He stiffened under her touch. He lowered his arm and looked at her, his eyes cold and hard. "Next time you plan to trap a man into marriage," he said, his voice like shards of glass, "make sure you have the guts to go through with it."

Ellie's hand fell to her side. "What are you talking about?"

He stood up and gestured toward the door and where her cousin had positioned himself outside. "The shotgun wedding. The reluctant bride. I thought I'd seen every trick in the book when it came to women trying to ensnare me, but this one, I admit, was brilliant." He looked down at her, his gaze traveling from her face to her chest. "You're one hot little witch when you want to be."

Realizing her blouse was hanging open, she flushed and pulled the edges together. Then she paled. "Surely you don't think I *planned* this. You're the one that barged in here—"

"Yeah, after you left that message that ensured that I would—I was actually feeling guilty for having used you—for misjudging you. But I got it right the first time, didn't I? You're a greedy, manipulative little gold digger, out to make a quick buck."

"I don't care about your money—"

"It's a little late for the innocent act. You set me up. You don't really expect me to believe that your witless cousin came up with this marriage idea on his own? Or that the presence of Caspar, the friendly minister, was merely a coincidence? Oh, and let's not forget the icing on the wedding cake—you, the *pregnant* bride. Tell me something—are you really pregnant? Did some guy knock you up and you decided to pass the baby off as mine? Or was the whole thing a story you invented to get your cousin and his friend to go along with your plan?"

Her face felt frozen. "You...you conceited ass. This whole mess is *your* fault. None of this would have happened if you hadn't decided to play such a nasty trick on your sister. Even if I *were* pregnant, I would never marry you. I wouldn't marry you for all the sculptures in the Metropolitan. I wouldn't marry you for all the paintings in the Louvre. I wouldn't marry you—"

"I get the idea. If you don't mind, I'm going to get some sleep. I have to work tomorrow."

She hated the indifference of his tone. She hated

even more that she couldn't match it—her voice sounded slightly shrill as she asked, "But where are you going to sleep?"

"In the bed, of course." He picked up the pillow and punched it.

"This is *my* bed."

"I'm willing to share. Your virtue is safe with me."

She glared at him. "You can sleep on the floor."

"I'm not that chivalrous. *You* sleep on the floor."

She watched with fury and dismay as he turned back the hand-stitched quilt Aunt Alma had made and sat down to shuck off his shoes. The jerk. The cad. The—

His hands went to the buckle of his belt.

Her cheeks burning again, she practically leaped off the bed and stood with her back to him. A few seconds later she heard the rustle of sheets and the click of the light. The room went dark.

Ellie hesitated, trying to decide what to do. She was *not* going to share a bed with him. But the only other option was the bare wooden planks of the floor.

She considered marching out into the living room and taking the couch. She knew Robbie wouldn't stop her. The only problem was, he would probably come in and shoot Garek. Oh, she didn't think he would kill him—at least not intentionally. But it would be just like Robbie to accidentally shoot Garek in the foot or the hand. Or the rear....

She glanced at the black silhouette in her bed. For a second, she was tempted to go to the couch and leave Garek to his fate.

She sighed. She couldn't do that. No matter how much she hated Garek, she couldn't allow Robbie to shoot him.

An hour later, though, turning on the hard floor, she wasn't so sure. She was so cold, her bones ached with it. She couldn't stop shivering. She pulled her knees up to her chest, trying to conserve her body heat. She didn't remember ever being this cold. The clunky furnace must have conked out again. She would probably freeze by morning....

Warm arms suddenly encircled and lifted her. She gave a little squeak, all she was capable of at the moment since she was shivering so badly. "Wh-what are you doing?"

"The chattering of your teeth is keeping me awake," he growled.

"W-well, isn't that just too bad?" She yelped as he dropped her and she hit the mattress. "I would rather freeze to death than share a bed with you," she informed him haughtily.

"If you insist. At least you'll save me the cost of a lawyer to dissolve this marriage. Just do it quietly."

Outraged, she sat up and glared through the dark at him. Suddenly, she was determined *not* to freeze to death. She wouldn't give him the satisfaction.

Not to mention the warmth of the bed was so heavenly, she didn't think she could get up if she wanted to.

Carefully, she eased herself, still fully clothed, between the blanket and the sheet, trying to ignore the black bulk sprawled beside her in the spot on the mattress where she usually slept.

"You know," he drawled, "you might have grounds to claim the marriage is valid if we consummate it—"

"No, thank you!" she snapped.

He laughed softly, sardonically.

She turned on her side and scooted to the very edge of the mattress.

If he made *one move* toward her, she would shoot him herself.

* * *

Ellie woke up slowly, aware that something was different than usual. Her nose twitched. What was that smell? It wasn't unpleasant exactly. It was more earthy. Musky. Masculine…

Her eyes flew open.

A brawny shoulder was only a few inches away from her own. Instinctively, she pulled away, then, as Garek stirred and rolled over, she grew still, holding her breath.

He didn't wake up, however, and she stared at him. In the clear light filtering through the blinds, she could see every detail. A cowlick spiked up on top of his head. His hair grew back from his wide forehead in a straight line. He frowned, even in his sleep, a crease showing between his eyebrows. He had short, dark lashes, a reasonably well-shaped nose and ears that stuck out slightly, giving him an almost boyish look. The boyishness was instantly belied, however, by the dark shadow of beard and mustache, and the clean line of his upper lip and the full, amazingly sensual curve of his lower lip.

Her chest began to hurt. Two days ago, she'd thought he was someone special. Two days ago, she might have welcomed last night's crazy ceremony—only without the gun.

How could she have been so stupid?

But there was no point in crying. She'd cried over Rafe. She wasn't going to cry over Garek Wisnewski.

She climbed out of the bed. Straightening her spine and smoothing her creased and twisted skirt as best she could, she went to the door and peeked out.

No gun-wielding madmen lurked in the hall.

She checked the other bedroom but saw no sign of

Robbie or his friend. They must have decided to make themselves scarce.

Wisely, thought Ellie as she went into the kitchen and started some coffee. She was going to kill Robbie when she got her hands on him....

A sound made her turn. Garek stood in the doorway, buttoning his shirt, his coat over his arm. His hair was wet and slicked back, but dark stubble still covered his jaw.

"Your cousin decided not to stay for the rest of the honeymoon?"

Ellie turned away from the sardonic tone in Garek's voice. Opening a drawer, she stared down at the contents. She wouldn't let him bait her, she told herself grimly. She'd done nothing wrong. "Would you like some coffee?"

"How wifely you sound."

Closing the drawer with a small bang, she turned to face him. Then paused. She took a deep breath. "Look, I'm sorry about what happened. Robbie is sometimes a bit...impulsive. But he means well."

"I'm sure Al Capone and Bonnie and Clyde had pure motives, also."

She clenched her jaw until the filling in her back molar ached. "I'm sorry you were forced to spend the night here, but no harm done, right?" She pasted a smile on her face. "As you said, the marriage wasn't valid."

He didn't smile back. If anything, the angles of his face grew harsher. "My lawyer will take care of any legalities involved. I am instructing him, however, not to give you a single penny."

"Fine," she said. "I don't want anything from you."

His eyes narrowed. "You really expect me to believe that you're not going to make some claim against me?"

"I don't care what you believe, but that's the truth."

"That's good," he said. "Because you're not getting anything."

"Yes, you already said that." She was tired of his accusations, his suspicion. She stalked out of the kitchen, stepped to the front door and opened it, letting in a blast of cold air. Turning, she spoke across the small space to where he stood in the kitchen doorway watching her. "You better go now and get your lawyer working on it right away."

Garek frowned as he approached her. She played the innocent so well. But he wasn't falling for it this time. "Very well. My lawyer will be in touch with you." He pulled on his coat and gloves. "I'm going to make certain that you're prosecuted for attempted fraud."

"Fine!" she said through gritted teeth. "Just go!"

Garek stepped toward the door. "My lawyer will also make certain that your lunatic cousin is sent back to jail—"

"Robbie?" For the first time Garek saw a crack in her facade. She shut the door abruptly. "You can't do that. Robbie didn't mean any harm—"

"Holding a gun on a person usually qualifies as intending harm. He belongs in prison—"

"He just needs a chance," she said fiercely. "If you do anything to hurt Robbie, I'll…I'll tell the whole story about our marriage to the tabloids."

So *that* was how she intended to turn the situation to her advantage. He'd known she must have some plan up her sleeve. His anger, which had begun to fade, flared up to new heights. "Do whatever the hell you like," he snarled. "I really don't give a damn."

He opened the door and strode out of the apartment. Head bent against the cold wind, he silently cursed himself for believing, just for a moment, that she was as innocent as she looked.

Chapter Ten

Garek worked long, hard hours the next week. Other than giving his lawyer a terse explanation and an even terser set of instructions, he did not think of Eleanor Hernandez at all—except, perhaps, when he chanced to glance at the abstract painting hanging on his wall. Then he couldn't quite control the acid burn in his stomach.

He was searching his desk drawer for a roll of antacids as he talked on the phone to his production manager late Friday afternoon, when the door opened and Larry Larson, head of the legal department for Wisnewski Industries, entered the office.

"Let me get back to you, Ed." Garek hung up the phone, his gaze on Larry's face. "Well?"

"I've got good news and bad news." Larry sat down, carefully positioning the fall of his jacket as he seated himself. He had a fondness for expensive suits and a tendency to comb his hair across the bald spot on his crown, but he was an excellent lawyer, intelligent and efficient, and Garek knew he could count on him for sound advice.

"Go on," Garek said.

"The good news is that I spoke to several experts and they confirmed what I told you initially—any marriage involving coercion is automatically invalid. Also, after careful research, I've discovered that virtually every state refuses to recognize Internet marriage licenses. Ms. Hernandez will have a very difficult time making any claim against you."

Garek leaned back in his chair, his hard gaze not leaving the lawyer's face. "And the bad news?"

"The bad news—ah." Larry cleared his throat and adjusted his cuff. "The bad news is that coercion can be a difficult thing to prove. She could claim that the two of you married of your own free will. Then it would be her word against yours. Also, one or two states do recognize Internet marriage licenses. Vermont, for example, recognizes just about anything as a marriage. And unfortunately, Caspar Egilbert *is* a legally ordained minister, even though the university he obtained his degree from is somewhat suspect. The unpleasant truth is that although I have no doubt that we would ultimately be successful, I'm afraid Ms. Hernandez could involve us in a very messy, very embarrassing court case and the resulting publicity would not be good for the company. Stockholders want their CEOs to be above reproach these days—"

"I don't care about the damn stockholders." The anger Garek had been controlling all week flared dangerously high. "I'm not paying her one dime—"

"Yes, yes," Larry said hastily, fingering the knot of his tie. "Fortunately, that won't be necessary. If you'll look in this file, you'll see that I've taken care of all the paperwork."

Hard satisfaction replaced the burn in Garek's stomach. He took the thick file from Larry and opened it. Inside on top was a document giving him ownership of the gallery. He picked up a pen. "Did the accountant go over the books?"

"Yes, everything was in order. Although there was one thing that seemed a bit odd…."

Tensing, Garek glanced up. "What?"

"A donation to the Art Institute a few days ago."

"What's so odd about that?"

"The artist was paid five thousand for the work. Coincidentally, a check you'd made out to Ms. Hernandez was cashed the same day…."

Garek's grip tightened on the pen.

"I called the Art Institute and discovered that the donation had been made in *your* name. I asked what exactly the donation was, and the woman said it was a sculpture of a giant…" Larry paused.

"A giant cockroach?" Garek guessed.

Larry's nearly nonexistent eyebrows rose. "You knew about this?"

"Not exactly." Narrowing his eyes, Garek signed the deed and set it aside. He stared down at the next paper, a document stating that one Eleanor Hernandez relinquished all claims on him. "This is already signed," Garek observed.

"Yes," Larry said, his satisfaction evident. "I spoke to her this morning."

"Did she give you any trouble?"

"Surprisingly, no. I think she realized she was beat. She read through the waiver and the annulment papers, then signed them both. She did ask me to remind you what she'd said about her cousin, though."

"Ah, yes. Her cousin." Garek set Ellie's waiver aside and glanced at the next document—a statement against Robbie. Phrases like *assault with a deadly weapon* and *criminal confinement* leaped out at him.

He'd been too furious about the whole shotgun marriage and her threat to sell her story to the tabloids to think about Eleanor Hernandez very clearly. All he'd thought of this last week were ways to squash her gallery, her cousin and—most especially—her.

But now, something nagged at him, something that had been niggling at the back of his brain all week.

She'd been extremely upset when the reporter had taken a picture of Garek and her, insisting that he go after the man and get the film. She'd even refused to be interviewed when it could have helped her precious gallery. She'd claimed she wanted the attention focused on the artists and their work, but the more he thought about it, the more certain he was that she found the idea of appearing in a tabloid as distasteful as he did.

Garek frowned.

If she was trying to blackmail him, she wasn't doing a very good job of it. She should have threatened to go to the tabloids if he didn't give her money—not to save her cousin. If money was what she was after, she should have cashed that five-thousand-dollar check weeks ago, not squandered it on a ridiculous donation to the Art Institute, a donation designed to…what? Embarrass him? Make some point?

If she wanted to make any kind of claim on him at all, she should have refused to sign these papers. She should have let him make love to her that night, encouraged him to consummate their "marriage"....

It didn't make any sense. *She* didn't make any sense—

"Ahem."

Garek looked up to see Larry watching him. The lawyer pointed to the line at the bottom of the complaint. "You just need to sign there—"

Garek pushed the paper aside. "I've changed my mind. I'm not going to have Roberto Hernandez arrested. I want to leave him out of this."

Larry's mouth fell open. "But why?"

"I don't want to have it on public record that I was coerced into marriage at gunpoint."

Lines formed on the lawyer's forehead. "Since when have you cared what anyone thinks?"

Garek's eyebrows lifted. "You should be happy—you're always telling me I should worry about it."

Larry's frown deepened. "You can't let this man off. He's a menace, a danger to society—"

"You're afraid he'll go all over town forcing men to marry his cousin?" Garek asked sardonically. "Somehow, I'm not too concerned."

"I don't think it's wise," Larry said unhappily. "Without the legal complaint, it will be easier for Ms. Hernandez to claim that you weren't coerced."

"She's already signed away all claims."

"That doesn't mean she couldn't change her mind. If she gets herself a sharp lawyer, she could—"

"I'm willing to take that chance," Garek interrupted. "I've made my decision."

"Very well," Larry said, his voice as stiff as the hair covering his bald spot. "If you'll just sign the annulment papers, I'll go."

Garek glanced down at the last document, then set it aside also. "I have a meeting shortly. I'll do it later."

"All you have to do is sign it."

"I want to look it over," Garek said coldly. He turned his attention to some other papers. Without looking at his lawyer, he said, "That will be all, Larry."

When Garek heard the door close, he looked up. He stared at nothing in particular for several seconds. Then, slowly, he picked up the annulment papers again. He flipped to the back page where Ellie had signed the document.

He studied her signature for a long moment—the delicate pen strokes, the looping "E" in "Eleanor," the elegant "H" in "Hernandez."

An image flashed through his head of the morning he'd woken in Ellie's apartment. He'd immediately been aware that something was wrong—the pillowcase under his cheek was cheap cotton instead of silk, cold air stung the parts of his skin not covered by a heavy, fluffy comforter, and there was a heady scent nearby—one that made his body harden instantly. He'd opened his eyes slowly.

He'd seen dark tousled curls; long, black lashes lying heavily on delicately flushed cheeks; and red, soft lips, slightly parted, inviting him to lean over and kiss her....

He'd closed his eyes again and waited until she got up and left the room. Only then had he risen and dressed. But instead of leaving immediately, he'd looked around her room, noticing the antique iron bed frame and old-fashioned quilt that contrasted oddly with the abstract paintings hanging on the wall. On the white-washed dresser was a small oval frame with a picture of two people. The man, blond with blue eyes, had a cheerful smile. The woman had dark hair and eyes and her face was solemn, a few lines giving her a more care-worn expression than the man. The two of them hadn't been looking at each other, but there was an indefinable aura about them, something about the way the man's hand held the woman's arm so tenderly and the way the woman tilted her head toward the man, that had made Garek stare at the picture for a long, long time....

Garek set the annulment papers down on his desk. Closing the file, he picked up the phone and dialed.

Chapter Eleven

She wouldn't talk to him.

Garek grew more and more annoyed as the day wore on and Ellie didn't answer the phone or return his calls. He went to the gallery, but Tom, the timid artist, told him in a quaking voice that she wasn't going to be in that day—or tomorrow, either. He went to her apartment, but either she wasn't home, or she refused to answer the door.

By the next day, he was at the end of his patience. He called and left a message on her answering machine.

"If you want to keep your job at Vogel's, you'd better present yourself at my office at 3:00 p.m. sharp this afternoon."

She called several times after that, but Garek told Mrs. Grist not to put the calls through.

That afternoon, at precisely three o'clock, she stalked into his office, quivering with indignation.

"What are you up to now?" Stopping by the leather

chair in front of his desk, Ellie glared at Garek. "Are you going to try to talk Mr. Vogel into firing me? He won't listen to you. He'll believe me—"

"I won't be talking to Vogel anymore at all." Garek stood up slowly. He looked more controlled than usual, his tie straight, his hair neatly combed, his jacket lying smoothly across his shoulders. His expression was harder and more remote than ever. "I just purchased the gallery from him."

Ellie grew very still, staring into his eyes. Surrounded by short, black lashes, they were as gray as the sky outside, as cold as the water in Lake Michigan.

She swallowed, even that small movement difficult and painful. "I don't believe you," she whispered. "Mr. Vogel would have told me."

But even as she spoke the words, Ellie knew they weren't necessarily true. Al Vogel was growing increasingly frail and forgetful—and although she hadn't wanted to admit it to herself, she'd known he would have to sell the gallery soon.

"Ask him."

Ellie felt stunned. Garek might be lying—but she doubted it. What would be the point? The office had seemed warm when she first came in, but now she felt cold in spite of her thick, cable-knit sweater. She pressed her forearm against her middle, against the queasiness in her stomach. The gallery—*her* gallery—purchased by Garek Wisnewski. She was at his mercy—as was everyone Vogel's supported.

And didn't he know it. He stood there behind his enormous desk, surrounded by his fancy furniture, like a king waiting to hear a penitent's plea. He was waiting for her to apologize, she realized. Waiting for her to beg for mercy. Her nails dug into the thick yarn of her sweater. As if she would *ever* give him that satisfaction.

"So," she said proudly, pressing her forearm more tightly against her roiling stomach. "Did you summon me here to fire me? Or to tell me you're closing the gallery? Or just to gloat?"

"All very attractive options, but first I want to ask you about something else. I understand you donated a certain sculpture to the Art Institute. In my name."

It had seemed like a good idea at the time. Although now, in retrospect...

But it was too late for caution, too late for regrets.

She lifted her chin. "Yes, I *did* give Bertrice's sculpture to the museum. I told them there was only one condition—they had to display your name prominently. Everyone who goes to the museum will look at that cockroach, then look at the name Garek Wisnewski. I'm sure that everyone who knows you will immediately understand the connection—"

"You may be right," he said in a disgustingly calm voice. "Tell me something—was it worth five thousand dollars?"

"It was worth ten times that amount!" She shivered, but from rage now, not cold. "I know this is beyond your comprehension, but I don't want your money, I never did! I only took that five thousand dollars because you were so rude. But now I'm glad I took it because it helped Bertrice, and I'm glad that out of all the misery you've caused, at least one person benefited, and I'm glad that the whole world can see now what an insect you really are—"

"Are you finished?"

She gripped the back of the leather chair. "Yes. I am.

Will you at least wait until I can find another place to take the art before you close Vogel's?"

"I'm not closing the gallery."

She thought she must have misheard him. "What did you say?"

"I want the gallery to stay open—and I want you to continue to run it."

Tense and disbelieving, she stared at him. "Why?"

"Maybe I'm afraid you'll sell your story about our marriage to the tabloids."

"I said I was only going to do that if you turned Robbie in," she pointed out.

"Are you saying that I can close the gallery and not worry about reprisals?"

"Yes. I mean, no…that is—"

"Would you go out to dinner with me?"

He couldn't be serious. And yet, his eyes were dark and intent, his mouth a straight, unsmiling line.

"I'm surprised you'd want to go out with a 'criminal' like me," she said, trying to gather her scattered wits.

"I'm making an exception in your case."

"Why?"

"Does there have to be a reason?"

"Yes," she said decisively. "There does."

He put his hands in his pockets. "I suppose I thought we could be…friends."

"Friends?" she repeated in disbelief. After using her, insulting her and accusing her of trying to trap him into marriage, he wanted to be *friends*? She didn't think so. "No, thank you," she said coldly. "I'm very particular about my friends."

He didn't seem offended by her rudeness. "I can be a very good friend."

"What's that supposed to mean?"

"I can put a lot more money into the art foundation. I can move your gallery to the fashionable part of town. I can—"

"Are you trying to bribe me into going out with you?" she asked.

"No, of course not."

"That's good. Because the answer is still no."

His gaze was inscrutable. "The silent auction Stacy Hatfield arranged is this Saturday at my sister's."

"So?"

"You have to be there. It's business."

"I'm sure Stacy can handle it."

"It's imperative that you be present. Donors like to see the people involved before they give money."

"They can see your sister and you."

His eyes narrowed. "I can also be a very bad enemy."

She gaped at him. "Are you *threatening* me now?"

"I'm only trying to ensure the foundation is a success," he said smoothly. "I've invested a lot of money in it."

"Yeah, right. I suppose I have no choice, then." She glared at him. "Tell me, do you always have to blackmail women into a date?"

"No," he said grimly. "You're the first."

"You should never have made me go through with this," Doreen Tarrington hissed at Garek as she smiled and nodded at a couple helping themselves to shrimp and prosciutto appetizers. "It's going to be a disaster."

"Perhaps. Perhaps not," Garek drawled in a bored tone. His sister had been nagging at him ever since he'd ordered her to go ahead with the dinner party. She'd whined and complained and dragged her size-ten feet, but in the end, when faced with the prospect of paying the cost of her next face-lift herself, she'd reluctantly agreed.

"I warn you, Garek," Doreen said in threatening accents, "if that tawdry little girlfriend of yours or her cartoon-character friend embarrass me in front of my friends I will never speak to you again."

Garek thought of several unkind responses, but managed to restrain himself. His object wasn't to be at odds with his sister all evening. "I'm sure Ellie and Caspar will behave in a perfectly normal manner," he responded, his gaze turning to the couple in question.

A slight frown creased his forehead. He hadn't expected Ellie to bring Caspar along. Apparently, Stacy Hatfield had told Ellie to choose an artist for the guests to meet. That would have been fine—if Ellie had picked just about anyone other than Roberto's friend.

Originally, when Garek's only purpose was to punish his sister, he would have been delighted by Caspar's presence. Now, he only wanted everything to go smoothly.

Looking at Caspar's gangly form and Ellie's overly bright smile and stiff back, he began to suspect that he'd made a few miscalculations…

Suddenly, Ellie turned her head and her gaze met his. Even across the crowded room, he could see the way her eyes flashed.

The dinner bell rang. She looked away and began to move with the other guests toward the dining room.

Garek followed, aware of a slight sense of trepidation.

Ellie didn't want to be there. She didn't want to be in this ugly, overly ornate house, with its fussy details and chairs and sofas that seemed to shout, "We are expensive pieces of furniture!" She did not want to talk and try to be polite to the snobbish Mrs. Tarrington whose nose quivered every time she came near and who seemed to regard her like an insect she'd found in her salad. And, most of all, she didn't want to be sitting in this dining room, eating bouillabaisse, forced to look at Garek Wisnewski every time she raised her gaze from her soup.

She glared across the table at him, but he didn't appear to notice, so deep in conversation was he with Amber Bellair, his blond ex-girlfriend. Amber's "little black dress" made Ellie's simple blue frock look like something from a thrift store—which, in fact, it was.

Garek, in his dark suit that fit snugly across his shoulders, made the perfect companion for the blonde—although the garish colors of the tie Ellie had given him for his birthday clashed horribly with Amber's simple elegance. Why was he wearing it? To remind Ellie how naive and stupid she'd been when she'd given it to him?

She couldn't imagine what he hoped to gain by this whole charade. She didn't believe for a second his sorry excuse that he just wanted to be "friends." More likely he wanted to continue with his plan to annoy his sister.

Well, she had no intention of cooperating. No matter how rude Mrs. Tarrington was.

Ellie looked a little anxiously at Caspar, who was sitting at the opposite end of the table. She'd originally intended to bring one of the gallery artists, but she'd felt obliged to warn them that the hostess did not care for contemporary art, and in fact was openly hostile toward it. They'd all refused to attend—no big surprise there. Caspar, however, had begged to come, saying that it was his big chance to make contact with some people who might buy his work. She'd been so angry at Garek, she'd finally agreed, thinking that the whole evening would be a farce, anyway. She'd thought that Garek and Doreen would probably like the ex-convict's vapid paintings.

But now Ellie regretted her temper. She hated to subject any artist—however questionable his talent—to Garek's snobbish sister. Fortunately, Caspar seemed oblivious to Doreen's gibes, and the other guests weren't as bad as Ellie had expected. Most of them, in contrast to their hostess, were very friendly. In fact, many were genuinely interested in art, and one or two were even extraordinarily knowledgeable.

But then there were a few…

Brandon Carlyle, a pompous, middle-aged lawyer, was presently telling everyone about his favorite restaurant.

"There's a place at the foot of the Swiss Alps," he droned at a peculiarly slow speed, "that I highly recommend. The food is all of the finest quality. They serve blue oxtail soup seasoned and cooked to perfection. I've had blue oxtail soup in New York and in Paris, but in my opinion, it's not quite as good."

"Oh, come on, Brandon." Sam Kroner, a man in his middle thirties with blond hair and smiling blue eyes, leaned forward to address the other man. "The *best* food is always the food you catch yourself. When Bonnie and I were on vacation in Alaska, we caught a trout that was the best I've ever tasted. Isn't that right, BonBon?"

Sam's wife nodded. "The only bad part was cleaning it—"

"The best fish *I* ever had was in Hawaii," Doreen interrupted, her loud voice carrying clearly to where Ellie sat halfway down the table. "It was absolutely delicious. Remember, Amber? You and Garek had dinner at that little place in Honolulu once, I believe."

"Yes, I remember. It was good. *Very* good."

Amber looked at Garek in a way that made Ellie think the blonde wasn't just talking about the fish.

"Tell us, Ms. Hernandez," Doreen went on. "What is *your* favorite restaurant?"

Ellie looked up and glanced at the faces around the table. Everyone seemed to be staring at her. "The Taco Palace," she said. "It has the best fish tacos you can imagine."

Sarah Carlyle laughed, causing some soup to drip from her spoon onto her white dress. Still smiling, she dabbed at the greenish stain with her napkin. "The Taco Palace? I've never heard of it. But I love fish tacos. Where is it?"

"Near the corner of Twenty-fifth and Kedzie in Little Village."

"I like Mexican food, too," Sam said. "Do they make enchiladas?"

"The best," Ellie assured him. "Although I have to warn you, I may be a little biased. My uncle owns the place."

Peter Branwell, who owned a national chain of restaurants, looked up from his soup. "Your uncle owns the Taco Palace? I've heard of it—it has an excellent reputation for inexpensive, high-quality food. Has your uncle ever thought of franchising?"

"No, he prefers to keep the restaurant family-owned and operated."

Doreen gave a tinkling laugh. "Family-owned and operated? You make it sound as if you've actually worked there."

Ellie met her gaze calmly. "I have. As a waitress."

"A waitress?" Doreen waved at the maid to remove the soup bowls. "Not a profession most people would aspire to. But perhaps you come from a long line of waitresses?"

"No, my mother cleaned houses."

"Dear me. And your father?"

A rueful smile curved Ellie's lips. "Poor Papa. He was most often unemployed, I'm afraid. His last job was as a used-car salesman."

"I've bought used cars for the last twenty years," Sam commented as the maid set a dessert plate in front of him. "Maybe I bought one from your father. Hernandez… Hmm, it doesn't ring a bell. What was his first name?"

"I doubt you knew him—we lived in Philadelphia." Ellie reached toward the two forks above her plate. She hesitated, then picked up one and took a bite of her dessert. "Mmm, cherries jubilee, my favorite."

"Ahem." Doreen cleared her throat delicately and pointedly picked up another fork. "After hearing about your background, I can see why some of the finer aspects of etiquette must be bewildering to you."

Ellie switched forks and smiled sweetly. "Oh, no, not at all. My mother taught me that truly good manners mean making other people comfortable."

Ellie thought she saw Garek smile, but then he covered his mouth with his hand and coughed. "It's time to proceed with the silent auction," he said, rising to his feet. "We have a special item this evening, from Vogel's Gallery. The artist, Caspar Egilbert, will tell you about it. Caspar?"

Caspar, who'd been deep in conversation with the Palermos at the other end of the table, stood also, pushing his lank brown hair back from his face. The motion caused the sleeves of his ill-fitting brown suit to hike up, exposing his bony wrists. He ambled over to the easel. "I created this painting especially for this occasion. It is symbolic of the many influences in my life, and my love and appreciation for my mother." He whipped off the covering, revealing…breasts.

Hundreds of them.

Pointy, sagging and siliconed breasts. Brown, pink and one pair of blue breasts. Lopsided, tattooed and hairy breasts. Breasts with nipples that, through some trick of perspective, always seemed to be pointing directly at the viewer no matter where he or she stood—or sat.

Mrs. Branwell's fork clattered onto her plate. Her husband leaned forward and craned his neck to get a better look. Amber folded her arms over her chest. Doreen emitted an odd, muffled noise.

Garek burst out laughing.

"I'm glad you found the evening so amusing," Ellie said several hours later as Garek was driving her home. "I don't think your sister did. But that was your intention, wasn't it?"

"At first, perhaps," he admitted. "What about you? Did you enjoy yourself?"

"It could have been worse," she said, not very graciously. But she didn't want to admit that she *had* had a good time. After Garek burst into laughter, everyone had seemed to loosen up. The silent auction had gone well, with George Palermo and Sam Kroner getting into a bidding war over Caspar's painting. Through it all, Ellie had chatted with the guests. Amber had left early,

but everyone else had appeared to enjoy themselves—
everyone except Doreen.

Looking stiff and mortified, Doreen Tarrington had
barely spoken a word to anyone the remainder of the
evening. Unfortunately, the one person she did speak to
was Ellie. The older woman pulled her aside at one
point to "warn" her about Garek. He had committed numerous sins, according to his sister, including neglecting his duty to his family and his position in the
community, as well as cheating her out of her fair share
of their father's company.

Garek turned the car onto Ellie's street and parked
under a streetlight. It provided dim illumination through
the sleet-filled night, but enough that she could see Garek's serious expression as he turned to her.

"I apologize for Doreen," he said quietly.

His words surprised her. "You don't have to. She
didn't bother me."

He shot a skeptical glance at her. "Oh? You didn't
mind being interrogated about your family, having your
manners attacked and being cold-shouldered by your
hostess?"

"Not really. I feel sorry for your sister."

"*Sorry* for her? What on earth for?"

"I see a sad and lonely woman who is trying very
hard to buy her place in life. She doesn't seem to understand that money can't make her happy."

He stared at her. "You honestly think someone with
no money can be as happy as someone with a large
bank account?"

Ellie thought about some of the hardships she'd experienced since coming to Chicago—working twelve-
and fourteen-hour days; eating nothing but rice and

beans in order to make her rent payment; and the sick feeling in the pit of her stomach at the end of every month when she balanced the gallery's books and saw the steadily increasing red ink. "I suppose money can smooth the way," she admitted. "But haven't you ever noticed that no matter how much people have, they always want more? If they make ten thousand dollars, they want thirty thousand dollars. If they make a hundred thousand dollars, they want a hundred and fifty thousand dollars. They're never satisfied with what they have."

He stared at her with an odd expression she couldn't quite define. She expected him to argue with her, to ridicule her for being naive and simplistic.

"It's kind of you to say Doreen didn't bother you," he said, directing his gaze toward the sleet-battered windshield. "But I know that's not true. I saw how nervous you were."

She glanced at him in surprise. What was he talking about? She hadn't been nervous. Angry, maybe, but not nervous. "Did I seem nervous?"

"Yes, you did." He turned his gaze back to her, watching her closely. "I could tell, because in all the time I've known you, as many restaurants as I've taken you to, I've never seen you use the wrong fork before."

"Oh!" Her eyes skittered away, then returned to his. She smiled a little ruefully. "Well, maybe I did egg your sister on a bit. I really shouldn't have."

He didn't say anything else. He got out of the car into the raging sleet and wind. He opened her door for her and ran with her up to her apartment. Sheltered somewhat by the roof, he took her hand. "Will you go to dinner with me tomorrow night?"

She stared at the large hand enveloping hers. Did he really think she could ignore everything that he'd done? Did he really think they could go on as though none of it had happened?

"No," she said, then braced herself, expecting him to argue or try to kiss her.

Instead, he gazed down at her for a long moment, a slight frown between his brows. Suddenly, he raised her hand to his lips and lightly kissed the back of her glove.

Then, without a word, he left, leaving her feeling angry, upset…and strangely confused.

Garek returned to his sister's house to find her pacing the marble tile of the entry hall.

"There you are!" she greeted him accusingly. "I'm surprised you didn't stay all night with your little girlfriend."

"Perhaps I should have."

Doreen gave him a sharp look. "What's going on with you and that girl?"

"Nothing. Absolutely nothing."

"You would like there to be, though, wouldn't you?"

"Is this why you asked me to come back here tonight? So you could interrogate me about my relationship with Ellie?"

"Yes…no! I asked you to come here so I could tell you what I think of you, you bastard! I never should have let you talk me into going forward with this—if I hadn't needed that money so desperately…oh! What my friends must have thought!"

"Your friends appeared to enjoy themselves," Garek said coolly.

"No, thanks to your girlfriend and that horrible artist person. When he unveiled that obscene painting…and you! You were no help, laughing the way you did. I was mortified, absolutely mortified. You knew how much this evening meant to me—and yet you couldn't even be bothered to wear a decent tie!"

He glanced down at the scrap of fabric in question. "I'm beginning to like it," he said. "Ellie gave it to me."

"I'm not at all surprised. You cannot be serious about that girl—oh, don't pretend you don't know what I'm talking about. I saw the way you were looking at her all evening. I admit, she's attractive in a low-class sort of way, but she would never fit in. Just look at her family—her mother a house cleaner, her father a used-car salesman, her uncle a taco maker. Who knows what other distasteful details we'll discover about her background?"

At least one more, if his suspicions were correct, Garek thought, remembering the picture of Ellie's parents in her bedroom.

He looked at his sister. If they'd had this conversation yesterday, he would have been furious. But now, after his conversation with Ellie, he could only think of what she'd said. Doreen's face had the smooth, blank look of someone who'd had a face-lift; there were no smile lines by her eyes, only tiny vertical grooves above her upper lip that made her look bitter and dissatisfied. What had made her that way? he wondered. Out loud, he said, "Ellie fit in perfectly tonight."

"She was tolerated, nothing more. And only because my friends are too polite to say anything. You must watch out for this girl. You know she's only interested in your money. Did you see the way she was eyeing the furniture, as if she was assessing its value?"

"You don't know her," Garek said.

"I know her, all right. Her type is obvious. She's the type to get pregnant and trap a man into marriage."

"No, she's the type to have a cousin who forces her to marry a man at gunpoint."

Doreen's mouth dropped open. "What are you talking about?"

A glimmer of a smile curved Garek's mouth at the sight of Doreen's aghast look. "I'm saying, sister, dear, your warning is too late. Ellie and I are already married."

Chapter Twelve

Ellie looked at the giraffe, wishing she could wring Garek's neck until he looked like a twin of the penned animal in front of her. "Why haven't you signed the annulment papers?" she asked, turning her gaze back to the aggravating creature next to her.

He shrugged and led her to the next enclosure, not responding to her question—another bad habit of his, she thought darkly. When she'd called his office this morning and demanded to speak to him, his assistant had put her on hold, then come back on the line saying Garek was too busy to talk right now, but he'd be glad to meet her at lunchtime at any spot she chose.

"He can talk to me now," Ellie had said sweetly, "or meet me at the zoo."

She hadn't thought the big ape would actually *agree* to her suggestion. She'd been tempted to stand him up—and she probably would have if the matter hadn't been so urgent.

"Why haven't you signed the papers?" she asked again.

"There's been a glitch." He threw a peanut to one of the baboons.

Probably a close relative of his, Ellie thought. "What kind of glitch?"

"Some legal technicality. It should take only a week or two to correct."

"A week or two?" she repeated blankly. For the last couple of days, ever since Doreen Tarrington's dinner party, Ellie had been feeling like she'd fallen down the rabbit hole. First there'd been the influx of customers to the gallery—virtually all of the dinner guests and a multitude of their friends had descended upon Vogel's and purchased at least one art piece. Tom, Carlo and Bertrice were ecstatic.

Ellie should have been delighted too. And she was. Only…she wished Garek wasn't the one largely responsible for the gallery's sudden success. She didn't want to have to be grateful to him. She didn't want to have to even *think* about him. But it was amazingly difficult not to. Especially after the visitor she'd had at the gallery yesterday.

Ellie had just opened, when the bell on the door jingled and a teenager walked in. The tall girl with hostile gray eyes looked vaguely familiar, but it took Ellie a moment to place where she'd seen that thin face and straight brown hair before.

"You're Karen Tarrington, aren't you?" Ellie said.

The girl looked shocked, then suspicious. "How'd you know that?"

"Your uncle showed me a picture of you once."

"He did?" Some emotion flickered in the girl's eyes—but only for a moment. "I didn't know he had one. Mom must have given him my stupid school picture. I'm surprised he didn't throw it away." She glanced disdainfully around the gallery. "What a bunch of junk!"

The girl was as charming as her mother, Ellie thought wryly. "Your family appears to be completely unanimous in that opinion."

Karen stared at a chair covered with beads and bits of glass. "Yeah, Mom's pretty upset. This is going to kill her chance of getting in the Social Register for sure. Are you supposed to sit on this chair?"

Ellie blinked. "No, not really. It's more for decoration. What does Vogel's have to do with your mother and the Social Register?"

"That's why Mom wanted Uncle Garek to start an art foundation. So she could get her name in the Social Register. Uncle Garek thought it was a stupid idea."

For once Ellie had to agree with him. "I'm surprised he didn't refuse her request, then."

"He couldn't. Mom threatened to screw up some business deal he was working on. Uncle Garek was pretty hot under the collar about it."

Appalled, Ellie stared at Karen. "How do you know all this?"

"They were arguing about it on Christmas Eve. They argue a lot. Uncle Garek hates my mom."

"I doubt that's true," Ellie said automatically, then paused. "I think he's just very angry at her for trying to hurt his business," she said more slowly.

Karen shrugged. "Same difference. He hardly ever comes over to our house anymore."

"Did he use to?"

"Yeah, when I was a little kid. He took me to the park and baseball games and stuff like that. Once he took me to the symphony."

"The symphony?"

"Yeah. For my birthday. I was thirteen years old and he bought me a white lace dress with a blue satin bow." Once more, the cynical expression slipped, revealing pure, naked emotion. For a moment, the girl's face was full of such wistfulness, such yearning, that Ellie's breath caught. Then the mask descended once more and Karen sneered. "It was a little kid's dress. I didn't want to wear it, but Mom insisted. I hated it and I hated the stupid symphony. All that lame classical music. Uncle Garek stopped coming by after that. He said he had to work."

Ellie said gently, "That was probably true."

Karen shrugged again. "Yeah, right. At least he buys good presents. He got me a computer for Christmas, and he bought my mom an emerald and ruby necklace. Actually, I thought the necklace was kind of ugly, but Mom didn't care. She always returns everything he gives her for the cash."

Ellie remembered the gaudy necklace with shock. She'd imagined his sister treasuring the ugly jewelry as a sign of his affection—instead, it appeared the woman only cared about the monetary value. Did Garek know? Probably. His anger at his sister obviously went back a long way. But oddly enough, in spite of all the anger and bitterness, she sensed that he really did care about Doreen—

"So what's the deal here?" Karen asked, bending over to look more closely at a fishbone hung in a frame. "Are you my aunt now, or what?"

Ellie froze. "What are you talking about?"

"You and Uncle Garek are married, right? He told Mom last night. She's absolutely livid."

Karen's warning should have prepared Ellie for the phone call she'd received shortly after the girl left—but it hadn't. Remembering the unpleasant conversation, she glared at the South American rodent in the enclosure in front of her, then turned her gaze to its North American counterpart standing next to her. "Did you have to tell your sister?" she asked.

Garek slanted a glance at her. "She gave you a hard time, I take it."

"Did she ever!" Indignation rose in Ellie at the memory. Karen had given her a blatantly skeptical look when Ellie denied the marriage and had left the gallery a few minutes later; Doreen hadn't been nearly so restrained. "The names she called me! And when I finally got her calmed down enough to explain that the ceremony was invalid, that we weren't really married, she called me a liar!"

"Sorry about that," he murmured.

She looked at him suspiciously. "But why did you tell her?"

"It just slipped out."

Ellie gripped the iron railing. "You've never struck me as the type to let things slip."

"Maybe you don't know me as well as you think."

"I know as much as I want to know."

"Are you so sure, Ellie? Why won't you give me a second chance?"

"Why should I?"

"I don't know." He ran his fingers through his hair. "I just know that I don't want you to disappear from my life until we've had a chance to explore this attraction between us."

She glared at him. "Is that what this is all about? Are you still hoping to get me into bed? Well, you won't. I wouldn't go to bed with you if the world was about to end. I wouldn't go to bed with you if the survival of the human species depended on it. I wouldn't go to bed with you if—"

"Okay, okay," he said. "I get the idea."

"I don't think you know how to be friends with a woman."

"You could teach me."

"I don't want to teach you anything." She headed for the door that led out of the Large Mammal House. Freezing-cold wind bit at her face as she started up a winding path. "I've had a revelation. I've realized that sex before marriage is a big mistake. My new philosophy in life is no sex without a wedding ring. What do you think of that?"

"I still want to go out with you."

He must not have heard her. "There would be *no sex*. And no spending lots of money, either. Could you live with that?"

"Yes," he said meekly.

She didn't believe him. He would get tired of a relationship based on nothing more than friendship. She doubted he would last more than a month, if that.

She glanced up at him as they approached an outdoor animal enclosure. "There's a foreign film playing at the college on Saturday and the Azalea Flower Show at Garfield Park the week after that. You can come with me to those," she informed him.

He winced a little, but nodded.

"You understand, no sex," she reiterated.

He nodded again.

Satisfied, she turned to look at the animals in the enclosure.

Two huge polar bears were vigorously mating.

Ellie's eyes widened. She froze. The bears continued their business with the utmost nonchalance.

She sneaked a glance at Garek.

"Unless, of course," he said, completely straight-faced except for a gleam in his eye, "you can't bear to go without."

Chapter Thirteen

"So what do you think?" she asked him one month later during the intermission of the free concert being held at a local college.

Garek eyed the stale doughnuts and cold coffee being sold by some student group in the dingy hallway. He decided against refreshments.

"To be perfectly truthful," he said, turning his gaze back to Ellie, "it's incredibly boring."

He saw the shock register. She stared at him, her lips pursing in an expression of disapproval. But then, her mouth softened, and she laughed. "At least you're honest. But you're spoiled. You're used to easy entertainment. Sometimes you have to make an effort."

"An effort how?"

"You learn about the music, to appreciate it. You imagine a story as it's playing. Or what the music makes you feel. What did you feel with the music we just heard?"

"Sleepy."

She laughed again, but shook her head. "That wasn't much of an effort."

"I save my effort for business."

She looked at him curiously. "Is that the only thing in your life worth exerting yourself for?"

He frowned. A few months ago he would have said yes. Now, he wasn't so sure. "Running a company requires total commitment. Art and music are completely frivolous."

"You're wrong. Art teaches you to observe, to look beyond the surface. Music teaches you to listen, to hear more than what's being said."

A pimply-faced student announced that the music was about to begin again and Ellie didn't say any more, but her words stuck with Garek through the second half of the concert.

Perhaps the business had lost some of its attraction. The company had always demanded a lot of his attention and he'd never minded before. But lately he'd been aware of a vague sense of dissatisfaction. Sometimes he felt as though he was in a dark tunnel, one that was getting narrower and narrower as he proceeded. He couldn't go back, but sometimes he thought that if he kept going forward, the concrete walls would start to press against him, squeezing him until he couldn't breathe....

Maybe that was why he was finding it strangely appealing to go out on weird dates with a woman he wasn't even sleeping with.

She wouldn't let him take her anywhere expensive; they went to museums, lectures and cheap restaurants. It reminded him a little of his childhood, before his fa-

ther had started the company. Every Saturday, he, his
sister and parents had gone to the Navy Pier. Doreen had
saved her baby-sitting money and took him for rides on
the Ferris wheel and bought him funnel cakes.

He had a lot of good memories of Doreen. She'd
been different then; she'd helped their mother cook and
clean their small house and flirted with the son of the
auto mechanic next door.

After his father started his own business, everything
had changed. The business had been wildly successful,
and his father had worked long hours and weekends.
They rarely saw him after that, but at first Garek really
didn't notice. That first year had been like a constant
stream of Christmas mornings. His father got a new car,
his mother a housekeeper. Garek and his sister received
TVs, toys, whatever they wanted. They moved into the
fancy Gold Coast neighborhood of Chicago. Only, there
hadn't been many kids to play with there, and he'd felt
awkward at his new fancy private school. His father became totally immersed in the business; his mother got
involved in her own projects. Doreen had dumped the
auto mechanic's son and married blue-blooded Grant
Tarrington. She'd been dazzled and impressed by her
taste of high society.

Garek shook his head and glanced over at Ellie. She
was wearing jeans and a sweater instead of an evening
gown, but she sat as still and straight as she had at the
symphony, listening to the music with every sign of
pleasure.

Unlike Doreen, she never seemed impressed by
wealth or status. He wondered how she'd gained such
poise. She couldn't have had an easy life. In the last
month he'd learned a lot about her family—how her

mother's parents and siblings had come to this country from Mexico, and how they'd all worked hard to get jobs and educations.

Garek had heard all about Ellie's six cousins and their marriages and their offspring. He knew that her cousin Julio's six-year-old daughter had gotten an award at school for being "conscientious." He knew that her cousin Pedro's four-year-old son collected Pokémon cards.

But as much as Ellie talked about her cousins and their children, she rarely spoke of her mother and father.

The little he'd been able to glean was that her father had loved art and the violin, taken her to see symphony rehearsals when she was very small, and failed at just about every job he tried. Her mother had been kind and loving, but worn down by being virtually the sole support of the small family. And every summer she took Ellie on a bus to visit her family in Chicago.

Garek had guessed that her parents never married. That had been easy to deduce from the fact that she had her mother's last name and her reticence about her father's family. He also guessed that worry and uncertainty had shaped a large part of her early years.

He also guessed that the turmoil of her childhood was what had formed two of her most prominent characteristics: a love of her family and an ability to find enjoyment in even the most mundane activities and pastimes. She seemed to take pleasure in every aspect of her life.

Garek shifted on the hard folding chair. Perhaps that was the secret of her appeal. He didn't know what else it could be. Over the past four weeks he'd kept his word and hadn't tried to kiss her or touch her, even though sometimes it nearly killed him not to do so. He was aware of her all the time. At the art lecture they'd gone to last week, the chairs had been so close together that she'd brushed against him every time she moved. It had been extremely difficult to listen to the instructor.

He'd made an effort though, because he knew she would quiz him afterward. Professor Jameson had been exceedingly boring, but to Garek's surprise, the guest speaker had actually been interesting. The European woman had showed slides of her modern-art collection. She'd grown up with the Old Masters and loved them, but now preferred contemporary art because it was new and different and exciting. She'd talked about line and form, negative space and motion, color and connections. She'd showed how rational analysis could be applied to the way the art was structured, but also pointed out that logic could never explain the magic of the content contained within.

Garek had wanted to scoff at the woman's words, but somehow he couldn't. He'd been thinking of them when he went over to Doreen's the next night and offered to help Karen with her computer. The visit had been less than magical—Karen had been sullen and uncooperative—but Ellie had looked pleased when he told her about it.

"You can't expect miracles," she'd assured him. "Especially with a teenager."

"But why does she always seems so angry?"

"She's probably not very good at expressing her feelings. Or maybe she's just afraid to. Some kids have trouble with that."

"So you're saying I should just give up until she's an adult?"

"Adults can have the same problem." She gave him a pointed look, and he frowned, still not really understanding. She sighed. "Think of it like starting a business. You wouldn't work for one day and expect to make a million dollars, would you? You have to spend a lot of time and effort before it starts to pay off. A relationship is the same way."

Once again, her words stuck with him. He'd gone over to help Karen a second time—and had even stayed for dinner.

Doreen had been astonished.

The meal had been full of wary glances and awkward silences, but she'd invited him back the following week, and it had been easier that time. He'd been telling Karen about the time one of Doreen's boyfriends had come to the house to take her on a date. While Doreen was getting ready, Garek—still in junior high and barely five feet tall—had taken the brawny twenty-two-year-old Joe Pulaski into the living room and proceeded to ask him about his job, his income, whether he was planning to go to college, what his plans for the future were, and exactly how did Doreen fit into those plans? Joe, sweating and squirming, had leapt to his feet when Doreen came down, and rushed her out the door.

Karen had listened to the story expressionlessly, while Doreen sniffed and said what a little pest Garek had been…but then, unexpectedly, she'd smiled. And he'd smiled back. And then, suddenly, they'd both started laughing, and Karen, her mouth agape, had stared at them with wide, bewildered eyes—

A burst of applause interrupted Garek's thoughts. He glanced at Ellie, who was clapping vigorously. She had a way of explaining that made everything seem so clear and simple. But at the same time, when he was with her, he felt confused. Looking at her, he felt the same way he did when he looked at *Woman in Blue*. He could almost see it. Almost get it. Almost…

The applause faded and everyone rose to their feet. Garek looked down at Ellie. Even with her heels on, the top of her head barely reached his chin. She was so small—and yet she was somehow becoming more and more important in his life.

"Will you let me take you to dinner?" he asked, raising his voice to be heard over the clanking scrape of metal chairs. She glanced over her shoulder, and he added with a smile, "Somewhere inexpensive, I promise."

For a moment, he saw an answering smile in her eyes. But then, just as quickly, it disappeared, and she turned away.

"I can't, I have other plans." She stepped into the aisle.

His smile vanished. Going after her, he caught her arm. "You have a date with someone else?"

"No…not exactly." She stared at the back of the man in front of her. "It's my cousin Alyssa's birthday. My aunt and uncle are having a party for her."

"I see."

Ellie shifted uneasily at the cool note in his voice. She'd thought about inviting him, but quickly decided against it. She couldn't imagine him with her family. They weren't rich. They were hardworking, respectable people, but she didn't know how he would react to them. A month ago, she would have thought he would look down his nose at them. Now, she wasn't quite so sure.

He'd surprised her these last few weeks. Now that the blinders were off, and she knew who and what he really was, she'd expected that spending time with Garek would banish any lingering feelings she had for him. Instead, she'd noticed a change in him. He wasn't as flip, as glib as he'd been before. He no longer seemed to be trying to charm her—but instead of liking him less, she actually liked him more. He no longer seemed as guarded, the remoteness she sometimes sensed in him seemed almost to have vanished. It only returned occasionally, like now. But this time, unlike before, she recognized what it meant—he was hurt.

The expression in his eyes bothered her more than she liked to admit, even to herself. He was trying really hard to establish a relationship with his sister and niece, but it was an uphill struggle. He seemed so...*alone* sometimes. As if he had no family at all.

But he probably liked it that way, she told herself. He would probably despise attending a fourteen-year-old's birthday party. It would only be a lot of silly games. And yet...she supposed it wouldn't hurt to ask him. He would probably say no. But at least she would have asked....

"Would you like to come with me?" she asked when they reached the entrance hall of the building and the crowd thinned out a little.

He stopped and stared at her, an expression that was hard to read in his eyes.

"You don't have to," she added hastily. "It would probably be embarrassing. Robbie will be there, and even though I made him promise not to tell anyone about what happened, he might let something slip—"

He pressed a finger to her lips. "I would be delighted to go."

He removed his finger immediately, but she was aware of a lingering tickle. Her lips felt dry, she wanted to lick them, but seeing how he was looking at her mouth, she didn't.

She wished she could stop remembering what it had felt like when he kissed her. She wished she could control the silly lurching of her stomach when he looked at her just so. She wished her heart didn't flutter happily to see the remoteness gone from his eyes.

She wished she'd kept her mouth shut.

And that feeling only intensified when they arrived at her aunt and uncle's and found Robbie out on the front porch, a beer in his hand.

He stood up, his eyes narrowing when he saw Garek. But then he smiled and slapped the other man on the back. "How's it going, *primo?*"

"He's not your cousin," Ellie said. "Remember what you promised me."

"Yeah, sure, Ellie. Come on inside, everyone else is already here."

Ellie relaxed a little. Everyone was going to be curious enough about Garek. The last thing she wanted was for them to find out about her silly "marriage"—

"Hey, everyone, look who's here," Robbie announced as they entered the crowded living room. "Ellie and her new husband!"

Several hours later, Ellie was exhausted. All evening she'd had to explain over and over that she and Garek *weren't* married, that it was just a joke on Robbie's part.

But in spite of her explanations, everyone still seemed to think Garek was her husband.

"I like your husband," Great-Grandma Pilar said at one point late in the evening. "He's a very nice young man. But you should have invited me to the wedding."

An image of Grandma Pilar—all four-foot-ten wizened inches of her—standing next to Caspar's tall, lanky frame as he intoned the ceremony popped into Ellie's head. Shuddering a little, she wondered how Grandma Pilar had formed any opinion at all of Garek since she spoke only Spanish. But she didn't ask. Instead, in the same language, she replied, "*Abuela*, he is *not* my husband."

But Grandma Pilar didn't seem to hear her. "A fine young man. He'll make fine babies. Are you pregnant yet?"

"No, Grandma," Ellie said resignedly.

"Better not wait," the old lady advised. "You're not getting any younger, you know."

Ellie muttered she was going to get something to eat.

Robbie was by the table, piling *carnitas* onto his plate. "I knew he was the one for you, Ellie. As soon as he punched me, I knew."

She might punch her cousin too if he didn't shut up. In desperation, she looked around for Garek.

He was dancing with Alyssa. Alyssa, all knees and elbows and braces, looked as though she was in seventh heaven—or maybe even eighth or ninth. Garek laughed at something the girl said, then, as if he felt her gaze on him, looked across the room straight at Ellie.

Their eyes met. He flashed a smile at her, then returned his attention to Alyssa, whirling her away in the dance.

Ellie inhaled sharply. She felt dizzy. She felt sick. In that split second, she knew the truth, the truth she'd been trying to deny.

She loved him.

In spite of everything, she loved Garek Wisnewski.

"I like your family," he said as he drove her home later that evening. "You're lucky to have a family like that."

"Yes, I know," she said. She did know it. But why did *he* have to recognize it, too? A ruthless businessman like him shouldn't have been able to see beyond the cramped house and poor clothes to the love and joy her family had. But obviously he had.

She stared out the window at the houses zipping by. She never should have agreed to keep going out with him. She was a thousand times a fool. But how could she have known her heart would be so treacherous?

He was arrogant and ruthless and bad-tempered. She'd thought she couldn't possibly fall in love with someone like that. But during the last few weeks she'd realized that his callous facade wasn't a true indication of his character. Rather, it was a form of protection. Against being hurt.

And he had been hurt. Not necessarily in large, traumatic ways, but in small, thoughtless ones. Not very many people had been kind to Garek Wisnewski. Whenever he talked about his parents, his sister or his ex-fiancée, there was a blankness to his expression. At first, she'd thought he just didn't care. But in the last few weeks, as he let his guard down more and more, she could sometimes see the pain in his eyes, the bewilderment. Sometimes she just wanted to put her arms around him and hold him as tightly as she possibly could.

He would be horrified if he knew what she was thinking. He would scoff at the idea that anyone had hurt him. In that respect he was a lot like his niece—both of them seemed determined to squash any and all emotions. Ellie suspected that to do so had become such a habit that they were now finding it difficult to recognize, let alone express their feelings. She doubted Garek would ever willingly talk about his feelings. Certainly he would never admit to something so sappy as love. He would never make himself so vulnerable.

Which meant that *she* was completely vulnerable.

They arrived at her apartment and he walked her to her door. "Thanks again for inviting me," he said, the dim porch light illuminating his face as he smiled down at her. "I'll pick you up tomorrow at noon."

"I…I can't see you tomorrow," she said, some sense of self-preservation belatedly kicking in.

He frowned. "Why not?" he asked bluntly, as incapable as ever of accepting a refusal graciously.

"Um, when I was talking to my uncle, he said he's shorthanded at the restaurant tomorrow and I told him I'd help out," she lied.

Garek's frown deepened. "Can't your uncle find someone else?"

"Everyone else is busy."

"That's not acceptable."

She stiffened. "What do you mean?"

"I mean, I don't want you working at the Taco Palace," he snapped.

"*You* don't want me to?" she snapped right back. "You have no right to tell me what to do."

"I'm your employer. I don't want you showing up at the gallery on Monday too exhausted to work."

"Oh, I should have known. You're worried about *business*. Heaven forbid I should botch a sale because I yawned in a customer's face. It's obvious you'll never change. I don't know why I ever thought you could." She crossed her arms across her chest, trying to protect herself against the wind. "Just go away."

"No. I want to talk to you."

"Well, I don't want to hear whatever it is you have to say."

His face was pale, his voice grim. "That's too bad, because you're going to have to listen."

"*Have* to?" she cried. "Why is that?"

"Because we're getting married—for real this time."

Chapter Fourteen

Ellie stared at him in astonishment. "Was that a proposal?"

"Yes."

His tight-lipped response was not exactly romantic. "It sounded like an order."

"Ellie…I…that is…oh, dammit." He closed his eyes and took a deep breath. When he opened them again, they looked a very dark green.

"I can't live without you, Ellie. Will you please marry me?"

The cold wind had stopped blowing at the beginning of his uncharacteristic, stammering speech. By the end, the clouds in the sky had parted and a moonbeam streamed down onto the porch. It danced over her skin and slipped inside her veins, making her feel as though she were lit from within. "Garek," she breathed. "Oh, Garek!" and hurled herself into his arms.

She saw the tension in his face disappear and an expression she'd never seen before light up his eyes, before his arms closed around her and he was kissing her fiercely.

She returned the kiss with equal strength, until she could barely breathe. She felt as though she were going to float up off the ground, her happiness was so intense.

With a choked laugh, he broke off the kiss. "I don't want to spoil your 'no sex before marriage' policy at this late date. Can you be ready tomorrow?"

She blinked up at him, surprised and rather disappointed. "Tomorrow?" she repeated vaguely, trying to resist the urge to unbutton his coat. "For what?"

"For our wedding, of course."

She gasped, his words dispelling her sensual haze, somewhat. "You want to get married tomorrow? That's impossible!"

His jaw tightened in that stubborn way she knew so well. "Why?"

A choked laugh escaped her. "I have to buy a dress, I have to give Martina time to find a new roommate, I have to get time off work—"

"I'll pay the rent for Martina and you can quit your job." His eyes dark and sensuous, he whispered, "I can't wait much longer, Ellie."

A shiver coursed through her. Of course, she wasn't going to quit her job or let him pay her rent. But the truth of the matter was, *she* didn't want to wait either. "Give me a week."

For a moment, she thought he was going to refuse. But then he said, "You've got your week—but I warn you—" his eyes gleamed "— I'm kidnapping you after that."

She laughed. "A week doesn't give me much time. I'm really going to have to cancel our date tomorrow."

"If you insist. But you'll have to make up for it now."

He kissed her—extremely thoroughly—until they were both breathing hard.

"Maybe it's better that I don't see you this week," he said huskily, resting his forehead against hers. "I can't take too much of this."

"Do we really have to wait?" she asked, still breathless. "Why don't you come inside?"

"Ellie…" He leaned back, his hand cupping the curve of her cheek, his gaze dark and serious. "For once in my life, I want to do the right thing. I'm going to marry you first."

She would have laughed at the grim determination in his voice if her throat wasn't suddenly so impossibly tight. "Oh, Garek," she whispered, blinking back foolish, happy tears.

He groaned. "Don't look at me like that, or I won't be able to help myself." He kissed her hard, then again, more slowly. "I can't go a whole week without seeing you. We can at least have lunch together. Monday. Come to my office around noon?"

She nodded. With one final kiss, he released her and thrust his hands into his pockets, as if to prevent himself from reaching out for her again. She went inside and closed the door, but couldn't resist running to the window to watch him go. He strode down the stairs to the sidewalk, looking tall and strong and handsome.

She hugged her arms around herself. She couldn't believe this was happening.

She supposed she shouldn't have said yes so quickly.

After all her doubts, after all their differences, she should have at least asked for some time to think it over.

But she hadn't been able to think. She'd been too surprised and too happy—too deliriously, ecstatically happy. She loved him. And he loved her.

She believed that with all her heart.

Whistling, Garek entered his office late Monday morning. Larry and Mrs. Grist were already there.

Garek smiled. "Good morning, Mrs. Grist, Larry," he said cheerfully.

Mrs. Grist responded civilly, but Larry only stared at him in astonishment.

"Mrs. Grist," Garek continued, ignoring Larry's silence, "would you please clear all appointments for two weeks—no, make that a month—starting next week. I will not be available."

Now Mrs. Grist looked startled. "But what about the meeting with the Lachland lawyers? They want to go over the independent auditor's report in detail. Most of the auditor's points are perfectly ridiculous, but the lawyers have a lot of questions—"

"Reschedule the meeting for this week," Garek said. "If they can't make it, suggest a teleconference."

Larry frowned. "What's happened?"

Garek looked at the two anxious faces before him. "Nothing," he said. "Except that Ellie and I are getting married."

An exclamation escaped Mrs. Grist. She beamed like a hundred lightbulbs. "Well, it's about time! Congratulations, Mr. Wisnewski. She's a fine young woman, and I'm sure you'll be very happy together."

Garek smiled back. "Thank you, Mrs. Grist." He glanced at Larry.

Larry, in contrast to Mrs. Grist, did not look at all pleased by Garek's news. In fact, he looked downright worried.

Garek arched an eyebrow. "Something wrong, Larry?"

"What? Oh, uh, no. Congratulations," Larry said hurriedly. "Uh, could I see you in your office?"

"Certainly." To Mrs. Grist, Garek said, "Ellie is coming to meet me for lunch. Have her come up immediately when she arrives."

In his office, Garek sat at his desk and looked at Larry's concerned face. "Yes?"

Larry hesitated a moment, then launched into speech. "This girl, Eleanor Hernandez—do you know anything about her finances?"

Garek arched a brow. "I haven't looked at her bank statement, no."

Larry's frown deepened. "I dislike having to be the voice of caution, but that is part of my job. You must get her to sign a prenuptial agreement."

Now it was Garek's turn to frown. "I hardly think that's necessary."

"It *is* necessary. You know as well as I do that fifty percent of all marriages end in divorce—"

"I have no intention of getting a divorce."

"No one does, Garek. But you've got to realize that people change, things go wrong, you can't always predict what your feelings will be five, ten, fifteen years from now."

"We're not getting divorced," Garek said, steel in his voice. "But even if we did, I would treat Ellie fairly."

"Yes, I'm sure you would. But her definition of fair

might be very different from yours. Believe me, after four divorces, I know what I'm talking about. Women can be very vindictive when they're angry."

"Ellie's not like that."

"Maybe not—but she would legally be entitled to a portion of all your assets—she might even try to go after your business. You owe it to your stockholders, if not yourself, to protect the company."

Garek frowned. As much as he hated to admit it, what Larry said made sense. He had a responsibility to the company. He couldn't shirk that just because he was getting married.

"How long will it take you to draft an agreement?" he asked abruptly.

"I'll have to consult with a prenuptial expert, get a financial statement from your accountant, write out a schedule of separate property and an expense-payment schedule and a waiver of interest in the business...although maybe it would be safer to establish a trust to protect Wisnewski Industries. I'm guessing a month, maybe two—"

"You have until Thursday."

"Until Thursday! But—" Larry stopped midsentence. Something in Garek's expression must have made him rethink what he was about to say.

"Very well," the lawyer agreed. "I'll have it ready."

Larry left, and Garek stared for a moment at the painting of *Woman in Blue*, before turning his gaze to the independent auditor's report on his desk. He could guess what it contained. Trouble. Lots of trouble.

The Lachland buyout had been progressing so smoothly—perhaps too smoothly. He damn well should have known that no deal ever happened that easily.

He picked up the phone.

"I'm going to have to spend the day going over the auditor's report," he told Mrs. Grist curtly. "Call Ms. Hernandez and cancel our lunch."

Chapter Fifteen

Ellie's treatment when she entered Wisnewski Industries on Thursday was very different from the first time she'd gone there. The security guard escorted her up the elevator himself, telling her that if she needed anything to just let him know.

"Thank you," Ellie responded, only half aware of his eager solicitude. She was thinking of Garek.

It was probably just as well that he'd canceled their lunch on Monday. She'd been terribly busy that whole day—and on Tuesday and Wednesday, also. She'd had to cancel her lease since Martina had decided to move in with friends who needed a third roommate. She'd also had to notify the utilities and the newspapers, both the *Tribune* and the *Sun Times*, and buy herself a wedding dress; she'd found a beautiful white lace frock in a small boutique off Michigan Avenue for half price. Ellie'd also arranged for Bertrice to fill in for her at the gallery while she was on her honeymoon. Bertrice had been reluctant at first, but had changed her mind when she heard how much Garek was paying.

The power of money, Ellie thought.

But the idea didn't bother her as much as it once had. She could put Garek's money to good use, she realized. She appreciated that now in a way she hadn't been able to a year ago. It had been silly of her to fear wealth. Money couldn't destroy what she and Garek had. She wouldn't let it.

But of course, that brought her to her other problem—there were a few things she should tell Garek. None of them was really relevant to their relationship, but he had a right to know.

She'd intended to tell him on Monday, but then his assistant had called to cancel. She hadn't thought too much about it, imagining that he must be extremely busy. She'd expected he would call her that night.

When he hadn't, she'd been half disappointed, half relieved. But then, when another day passed, and he still didn't call, she began to feel more and more uncertain.

Why didn't he call her? True, they'd agreed not to meet, but did that preclude telephone conversations, as well? Was he having second thoughts? Now that she thought about it, he hadn't really said he loved her. The words hadn't seemed necessary at the time. They'd been implicit in his actions.

Hadn't they?

Of course they had. She was acting like a ninny. She should just call him....

And so she had. He'd sounded a bit curt at first, but when she told him she wanted to meet him for lunch, he'd agreed.

"Tomorrow would be good. There's something I need to talk to you about," he'd said.

"Me, too." She hesitated a moment, then asked, "Is everything okay?"

"Yes." And then, "I just hate this damn waiting."

The frustration and longing in his voice had sent her spirits soaring. She'd been smiling when she hung up the phone.

He did love her, she thought now as she stepped off the elevator. And she loved him....

His assistant, talking on the phone, smiled and motioned her toward the office. Ellie entered quietly and saw him sitting at his desk, his hair rumpled, his tie askew, his jacket straining across his shoulders as he bent over some papers.

Dear heaven, how she loved him. For a moment, the emotion almost overwhelmed her. She felt fluttery and elated and buoyant just looking at him. How could she have doubted it for a second?

"Hello, darling," she said, a smile trembling on her lips as she stepped forward.

He looked up. Something blazed in his eyes, but he didn't return her smile. He had a tense look about his mouth and jaw. She heard a low cough. Turning, she saw a short man in a tailored suit rising from a chair.

Garek stood also. "Ellie, this is Larry Larson, the company lawyer. He has something for you to sign."

"Something for me to sign?" Ellie repeated in confusion. "What is it?"

Garek met her puzzled gaze steadily.

"A prenuptial agreement," he said.

Garek watched Ellie as Larry explained the contract to her. She was very quiet. She'd barely said a word since he'd first told her about the prenuptial agreement. She sat in the chair across from him, her face very pale.

What was she thinking? He didn't know. Except for one stunned glance at him when he'd made his announcement, she hadn't looked at him. She looked hurt. She looked as though he'd done something unspeakable.

Dammit, he thought angrily. She had no right to look like that. No right at all. It was common sense to settle their financial matters before they married. It made no difference to their relationship. Couldn't she see that?

Larry finished his explanation. He flipped to the back page of the document and showed her the signature line. "You just need to sign here," he said, holding out his pen.

Ellie didn't take the pen. Instead, she rose to her feet and gathered up the pages.

"Is something wrong?" Larry asked.

"No, not at all," she said calmly. "I just want to take it home and read through it."

Larry frowned. "But I explained all of the clauses to you."

"Yes, I know. I still want to read them over on my own."

Garek frowned also. "Is there something you don't understand?"

"No, not really."

"Then there's no reason to delay signing," the lawyer said, his voice a trifle chilly.

Her voice was equally cool. "I disagree. You've explained to me the necessity for this. Your reasons were practical. But I must be practical, also. It's only common sense to read something before I sign it, perhaps have my lawyer look it over."

Larry gaped at her.

She gave Garek a slightly shaky smile. "Do you mind if we skip lunch? I'm not very hungry…" She turned and walked out of the room.

Garek went after her.

"Ellie," he said, catching her elbow in the hall outside Mrs. Grist's office. "Dammit, it doesn't have to be like this—"

"Like what?"

Her expression was cool and remote—except for her eyes—her eyes were big blue pools of pain. Releasing her, he shoved his hands in his pockets and stepped back. "I can't take chances with the business."

"I know. I'm not mad, honestly. It's just that…oh, why does money have to ruin everything? Why does it make everything corrupt and ugly?"

He frowned at her. "You're exaggerating."

"I know. I know. I guess I'm still in shock. I wish you'd told me about this sooner."

"I've been busy." It was difficult suddenly to meet her gaze. "I just signed the Lachland buyout this morning. It means a lot to Wisnewski Industries."

"Does it? I'm happy for you, then." She turned her face away, brushing the dampness from her cheeks. "I'm sorry. I have to go." She hurried out the door.

"Ellie…" He started after her again, but a hand on his arm stopped him.

It was Larry.

"Let her go," the lawyer said. "Don't fall for the tears."

Garek glared at him. "What the hell are you talking about?"

"The tears." Larry shook his head. "Men fall for it every time. I fell for it four times myself. Leave her alone—she'll sign the prenup and she'll forget about it, believe me. Until the divorce. Um, *if* there's a divorce," he added hastily.

"Get the hell out of here," Garek snarled.

Larry beat a hasty retreat.

For the next several hours, Garek tried to concentrate on his work. He had plans to make now that the Lachland buyout had taken place. He could easily spend the next six months working out all the details. This was an exciting, challenging time for Wisnewski Industries. He should have had no trouble focusing on his work.

But then, he'd never been in a situation like this before.

He pushed away the profit-and-loss statements he was studying and leaned back in his chair. He wanted to marry Ellie. He'd made the decision impulsively, but he'd thought it was the right one. Only now he wasn't so sure.

Ever since Larry had brought up the subject of the prenuptial agreement, needles of doubt had poked at him. This whole marriage thing was more difficult than he'd thought it would be. He didn't like having demands put on him. And in her own way, he realized suddenly, Ellie was more demanding than Doreen and Amber combined.

He almost wished she did want money—that would have been easy to give. But Ellie wanted something more complicated than that.

He wished he'd just slept with her.

Only somehow, that wasn't enough. He wanted more, also. He wanted…what exactly? He didn't know. What the hell was the matter with him?

He frowned at the painting on the wall across from him.

Woman in Blue.

He'd disliked it at first. He'd thought it was silly and stupid and pointless. But somehow, over the last few months, it had begun to grow on him. It brightened up his office, made the room seem less dull, less enclosed. It was like having a window into an alternate reality.

As he looked at it now, he saw how the colors moved in sinuous tendrils and rhythmic scalloped patterns and how the blue became more and more intense as it moved toward the center of the painting. There was no one spot where you could see a change in hue, but the blue slowly, gradually, became brighter and brighter until in the very center it was an intense, bright sapphire....

And suddenly he understood.

Garek tried all afternoon and all evening to reach Ellie, but she seemed to have disappeared from the city of Chicago. Her phone had been disconnected and when he went to her apartment, the windows were dark and no one answered the door. He went to the gallery, but the idiot girl there said Ellie was on vacation. He even went to her aunt and uncle's house, but they only looked at him coolly and said they had no idea where she was.

The coolness made him think they were lying, that they knew something. He parked at the end of the street and lurked there for several hours, but there was no sign of Ellie.

He drove back over to her apartment and waited...and waited. Finally, at 3:00 a.m., he pounded on the door of the downstairs flat where Ellie's landlord lived, and convinced the man to unlock her door in case she was hurt.

Squinting in the glare from the kitchen lights, Garek looked at the bare walls, the packed suitcases.

"She said you two were getting married tomorrow," the landlord said. "You think she's changed her mind?"

Garek's gut twisted, squeezing the air out of his lungs and making it difficult to breathe. "No," he said more sharply than he'd intended.

"Uh-huh." The landlord looked pityingly at him.

Garek felt a sudden, strange sense of disorientation. The cramped, dark apartment faded from his consciousness, replaced by a memory of a different place—a brightly lit place with stark white walls. He'd been standing outside the hospital emergency room where the surgeons were operating on his father, waiting for someone to come out and tell him what was going on. The minutes had ticked by, turning with agonizing slowness into hours. He'd alternated between trying to calm his mother's and sister's hysterical crying, assuring them over and over again that the hospital had the city's finest doctors, that everything would turn out all right. They'd both finally fallen asleep on the couches in the waiting room. So he'd been the only one to see the expression in the doctor's eyes when he'd come in to talk to them—an expression very similar to the one in Ellie's landlord's eyes.

"No," Garek said again.

But this time his voice emerged a harsh, cracked whisper.

"I always thought he was a jerk," Robbie growled. "You should have let me smash his face that first time—"

"Robbie!" Ellie shifted on the dingy couch in his apartment. Her back still ached from sleeping on its springless cushions and she had a headache from Robbie's cologne, which he had a tendency to apply too heavily. She was in no mood to listen to his threats. "I need advice, not violence. I need logic and common sense."

"And you came to me?" Robbie, sitting on the couch next to her, dumped some more salsa on the cold taco he was eating for breakfast. A diced tomato flew into the air and landed on the prenuptial agreement lying on the coffee table next to his plate. "Hmm, well…" He grimaced. "You need to talk to your grandfather. He would know about this kind of stuff."

"No." Ellie brushed the tomato off the document and frowned at the slight red stain left on the paper. "I can handle this myself."

"But you can't," Robbie pointed out with impeccable logic. "Otherwise, you wouldn't have asked me for advice."

Ellie glared at him while he chomped on his taco. Yesterday, she'd just wanted a place where she could think without having to explain everything. But this morning, she wanted to talk about it—she wanted advice.

"You know, Ellie," Robbie said, swallowing a large bite, "I don't think you can really blame the guy for trying to protect his company."

"I don't. Not exactly. It's just…" She paused, struggling to put her feelings into words.

"It's just what?" Robbie asked.

"It's just that Garek has obviously put a lot of thought and time and consideration into his company." She swallowed the sudden lump in her throat. "I just wish he'd spare the same thought and time and consideration for me."

Robbie sighed. "Look, if the guy doesn't love you, he's an idiot and you should dump him."

"I think he does love me. I just don't think he knows *how* to love me."

"He's a virgin?" Robbie glanced down at his limp taco. "Well, if you want me to give him a few pointers—"

"No, that's not what I mean," Ellie said. "I mean he doesn't know how to have a relationship. I don't think he knows how to discuss things, how to compromise, how to allow himself to be vulnerable."

A doubtful look crossed Robbie's face. "Does any guy know how to do those things?"

"Maybe not." Ellie felt a burning behind her eyes. The sad thing was that she suspected that if Garek ever let down his guard, he would be more than capable of all those things—and much, much more. But it would take a long time for her to breach the walls he'd erected around himself. If she were lucky, in five or ten years, maybe—maybe—he would actually admit that he loved her.

Was she just wasting her time?

That's what she needed to know.

She never should have come to Robbie. She should have called Martina. Or Aunt Alma. Robbie was hopeless when it came to advice. He'd never had the least bit of common sense. He never let logic, or anything else, get in the way of his feelings.

But then again, maybe that was exactly the answer she was looking for.

Chapter Sixteen

Garek sat at his desk, staring bleary-eyed at the paper in front of him, the words running together in an unintelligible mess. He'd been trying to read it for the last hour, but his aching eyes and pounding head refused to cooperate. It was almost four o'clock in the afternoon and he still hadn't heard from Ellie. He'd told Mrs. Grist not to put any call through unless it was from her. So far, the phone had been completely silent.

He yanked at his tie, then pulled it off completely. He rose to his feet and paced around the room, rubbing his unshaven jaw. He'd left a note at her apartment. "You don't have to sign anything," he'd scrawled hastily. "Call me." Her landlord had promised to give it to her when she came back for her suitcases.

Garek had gone home after that, but he hadn't been able to sleep, so he'd come to the office. He had plenty of work to do.

Only, he hadn't done any of it.

He paced back to his desk, picked up the phone and dialed a number.

"Hello?" a slightly accented voice said.

"Mrs. Hernandez, this is Garek Wisnewski," he said. "Have you heard from Ellie?"

There was a slight pause. "In the fifteen minutes since you last called? No," she said.

"Will you please call me if she contacts you?"

"Yes, I will," she said, her voice a mixture of sympathy and impatience. "Goodbye, Mr. Wisnewski."

He sat back down, resting his head on his hands. The same fear he'd felt last night standing in her apartment was twisting his gut again, only more tightly, more viciously than before.

Had he lost her?

An image floated in his head, a vision of how she'd looked the day before, her face pale, her eyes wide and dark with hurt.

He squeezed his tired, burning eyes shut, trying to banish the picture. He hadn't meant to hurt her. He never should have given her that prenuptial agreement. He was an idiot. If she would just come back, he would apologize, tell her what a fool he'd been. He would make it up to her....

If he ever got the chance.

Why didn't she call?

Maybe something had happened to her. What if she'd been in an accident? What if she'd been mugged and her purse snatched? She was a fool for going around the city in that damn train at all hours of the day and night. What if she was in the hospital right now, critically injured, with no identification, unable to speak—

He jumped to his feet, picked up the phone and buzzed Mrs. Grist.

"Mr. Wisnewski!" her voice came on the line. "I was just about to ring you—"

"Has she called?" Hope flared in his chest.

"No, but Mr. Larson wants to talk to you—"

Hope turned to ashes. "Tell Larry to go to hell," he growled. "I want you to call the local hospitals. See if anyone answering to Ellie's description has been admitted in the last twenty-four hours—"

"Yes, Mr. Wisnewski, but—"

"No buts. Call the police, too. See if there've been any accidents—"

"But Mr. Larson said it was about Ellie—"

"And have security see what they…Ellie? What about Ellie?"

"I don't know exactly. He just said you need to come down to the conference room. He said it's important."

Garek frowned. Had Larry found out something? Was Ellie *here?*

He hurried down to the second floor, but when he entered the conference room, there was no sign of Ellie—just a phalanx of gray-suited, black-briefcased businessmen. They looked like robots—except for the short, red-faced man in a green plaid suit at one end of the table.

The man looked familiar, although it took Garek a moment to place him—Calvin G. Hibbert, financier and wealthy scion of the blue-blooded Hibbert family. One of his companies had been competing with Wisnewski Industries for the Lachland Company. What the hell was he doing here?

"Ah, Garek, there you are!" Larry's usually neatly

combed hair was disheveled, the bald spot in plain view. In an undertone, he added, "You are not going to *believe* what's happening—"

"Mr. Garek Wisnewski?" One of the robotic clones spoke when he heard Garek's name. "I am Rex Rathskeller, senior partner of the firm Rathskeller, Broad and Campbell. These gentlemen are Mr. Broad, Mr. Campbell and our associates, Mr. Pesner, Mr. White and Mr. Kiphuth."

Garek frowned. He'd heard of the firm. Headquartered in Philadelphia, it was considered one of the best in the nation. "If this has something to do with Lachland—"

"Lachland?" The lawyer appeared confused until one of his colleagues whispered in his ear. His forehead cleared. "Ah, I see. No, Mr. Wisnewski, this has nothing to do with your company's business. No, we've been hired by our client to discuss a prenuptial agreement—"

A ringing sounded in Garek's ears, obscuring the rest of the man's sentence. He'd spent the last twenty-four hours rushing all over the city looking for Ellie, half out of his mind with fear and worry—and she'd been off hiring a pack of lawyers? And not just any lawyers. She'd hired the most experienced, most cutthroat, most *expensive* lawyers in the business. She'd certainly changed her tune—

Larry's frantic voice penetrated the haze. "Mr. Rathskeller claims that Ellie isn't penniless. He claims that she has money of her own. He claims that—"

"He doesn't claim anything," the old man in green announced coldly. "He states facts. I am Calvin G. Hibbert, and Eleanor Graciela Hibbert Hernandez is my granddaughter. And she possesses a trust fund in excess of two hundred million dollars—"

Larry's eyes bugged out. "Two…hundred…million…!" he gasped, sinking into a chair.

For a moment, no one spoke, the silence broken only by Larry's choking noises.

Then, suddenly, the door to the conference room swung open.

A small woman with tousled black curls and large blue eyes peered in. For a moment, she appeared startled by all the men in the room. Then she saw Hibbert.

"Grandpa?" she gasped. And then, "Grandpa!"

Suddenly, she ran to the head of the table and threw herself into his arms, laughing and hugging and kissing him. "Grandpa, what on earth are you doing here?"

Chapter Seventeen

Garek's immediate reaction upon seeing her had been relief that she was all right. But before the relief could even sink in, she'd flown into the old man's arms, hugging and kissing him. Garek clenched his teeth. Not only had she *lied* to him…she hadn't even *noticed* he was in the room.

All her attention was wrapped up in the old man. Calvin G. Hibbert. One of the wealthiest men in the country. Her *grandfather.*

"Your cousin Robert called me," Hibbert was explaining. "The first time in his life that young man ever showed any common sense, I'm sure. *He* told me that my only granddaughter was getting married."

Ellie blushed guiltily. "I'm sorry, Grandpa. I wasn't sure—"

"I came straightaway," he said, waving away her faltering explanation and casting a disparaging glance at

Garek. "I wanted to meet this fiancé of yours. I must say, Eleanor, I don't think much of your choice—"

"Grandpa—"

"But Robert says he's better than the last one. At least he appears to have a little bit of his own money. I don't like the sound of this prenuptial agreement, though. I don't want you to get cheated out of your inheritance."

"What inheritance?" Her smile faded and her tone grew cool. "You disowned me, remember?"

It was Hibbert's turn to blush, the hue of his skin changing from red to scarlet. "Nonsense," he blustered. "You know I didn't mean it. I was just angry."

"You meant it when you disowned my father."

"Well, harrumph, I learn from my mistakes." His voice turned gruff. "You're all I have, Eleanor."

Her eyes grew misty. "Oh, Grandpa…"

"Ms. *Hibbert,* I hate to interrupt this touching reunion," a sarcastic voice intruded. "But may I speak to you a moment? Alone."

Ellie glanced up to see Garek holding the door open to a small adjoining office. Black bristles stood out on his tightly clenched jaw. His eyes were narrow red slits.

Uh-oh.

She walked the length of the room, conscious of the roomful of lawyers watching her, and into the office. Garek closed the door and leaned back against it, his arms folded across his chest.

"Well?" he demanded.

She glanced at him uncertainly. "What happened to you? You look awful—"

"Don't try to change the subject…*Eleanor.*"

She looked down to where her fingers were twisting the strap of her purse. "I suppose I should have told you—"

"You *suppose?* Exactly when were you going to tell me that you had *two hundred million dollars* sitting in the bank?"

"It wasn't like that. My grandfather and I had a fight when I moved out. I haven't even seen or talked to him in over a year. I didn't want to be controlled by him and his money anymore. He disowned me, and that was fine with me."

"He doesn't appear to consider you disowned."

"Apparently he changed his mind."

"You must have known that was likely."

"Actually, it seemed highly *un*likely. He did the same thing to my father. My parents lived in poverty because Grandpa disapproved of his son's marriage to a Mexican house cleaner. It wasn't until my mother and father died that he took me in. And he soon let me know who was in control. He picked my school, my friends, even the men I dated. When I couldn't stand it anymore, I moved out."

"That really doesn't explain why you didn't tell me about all this."

She darted a quick glance at him. "Sometimes people act…differently toward me when they know how much my grandfather is worth."

"I see. So I had to believe that you loved me for myself and not my money, but you weren't willing to extend the same trust to me?"

"It wasn't like that! It didn't seem important. Especially since Grandfather had disowned me. I would have been perfectly happy if it were true. Money spoils everything."

"That's bull." Garek took a step forward. "Everyone has to have money to survive. You just want to live in a fairy-tale world where you can pretend money doesn't exist, where you don't have to accept responsibility for your own survival. Money makes everything better."

"Not everything," she said quietly.

"Get over it," he said curtly. "So maybe your grandfather tried to control you—there's lots worse problems—like not having enough food to eat, not having a home."

She nodded slowly, remembering her father's futile efforts to hold on to a job and how tired her mother had been coming home after cleaning houses all day. "I know I shouldn't complain…but it's not just the control. When I moved in with my grandfather, everyone treated me differently. People who never would have given me the time of day suddenly sought me out. Everyone laughed at every stupid joke I told. Men told me I was the most beautiful, exciting, wonderful woman ever to walk the earth. I never knew for sure who really meant what they said."

Garek opened his mouth to dismiss her excuse, then paused. Actually, what she said had some truth in it. He'd experienced it himself.

"Rafe told me he loved me, but he couldn't dump me fast enough when my grandfather disinherited me," she continued, not noticing his distraction. "People *think* about me differently, knowing I have all that money. *You* probably think of me differently."

Again, he started to deny it, then paused, realizing that it was true. In a few, fundamental ways, their relationship had completely changed. No longer was he the wealthy businessman rescuing the poor working girl from a life of poverty. In some way that he hadn't even recognized until now, his money had given him an advantage over her. A sense of superiority, perhaps, a sense that she should be *grateful* to him.

His financial status no longer gave him that edge over her—in fact, the exact opposite was true. *She* had more money than *he* did. The thought wasn't pleasant.

Frowning, he looked at her. "I suppose it does change things—"

She stepped back, a stricken look coming over her face. "I understand—"

He reached out and grabbed her arm. "No, you don't, Ellie. I can't deny that it changes how people will look at us. But it *doesn't* change how I feel about you."

She looked at him. "And exactly how do you feel about me, Garek?"

He let go of her arm. He stood silently, not speaking. Ellie felt as though her heart was cracking in two. She turned again to leave, but then he spoke, his voice quiet.

"That painting," he said. *"Woman in Blue."*

She stopped in her tracks.

"I didn't like it at first. It made no sense, the colors and shapes seemed haphazard and inexplicable. But when I looked harder, I noticed a balance in the picture, an equilibrium that somehow connected all the elements together. And then I noticed how intense the blue was. How bright. How true."

She felt him standing behind her. "It's you, isn't it, Ellie? *Woman in Blue* is you. It took me a long time to figure it out, but I finally did. And that's when everything became clear."

He took her shoulders and turned her to face him. "I've made a lot of stupid mistakes, Ellie, like asking you to sign that prenuptial agreement. You gave me a second chance once, and now I'm having to ask you for a third one. This relationship business is a lot harder than I realized. But I'm willing to learn. I'm a hard worker and I'll do whatever it takes to make our relationship work because I love you, Ellie. I love you, and if you'll marry me, I'll spend the rest of my life proving it to you."

"Oh, Garek." She smiled shakily. "I love you so much."

And then, suddenly, she was in his arms and he was kissing her as if she was more valuable, more beautiful, more precious than a museum full of the finest art in the world.

"Oh, Garek," she sighed again when they finally had to come up for oxygen. Her cheeks stung from the scrape of his whiskers, but she was too happy to care. "Let's give the lawyers the prenuptial agreement and go."

He brushed a curl back from her forehead, his fingers lingering on her skin. "What prenuptial agreement?"

"The one Larry prepared. When I really thought about it, I realized that I've let money control me. I believed money was causing all my problems. But it was me and my own fear causing the problems, not the money. I knew I loved you too much to let anything spoil what we had. I have the contract right here, all signed." She pulled the sheaf of papers out of her purse.

He looked at the documents, then at her. "You signed it even after I told you not to?"

She stared at him. "You told me not to sign it?"

"In the note I left with your landlord this morning." His forehead creased. "Didn't you read it?"

"I haven't been home." She looked up at him, touched beyond words that he'd trusted her enough to tell her not to sign the agreement. "But it really doesn't matter now. Let's give it to the lawyers."

He frowned. "That's not going to work. We need a new prenuptial agreement."

Her smile faltered. "But why?"

"To protect your inheritance."

"I trust you."

"I know you do." He looked down into her troubled eyes. "It's only practical," he said gently.

"It just seems so sordid," she sighed.

He stared at her thoughtfully. "Why don't we let the lawyers hash out the money issues and we come up with our own agreement."

"Our own agreement?" Frowning, she watched him pull a pen and paper out of a drawer and motion her to sit down at the desk. She sat down uncertainly. "What do you mean?"

"I mean—write this down—you must never take me to a lecture by Professor Jameson again."

A smile began to curve her lips. Obediently, she wrote down, *Eleanor G. Hibbert Hernandez promises never to take Garek Wisnewski to a Jameson lecture.* She then went on to write:

Eleanor G. Hibbert Hernandez gets to choose all the art for the house.

"Hmm." He pretended to consider that one. "Very well—as long as you don't buy anything from Caspar."

She glanced up at him, smiling. "Not even for the bathroom?"

"Especially not for the bathroom. I want that in writing."

Laughing, she complied. "Very well…but we have to spend Christmas Eve at my family's."

"No argument from me there." He paused a moment, then added slowly, "I'd like to invite my sister and niece, though."

She smiled at him. "That's a good idea."

He grimaced a little. "I'm not so sure. I may live to regret it."

"No, you won't," she said firmly.

He looked at her, a smile quirking the corners of his mouth. "I believe you. Speaking of holidays, that reminds me... You must never buy me a tie again."

"I thought you liked the tie I gave you."

"I do," he said firmly. "I like it so much I want it to forever be unique in my closet."

"But I could find something different—"

"No."

She pouted a little. "All right. But you can't buy me any jewelry then."

He crouched beside her and looked into her eyes. "I'm afraid I already broke that one." He pulled a small box out of his pocket and handed it to her. "Open it, Ellie."

With trembling fingers, she lifted the lid. Her breath caught. A simple platinum ring with a small, exquisitely cut sapphire. "Oh, Garek, it's beautiful." She looked up at him, tears in her eyes. "Maybe I'll make an exception—just this once."

He pulled her out of the chair and kissed her.

A while later, they came out of the office into the conference room and headed for the door.

Hibbert watched as the couple, smiling at each other, strolled toward the door. He frowned. "Where are you two going?"

"To the courthouse," Ellie replied. "To get married."

"B-b-but what about the prenuptial agreement?" Larry sputtered.

"Ellie and I have written up our own arrangement."

Garek looked at the roomful of lawyers. "You have this afternoon to come up with an agreement acceptable to both sides. Otherwise, you're all fired."

Without another word, Garek and Ellie strolled out of the room.

"This afternoon!" Mr. Rathskeller exclaimed. "That's impossible."

Hibbert, who was still staring after the couple thoughtfully, turned his eaglelike gaze on the lawyer. "Nothing's impossible. Write up something fair and equitable. That's all you have to do. But you'd better get to it instead of sitting around bellyaching."

The lawyers grumbled as they opened their briefcases and pulled out sheaves of paper.

"Love," one of them muttered in disgust.

Hibbert moving over to stand by the window, frowned deeply, his eyebrows beetling. He was about to make a comment, when he saw Garek and Eleanor come out of the front door of the building. Apparently too impatient to wait for the limo, Garek hailed a taxi and the couple climbed in. As they drove away, through the rear window Hibbert could see the two of them kissing.

The corner of his mouth lifted.

"Yes," he murmured, sounding wistful. "Love."

* * * * *

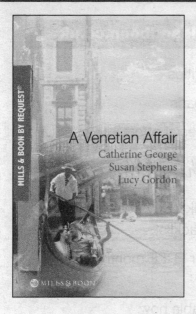

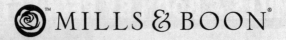